The Reluctant Canadian

Inspired by the true story of a Canadian Home Child

a novel by Brad Barnes

Brad Barnes, MARCH 23, 2013

First Edition –January 2013

ISBN
978-1-4602-1145-8 (Hardcover)
978-1-4602-1146-5 (Paperback)
978-1-4602-1147-2 (eBook)

Produced by:

FriesenPress
Suite 300 – 852 Fort Street
Victoria, BC, Canada V8W 1H8

www.friesenpress.com

Distributed to the trade by The Ingram Book Company

Special thanks to Elizabeth Bond for her editorial advice.

Dedicated to the memory of my father

George M. Barnes

1933-1997

Preface

For as long as I can remember, my father was always curious about his roots and about his own father, the man who'd abandoned him and my uncle when they were both just babies. No one in the family ever talked about my grandfather, not even my grandmother. After all those years of not knowing about his ancestry, dad finally discovered that his father was still alive and living in British Columbia. In 1993, dad travelled to the Penticton hospital to meet his father for the first time. Eighty-eight-year-old Sid died an hour later. No words were spoken, but Sid did acknowledge my father by holding his hand for the first time in his life. Until then, I had never heard of the child migration scheme. After discovering that my grandfather was one of these children, I was compelled to write The Reluctant Canadian.

By all accounts my grandfather was a bastard, a cowardly man who abandoned his family and wasted his life on booze, loose women, and cards. But this is all hearsay; truth be told, I never even met the man. Well, that's not entirely true. I met him once, an hour before he died. And it made me wonder, can a lifetime of disappointment be reversed in the mere squeeze of a hand? Is that all it takes to be forgiven, and to forgive? Or are we all masters of our own deception, just waiting for a gesture to set us free from the prisons in which we've trapped our past selves?

I'll let you be the judge.

Prologue

He was lying there motionless, eyes closed, desperately sucking in shallow gulps of air over his toothless gums. He was gasping for every breath that he knew might be his last.

His eighty-eight-year-old withered arms lay limp by his side over top of the single white bed sheet that covered him up to his chin. He was tucked in like a little boy; he was seen and not heard.

Isn't it funny how we leave this world the same way we entered it? he thought in a fleeting moment of clarity. If that was the case, then perhaps all of his sins would be forgiven, though he knew they would never be forgotten.

March 19, 1993

They arrived at the Penticton hospital at nine o'clock that night, exhausted from the ten-hour drive across the mountains. They didn't take time to find a room. The two men, especially George, were anxious to meet the person who had ruthlessly dominated over their family, not with an abusive presence, but with a selfish absence.

As the nurse led them to his room, George's heart rate accelerated. He'd been both dreading and looking forward to this moment for as long as he could remember. The time had finally come for him to face the man who, until then, had only existed in his mind, because he had to, because he, George, existed. It came down to biology, heredity, genes. It came down to the root of everything.

As George walked into the hospital room followed by his eldest son, he saw the frail, wheezing, rice paper-skinned man. So this was his enemy. This was the man who had sabotaged George's life with cruelty and cowardice.

As much as this moment was a turning point in George's life, the old man didn't seem to even know that he was there. That George had waited his whole life just to get a glimpse of him. Perhaps the old man didn't care. Perhaps he never had. Maybe George would never know the truth.

The two men stood next to the bed, closing in on their shared enemy. Feet were shuffled. Throats were cleared. A moment of terrible anti-climax settled in.

George broke the silence. "What should I say to him?" he asked, lifting his head and looking at his son for an answer.

"Just introduce yourself." It seemed so simple.

George looked back to the old man and took a deep breath. "Hi Sid, I'm George. I'm your son."

No reply, only a feeble gesture. The old man slowly raised his arm and offered his hand, silently inviting his son to take it. Was he simply saying hello, goodbye, or was he asking for forgiveness? George would never know for sure. Within an hour, the old man was dead.

Chapter One

The Meeting

He rubbed his palm, savouring the warmth that was still passing through it. He turned his hand into a fist to hold onto the sensation.

"Excuse me, sir, but is your name George?"

The voice startled him more than the tap on the shoulder did. The voice, though weakened with age, was insistent.

George turned around in the motel hallway to find a petite, grey-haired lady with startling emerald eyes that burned into his. Behind her, he noticed another similarly aged woman watching them intently.

"Yes, I'm George," he answered, taken aback by the query. "And you are?"

"My name is Mary," she said. "Are you Sid's son?"

George sucked in a deep breath. Nobody had ever asked him that before. After a few false starts, he finally said, "yes. In fact, we just left him at the hospital."

"Oh, I know. We need to talk," she said.

By then, their conversation had captured everyone's attention. The other lady inched in closer from down the hall while George's son stepped out of the motel room doorway. Mary's excitement was unmistakable. It was as if she had just met a long-lost friend.

"I have some news from the hospital." Mary suddenly stopped herself, put her hand on George's shoulder and looked straight into his eyes. "Sid, your father, he passed away just a few minutes after you left him."

George suddenly felt terribly confused. "How do you know my father?"

"I'm sorry," she apologized, the deep creases around her eyes softening. "Let me explain. My name's Mary and I've known Sid for many years," she said. "More than I even like to admit." She caught her breath before she continued. "I've been his live-in housekeeper for the past fifteen years. We live over in Princeton. It was me who brought him down here to the hospital last week. My friend Ethal and I have been staying here since; I suppose just waiting for the end. Ethal and I were just getting ready for bed when the nurse called to tell us that Sid had passed. We must have just missed you at the hospital. They told me that Sid's son had left only a few minutes before he died and asked me if I could track you down. Well, you can imagine my surprise," she said. "Sid's son! I told them I'd try."

"How'd you do it, and so quickly?" George asked, still disoriented from everything that had happened, and was still happening that night.

"Well, it seems that we not only booked into the same motel, you got a room right next to ours," she smiled. "And once I saw you, it was plain as day that you were the one. You're a dead ringer for your father."

George raised his eyebrows as he gazed back at Mary. No one had ever told him that before, and for the first time that night, he felt tears welling in his eyes. He turned his head away to compose himself. "Well, I suppose we'll need to make arrangements," he said.

"Oh, Sid looked after most of it years ago," Mary advised. "There are still a few things that will need to be done. Are you going to call Lauren, or shall I?" she casually asked.

George once again raised his eyebrows. "Lauren?"

Mary raised a hand to her mouth. "Of course, what a fool I am!" She reached out and took both of his hands in hers. "I know you've already taken in a lot tonight, but there are some things you should know--for instance, Lauren, Sid's daughter. She'd be your half-sister."

"My sister?" George muttered. He suddenly felt like he'd been bowled over by a train. His son reached out and put a hand on George's shoulder.

"Yes, Lauren. She lives in Burnaby with her two kids. She just barely scrapes by on welfare, actually. You also had a brother, Frank, but he's passed now."

George felt like he needed to sit down. He'd just found out that he'd lost a father and a brother in the same evening.

Mary seemed to sense his shock. "George, dear, I can see I've said too much for one night. Why don't you rest now, and then in the morning, if you like, you can follow us back to your father's house in Princeton and collect some of his things. It's less than two hours away," she said.

George found himself nodding his head in agreement. He was going to see where his father lived, a father who up until the hour before, he'd never said a single word to.

"Excellent. That should give you some time to let everything sink in. Here, let me write down the address for you, in case we get separated." Mary's friend was quick to hand over a pen. Mary wrote down the address on a motel brochure that was resting on the table nearby. "Why don't we leave at say, ten o'clock, after breakfast. And George, dear, Lauren really should be notified tonight. I understand if you'd like me to do it," Mary offered.

George shook his head. "No, it's alright. I should do it. I should call my sister." The words sounded foreign in his mouth. He'd never had a sister before.

Mary bobbed her head in approval. She fished in her purse for a little folded piece of paper. "I knew the day would come when I'd need this number handy," she said sadly. Mary copied down Lauren's number and handed it to George.

George perched on the edge of the hard motel bed, the phone in his hand. After three aborted attempts, he was ready to do it. He dialled the number and suddenly, he panicked. Maybe he wasn't the best person to call after-all. He'd never even heard of Lauren before that night. Maybe Mary should do it, he decided. But it was too late. The number had been dialled and a woman's voice answered.

"Hello."

"Oh, Hello, is this Lauren?" George inquired. A brief but awkward silence followed. "Hello, my name is George. I'm Sid's son," he blurted.

There was a longer and a considerably more awkward silence. Finally, she responded. "Pardon me?"

"My name is George. I'm Sid's son," he repeated. "Is this Lauren?"

"Yes, my name is Lauren," she cautiously replied.

"My name is George. I'm your half-brother."

Again, no response. George suddenly realized that this wasn't going to be the joyful first encounter that he had hoped for. He hastily tempered his enthusiasm and matter-of-factly told Lauren the news of Sid's passing, quickly followed with an offer to pay her way to the funeral.

"Thanks, but no thanks," she hastily replied. "I want nothing to do with that son of a bitch, dead or alive." And then the phone went dead, along with George's elated expectations.

~~~

The following morning, George pointed the car up the long gravel driveway that lead to his father's house. His son shifted nervously in the seat beside him, reflecting his own sense of anticipation. George followed the driveway to a small, dilapidated shack built on a hillside and overlooking the river. The otherwise pristine view was spoiled by the presence of an unsightly lumber mill below. They got out of the car and George took in a deep breath. He would soon be entering into Sid's world.

Mary had arrived earlier and met them at the door. She was a gracious host. Inside the small five-room dwelling, she prepared tea and placed homemade biscuits onto a tray. She ushered her guests into the tiny living room and urged them to make themselves comfortable.

George looked around, trying to imagine how his father would have spent his days there. Mary interrupted his thoughts by giving them a verbal tour. "That is my room," she said, pointing to a closed door. "And that is, I mean was, Sid's room." She pointed to another door. "You're more than welcome to go in and go through his things," she offered.

George hesitated. He still felt like a stranger to Sid's life and he wasn't sure he had a right to go through his things.

"Whenever you're ready," Mary said, sensing George's uncertainty. "Sid was a very private person. Not many people knew much about him," she said. "As he aged though, he seemed to want to share his story.
~~~

Lucky for me, I was the one around to hear it. I guess he grew to trust me," she presumed. "Near the end, it was all he wanted to talk about. And that's how I learned about you, George," Mary added.

George's mouth dropped open. He'd never imagined that his father would have talked about him, assuming that Sid had scratched him from his memory altogether.

"It's true," Mary said as she took a sip of Orange Pekoe. "If you'd like, I can tell you about him, and then maybe you'll come to understand."

"Yes, I'd like that," George quickly replied as he nestled himself into his father's old rocker. "I'd like to hear all about him."

"Alright! Well then, where to begin?" Mary pondered.

Chapter Two

The Beginning

Sidney came into the world at a time and a place that didn't favour him reaching the age of ten, let alone afford him opportunities for prosperity and success in life. The year was nineteen-o-five and the place was East London. At one time, not so very long before he was born, Sidney would have fared well in that picturesque and thriving area known as Bethnal Green, where silk weavers once prospered and market gardens were abundant. Families lived in grand houses bounded by beautiful gardens. Sidney would have attended a good school and would have been offered unlimited prospects and hope for his future. He would have attended church every Sunday, and afterwards, he would have wandered through one of the many bustling markets with his parents to buy fresh fruits and vegetables, fish and meat. Getting treacle treats and cinnamon buns would have been such a regular occurrence that it would have been inconceivable for him to think that every child did not enjoy such indulgences. Sidney's life would have been different. He would have known about family, and about love and caring, and he would have grown up to be a gentle and kind man, and a good father.

But that is not how Sidney's story begins. Bethnal Green had changed by the time he came along--it had become one of the poorest slums in London. The area was filled with tumbledown old buildings and overcrowded tenements. Few jobs and low wages ensured constant struggles for most families, even the lucky ones. Some were fortunate enough to be able to afford the basics of life, a roof over their heads and enough food on the table to stay one step ahead of starvation. Any extras were few and far between. And even then, a treat might comprise of a plum that was either stolen or discarded by a vendor because it was no longer fit for sale. But still, it was a treat. Sidney's family was considered one of the lucky ones, at least at first.

December 25, 1910

Sidney didn't know what time it was. He was still too little to read the Roman numerals on the small brass clock that sat on the mantel and that only his father was allowed to touch. But a feeling of excitement rushed through him and he knew that he could no longer pretend to sleep. He rolled over in the narrow bed that he shared with his older brother and gently touched George's shoulder.

"Wake up, George. It's Christmas morning," he whispered. He needed to be quiet so as not to disturb his oldest brother Reginald, who slept in a big bed next to theirs, and who Sidney knew would punch him hard in the leg if his sleep was disturbed.

George rolled over and rubbed his sleepy brown eyes with his small fist. Even though he was five years older than Sidney, their hands were almost the same size. In fact, Sidney nearly matched George pound for pound.

George smiled groggily before putting his finger to his lips and making an elaborate shushing sound, nodding his head towards the snoring mound in the other bed. As mean as Reginald could be to Sidney, he was worse to George when their father wasn't around.

George pulled back the quilts and struggled to swing his gimpy leg over the side of the bed and onto the ground. Sidney bounced out of his side of the bed, scampering across the floor and down the stairs, too excited to wait for George like he usually did. Sidney was already nearing the small tree in the family room by the time George's familiar thud-THUD was sounding on the stairs.

The air was filled with the sweet smell of tea and biscuits as Sidney's mother emerged from the kitchen, wiping her hands on her apron.

"Happy Christmas, mother!" Sidney called, jumping up and throwing his arms around her knees. Eleanor laughed as she bent down to nuzzle him, her long, thick black hair tickling his nose and her scratchy woollen skirt itching at his cheeks.

"Happy Christmas, Sidney," she returned, kissing him on the crown of his head with a loud smack. Eleanor held Sidney at arm's length. "Such a handsome boy," she said. "Those chocolate eyes, that fiery hair. You surely did get your father's looks. And Happy Christmas, Georgie," she said, opening her arms to George, who had just managed to step off the bottom stair.

The sound of Frederick's harsh cough caused Eleanor to look up the stairs. "Here, Sidney, let me fetch you a cup of tea to bring up to your father," she said. "The hot is good for his throat."

"Yes, mommy," Sidney obediently replied, following her into the kitchen.

"Now be careful, it's hot," she said. "And give your father a big Christmas hug. It'll lift his spirits."

"Yes mother." Sidney carefully balanced the delicate tea cup on the chipped saucer. As he approached his parent's bedroom, an unsettling angst swept over him. He wasn't used to not having his father up and about in the morning, cheerfully greeting him, giving hugs and kisses, and especially not on Christmas morning. "Good morning father," he said as he gently pushed open the door with his hip. A chill rushed through him as he entered the cold room. "I've brung you some hot tea father, for your cough." Sidney set the cup and saucer on the bedside table. Frederick was buried under a pile of heavy wool blankets--only his neck and head stuck out. His face was pale and gaunt.

"Good morning lad," Frederick whispered, his voice weak and wheezy. "And Happy Christmas." He turned away abruptly and coughed incessantly. Uttering those few words seemed too much for him at such an early hour. When he was done, he turned back towards Sidney and feebly pulled the blankets down to his chest. "Come over here lad," he said, gesturing for Sidney to sit on the edge of the bed.

Sidney cautiously complied, hoping not to do anything that would cause another coughing spell. He carefully climbed up, leaned over his father and wrapped his short arms around him. "Happy Christmas father," he said. Sidney could feel every rib. It was like there was no meat left on him at all and he hoped his father hadn't notice when he hastily pulled away. "Will you be coming down for gifts and Christmas dinner?" he asked, feigning a quick smile.

Frederick forced himself to sit up in the bed. "Well, you don't think I'd miss Christmas dinner do you lad!" he said, with as much joviality as he could muster. "Besides, I've made you something very special this year and I want to be there when you open it."

A relieved smile spread across Sidney's face. The sudden burst of energy and the mention of a special gift instantly lifted his spirit. For as long as he could remember, Sidney had been excited to receive the wooden toys that his father made for him each Christmas. Frederick's trade as a respected furniture maker and wood carver made certain that his handcrafted creations were the envy of every other child in the neighbourhood.

"Okay, now go down stairs and have a treat. Tell Eleanor, I mean, tell your mother that I'll be right along," Frederick instructed. "And save a biscuit for me," he teased.

Sidney jumped off the bed and ran towards the door. Father made it alright, like he always had. *Everything was going to be just fine*, he thought.

Frederick slowly made his way down the stairs and into the living room just as Eleanor was bringing in another tray of hot biscuits. Sidney saw the delight on his mothers face when she saw his father enter the room.

"Well, good morning darling and Happy Christmas," she cheerily greeted, setting the tray down. Sidney felt a sense of warmth rush over him as his mother hurried over to his father and put her arms around him. Frederick kissed his wife and they held each other until Eleanor knew that it was time for him to rest. "Now sit," she said. "I'll bring you another cup of tea."Sidney jumped out of the old arm chair that he had previously claimed. "I kept it warm for you father," he said.

As Frederick slowly nestled himself into the chair, he looked over at the tree. "Well now, what do you suppose could be under there? And where is Reginald?" he said, gasping for a bit of air.

Sidney saw the frightened look on his mother's face as she handed Frederick his tea, the same look he saw only a month prior when he witnessed his oldest brother raise his hand to her in the kitchen, before angrily stomping out of the house.

"Don't you tell your father about this Sidney, do you hear?" he remembered her saying when she realized he was spying on them from just outside the kitchen door. Sidney didn't understand why mother would want to keep such a secret from his father, but he was also taught to obey her, so he never mentioned the incident to anyone.

"I don't think Reginald will be joining us this morning," Eleanor said, her voice wavering. "I heard him leave the house just after I sent Sidney up with your tea."

Sidney's heart sank as the fragile smile left his father's face. As afraid as he was of his oldest brother and glad that Reginald wouldn't be there, Sidney sensed the hopelessness his parents felt due to their eldest son's increasingly aberrant behaviour.

Fredrick fidgeted in his chair and dolefully looked up at Eleanor. "The boy is only twelve. I just don't know what to do with him. He comes and goes as he pleases. The police bring him home in the wee hours. I am weary Eleanor. I don't have the strength to punish him." Frederick shook his head. "At least the boy could stay home on Christmas morning."

The sadness in his parents eyes troubled Sidney and he wished he had something encouraging to say to them.

"Well then!" Frederick piped, seemingly regaining the festive spirit. "I don't suppose the rest of us should do without Christmas on his account. Sidney, this year you can pass out the gifts." Eleanor perched herself on the soft arm of the chair beside her husband and put her arm around him.

Sidney dashed over to the tree and rummaged through the small pile of carefully wrapped presents. "These two are for George. I know what this is," he boasted as he passed the long skinny package to his brother. "This one looks like a box," he said, quickly handing over the second one. "And this one, this one is mine," he hollered as he eagerly pulled out a large parcel. "It weighs as much as me. I wonder what it is?" He held it up and examined it from all sides. Sidney tore the wrapping off and a puzzled look came over him as he stared at the wooden contraption.

"It's a boat lad," his father finally informed. "And not just any boat. It's Noah's Ark. Open that little door at the back. There's more inside."

"Oh yes, Noah's Ark. Noah saved the animals, right mother?" Sidney shouted, recalling her telling of the story.

Eleanor smiled and confirmed his assertion with an affirmative nod.

Sidney opened the door and dumped out five intricately carved animal figures. "Look George," he shouted. "Noah's Ark, with animals and everything." Sidney held up one of the carvings and again had a puzzled look. "What is this animal father?" he asked.

"That's a cow lad," Frederick chuckled. "We don't see many of those beasts around here, do we? Someday Sidney, I'm sure you'll meet one."

Sidney cringed. "I sure hope not father." He looked over at his brother, who had been silent while he enthusiastically rambled on. "What did you get George?"

George held up a finely sanded wooden box with a delicately engraved lid. "It's a treasure box," he proudly proclaimed, "to save my pennies in."

"And a new crutch," Frederick interrupted. "He's been without far too long."

Sidney understood why George tried to hide his disappointment. Even though father meant well, Sidney knew that the crutch would give others in the neighbourhood, children and adults alike, more reason to mock his crippled sibling. *It was a fine gesture*, he thought, but one that would not only cause trouble for George, but for Sidney as well. Sidney looked out for his older brother and always stood by him when there was trouble. His thoughts were suddenly interrupted by a knock at the door.

"I wander who that would be on Christmas morning?" Eleanor said as she started to stand.

"Sit Eleanor," Frederick snapped, pulling her back onto the chair, trying to conceal his grin. "Sidney, come over here." He pulled Sidney close and whispered in his ear. "That will be Earl, from the factory. He'll have something and I want you to help bring it in. Go boy, answer the door."

"Yes father." Sidney didn't know what he was going to bring in, but he anticipated that it was something special for mother. Father always saved his best work for her, and over the years, she had acquired a sizeable collection of his finest pieces: tables, jewellery boxes, tea trays, picture frames, anything he could make from left-over scraps of wood from the furniture factory where he worked. And Sidney knew that his mother cherished every piece. He opened the door and froze as he looked upon the most beautiful rocking chair he had ever seen. Excitement filled him as he anticipated his mother's reaction.

"Happy Christmas Sidney," Earl said. "Now, help me get this inside lad. Happy Christmas Eleanor, Frederick, George," he shouted as they carried the chair into the living room. Earl smiled at Eleanor and then looked over to Frederick. "It's one of your finest pieces yet Frederick," he said.

"Well, thank you Earl," Frederick said. "Stay for tea and biscuits?"

"Thank you, but no time Frederick. I'm off to gran's for a bit of Christmas cheer. Nice day to you all, I'll see myself out."

Eleanor walked over to the chair and silently looked at it for what seemed an eternity to Sidney.

"Maybe you should sit in it," Frederick finally said.

Without uttering a word, Eleanor went to her husband and wrapped her arms around him.

Sidney could hear her sobs as she squeezed his father tightly. The love he saw between his parents at that moment made him feel safe. He was glad to have such a family. Suddenly, he felt compelled to know how it all came to be. "Father, how did you and mother meet?" he blurted.

Eleanor released her embrace and seemed pleasantly shocked at Sidney's query.

Frederick coughed, and then smiled. "Well, your mother's the storyteller," he said, gesturing for Eleanor to sit in her new chair. "Maybe she would like to tell it."

Eleanor got up, pulled the chair to the centre of the room and sat. "This is beautiful," she said, gently rocking back and forth, wiping the last of her tears away. "Of course I'll tell the story."

Sidney huddled on the floor close to her while George hobbled over to the arm chair and sat with his father.

Eleanor playfully looked at Frederick and furled her brow. "Well, if it wasn't for Barney Rose, your father wouldn't ever have known I existed," she laughed.

"You mean Mr. Rose, the cobbler?" Sidney cut in.

"Yes Sidney, that's right, Mr. Rose. Well, your father and I met in the year of eighteen-eighty-nine, long before you boy's came along," she said. "Both of us just twenty, I remember like it was yesterday. It was a Saturday evening--my girlfriends and I weren't familiar with taverns, but that night we decided to step into a little pub, you know, to see what all the fuss was about. Well, I saw your father right off," she said. "There he was, as handsome a man as I'd ever laid my eyes on. Big and strong, and he had the most beautiful voice. He was standing on a table, swinging his glass, back and forth, like he was Father Francis conducting the church choir, and singing so loud you could hardly hear the band. Everyone loved his songs. And your father would have sung the whole night away without ever taking notice of a lass such as myself," she laughed.

So, what about Mr. Rose?" Sidney asked.

"Yes, Mr. Rose. Well, Mr. Rose considered himself to be a bit of a lady's man in those days," she said. "And he wasn't very well mannered either, nor could he handle his drink. We were all having such a good time, even though your father still hadn't noticed me," she said, glaring back at Frederick. "Mr. Rose-" Eleanor stopped herself. "Now you boys don't go telling this story to your friends."

"Yes, mother," they replied in unison. Sidney would have agreed to anything so that she would continue.

"Alright then! Well, by ten o'clock, Mr. Rose had his fill of beer and he started to become, shall I say, rude towards me," she said. "So, I slapped his face."

Sidney and George laughed loudly at the idea of mother slapping a man in the face. "Did you knock him over mother?" Sidney asked.

"No Sidney, I didn't," she said. "But, he knocked me over. Barney sent me clear across the room and down to the floor. Cut my lip wide open, he did."

The boys perked up and Sidney's gut churned. "What happened next mother?" he frantically asked.

"Well, that's when your father noticed me," she chuckled. "He hit Barney Rose so hard that he didn't wake up until the next day." Eleanor winked at Sidney. "You see, your father doesn't take kindly to a man striking a woman," she said.

Sidney took quick notice of his mother's look. *So that's why she didn't want him to tell his father about Reginald's behaviour in the kitchen that day*, he thought. *These days, her concern was more likely for her husband's sake than for Reginald's.*

"That was more than twenty years ago," Frederick interrupted. "There's one thing not right with your mother's story," he added, playfully glancing her way. "I set eyes on her the moment she walked into that pub. How could I not notice the most beautiful woman in the place? And when I took her hand to help her from the floor, I knew right then that she would be my wife, and the mother of my children."

Sidney saw the devotion in his father's grey eyes as Frederick looked at Eleanor.

Two unopened gifts remained under the tree.

Following all of the Christmas morning festivities and after the tea and biscuits were gone, Sidney hurriedly bundled himself into his overcoat and boots and ran out the door to find Alfred. Alfred had been Sidney's neighbour and best friend forever. He banged his mittened fist on the neighbouring door, and after a long pause, Alfred's small puckered face appeared in the crack.

"Happy Christmas Alfred," Sidney greeted. "Can you come out?"

"Sure, why not?" Alfred said.

From behind Alfred, Sidney heard the sound of pots banging, followed by loud cursing. He peered over his friend's shoulder. "Where's your Christmas tree?" he asked.

Alfred lowered his head. "Na, we don't have Christmas trees. Da says they're no use."

"Oh," Sidney mumbled.

"Alfred, close that bloody door! You're as dumb as your no-good father sometimes!" shouted Alfred's mother.

Alfred grabbed his boots and a thin coat and slammed the door behind him. He sat down on the step to put on his boots and then made a wicked face at the closed door. The two youngsters howled in laughter, then ran as fast as they could, four full blocks to the big house where the old lady, Mrs. Moseby, would be waiting for her Christmas carols.

As everyone in Bethnal Green knew, Mrs. Moseby gifted a piece of toffee to every child that sang a carol for her on Christmas morning. Sidney and Alfred weren't about to pass up this treat. They approached the enormous house that, to Sidney, looked more like a castle built for kings than home for one old lady. When Mrs. Moseby answered the door and the boys had each sung their song, their reward was handed to them, neatly wrapped in a piece of plain brown paper, another Christmas gift to brag about.

"You're Eleanor's boy," she said as she handed Sidney his treat.

Sidney glanced up at the old lady's smiling face. "Yes, ma'am," he quietly responded.

"And how old are you, boy?" she asked.

"I'm five," Sidney boasted.

"And how is your mother?" the woman asked, her voice soft and caring.

Sidney shuffled his feet, trying to come up with a suitable response. He didn't want to tell the old lady that his mother was tired from caring for his sick father or that she needed to find occasional work to help out with the family's needs.

"Your mother, how is she?" the lady insisted.

"Ah, she's fine, ma'am," he blurted. Alfred fidgeted by his side. *I wish she'd just let us leave already*, Sidney thought, growing more uncomfortable with every passing second.

"I understand that your father has been ill," she said, bending down to touch Sidney softly on the shoulder. "Tell your mother to stop by soon. Tell her I have work for her."

"Yes ma'am, thank you ma'am," Sidney politely acknowledged.

The boys briskly turned and started towards home. As soon as they thought they were out of sight of the old lady, they opened their packages and began biting into the sweet candy. It was good. The boys laughed, licking every grain of sugar from their fingers as they skipped down the street towards home. They gently tapped each other on the shoulder in a back and forth game of tag--Sidney chased Alfred for a ways and then Alfred would take his turn at catching Sidney.

"Tag! You're it!" Alfred cried. He was eight, maybe ten steps ahead when Sidney stopped short. Something caught his eye down the alleyway they had just passed.

"Sidney, come on or we'll be late!" Alfred shouted, stressing his authority with a stomp of his foot.

Sidney didn't respond. He just stood there, staring down the lane.

Alfred walked back to where Sidney was standing and looked down the alleyway. "What are you looking at Sidney?" he asked, as he took a second glance.

Sidney saw the worried look on his friends face as they both stared at the group of street dwellers huddled around an open fire.

"Let's go Sidney," Alfred quietly demanded, trying to avoid undue attention from the unsightly group.

Sidney looked at Alfred and then back to a woman and young boy who stood just away from the others. The woman was tightly cradling the boy in her arms. The pair looked dirty and tired.

"That looks like the boy who moved into our neighbourhood last summer," Sidney said. "You remember Alfred, the one who couldn't play."

Alfred took a closer look. "Yes Sidney, I remember, his name is Nigel. His mother said cruel things to us." Alfred suddenly looked confused. "Why are they having Christmas here, Sidney? Why are they in the alley?"

Sidney wasn't paying attention to Alfred's inquiries. He could only stare at the unusual sight. The two of them stood silently, watching Nigel and his mother as they mingled with the homeless, huddled in each other's arms, trying to stay warm on Christmas morning. "Where's his father?" Sidney muttered.

The boys took another look to confirm their observations. It was him alright. It was Nigel and his mother. The boys stared at the odd sight for a moment before carrying on.

"Do you think you'll ever live on the street Sidney?" Alfred asked as they slowly walked away.

"Oh, I could never live on the street," Sidney matter-of-factly responded. "Father would never allow it. Besides, only people with no home to go to live on the streets," he reasoned. "I have a home."

The boys continued on their way, neither saying another word about what they saw. Sidney felt sad for Nigel, but he didn't know why. Afterall, he never did get to know him.

As they approached their houses, Sidney could see that George had taken his usual place near the front window and was watching the activities taking place on the street out front. Sidney felt a surge of love for his brother and he wished he'd saved some of his toffee to give to him as a Christmas gift. *Next year I will*, he promised himself.

Chapter Three

Desperate Times

"More tea George?" Mary asked.

"Yes, thank you," he said, passing his empty cup over. "It seems my father was a happy boy, with a loving family. Eleanor, Frederick, my grandparents," he said with a smile.

"Yes, George. By Sid's account, he was a very happy boy. But life soon changed for him, for all of them," Mary sadly replied.

With Christmas barely a month behind them, Frederick's health took a turn for the worse. By early February, his breathing had become so shallow and laboured that he was unable to get out of bed at all. His cough was raspier. His body burned with fever.

The family had no doctor to tend to their ills, but Frederick was seen by a qualified physician. The doctor assured Frederick that money was not a concern, so he consented to the examination. Following a brief going over, the diagnosis was certain, and the news was not good. Frederick had pneumonia. He was not likely to recover.

Eleanor was informed that the best she could do was to keep her dying husband comfortable and wait for the end. On February 11, 1911, Frederick died in his bed with Eleanor by his side. He was forty-one years of age.

February 18, 1911

A week passed since Frederick's death. Sidney and George spent much of that time sitting with their mother, who hadn't left her bed at all. She slept mostly, and when she was awake, she wept. Sidney felt alone and afraid--the safety he felt from his family was suddenly gone. His stomach churned as he hadn't eaten a decent meal in all that time, aside from the few morsels delivered by the occasional passer-byer. Some he recognized from church, some were so-called friends of the family. *Mother and father were always there to help others in time of need*, he thought. *Where were they when his family needed help*?

A sharp knock echoed through the house and Sidney ran to the front door to answer, eager to see who had come to visit, and desperately hoping that it was one of the neighbours bringing them something to eat. He gingerly swung open the door and to his surprise, it was the old lady, Mrs. Moseby, and another woman. Each woman carried a large wicker basket covered by sheets of white cloth.

Sidney sucked in the aroma of fresh baked bread and other delicacies oozing from the baskets. It was as if he were standing right in the middle of a bakery. He turned momentarily, trying to hide the rumbling in his stomach as he envisioned biting into a hot roll smothered in creamy butter. He felt relieved that the ladies didn't seem to hear, or at least pay much mind to the sounds coming from him.

Mrs. Moseby's friend set her basket down and went back to the carriage to fetch yet another, which she promptly delivered the front door. By this time, George had made his way down the stairs to see who had arrived, thud-thudding his way to the door. Mrs. Moseby watched George's progress with a pained look before turning to Sidney. "Do you remember me?" she asked. Her smile shone down on Sidney and the warmth it delivered momentarily made him forget his pitiful state of affairs.

"Yes ma'am, you're the old lady with the toffee." As the words came out, Sidney could feel the blood rush to his face. George elbowed him in the ribs. "I mean, yes ma'am, you live in the big house up the way." He couldn't remember the her name, but he thought his second response might have been satisfactory.

"Yes, well," Mrs. Moseby started. "I heard of your father's passing. This surely is a difficult time for your family. Is your mother at home?"

Sidney was having a difficult time focusing on the woman as his thoughts turned back to the smells coming from the baskets that sat on the floor between them.

Luckily, George spoke up. "Oh, yes ma'am," he said in his best grown-up voice. "She's in her room."

"Mother hasn't been out of bed since father died," Sidney added, not wanting to let his brother show him up. George elbowed him in the ribs again, and suddenly Sidney felt embarrassed by revealing their mother's condition.

Mrs. Moseby gestured to her companion to take the baskets of food into the kitchen. "You show Miss Laurentide where to put the baskets," she instructed George. Then she took Sidney's hand. "You show me to your mother's room."

As Sidney led Mrs. Moseby towards the stairs, he noticed that she was pausing in front of the treasures that his father had made for mother. Sidney heard Mrs. Moseby cluck her tongue as she tenderly ran her fingers over the finely polished wood.

"My, oh my," she murmured.

Observing Mrs. Moseby's interest in the work, Sidney spoke up. "Father made it all," he proudly proclaimed. "He used scraps of wood from the factory, but mother says it's all as good as if they'd bought it from the finest furniture store."

Mrs. Moseby nodded. "Yes in-deed. I can see that."

Sidney could tell from the look on her face that the rich lady liked the wooden collection as much as his mother did. At the top of the staircase, Sidney turned the doorknob and they entered the dark room.

Mrs. Moseby turned to him. "Thank you, dear. Now go along down to the kitchen and have a bun with cinnamon."

Sidney didn't need more of an invitation than that. He backed out the door and as he headed down the stairs, he heard Mrs. Moseby pull his mother's door closed behind him. "Really, Eleanor, you have responsibilities," he heard her say before racing down towards the wafting smells.

In the kitchen, Sidney and George ate heartily until their stomachs ached, now from indulgence. Before long, Mrs. Moseby entered with their mother in tow. Sidney looked up at her and a broad smile instantaneously blossomed across his face.

Mrs. Moseby directed Eleanor to sit. "Give the woman a cup of tea would you Miss Laurentide," she said. "Now Eleanor," she continued. "You stop by the house tomorrow. I'll put you to work in my kitchen. And bring the boys along. I'll see to it that they have two hot meals a week."

Eleanor humbly looked up at the woman and with tears in her eyes, looked at her two sons. "Yes ma'am, thank you," she softly replied.

"Alright then, that's settled," Mrs. Moseby said. "Miss Laurentide, time to leave. Good day Eleanor, children. We'll see ourselves out."

Sidney felt relieved by Mrs. Moseby's generosity. *Life would be back to normal soon*, he thought. But there was something about her though, that made him feel unsettled.

"Oh, one more thing, Eleanor," Mrs. Moseby casually declared as she started for the front door. "If it becomes necessary for you to sell those quaint sticks of furniture and decoratives scattered about the sitting room, I'll see to it that you are paid an equitable price for the lot. Don't expect too much. After all, they are amateur pieces of inferior materials, but I could try to get you at least something for them." She gave a polite smile before turning her back on Eleanor and the two boys. The ladies left the three baskets, enough food for at least four days if they rationed it well, and grandly strolled back to the waiting carriage.

The old woman's comments made Sidney feel queasy. *Mother would never sell her treasures*, he imagined. *Not the rocking chair. I don't care how kind she is to us. How dare she make such a suggestion*, he thought. Sidney was glad to see the ladies leave. Despite his displeasure, however, for the first time in many days, he didn't feel a heavy sadness suffocating him. His tummy was full and there was plenty of food left for tomorrow and another tomorrow and another. Sidney felt safer now that mother was up and about and that she had a job to go to at the big mansion.

That night, as their mother sat in father's tattered arm chair, Sidney and George curled up close on her lap. She held them tight and told them that she loved them. They fell asleep together. That night, for the first night since his father's death, Sidney drifted into a contented slumber.

~~~

Sidney and George both jumped up from the chair at the same time, shaken from their sleep by a piercing scream coming from the kitchen. The shriek was directly followed by a loud thump, and the apartment shook as if someone had thrown a large sack of flour against the wall. Then a door slammed shut and there was eerie silence.

Sidney ran ahead of George, who thud-thudded after him. He entered the kitchen to find the table overturned and chairs scattered everywhere. Mother was sitting on the floor with her back against the wall, her hands cupped over her face--she was crying and trembling, uncontrollably. When George arrived, he stopped short, surveying the scene. Sidney didn't know what to do. The sight frightened him terribly. George cautiously approached their mother. "What's happened, mother?" he asked.

Eleanor just sat there crying, her face still buried in her hands. By now, blood was dripping down her cheek and onto the floor beside her.

"What's happened, mother?" George repeated, his voice rising in fear.

Eleanor slowly lifted her head. Her hands were covered in blood and as her face came up, a large wound was revealed above her right eye. The side of her face had already turned black and blue.

"Get some cloth's Sidney!" George yelled.

Sidney hesitated, still unable to comprehend what was happening.

"Some cloth's Sidney!"

The urgency in George's voice shook Sidney to the core. He ran to the cupboard where mother kept a pile of cleaning rags and quickly handed them to his brother. As George was covering the wound and wiping away the blood, Sidney looked around the room, searching for clues to help him understand what had happened. He looked over at the counter. "Someone stole the baking!" he cried.

His mother looked up at him with a vacant look in her eyes. "It was Reggie," she said in a flat, serious voice. And then she broke down crying. "It was Reggie. It was Reggie," she repeated over and over through her heaving sobs.

Sidney looked down at her bloodied and swollen face. His face reddened as the reality of the situation began to set in--Reginald came
~~~

home to steal our food and beat mother. An intense rage suddenly enveloped him. "I hate him," he hollered as loud as he could. "I hate him, I hate him," he shouted over and over.

"Sidney, Sidney," Eleanor cried. "It's okay, it'll all be okay. I'm fine," she assured, forcing a smile, still crouched against the wall.

George reached under one arm and tried to lift Eleanor. "Come Sidney, help me get mother to bed." The two boys helped their mother to her feet and ushered her to her room. No one said a word. As they covered her, Sidney was overcome with fear that he had lost her once more and that he and George would be left alone and hungry again.

As if reading his thoughts, Eleanor gestured for the boys to lie with her. Sidney nodded and climbed atop the big bed, followed by George. Their mother held them as tightly as she had ever held them. They fell asleep together, though this time Sidney's sleep was uneasy. Uncertainty once again consumed him.

Chapter Four

Gutters and Alleyways

Mary's hands shook and her tea cup rattled loudly against the saucer as she fumbled to prevent it all from crashing to the floor. "I'm sorry George," she said, "but I get a bit edgy whenever I think about what Reginald did to your grandmother that night. And those boys, well, I just can't imagine what they must have been going through. But they still had hope."

Eleanor held true her promise to Mrs. Moseby and, more importantly, to her sons. She showed up at the grand house the following day to begin daily housecleaning work. Mrs. Moseby kept her end of the bargain, agreeing to pay Eleanor a small wage and provide two hot meals a week to her and the boys. Of course, feeding Reginald was not part of the agreement. Eleanor felt comforted in knowing that she and her youngest sons would be okay, at least for awhile. But she realized that her meagre income wouldn't be enough to keep her and the boys housed for long. Eleanor thought back to Mrs. Moseby's offer to purchase her cherished wooden gifts, and of course, Mrs. Moseby graciously agreed to keep her end of that bargain. The very next day, two men stopped by and took all of Eleanor's treasures, leaving behind anything that wasn't of value.

February 28, 1911

Sidney peered out the window and watched the familiar figure slowly amble up the walk. It was a visitor he had excitedly greeted many times in the past. "Mother, Mr. Smits has come to visit," he yelled.

Mr. Smits was a friendly man and had always been good to Sidney and his family. Sidney recalled his father saying that if it wasn't for Mr. Smits, 'we'd all be living on the streets.' Today though, *Mr. Smits looked grumpy*, Sidney thought. And today, he hesitated before knocking on the door.

"It's okay Sidney. I'll get it," mother shouted. The whisper of anxiety in her voice made Sidney feel uneasy. He grabbed onto her dress and tucked in behind, eager to hear what good news Mr. Smits had come calling with.

Eleanor paused for a moment and quickly straightened her hair before partially opening the door. "Well, good morning Mr. Smits. And how are you today?" she said, tilting her head slightly so that she could see him through the small opening she had allowed.

"Good morning Eleanor," Mr. Smits kindly greeted. "I am well. And how are you and the boys holding up?"

Sidney sensed anxiety in Mr. Smits voice as well. *Maybe there is no good news*, he thought. Sidney held onto his mothers dress a little tighter and snuggled a little closer to her. Now he was anxious.

"We're doing as well as can be expected," she said. "I am doing some work for Mrs. Moseby," she quickly noted. "She has been very kind to us."

"That's wonderful," Mr. Smits replied.

Sidney snuggled even closer to his mother as he looked up and saw Mr. Smits lower his head.

"Eleanor, we need to discuss the rent payments. I know you are in hard times, but February's rent is still owing and, now March is due as well. I'm sorry Eleanor, I cannot carry you any further," he sadly advised.

Sidney felt his mother quiver and he held on even tighter.

"Just give me a minute," Eleanor pleaded as she pushed Sidney away, leaving him alone with Mr. Smits.

Mr. Smits looked down at Sidney. His eyes were red and glossy. "I'm sorry son," he said, his voice cracking. "It's just that, well I have a family of my own to care for. I just can't let it go any further."

Sidney wasn't sure why Mr. Smits was talking to him that way, but thought he saw tears in his eyes just before mother pulled him back from the door.

"Here, Mr. Smits. This is what I have." Eleanor handed him the money that Mrs. Moseby gave her for the wooden treasures. "I need more time," she begged.

Mr. Smits looked at the money. "That's not nearly enough to pay half-a-month's rent," he said, sucking in a deep breath. "I'm sorry Eleanor. I have other tenants who will move into the apartment two weeks from today. You have until then. Keep the money for food," he offered.

Sidney's heart raced as Mr. Smits slowly turned his back on them and walked away. He didn't know what had transpired between mother and Mr. Smits, but suddenly, a sinking feeling enveloped him, warning of more hardship ahead. As Eleanor slowly closed the door, her sobs were all it took to convince Sidney that his fears were real.

March 9, 1911

Sidney answered the knock, and without hesitation allowed the doctor into their home. He didn't pay heed as to why the man wasn't carrying his usual black bag, but instead carried only a bottle. *The doctor is a good man*, he thought. *After all, he did try to save father.* Eleanor startled him when she entered the room.

"Oh, good day doctor," she warily greeted, her voice trembling. "And what brings you by this day?"

Sidney stood between them, not yet sensing his mother's uneasiness. He calmly stood by, hope in his eyes, waiting for the good news that the doctor had surely come with, the news that would make mother smile again. There was an awful stench coming from him, and the man did seem unsteady on his feet.

Just then, George walked into the room and stood by Sidney. "Good afternoon sir," he politely greeted.

The doctor quickly glanced at the boys and without speaking, turned to Eleanor. "Good afternoon Eleanor," he slurred.

Sidney had seen drunkards on the street many times before, the ones father warned him to stay clear of. *The doctor couldn't be one of those*, he thought.

The doctor invited himself into the apartment and looked around, re-familiarizing himself with the now nearly empty dwelling. "I'll get right to it Eleanor," he said. "I'm here on a matter of collections." He held up the bottle and laughed. "I brought a little something that'll get you in the mood."

Eleanor pulled the boys close. "I'm sorry sir," she said, "but I don't really understand what it is you're wanting from me. And this isn't a good time."

An eerie smirk spread across the doctor's face and he menacingly stepped towards the trio. "You didn't think my services would be free, did you?" he said. "Now, I think you should tell the boys to leave while we discuss our business."

Shivers ran down Sidney's back. Suddenly, the doctor's presence made him uncomfortable, and he was afraid to leave mother alone with him.

Eleanor nervously shuffled her feet for a moment before looking at her sons. "You boys go on outside while I talk with the doctor," she said, desperately trying to mask the terror in her voice that was by now, obvious.

Sidney looked at George, and then back to mother. Tears began welling in his eyes. "I don't want to go," he sobbed.

George quickly chimed in. "Me neither mother. We can go to our room while you talk to the doctor," he suggested.

"It'll be fine," she said. "Now both of you, go see Alfred for two hours, then come home and we'll have supper." Tears dripped from Eleanor's eyes. "Go," she yelled.

It was the first time that she had ever spoken to them that way. Sidney was terrified.

The boys slowly dressed for the cold and stepped out into the night. Sidney caught a glimpse as the doctor stepped in behind mother, his arms clumsily wrapping around her as she closed the door behind them. When they returned, they found her passed out drunk on a bare mattress, the sheets lying next to the bed in a tangled pile on the floor. The debt had been paid, in full.

~~~

The day had finally arrived. One week after the doctor cruelly collected his dues, the few furnishings Eleanor had left were sold and Sidney and his brother were moved out of the only home they had ever known. With nowhere to go, Eleanor found herself and the boys on the doorstep of a shelter. Frederick's family had succumbed to a fate he worked all his life to keep them from knowing. Without him, they were left to the mercy of the elements, the robbers, the rapists and the police. Eleanor vowed to do the best she could by her family, but she knew in her heart that wouldn't always be possible, and that her sons would need to learn for themselves how to survive in the streets of one of London's harshest neighbourhoods. She did know that they wouldn't be the only family struggling to stay alive in the gutters and alleyways.

Eleanor quickly learned the ways of the street and how to exploit her two boys to meet their basic needs. When there was no food, they begged for handouts or stole their supper. Folks were generous when a crippled ten year old was pleading for a morsel or a penny, and a five year old like Sidney could easily sneak around undetected. It was a matter of survival.

July 11, 1911

Sidney buckled over, his hands clutching his knees, gasping for air. His heart still pounded heavily against his chest. He managed a glimpse upward at his grinning brother, who seemed to find humour in the situation. It was cool there, in the alleyway, sheltered from the sweltering afternoon heat out on the street. "It's not funny George," he muttered.

"What did you bring?" George asked, struggling to hold back an all out laugh. "Did you get some fruit?"

Sidney caught his breath and stood straight. "Whatever I got, you shouldn't have any of it," he scolded. "That man chased me for six blocks." He hesitated for a moment, smiled and reached into his pocket.
~~~

"I got eight plums," he said with a huge gapping grin. He handed four of the plump ripe fruits to George. George immediately bit into one, allowing the juice to run over his chin and onto the torn and dirty shirt that he had been wearing since April.

"And what did you get today?" Sidney asked.

"Only a couple of pennies today," George said. "I put them with the others. There's enough to buy bread when the bakery opens in the morning." George paused for a moment. "I saw mother today," he said. "She will meet us tomorrow. We have a room at the shelter, all of us, together."

Sidney squatted, bit into a plum and smiled. He was always excited to be with mother, spending nights with her, the three of them together. An abandoned building or a dark doorway, it didn't matter. Sometimes, after Eleanor scrounged enough money, she would rent a room and they would eat a hot meal and curl up together in a soft bed. *The shelters were okay too*, he thought. *At least they were clean.*

October 11, 1911

Eight months had passed since his father's death. It was a chilly morning and Sidney was huddled with his mother and George, trying to steal some sleep in a doorway that until then had served them well for that purpose. Sidney was suddenly roused by a sour-faced constable poking him with his foot.

"Wake up!" he shouted. "I said, wake up!"

As Sidney rubbed his eyes and his mother and brother stirred to life beside him, he heard the officer mutter, "Can't take a step in this neighbourhood without tripping over some urchin or another."

Once on their feet, the constable unceremoniously dragged the brothers in the direction of the police station, with their mother close behind, begging him to let her sons go. At the station, Eleanor and the boys were ushered to a waiting area. "Sit here while I start the paperwork," the officer ordered.

"Paperwork! What paperwork?" Eleanor screamed.

"The charges," the officer replied. "You and the boys will be charged with wandering without visible means of subsistence--bloody vagrants."

Eleanor slumped back in her chair and started to weep. "What about my boys?" she asked. "What will happen to them?"

The officer looked down at her and shrugged his shoulders. "That'll be up to the Magistrate," he said as he walked away.

The three of them sat in silence in the noise filled room as officers scurried about, shouting commands and dragging other offenders around, mostly youngsters like Sidney and George. Sidney dared not get up to go to his mother.

Despite the commotion going on around him, Sidney immediately noticed the stylishly attired man that confidently strolled into the station. He was a giant. *Well fed* Sidney presumed, *a man of means and authority*. His silk top hat covered all but a ring of meticulously trimmed grey hair, and despite no visible ailments, the man carried a walking stick. His mere presence demanded respect--even the constables seemed to fear him.

"Superintendant, good day sir," the officer nearest to Sidney called out. Everyone in the room greeted him with similar reverence.

"Good day officers," the man cordially replied. "What do we have today?" he asked as he looked around the bustling room.

"Well sir, this pair just came in this morning, with their mother sir," a constable quickly informed, pointing to Eleanor and the boys. "The charges are being processed now," he said.

When the superintendant's gaze fell on their little group, Sidney felt his mother's body stiffen beside him. He immediately looked to the floor, hoping that by avoiding eye contact the man would pay them no attention. The immense figure ambled up to the trio and stopped right in front of them. Still staring at the floor, Sidney took note of the man's shoes--immaculate black leather, *polished that morning*, he guessed.

The superintendant examined them, one by one, and then set his gaze on Eleanor. "And what is your name?" he asked.

She slowly looked up at him. "Eleanor."

"I understand that these are your boy's," he said.

"Yes," this is Sidney and this is George," she said, looking over at the boys. "Is there a problem sir?" she asked.

"Well, if you consider sleeping in doorways a problem, then I suppose there is," he sarcastically replied. "How long has this been going on?"

Eleanor squirmed uncomfortably in her chair. "Only a short while sir," she said. "You see, my husband passed away and it's made things difficult. But I can assure you sir, I have work and the boys and I will have our own place soon," she lied.

"Yes, I see. But until then, the boys should have a warm bed and three good meals-a-day. Don't you agree?" he asked.

"Yes, I suppose so," she said. "But, well, right now, I just don't have the means and-"

The man quickly interrupted. "It'll be fine ma'am," he said. "I will see to it that your boys are looked after, you know, while you get things in order. Come with me to my office. There are just a few forms that need to be signed and it'll all be taken care of."

It sounded easy and Sidney felt his mother's body relax. *Maybe the big man wasn't so bad after-all*, he thought. And that was the first time he had heard his mother speak of having work and their own home soon. A morning that started out so terrifying suddenly seemed filled with hope and promise.

"Oh my, the charges!" Eleanor blurted.

"No need to worry about that either, Eleanor," the man said with a smile. "You see, I am the Superintendant of the Children's Organization. I can take care of that as well. Come along now. Let us get on with our business shall we."

The superintendant's office was only two blocks from the station, situated on the first floor of the enormous granite building. *A fortress, three windows high and four blocks around*, Sidney reflected as they approached the front door. He knew it well, at least from the outside. Sidney passed it daily in his search for things to steal, and he often imagined what horrible, dark deeds went on inside. It was an ominously cold, grey building, one that Sidney never imagined he would ever enter. Yet, here he was, with his brother, quietly seated in squeaky wooden chairs pushed up against the dark oak wall of the superintendants office.

The superintendant pulled another chair up to the desk. "Go ahead Eleanor, sit," he said, gently placing his hand on her back. He walked around to the other side of the desk and took his place in a large, high backed leather chair that swivelled. "Well then, let's get to it shall we," he said as he pulled two files out from the drawer and placed them on the desk. "These forms are just formalities Eleanor," he advised. "As I've already said, we will take the boys into our care. They will be expected to do a few daily chores, and in turn, they will be housed and fed. They will also be expected to attend school and church," he added.

Eleanor looked at the forms and then quickly glanced back at her sons, and then up at the superintendant. "I will be able to visit them, won't I?" she asked.

"Yes, of course," he said, "On the first Sunday of each month, right after service. Now, if you'll just sign here." The superintendant slid both forms across the desk and handed Eleanor a pen.

Eleanor started flipping through one of the documents and then stopped. "What is this, Canadian Clause?" she asked, pointing to the page.

"Oh, that is nothing," he said. "It's merely a seldom used option we employ, only for the most desperate of cases. I wouldn't worry about it Eleanor. Now if you'll just sign here, we can get the boys properly outfitted and orientated before lunch."

Eleanor looked back at the boys and then to the forms, and slowly added her signature, once to each document. "There, it's done," she said. "I hold you to our bargain sir." Eleanor stood up and walked over to her sons, giving them each a hug. "It'll be alright. I'll find work and a nice place for us all. We'll be together soon. I promise."

There was a glimmer of hope as mother walked out of the office. Her promise was comforting to Sidney and he knew she wouldn't let them down. At the same time, he was frightened and a sickening sensation churned inside, and for a moment, he imagined never seeing her again.

Chapter Five

The Home

Sidney stopped short and squinted, his eyes straining as the superintendant led them into the darkness of the long corridor. "Come along lads. Get a move on," he growled, not the same friendly voice he used with their mother. An eerie echo bounced off the cold stone walls with his every step, those shiny black shoes clicking out a sinister rhythm all the way. At the end of the hall, he shoved the boys into a large, dank room.

"It'll be okay, George," Sidney whispered, trying to sound brave, even though he'd never been so afraid in his life.

As the boys clung close to each other, they were briskly nudged towards a woman who seemed to be impatiently expecting their arrival. She was a tall, portly woman--her stature reminded Sidney of the many constables that had chased him. They were slow, but their brutality was legendary according to those who were caught. She wore a long drab dress and her head was wrapped in a dreary scarf that looked like a rag to Sidney. The scowl looked as if it had been frozen onto her face, and she held her arms straight down and close to her side, as if standing at attention. She rhythmically tapped a well-worn cane against her shin. She was an intimidating figure. Sidney's heart pounded hard inside his chest.

"This is Thelma. She is the senior matron here," the superintendant said. "You will do as she says. You will not speak unless you are spoken to. You will not make any trouble." The superintendant spoke with such authority that Sidney found himself nodding at his words. "Is that understood?"

"Yes, sir," both boys responded in unison.

The superintendant abruptly turned and left the room, leaving Sidney and George at the mercy of the fiendish woman.

The room was dimly lit and cold. A table, a couple of chairs and a large wash tub all occupied an area near the middle of the room. A few items hung on large hooks impaled into the walls. Sidney's street wise instincts told him to scream and run as fast as he could. But he couldn't move. There was no-where to go here. He was trapped.

Thelma looked both boys up and down, stopping for a few moments when she fully realized the extent of George's deformity. With her cane, she gave him two, short, sharp raps on the back of his knee. George winced in pain, desperately trying not to whimper for fear of receiving another blow.

"You won't be of much use around here like that, will you boy?" she muttered as she slowly walked around George, looking for other reasons to humiliate him. She let out a muffled grunt and stepped towards Sidney. "You, on the other hand, just might turn out to be good farm stock for Canada," she smiled, seemingly proud of her assessment.

Sidney was too afraid to pay much mind to what she said. He had never heard of a 'Canada' before and the woman's cruel demeanour emptied him of all curiosity.

Thelma instructed the boys to strip down. "Everything," she demanded. It was an unusual and daunting request, but Sidney didn't think it was the time or place to be defiant. He began to remove his ripped, muddy trousers. Just then, a short, fat man dressed all in black entered the room.

"Hello, Doctor," Thelma said, her voice suddenly sweet and welcoming. "They're just about ready for the examination." Thelma's cold stare warned Sidney to hurry undressing.

Sidney trembled when Thelma greeted the man. He remembered the night when another doctor came to visit. *Doctors are not to be trusted,* he thought.

"Good day Thelma," the doctor said as he marched directly to the table, dropping his bag on it. "Step over here, boy," he said, glaring directly at Sidney. His voice was gruff and uncaring. Thelma grabbed Sidney's arm and pulled him closer to where the doctor stood. The doctor took a step back, scanning Sidney's body, making a few grumbling noises while he examined his physical characteristics. He stepped forward and placed his cold hands on Sidney, squeezing here and poking there. After a few minutes, he nonchalantly nodded to Thelma. "This one's good," he said.

Thelma returned the nod as if to accept his opinion. "Step aside boy," she said. Thelma grabbed Sidney's arm and pulled him to one side. "You boy, come here," she said, violently pulling George over to the doctor.

Sidney squirmed uneasily as he watched his brother quiver. George's bad leg seemed even more twisted than usual.

The doctor immediately focused on the bent limb. He motioned for Thelma to pull a chair closer. "Sit, boy, so I can have a look at that," he said.

Thelma brusquely shoved George into the chair. The doctor firmly grabbed the deformity with both hands and forcibly attempted to straighten it. George cringed in pain while the doctor tried in vain to manipulate the leg into what he considered should be its normal position. When he let go, the appendage comfortably returned to its distorted place.

"Stop!" Sidney cried. "You're hurting him!"

"Quiet, boy!" Thelma snapped. She raised her arm and hit him on the backside with her cane. "That will be your last warning," she said.

The blow stung, and Sidney quickly realized that he had no choice but to silently stand by and witness his brother's agony.

After a few more minutes of twisting and pulling, the doctor stood back and exhaled a frustrated sigh. "This is no good," he finally assessed as he looked back up to Thelma. "This one is likely to be more of a burden than of any beneficial use," he declared.

Thelma again nodded in agreement with the doctor's assessment. "We'll find a proper place for him," she assured.

The doctor smiled, acknowledging Thelma's expertise in dealing with such matters. "Well then," he said, "I'll be on my way." The doctor grabbed his bag from the table and saw himself out.

Sidney and George stood naked and shivering, their arms wrapped around their chests. Without notice, Thelma grabbed each boy under an arm and led them towards the large tub. "Get in, the both of you."

The urge to defy her overwhelmed Sidney. He thought he might be able to defend himself, but he knew that George would suffer greatly for that. He helped his brother over the edge before climbing in himself. The water was icy cold. They faced each other, their bodies shaking, and Sidney noticed that George was starting to turn blue. They sat silently as Thelma was always within earshot. To speak would certainly be met with harsh consequences.

From a wire hook on the wall, Thelma grabbed a thick-bristled brush that looked more suited for scrubbing floors than for bathing a child. She lathered the brush with a generous amount of soap and commenced scrubbing Sidney's back. The sting of the coarse bristles grating back and forth against his skin was intense. He wanted to cry out, but intuitively knew that his cries would solicit an even harsher scrubbing.

"This will get the stink of the street off you boy," she scoffed.

Sidney was quickly learning that Thelma was not one to provoke lest he was prepared to pay the price. He sat closed mouthed as she turned the brush on George.

Ten minutes had passed before she was finished her work. "Get out," she said. "Take these towels, dry yourselves. There's more to be done." Thelma stood back and inspected them, making a visual estimate of their size. She briefly disappeared into another room and emerged with two piles of clean clothes. In each pile were wool pants, a shirt, a pair of socks, shoes and a wool cap. "Put these on," she barked as she rudely flung a pile at each boy. Sidney managed to catch his bundle, but George fumbled his badly and the clothes scattered across the floor. Sidney instinctively stepped forward to help pick them up.

"Step back boy," Thelma yelled. "He can look after his own."

Sidney moved away and winced when George bent over. The skin on his brother's back was red and raw, and there was a trickle of blood streaming down. The sight made Sidney forget his own pain.

Once dressed, Thelma scrutinized them again, ensuring that they looked presentable. She grabbed each boy by an arm and hurriedly steered them to a doorway at the other end of the room. "Into the court yard you go," she said, pushing them both through. George stumbled. If not for Sidney's quick action, his brother would surely have landed face down in the dirt. The heavy door slammed behind. Sidney looked up and came face-to-face with a hundred identically dressed boys, all curious to see the newcomers.

As he looked around the yard, Sidney's heart beat so hard that he thought it would rupture his chest. Two hundred eyes stared back at him, and from experience, he knew it was a crowd that would pounce like rabid rats at the slightest smell of fear. Sidney pulled on George's arm and they slowly moved towards a bench. Most eyes focused on George as he thud-thudded his way across the yard. Like so many times in the past, Sidney was prepared to fight to protect his older brother.

The two made it to the bench and George sat while Sidney stood his ground. No challenges were made, only a few unkind mutterings about the cripple. A few boys sauntered closer to get a better look, and then two, three at a time, the mob slowly dispersed. "Not much to see here," Sidney heard one of them say. While the others went back about their business, one boy remained and just looked at them. Sidney studied him for a moment. *About my age*, he thought. He was scrawny, like Sidney, but his hair was shiny and black, like mothers. And Sidney could look straight into his blue, eyes, the same blue as his mothers. But his eyes didn't smile like hers did.

"I'm James," the boy quietly muttered.

"I'm Sidney." He turned to George. "This is my-"

George cut in. "I'm George. We're brothers," he said. "What is this place?" he asked.

James looked puzzled. "This is the boy's orphanage," he said. "This is where they send you when no-one wants you."

"Not so!" Sidney retorted. "We just left our mother. She has work and she'll be coming for us soon, as soon as she finds a place for us to live."

"Oh," James said, lowering his head. "It's just that, well, none of the others have a real home."

Sidney and James took a place on the bench beside George and the three sat quietly for a few minutes.

"Our father is a carpenter," Sidney suddenly blurted. "Well, he was until he died. Father always seemed to be sick," he said. "After he was gone, we had to live on the streets. But mother's coming for us," he repeated. "Me and George will be home soon."

George wriggled on the bench. Sidney sensed that he might have been a little irritated with his abrupt haughtiness.

"So, what does your father do?" George asked.

James looked befuddled. "I don't know," he said. "I never met my parents. But my grandmother said he did the work of the devil, that he's a drunken bastard and that my mother is a whore."

"You never knew your mother or father!" Sidney said. The thought of anyone not knowing their own parents confounded him.

"Well, not that I remember," James replied. "My grandparents took me in when I was a baby."

"What were they like?" Sidney asked. "Did they sing to you, tell you stories?"

Again, James looked perplexed. "We sang hymns and prayed a lot," he said. "But mostly they were just old." James lowered his head. "Grandmother said I was a slow learner and that's why she needed to whip me, to beat the devil out of me," he said.

"Did they die?" George asked.

"No. They just got too old to keep me anymore, I suppose," James said.

"Have you been here long?" Sidney asked.

"Almost a year," James replied. "It's not so bad. The works hard, cleaning and scrubbing all day, and you have to go to school and church. But most of the staff are kind enough. Thelma is the one you need to watch out for," he warned. "She's cruel and she'll whip you for nothing."

Just then, the thundering clang of a bell rang out.

"Come!" James said. "Leisure time is done. We can't be late for lunch. This way."

Sidney and James helped George from the bench, and with one on each side of him, the three of them hobbled as fast as they could towards the dining hall. That afternoon, the boys sat down to their first meal at the home: fishcakes, potatoes, bread, and peas.

October 25, 1911

Sidney was awake before the house supervisor flipped on the lights and yelled, "everybody up, come on now, everybody off their cots."

It didn't take long for Sidney to become acquainted with the daily routine. The fear of punishment prompted him to stay one step ahead of any staff member's command, especially Thelma's. In these first two weeks, Sidney had seen her wrath rain down on other boys, *sometimes for no reason at all*, he thought. Sidney was even more fearful for George. It was obvious that the organization intended to keep the brothers apart. Upon coming in from the yard on the first day, they were immediately separated and assigned to different dormitories and work schedules and were even made to sit at different tables in the dining hall. They were able to get glimpses of one another from time to time, or share a whispered hello if their paths crossed close enough.

"Why do they make him do that?" James asked as he dipped his mop into the bucket he shared with Sidney. "He can barely walk. He's going to spill it all over."

Sidney dipped his mop into the bucket and casually looked down the hall towards the staff lounge. He watched as his brother slowly hobbled along, carefully balancing a fully laden tea tray. It was a chore that appeared to serve someone's cruel need for amusement rather than a duty suitable for a boy like George. "We were better off in the streets," he mumbled. "At least we had mother there."

October 26, 1911

Sidney took his place in the dining hall. Everyone else was seated for breakfast and the loud chatter of young boys filled the space. A few staff wandered about. Sidney scanned the room, looking for George. He wasn't at his usual spot. An uneasy feeling settled in his stomach.

Suddenly, Thelma appeared at the front of the room. "Silence, I'll have complete silence," she yelled. All went quiet. "There is one among you that has shown utter disrespect since the day he arrived, a stray whom God doesn't care enough about to endow with suitable abilities," she smugly proclaimed. "Because of his laziness and his carelessness, he has put an extra burden on all of you."

Sidney began to feel nauseous.

"This morning, you will witness his punishment, a reminder to all of you that you are burdens on society and will gratefully pay your dues with respect and obedience." Thelma motioned at two staff members to bring the offender in.

The dining hall filled with whispers, everyone speculating who the unlucky boy might be. Sidney knew.

"Silence," Thelma shouted.

Sidney could barely contain himself as he silently speculated what manner of humiliation his brother was about to endure. He wanted to jump up on the table and scream out, but fear glued him to his seat. He sat quietly with the others and watched as his brother was paraded to the front of the room.

George, visibly weak and wobbly, was barely able to limp the twenty steps to the front of the hall. His knees buckled and his crippled leg appeared even more twisted. He nervously looked into the crowded room as he was escorted directly to Thelma.

"Lower your trousers to your ankles, boy," she ordered. A quick flick of her cane connected hard on George's thigh, fervent notification that she meant business. Thelma's methods of getting one's attention were effective. George slowly undid his pants and pulled them down.

"Further! All the way down," she yelled.

Slowly, George complied.

"Now, bend over that table." Thelma pointed him towards a table directly in front of the group.

Sidney gripped the edge of the table until his knuckles turned white.

"Pull his shirt up higher!" Thelma screamed. "Hold his arms down firmly!"

The two staff members solemnly looked over to Thelma, then out towards the group, and then back to George. Even they showed signs of discomfort at the severe punishment unfolding before the room of boys. But they, too, did not resist her commands. They slowly pulled his shirt up to his neck and held his arms firmly onto the wooden slab.

Thelma wasted no time. She stood back and took a great swing with her cane, cleanly, solidly landing the stick across George's bare backside.

The sharp snapping sound pierced Sidney's ears. Tears rolled down his face as he watched his brother struggle, desperately trying to avoid the inevitable next blow. A large red welt from the first blow had already begun to rise as Thelma took aim for a second attack, and then a third, a fourth and a fifth. Sidney could see the agony on his brother's face, how George was struggling not to scream, but finally, he couldn't contain himself and he let loose a wail unlike any Sidney had ever heard. Powerless but hating himself for not being able to protect his brother, Sidney turned his face down to the ground. He was sure that George would never forgive him for letting him down. Even those boys in the dining hall who had themselves previously hurled barbs George's way turned their faces away from his punishment.

When she was done, Thelma scanned the stunned group with contempt in her eyes, brazenly looking for someone to challenge her authority. There were no takers. Suddenly, she set her icy stare on Sidney and started to walk towards him, steadily tapping the cane against her leg.

Sidney sat motionless as Thelma closed in, certain he would be her next victim, simply for the offence of being George's brother. As she drew nearer, his body tensed and he prepared himself for his beating.

"That's what happens to undisciplined brats," she said as she ominously towered over him, her cold, unsympathetic eyes staring directly into his. Thelma slammed the rod hard on the table, and then backed away. She again looked around the room. "Insolence will not be tolerated here," she shouted. Thelma stood silent for a moment, menacingly looking around the room. "Get on with breakfast," she finally barked, shifting her attention to the staff. "There's chores to be done."

Sidney felt relieved that he wasn't paraded to the front of the room, and disappointed. He felt shame for not being able to protect his brother. *At least he could have shared George's pain*, he thought. It would have been better than the guilt he felt.

Bleeding and crying, George was hauled away and that same day was sent to another orphanage. Sidney later learned that his punishment was for the crime of tripping and spilling the contents on the tea tray. His fate was inevitable, as if by design.

Time passed painfully slowly for Sidney from that day on and the promised visit with his mother was the only thing that he had to look forward to. He was impatient for the first Sunday of November to arrive. He couldn't wait to tell her about life at the orphanage, and of the brutality he had witnessed--about the torture of his brother, which had left his heart hardened like a frozen lump of coal.

At the age of five, Sidney was fast learning how unkind life could be. In the eight months since his father died, the seeds of hatred and mistrust had generously been sown and were beginning to take root. His mother was his only chance for salvation.

November 5, 1911

Sidney woke early with excitement, not because his sixth birthday was drawing near, but because it was the first Sunday of the month. He prayed that his mother would show up for a visit, and she didn't disappoint him.

Sidney was led from church to the area where she was waiting, impatiently tapping her foot. As soon as he saw her, Sidney broke away from the grip of his escort and ran as fast as he could into her open arms. He held her tightly, and suddenly, for the first time in many weeks, he felt safe.

His mother held him close while he cried uncontrollably. After a few moments, when the tears abated, she pushed him away to arm's length for an inspection.

"Are they treating you well, love?" she asked, un-fallen tears filling her blue eyes. "Are you eating well?" Without waiting for an answer, she pulled him back into her body. "I missed you, God how I missed you," Sidney heard her mumbling into his shoulder.

Sidney would have been satisfied to spend the entire visit curled up on his mother's lap without saying a word, just feeling safe, but she continued asking questions.

"How are they treating you here, Sidney?" she asked again.

"I'm fine, mommy, but they were horrible to George!" Sidney started to cry anew as he began to tell her the story.

Eleanor quickly interrupted. "Yes dear," she said. "I know. I've seen George. He's-" Eleanor turned her head away as her voice began to crack. She quickly wiped a tear from her eye and looked back at him. "He's fine Sidney," she calmly assured. "You certainly look healthy," she said. "Well fed."

"We'll, we have enough to eat," Sidney conceded, "but the food is always the same here." He still hadn't heard what he had hoped for--his mother to tell him that she'd be taking him home with her that day. He couldn't wait for the answer any longer. "Mother, can I come with you today?" he blurted.

Eleanor's eyes once again welled up. "Not today," she sadly replied. "I have many things to tend to before I will be able to take you with me."

Something about the tone of her voice made his stomach feel empty.

"But I will see you every month while you are here," she promised. "Come, let me hold you for a while."

Sidney, disappointed and discouraged, crawled up into his mother's arms, closed his eyes and savoured the temporary warmth of her body while she gently rubbed his head and whispered a lullaby in his ear. Their two hours passed quickly.

June 7, 1914

"Mother," he shouted. Sidney broke away from Mr. Dobbs and ran into her open arms.

As usual, Eleanor greeted him with her smiling eyes and a mighty squeeze. "Good morning love. Good morning Mr. Dobbs," she said, directing a friendly gaze towards Sidney's escort.

Mr. Dobbs was a short, fat, bald and generally unkempt man who bore the brunt of many jokes and rude comments amongst the boys, all behind his back of course. He had worked at the home for as long as any of them could remember and, in Sidney's estimation, was one of the more generous and kind workers there. "Good morning Eleanor," he replied, not in his usual cheery voice. Mr. Dobbs quickly turned his back on the pair and walked away.

Sidney noticed the baffled look on his mother's face, but he didn't pay much mind. She grabbed him up in her arms and gave him another hug. "And how was church this morning?" she asked.

"Fine," he said. "Father Thomas says that God will answer all our prayers, so I prayed all morning that you will be taking me home soon," a hopeful smile stretching across his face.

Eleanor fidgeted. "I'm sorry. Not today Sidney. I expect soon though," she said, turning her gaze to the floor.

Sidney smiled. He had been holding onto that promise for almost three years.

Their visit was abruptly interrupted when the superintendant stepped into the room. "Eleanor. I'm glad I caught you before you left," he said. "I have a bit of business to discuss with you."

"Good day sir," she greeted. "Business! What sort of business?"

The superintendant pulled up a chair and sat beside them. "Eleanor," he started. "We have done a review of your progress in the community, and, well it appears not much has changed since you gave up the boys, almost three years ago now. You're still living in shelters and you are unemployed much of the time."

Eleanor quickly stepped in. "Well, yes sir," she said, "but there is very little work and rents are so high. I do the best I can sir. I look every day and I always take what's offered," she added.

Suddenly, Sidney's feelings of hope began to weaken as the conversation between the adults unfolded. *They intend to keep me here forever*, he thought.

The superintendant wasted no time in getting to the point. "I'm sorry Eleanor," he said. "We have no choice. A ship is leaving for Canada in nine days. Sidney will be among seventy-five of our boys on-board."

Eleanor slumped in her seat, squeezing Sidney even tighter. "Canada!" she screamed. "Canada! Please, sir," she pleaded. "He's only eight. His family is here. He'll have no one there. I beg you, sir, please don't send my son away!"

Her words fell on deaf ears as the superintendant interrupted her pleas. "Eleanor! Eleanor!" he repeated. "The cost of keeping the boy here is high and he needs to start earning his own way," he said. "All of our lads are placed with good families in Canada. He'll have a much better life than you can give him here."

"No sir," she screamed. "You won't take him. I won't allow it. The courts will never allow such a thing," she insisted.

Her persistence relieved Sidney and a temporary calm washed over him.

"Eleanor," he sighed. "You signed the Canada Clause. We retain guardianship of the boy until he is eighteen years of age and we decide where his interests will be best served." The superintendant stood up and prepared to leave. "The ship sails from Liverpool on the sixteenth, at noon," he informed. "Passage has already been booked. If you are able to make the journey yourself, you will have time to say goodbye at the docks. Once he has arrived in Canada, we will forward all correspondence if you wish to remain in contact," he added.

Eleanor looked up at the superintendant's unyielding face and Sidney felt her tremble as the nauseating sense of defeat overwhelmed her.

Eleanor quietly held her son tightly, Sidney sensed for the last time. And then, the visit was done.

Chapter Six

The Voyage

June 15, 1914

Sidney took his place in line with seventy-four other boys in the dining hall. The fresh smell coming from the piles of new clothes stacked on tables up front filled the air. Mr. Dobbs seemed to be in charge of the proceedings. "Can I please have your attentions lads," he shouted.

Despite his senior position at the home, and despite his kindness, Mr. Dobbs was not well respected by some of the older, more rebellious boys. But on this occasion, everyone paid close attention. Fear of the unknown was high amongst the group. The room went silent.

Mr. Dobbs momentarily looked surprised by the collective obedience. "Well then," he started. "As you are all aware, we will be setting sail for Canada first thing in the morning. I know this is frightening for some of you, but I can assure you all, everything will be just fine. When we arrive, you will all be placed with fine families and you'll have more opportunities than you could ever imagine."

Sidney looked around the room as Mr. Dobbs spoke of the beauty of Canada and of the many riches there. A few boys seemed excited, even James. Others looked scared, like Sidney. His mind filled with thoughts of his mother and their monthly visits at the home. *Why can't she visit me in Canada?* he wondered, *just once-a-month.* Sidney detected a gloomy tone in Mr. Dobbs voice, as if he too was unconvinced of the merits for such ventures.

Sidney's full attention went back to the front of the room as Mr. Dobbs paused and looked over at the crowd, likely surprised that he hadn't yet been rudely interrupted.

"Alright then," he said as he motioned for two other staff members to stand with him. "Let's get you all outfitted for the journey."

One by one, each boy stepped up and was handed a pile. Sidney's issue was the same as everyone else's: a pair of knee-high wool pants, a shirt, one pair of socks, a pair of shoes, a jacket and a cap. Sidney was also given a small metal trunk inside of which was a second pair of socks, a shirt and pants, a bible, some writing paper and a pencil. Like all of the trunks, Sidney's had three words stamped on the side in big white letters. He stared at the letters, unable to make out what they said.

"Toronto via Halifax," Mr. Dobbs said.

Sidney looked up and saw Mr. Dobbs smiling at him. No matter what the other's thought of Mr. Dobbs, Sidney liked him. "Thank you sir. What does it mean?" Sidney asked.

"It means that our first stop in Canada will be Halifax, and then we'll travel overland to Toronto from there," he said.

Halifax, Toronto. Sidney had never heard of either. One thing that Mr. Dobbs said did grab Sidney's attention. "You'll be travelling with us sir?" he asked.

"Yes lad," Mr. Dobbs replied. "I've accepted a position at the home in Toronto. Now go on, take your things to your room and get to bed. We have a long day ahead." Mr. Dobbs patted Sidney on the top of his head and then moved on to assist other boys.

Knowing that Mr. Dobbs would be travelling with them made Sidney feel a little better, but it did little to quell the longing he still felt to be with his mother.

Sidney's sleep was restless that night. Panic consumed him as a beam of sunlight filtered into the dormitory. He listened to the others, still on their cots, some sniffling, some crying. Departure time drew near, for all of them. Sidney quietly rolled out of his cot and kneeled beside it. *Another prayer*, he thought. Another prayer for mother to put an end to this madness. She did promise that they would all be together again soon. *Why hasn't she come to put a stop to this talk of Canada*? The only thing that he wanted was to be with her. As his departure neared, Sidney felt more desperate than ever, but he was helpless with nowhere to turn. *Where is she*? he struggled. *Did she abandon me? Does she not care that I'm being sent away*? As these thoughts tumbled through Sidney's mind, hope was quickly slipping away.

Sidney ate little of his breakfast. While pushing the porridge around in his bowl, he noted a general mood of reluctance and fear among the boys who were set to leave for Canada. In a strange way, he felt comforted, knowing that he was not alone. At least there were others who were sharing his trepidation.

"Finish up," Thelma yelled. "We don't have all day."

Sidney contemptuously glared in her direction as she slapped the cane against her leg. *At least I'll be rid of her*, he thought. At the same time, he wondered what George was doing at that moment. *Was he being treated well? Was he happy? Was he being sent away too*? These thoughts only fuelled his anxiety. *Surely, he would never see his brother again*, he thought.

"Right then lads, time to go." Mr. Dobbs voice offered some comfort to Sidney. "Your belongings are at the station," he said. "Let's get you boys to the train."

Inside the train station, Sidney was surrounded by crowds of people in all directions. His head twisted this way and that, and his eyes focused in the direction of every woman's voice, keenly anticipating that his mother might come to rescue him. He was relentlessly disappointed.

Where is she? he wondered, for the thousandth time. His eyes searched for her right up until the last minute, even as they pulled away from the station, his face pressed tight against the glass. She was nowhere to be seen.

Aside from the constant rhythmic chatter of the train wheels rolling along the steel tracks, the trip was silent. Sidney had never been out of East London and all he could think about was how every passing building brought him farther away from George and his mother.

As the sludgy stench of the ocean filled the train car, Sidney sensed that they must be close to the ship that would take him away from everything he'd ever known. He couldn't even imagine a ship that would be large enough to carry all of the boys and their trunks across an ocean. The group disembarked from the train and boarded wagons that would take them the final leg to the shipyard. In the open air, the thick, heavy sea smell was almost strangulating.

"The ship!" yelled one of the boys, and Sidney looked up. Awe overtook him as the wagon pulled up next to an enormous grey liner that dauntingly clung to the dock. The loading ramps were down and large bundles of goods were already being packed into the belly of the huge vessel. For a brief moment, the enormity of the ship distracted Sidney's thoughts away from why he was there looking at it in the first place.

"Sidney!" a voice snapped his thoughts back like the crack of a leather strap. That time, when his eyes focused in the voice's direction, he clearly saw a familiar and inviting face. It was his mother. *She's come to free me after all!* he joyously realized. An overwhelming sense of relief flowed over him. He suddenly felt safe. *God had surely answered his prayers after-all*, he thought.

Sidney jumped off the wagon to run to her, only to be stopped short by one of the escorts, who grabbed him by his collar and yanked him back with a violent jerk.

"You'll say goodbye in due time, boy," the gruff voice behind him instructed as the escort's strong hands forced Sidney back into the wagon. For the moment, he could do nothing more than look over to where his mother stood and desperately try to catch her eye amid the sea of bobbing heads.

The boys disembarked from the wagons and were directed to carry their metal boxes to the end of the loading ramp. Only after the boxes were stacked and ready to be put on board were those children with family who had come to say goodbye allowed to visit.

"The boys will be loaded onto the ship in five minutes," the superintendant's booming voice informed. "All goodbyes will need to be said quickly."

Sidney was taken to his mother and he brimmed with excitement at the secret of knowing for certain that she was there not to say goodbye, but to take him home. Sidney reached out and tightly wrapped his arms around her neck. Tears were streaming from Eleanor's bloodshot eyes. Sidney's sense of urgency heightened and an emptiness filled his gut. "You are going to take me home, aren't you mother?" he anxiously asked.

Eleanor held him close and looked off into the distance. More tears flowed from her eyes and she began to sob. She cleared her throat. "I'm sorry Sidney. Not today," she said, squeezing him even harder.

Sidney fell limp in her arms, his last remnants of hope dashed. His voice was little more than a whimper as he grasped for anything that might save him from his inevitable fate, as if he were drowning and desperately struggling to find a life preserver that wasn't there. "But mother, you promised," he cried.

Eleanor held Sidney close and whispered in his ear. "You be a good boy, okay? Do as you're asked, and learn what they have to teach you." Before she could finish her sentence, she began to sob. "You'll come home soon," she assured him through her tears. "And I'll write to you every month."

Sidney's sadness left his mind paralyzed. The ship's horn sounded loudly, a deafening intrusion that abruptly signalled the end of their time together. Sidney clung to his mother, and she hung onto him just as determinedly. When Mr. Dobbs finally separated them, they were still reaching out to each other.

"Eleanor, I assure you that we'll take the very best care of your boy," he assured.

"How will I know that my letters will get to him?" she frantically shouted.

"I promise you they'll get to him. You can address them through me. I'll make sure they reach him."

With that, Mr. Dobbs pulled him away. Sidney was placed in the procession of boys that was being paraded up the ramp and onto the ship's deck. They were all lined up along the rail facing back towards the shipyard, separated from the hundreds of fare-paying passengers, all of whom seemed happy to be aboard the ship. *Why aren't they sad to be leaving*? Sidney wondered, not understanding how anybody could be smiling at a time like that.

From his spot near the railing, Sidney looked down from the towering ship to where his mother stood. He cried out as the ramps were pulled aboard and the ship began to slowly slip away from the dock. With all his heart he wanted to jump from the great height and swim back towards her. Suddenly, a sad, sorrowful tune wafted up on the light wind as the people on the dock below had started to sing:

God be with you till we meet again;
by his counsel's guide, uphold you,
with his sheep securely fold you;
God be with you till we meet again.

Tears blurring his vision, Sidney watched his mother's face straining back and forth, seeking him out. *I'm right here, mommy*! he wanted to cry, feeling lost in the sea of grey-clad boys.

The onlookers continued to sing:

Till we meet, till we meet,
till we meet at Jesus' feet;
till we meet, till we meet,
God be with you till we meet again.
God be with you till we meet again;
neath his wings securely hide you,
daily manna still provide you;
God be with you till we meet again.

As the ship gradually slipped further and further from the dock, his mother's frantic, searching face slowly disappeared from his sight.

God be with you till we meet again;
when life's perils thick confound you,
put his arms unfailing round you;
God be with you till we meet again.

God be with you till we meet again;
keep love's banner floating o'er you,
smite death's threatening wave before you;
God be with you till we meet again.

"Okay then, let's have your attention, lads."

Sidney immediately recognized the booming voice that was calling from behind him. It was Mr. Dobbs.

"Listen up, lads," he shouted, making sure he had everyone's ear. "I have a list of rules to follow while on the ship and I want you all to pay close attention." His befuddled and disoriented audience focused on every word. "You will be allowed to come on deck during the trip, but you will not stray from this area." Mr. Dobbs made a well-defined sweeping motion with his arm, identifying the area to which the boys would be restricted. "And you will under no circumstances mingle with any of the other passengers," he proclaimed. "Is that clear?"

Sidney felt his lips automatically move in time with the collective and obedient "yes, sir" that resounded from the group.

Mr. Dobbs paused. Satisfied that he was adequately understood and happy that not one of them challenged his authority, he continued. "Right then." Mr. Dobbs scanned the area and looked baffled, as if he had suddenly become lost. "Well now," he said. "As soon as I can locate a crewman to show us the way, we'll be off to our quarters. Yes, there's a fellow there," he said, pointing to a uniformed man. "Stay put lads. I'll be right back."

"Bloody scandalous!"

Sidney and James simultaneously turned their heads, both looking in the direction from which the woman's voice came. Until then, they hadn't noticed how close they were to the rail that marked the boundary between their group and the rest of the ship, or the four adults that happened to be standing right behind them on the other side.

"Bloody scandalous," the woman repeated as she contemptuously fixed her gaze on Sidney.

Sidney's attention was immediately drawn to the broad brimmed hat she wore, tightly pulled down over her head, nearly covering her eyes. It was garishly decorated with plumes of white feathers, bunches of pink flowers and thick puffy bands of purple silk that eventually turned into big, floppy bow, and she held onto it tightly, obviously fearing that it would be blown off her head and forever lost at sea.

Sidney nearly broke into all out laughter at the sight, but managed to restrain himself to just a snicker, which he indiscreetly tried to conceal by looking at James. Seeing that James was having a similar reaction made it even harder for him to contain himself.

The woman haughtily averted her gaze from Sidney, clearly incensed by his disrespectful mannerisms. "It's bloody well not acceptable that we should have to travel with this bunch." The woman turned to the others in her group. "Not only will they steal anything that's not secured, these waifs are infected with god knows what diseases and contagious mental insufficiencies." The other adults scanned the boys, their grimaced faces revealing that they concurred with her assessment. "Bloody scandalous," she repeated as they turned and walked away.

The brief encounter stunned Sidney and he didn't immediately grasp what the woman was going on about, or why she stared at him with such disdain. He and James stood motionless, both trying to decipher what had transpired.

"What did she mean?" James asked. "I don't have a disease."

Sidney smiled and looked at his friend. "She was right about one thing," he said. "I'd steal her purse and everything in it." Sidney began to laugh. "I'd leave her the hat."

Sidney and James turned their attentions back to the others, their spirits temporarily lifted. They playfully shoved one another and lightly punched each other's arm, waiting for Mr. Dobbs to return with further instructions.

"Let's move on to the sleeping quarters, shall we?" Mr. Dobbs yelled as he moved towards a nearby door. In single file, Sidney and the others started on a gruelling trek down several flights of narrow iron stairs. *We must be near the very bottom of the ship,* Sidney thought, almost panicking at the notion that they must now be below sea level. The further down they went, the louder the clanging and rumbling noises of the giant engines became. The pungent smell of oil and grease became stronger as they ventured further still into the bowels of the boat.

The stench filled Sidney's nostrils, making him feel sick to his stomach. Looking around in the dim light, he noticed that some of the other boys had already started to take on an unusual shade of green. The ship heaved suddenly and the boys all lurched to the right.

Mr. Dobbs only just caught himself from tumbling down the stairs. "Let's be careful, shall we?" he noted, his voice a bit shaky. "But don't be afraid. Sailors say that sleeping at the bottom of a big ship like this is like sleeping in your mother's belly."

Sidney's nausea momentarily abated as his thoughts turned back to his mother, imagining her arms wrapped around him, holding him tightly. He briefly felt the safety of her company and for a moment, he felt her presence just as if she were with him then. Despite the nagging feelings of emptiness and loneliness he felt inside, Sidney still believed that she would save him someday soon. He still had hope.

Suddenly, a violent swell knocked Sidney back into the moment, causing him to slam brusquely into one of the other boys. He fell, solidly banging his knee against the handrail. "Sorry, mate," he blurted as he sprang back to his feet. It was James. The two exchanged fearful glances and pretend smiles. The terror on James face only served to fuel Sidney's fright even more. He reclaimed his place in line, trying to balance himself as the ship swayed unremittingly in the rolling sea. He continued to follow the group as they dutifully allowed themselves to be sucked further into the vessel's growling belly. Sidney's bruised knee was a minor discomfort compared to the sickness he felt in his stomach and the throbbing pain that was building in his head.

After descending deep into the ship's hull, Mr. Dobbs opened a door that led into a long and narrow hallway. Off each side of the hall were five smaller doorways. One by one, Mr. Dobbs opened the doors.

Sidney squeezed in amongst the others, all of them cramming together, trying to see inside the rooms. Sidney looked in and saw a cramped sleeping cabin, the space almost fully occupied by six small wooden bunks each with a thin mattress covered by a grey wool blanket. The air was thick and Sidney found himself nearly choking. There were no windows or vents to provide fresh air.

"Right then, lads," Mr. Dobbs muttered as he carefully scanned the confined and smelly lodgings. Mr. Dobbs himself appeared bewildered by the restricted space and revolted by the smell. He paused for a moment and looked back at the line of boys pushing through the tight doorway.

"Well, then, let's start with the first six," he shouted. He counted off the first half-dozen heads he came to, calling out each boy's name in turn. "You boys will have the first cabin. One, two, three..." Mr. Dobbs counted off the heads.

Sidney was among the boys in the last group of six to get a cabin. He breathed a sigh of relief that he had been chosen for a bunk, but wondered where the leftover boys would go.

Mr. Dobbs also seemed to be wondering and he looked perplexed. He opened another door at the end of the long hallway and peered in. "This must be the common room," he said. "I suppose the rest of you will have to sleep on the floor in here, or wherever else I can find for you," he glumly muttered. Mr. Dobbs sighed as he stepped into the common room. Sidney couldn't quite hear everything that Mr. Dobbs said before disappearing, but he thought he heard words that he was taught were reserved for adults.

In his cabin group was James, a comforting detail considering that the other four boys were amongst the oldest of the group. One by one, Sidney and his bunkmates filed into their cabin, each choosing a bunk. Sidney climbed onto his lumpy, itchy straw mat, hoping that he would feel better if he lay down. He didn't as the stench from below sustained its unrelenting attack.

Just as they settled in, one of the older boys hunched over a small bucket in the corner and proceeded to expel what little contents he had in his stomach. The sour stink of vomit soon invaded the small space, competing with the repugnant stench coming from below. As the odour hit Sidney's nostrils, he started to gag, nearly banishing the acrid contents of his own stomach. He managed to confine his urges to a few morsels that made it part way up before quickly being swallowed.

Sidney regained his composure and looked around the cabin, making a quick assessment of the others. He didn't know any of them well, but was happy to observe that none among them were troublemakers or bullies. His attention focused to James, who by then was lying on his own bunk, obviously just as frightened and bewildered as Sidney himself was. Sidney contemplated speaking to James, but reconsidered given the silence in the room.

Over the next couple of days Sidney survived on a diet of dry biscuits, tea and the occasional plum, his appetite tainted by both sea sickness and heartache. Even those bits of nourishment frequently ended up in the bucket. He preferred the fresh sea air of the open deck and ventured there whenever he could.

Sidney stood for many hours by himself at the rail, looking back over the endless expanse of ocean that separated him from his mother and remembering her embrace, her loving words, and her promises. As the days slowly passed, his hope of being reunited with her faded little by little as the ship heartlessly pushed towards Canada.

One afternoon, he was passing the time at the rail as usual by trying to imagine what life would be like in Canada. *Would things really be as wonderful for him as the adults at the orphanage had told him they'd be*? He tried to imagine himself sitting around a dinner table with a smiling, handsome family, the dark-haired mother putting more roast beef on his plate while the well-dressed, healthy father tussled his hair. Even in his vision, however, he was sad from missing home.

Suddenly, a gentle voice brought him back to the ship. "How are you managing, lad?"

Sidney turned to see Mr. Dobbs leaning against the rail beside him, a worried look on his face. "I'm fine, sir," he mumbled as he turned away and looked back out to the open sea. He didn't like lying to Mr. Dobbs.

There was a long silence. "We're all in God's hands, Sidney. None of us are in command here," Mr. Dobbs finally uttered.

Sidney curiously looked at Mr. Dobbs, unsure of what he was talking about.

"You're a good boy, Sidney. Everything will be fine, you'll see. You'll be happy in Canada, and I'm sure we'll find you a good family to live with," he assured.

Sidney looked back at Mr. Dobbs, wondering if the man had just read his thoughts. He tried to take comfort in the adult's words, but he knew that no family, no matter how perfect, could ever replace his mother and brother. A surge of courage washed over him. "When will I see my mother again?" Sidney asked, taking the opportunity to get the answers he desperately needed. "When will I go home?" he uttered, anxious with anticipation that Mr. Dobbs would relieve him of his torment.

Mr. Dobbs lay his hand on Sidney's shoulder. "I don't know, Sidney," he said. "I don't know." Mr. Dobbs hung his head and turned away, and

Sidney turned back to the rail and looked out to sea, his mind drifting back to his mother and home.

July 01, 1914

"Are you afraid?" Sidney asked.

"Yes, a little," James said. "I've never been away from home before."

Sidney moved closer. "I'm glad we're friends," he said. "We'll have each other when we arrive in Canada. We'll stick together."

James glanced at Sidney and smiled. "Yes," he confirmed. "We'll be friends forever."

"Well, how about that!" Mr. Dobbs exclaimed as he made his way over to the two boys, clapping a hand on each of their narrow shoulders. "We've arrived in Canada!"

By then, the rest of their group had gathered on deck for their morning dose of fresh air. The chaotic chatter quickly faded to absolute silence as they assembled along the rail watching the fog-drenched silhouette of their new home come into view. As the ship neared even closer, the boys could clearly see its coastline, stretching beyond unimaginable distances in two directions. Sidney was both elated and saddened by the sight.

"In just a few hours, we'll be in the harbour and you boys will be welcomed to your new homeland," Mr. Dobbs went on. Sidney was looking forward to setting foot on dry land, to feeling steadiness under his feet and stillness in his gut.

Canada greeted the boys with sunshine and calm as the ship's captain slowly positioned his vessel next to the dock. It was ten o'clock in the morning by the time she was securely moored. Sidney and most of the other boys had already gathered on deck with their trunks, all anxiously waiting for Mr. Dobbs to lead them off the ship.

Sidney peered over the railing. The dock below was a bustle of activity as dozens of workers milled around. A crowd of eager men and women had gathered, their faces turned up in search of people they knew.

Sidney and his group stood and watched patiently as the ramps were lowered and the fare-paying passengers disembarked, followed by their luggage.

"Can I have your attention, lads?" Mr. Dobbs shouted. Sidney held his breath. The group looked on attentively, waiting for their instructions to go ashore. "There'll be a bit of a delay before you boys can leave the ship," he announced. A collective groan escaped around Sidney. "I will go ashore myself and ensure that your trunks are properly loaded onto the train," Mr. Dobbs continued, raising his voice to be heard over the din of the boys. "You lads make yourselves comfortable here until I return."

Mr. Dobbs scanned the exhausted group, ensuring that everyone had heard and understood the instructions, and then he quickly turned and started towards the ramp. Sidney saw him hang his head, seemingly saddened that his boys were left stranded on the ship while the other passengers were so quickly unloaded and ceremoniously greeted below. Sidney watched as Mr. Dobbs walked off the ramp with the rest of the passengers and made his way to some waiting wagons.

A long hour passed, and Sidney and the others waited patiently as workers unloaded the cargo hold. Sidney and James made themselves comfortable, squatting on the filthy deck, their backs against the railing. Another two hours passed. The bustle below faded to a few men moving the last of the ship's cargo to its place.

"Maybe they've decided to send us back home," Sidney remarked, a glint of excitement obvious in his voice. "Maybe that's why they're keeping us on board!"

James's eyes widened at the thought. They jumped up and looked over the railing for clues that the ship was preparing to turn itself around. Their hopes were immediately dashed as they saw their metal trunks being loaded onto wagons on the dock below. Sidney let out a resigned sigh.

From their vantage point, the boys could see Mr. Dobbs, who seemed to be energetically involved in a vigorous discussion with three well-dressed and imposing men. Although Sidney couldn't hear what was being said, he could see that Mr. Dobbs was displaying an unusual amount of body language and he frequently pointed up towards the youngsters.

Finally, after three and a half hours had passed, Mr. Dobbs returned to the deck and announced that they could go ashore. "But first, I'll need to count heads to make sure I'm delivering all my cargo." His attempt at a joke fell flat with the exhausted boys.

Sidney was in the middle of the line of boys descending the ramp. Once on the dock, they were rudely greeted by one of the men with whom Mr. Dobbs had been in conversation with earlier.

"Stop right where you are, boys," the stern-looking man barked. "I'm the head immigration agent here. Before you take one step further, you'll all need to pass inspection."

Sidney's gut clenched. His mind flashed back to the gruff inspection he and George had undergone at the orphanage when they first arrived.

"This inspection will be done quickly and respectfully, I trust," Mr. Dobbs insisted.

The agent glared at him with a look of annoyed disapproval and then turned to the group of young grey-clad boys. "This way!" he ordered. The ill-tempered and thoroughly irritated man led them to a shed. He shuffled his feet impatiently until all of the boys were gathered into the confined space. "These doctors will examine you all before you will be allowed any further into Canada," he announced, pointing towards two similarly stern-looking men that Sidney had seen talking to Mr. Dobbs earlier. "You will all be co-operative with these gentlemen. Is that clear?"

One by one, the doctors looked each of the boys over, poking and prodding, noting any obvious defects. Sidney waited for his turn with dread, but his exam was rather uneventful, the doctor only commenting on the conspicuous ailments brought about by two weeks at sea before briskly shoving him to the side.

Sidney caught sight of James and crept closer to him, and together the friends waited for the rest of the boys to be inspected. Two full hours passed before the procedure was completed.

"Congratulations," the immigration agent bellowed. "You're all fit to enter Canada." With that, the two doctors exited the shed, slamming the door behind them.

"Okay boys, listen up. Let's have your attention please," Mr. Dobbs shouted. "There's one more matter to deal with before we continue on our journey. Twenty-five of you will be staying on in Halifax to live with families here. The rest of you will be coming with me on the train to Toronto. Please listen closely. I will call out the names of those who will be staying here. Would those boys please stand over here when their names are called." Mr. Dobbs pointed to an area on the opposite side of the shed.

Sidney and James stood close, neither saying a word. Sidney was silently fearful that one of them would be called but not the other. He counted on his fingers as Mr. Dobbs called out the names: "Martin, Gordon, Terrance, Kevin." Mr. Dobbs paused for a moment and looked over at the two friends. He looked back to his list and hesitated. "James," he read out. He paused for another moment and without looking up again, he continued. "Mark, Lucas, Brett." After all twenty-five names were called, Mr. Dobbs stepped back and looked over towards immigration agent. "That's all of them sir," he respectfully reported.

The agent casually sauntered towards the smaller group, carefully inspecting each boy as he drew closer. "There are only twenty-four boys here!" he hollered, spittle forming at the corner of his mouth. "Who is missing?"

Mr. Dobbs again looked over to the two boys and hesitantly pointed to James.

The man briskly walked over to James and grabbed him by the arm. "We don't have all day here, boy!" he yelled. He roughly dragged James to the area where the other Halifax-bound boys were standing. Sidney didn't get a chance to say goodbye to his friend. As with his brother, Sidney hadn't been able to save James, either.

"Try to get comfortable," Mr. Dobbs advised as he walked down the aisle of the car that was reserved for his group. "It's a long journey to Toronto." Sidney slouched in his wooden seat and fell into a deep unconsciousness that not even the train's resounding whistle could disturb. He remained there until the warmth of the sun's rays beat directly onto his face the following morning.

Three days later, the train reached its destination. As it pulled into the Toronto station, Sidney was overcome by a wave of intense afternoon heat. The air all around him was thick and sticky, and the sky was dark with ominous black storm clouds threatening to unleash all their fury.

As the group waited for their trunks to be unloaded, they were greeted by a portly, well-dressed man who appeared to Sidney to be friendly enough. He pumped Mr. Dobbs' hand in greeting and then smiled and laughed abundantly as he hustled the boys together.

"I'm Mr. Donnelly. I'm in charge of operations in Canada," he proudly announced. He seemed elated to see that his party of soon-to-be farm hands had arrived safely and mostly in-tact. "Welcome to Toronto, lads," he cheerfully proclaimed, vigorously waving his hands around as he spoke.

Sidney watched him through heavy, exhausted eyes, then scanned the ragged-looking bunch of boys on all sides of him.

"Okay, then," Mr. Donnelly concluded, seemingly disappointed at his failure to evoke a more cheerful response. "Let's get into the wagons and over to the school before these clouds open up on us, shall we?" he said, gesturing towards the sky.

Sidney and the others followed him to six horse-drawn wagons that were at the ready to transport the group. No one spoke as they loaded onto five of the wagons and their metal trunks were placed onto the sixth.

"Okay lads, twenty more minutes and we'll be there!" Mr. Donnelly called, motioning for the drivers to get moving.

For the next twenty minutes, as the wagons bumped and jerked along, Sidney's mind focused on the looming storm clouds above.

Chapter Seven

A Brief Reprieve

The Toronto home was abuzz with activity during the first week following the group's arrival, with men and women, farm families mostly, arriving at the home to retrieve their boys. A few of those first meetings seemed friendly enough, but most were awkward and detached, as if some of the farmers weren't happy with their pick of the lot.

Three weeks after his arrival, Sidney and two other boys his age were the only ones who hadn't been placed with a family. With each passing day, he was more convinced that they'd simply have to send him back to his mother if there was no home for him in Canada.

In a way, Sidney felt sad to see the others go, but he and his two young companions did have the run of the place, almost. They still needed to tend to their chores. Mr. Donnelly was very strict about that. Nevertheless, the boys had more time to themselves than they'd had at the home in England. They ate well, and Mr. Donnelly wasn't cruel like Thelma had been.

July 26, 1914

"Come, Sidney," Mr. Dobbs called from across the dining hall. "You will come to the market with me this morning."

"Yes, sir! Right away, sir," Sidney chirped. He had one more table to clean, and then he'd be done with his morning chores. "Will we be walking, sir?" he asked.

"Yes, Sidney. It's a lovely morning and we won't be bringing much back," Mr. Dobbs advised. "You can bring a penny for a treat," he offered.

"Oh, yes sir, Mr. Dobbs!" Sidney cheerfully shouted. "I'll just need to go to my room first." Finishing the last table, Sidney scurried off to get some of the money that Mr. Dobbs had paid him for doing extra chores around the home. Sidney had never been paid for doing extra chores before, but he happily accepted Mr. Dobbs' pennies.

Sidney retrieved his penny and he and Mr. Dobbs walked out the back door together. The pair strolled leisurely down the street, neither saying much as they soaked up the warmth of the early morning sun. Sidney was looking forward to helping Mr. Dobbs pick up a few provisions at the market, but it soon became clear that Mr. Dobbs had other reasons for wanting to walk with Sidney that morning.

"Well now, Sidney, how are you liking Canada?" Mr. Dobbs asked.

"It seems fine here, sir," Sidney quietly answered. Then another thought entered his mind. *Perhaps Mr. Dobbs is about to tell me they're sending me back to England*! "I do miss mother terribly sir," he added for good measure.

"You know, Sidney, I'm sure your mother thinks of you as often as you think of her. In fact, I'm sure she is thinking of you at this very moment," Mr. Dobbs chuckled as he gave Sidney a reassuring smile.

That was not quite the response that Sidney had been hoping for. "I do hope so, sir," Sidney said with an exaggerated sigh. "I think she will be making plans for me to return to England soon," he supposed, forcing the subject further.

"Perhaps, Sidney." Mr. Dobbs' response wasn't very convincing.

Sidney sighed again, for real this time.

Mr. Dobbs cleared his throat. "Well Sidney. Mr. Donnelly has informed me that there is a couple, a nice young couple," he qualified, "that is interested in taking you into their home near Aylmer. How do you feel about that?"

All of the air left Sidney's lungs and he suddenly felt like he was suffocating. His legs stopped short on the sidewalk, unable to move.

His young mind suddenly filled with a thousand mangled thoughts. He wasn't sure what to say. He looked up at Mr. Dobbs, again hoping for some answers. Then the way out became clear to him, as clear as day. *I can't go anywhere*, he thought. *Mother will be sending for me soon to take me back to England, and I need to be ready.*

"Thank you sir, but I think I will stay here with you until mother sends for me," Sidney replied in his most polite voice.

Mr. Dobbs hung his head. "I'm afraid that won't be possible, lad," he said, his voice suddenly firm. "It has already been arranged, Sidney. You will leave the day after tomorrow."

Sidney glanced up at the man he'd considered his friend with a look of solemn resignation.

Mr. Dobbs took Sidney gently by the arm and led him to a bench just outside the market. "I know that you're afraid, Sidney, but I have been assured that Mr. and Mrs. Olson are a fine couple and they will give you a good home. You will go to school every day, and to church every Sunday. Those are the terms they have agreed to."

Sidney looked up. It was clear from Mr. Dobbs' face that there was no way out of it. "And they will come for me in two days?"

"No Sidney. You'll be leaving in two days," Mr. Dobbs corrected. "They cannot come here to pick you up. You will need to travel by train yourself to London."

Sidney's ears immediately perked up. "London!" he shouted. It sounded too good to be true, he was going back to England after all.

"Yes, well, to a place called London not far from here," Mr. Dobbs said. "Canada's London. A very nice town," Mr. Dobbs clarified. "They will pick you up there. It's only three hours away," he quickly remarked. "You'll be fine, lad."

A dreadful emptiness filled Sidney's gut. "Oh, Canada's London," he mumbled. Sidney's hopes of ever seeing his mother again had been dashed yet again.

The pair got up from the bench and slowly started back the way they came, the market forgotten.

"Would you like to stop for a treat on the way back?" Mr. Dobbs offered.

Sidney stared down at the sidewalk as they plodded along. "No thank you, sir. Not today."

Mr. Dobbs put his arm around the youngster and laid a hand on his shoulder. A cool breeze chilled them as the sun slipped behind the clouds that were drifting in off the lake.

The pair silently returned to the home. Sidney withdrew to his bed in the dorm and stared at the ceiling until supper time.

"Wake up Sidney. Pull out your trunk," Mr. Dobbs cheerfully shouted.

His booming voice startled Sidney, causing him to sit straight up in his bed. Bleary eyed and still half asleep, Sidney stretched and let out a big yawn. *What's all the commotion about*, he wondered. When he was finally able to focus on Mr. Dobbs smiling face, his first thought was that his friend had come with good news. *Maybe they've changed their minds*, he thought.

"Well, good morning lad. I have some things for you." Mr. Dobbs was carrying a bundle of clothes, and he held up the garments one by one. "These are overalls for work, this is an extra wool coat, some extra socks, and an extra shirt." Mr. Dobbs set the clothes on the bed while Sidney pulled his trunk out from underneath. "Oh yes, and a pair of rubber boots as well," he added.

"Thank you, sir," Sidney said, doing his best to integrate some excitement into his voice. He knew that the gesture was Mr. Dobbs' way of boosting his spirits. Sidney opened the trunk and Mr. Dobbs helped him pack the extra items inside. There wasn't much room left after everything was in, and the trunk was considerably heavier than it was before.

"How will I carry it, Mr. Dobbs?" Sidney asked as he strained to lift one end off of the floor.

"It's okay, Sidney," Mr. Dobbs said as he grabbed a handle to check the weight of the box for himself. "I will go with you to the station in Toronto and help put your trunk on the train," he assured. "I'm sure Mr. and Mrs. Olson will be generous enough to assist you at the other end."

Early the following morning, Mr. Dobbs loaded Sidney's trunk onto the wagon that would transport them back to the same station they had left behind three weeks earlier.

Before Sidney climbed onto the wagon, Mr. Donnelly approached him and fastened a bright red tag onto his grey woollen coat. "This is how Mr. and Mrs. Olson will recognize you, lad," he said. "Don't lose it."

"No, sir," Sidney politely replied. He climbed aboard the wagon and Mr. Dobbs gave the command for the horse to start. As the wagon jerked forward, Sidney looked back at the Donnelly home, the only place where he'd truly felt safe during the previous two years. His brief reprieve was over.

Mr. Dobbs carried Sidney's trunk onto the train as promised and placed it neatly under the wooden bench. From his satchel, he pulled out a bag containing a sandwich and a few pieces of fruit and handed it to the boy. "This will keep your belly full until you are home," he said. "The conductor will see to it that you get off at the right station. Don't leave the train until he tells you to."

"Yes, sir. Thank you, sir."

"Do you have any questions, Sidney?" Mr. Dobbs asked in his gentle way.

Sidney thought for a moment. "Just one, sir. What if mother sends a letter? How will I know?"

"We'll forward any letters to Mr. Olson, lad," Mr. Dobbs promised. "He will see to it that you receive them." Mr. Dobbs' eyes softened as he looked at the boy. "Best wishes, lad. May God be with you." At that, he quickly turned away and stepped off the train, leaving Sidney alone to stare out the window as the engine started to pull away from the station.

Sidney felt the tears well in his eyes as he watched Mr. Dobbs slowly disappear from his sight, just as mother had at the dock in Liverpool only six weeks before.

The train quickly pushed up to speed, its loud horn sounding to warn of its powerful presence. Sidney looked around at the other passengers in the car. An elderly couple sat in front of him, both beaming as if they had just met, enthusiastically engaged in private chit chat. He looked over to the well-dressed man just ahead in the opposite row, immersed in a book and seemingly oblivious to everything and everybody around him. Sitting across from him was a young family, a mother and father and their daughter, a girl a few years younger than himself, he surmised. She seemed quite interested in Sidney and stared at him intently.

"Mother, why is that boy dressed so strangely?" she asked, tugging at the lady's dress to get her attention.

Sidney immediately reddened. He had long ago noticed that none of the other kids he'd seen in Canada dressed the same as the boys from the home. He knew that his short wool pants, the black socks pulled nearly to his knees, the double-breasted wool jacket and the funny little cap certainly did make him stand out in a crowd. Suddenly, he was acutely aware that he was totally alone for the first time since he arrived in Canada.

"I'm sorry honey, what did you say?" the lady said, picking the girl up and setting her on one knee.

"Why is that boy dressed so strangely?" she repeated, pointing directly over to Sidney.

The woman looked at Sidney and quickly pulled her daughter tight to her body. "Pay no attention to him, darling. Those kind are nothing but trouble," she scolded. The young girl's father glanced over and gave Sidney a stern look. The family went back about their business, the little girl occasionally sneaking a curious look at the strange young fellow.

The woman's comments made Sidney feel small and irrelevant. He turned away and stared out the window, oblivious to the lush green countryside rushing by.

At precisely twelve noon and as scheduled, the train pulled to a stop at the London Train Station. Looking out from his window, Sidney could see the crowd gathered on the platform, eagerly waiting to greet the other passengers as they prepared to unload. He scanned the mass to see if he could find a young couple that looked as if they were expecting to greet a young boy travelling alone.

The smiling priest tightly squeezing his bible close to his chest and standing by himself didn't draw Sidney's attention. Neither did the two elderly women sitting quietly on a bench. And then, a smiling young couple holding hands caught his eye. Sidney watched them closely, and confirmed that they seemed to be waiting for someone special to come off the train. *That must be them. That must be Mr. and Mrs. Olson.*

"Okay, lad, this is your stop," the conductor informed, wobbling up the narrow train aisle. "Here, let me help you with that trunk," he offered. The conductor reached under the seat and pulled out Sidney's metal chest and together they walked down the aisle and stepped out onto the platform.

"I'll just set your trunk over here. Did you see your people?" he asked.

"Yes sir, I think so, sir. I think they are right over there." Sidney pointed at the crowd in the general direction of the young couple.

"Okay, then. Well, best of luck to you, son," the conductor said as he stepped back onto the train.

Sidney turned towards the crowd and struggled to find the couple. Straining, he looked over and under the shifting crowd. Finally he spotted them, still looking towards the train, obviously still waiting for their party. *They mustn't have seen the red tag on my jacket yet*, he thought. He started to walk towards them, and then stopped short, not wanting to leave his trunk unattended. *Maybe when the crowd is smaller*, he decided. *They will surely see me when there were fewer people on the platform.*

Suddenly, the couple threw up their arms and broad smiles covered their faces as they ran to greet the old man who had just been helped from the train by the same conductor who'd helped Sidney off a few minutes earlier.

Disappointment enveloped him as he watched the couple and the old man walk away and disappear into the crowd. Sidney sat heavily on his trunk, scanning the crowd to see if there were any others who might be there for him. But he spotted no one. The crowd slowly disappeared and still no one came for him.

Nearly an hour later, Sidney was still sitting alone on the platform at the London Train Station with tears welling in his eyes, waiting for the Olson's to come and take him to a place that he was sure would never feel like home.

Chapter Eight

The Hand of the Devil

George's thick, working man hands wrapped tightly around the still nearly full tea cup--they had by now absorbed all of its heat. His focus was intense as Mary shared with him the details of his father's early childhood.

"Oh my!" she said. "You must be ready for more." Mary stood and reached for George's cup.

"Yes, thank you," George replied, careful not to spill what was left of his luke warm tea over to her. "There must have been a process," he said, "you know, for placing these young boys. They must have ensured that their best interests were being considered."

Mary pondered for a moment as she poured them both another cup of tea. She delicately handed George his cup and sat back in her chair.

"Well, according to your father, the process for procuring a boy was rather simple," she said. "One just needed to make application, agree to a few general terms and provide some form of reference, like a letter from the local clergy. Under the terms of the program, farmers only needed to ensure that boys under the age of fourteen went to school and church and were reasonably well clothed and, of course, fed. In exchange, the boy would perform labour around the farm for his keep. The older boys were paid a nominal wage for their work," she added. "In any case, all of the youngsters were indentured until the age of eighteen."

"Someone surely checked on them now and again," George said.

"If possible, I suppose," Mary said. "An agent from the organization was supposed to visit each family once a year. It's unfortunate that no-one ever did follow-up with your father," she said. "His story might have been much different if they had."

July 26, 1914

Sidney sat on his trunk, biting into the last apple from the bag that Mr. Dobbs had given him. The town clock sounded twice and still no one had come for him. He finished the apple and dragged his trunk to another area of the platform, setting himself up under a small awning that offered some shade from the scorching afternoon sun. He walked to the end of the platform to see if anyone was approaching.

The only sign of movement, however, were those off in the distance going about their business. Not one of them was concerned that he was stranded there with nowhere to go. The station itself was deserted, except for the station master, who Sidney occasionally caught peering out the window at him with a gentle look on his face.

"You have been sitting here for quite some time, son," came a voice.

Sidney jumped back, startled by the man standing over him.

"Are you expecting someone?" the station master asked.

"Oh, yes sir," Sidney blurted. "Mr. and Mrs. Olson are coming for me," he said, as if the man would know who they were.

"Well, those clothes you're wearing don't seem suited for this hot weather," the man observed.

"Yes sir," Sidney replied. "But I can't take off my jacket, sir, or else the Olson's won't be able to see my red badge."

"Oh, I see. Would you like a glass of water?"

"Yes, thank you sir," Sidney gladly accepted. He hadn't had a drink since he left Toronto.

The station master went inside and momentarily stepped back out with a large glass full of ice-cold water. "Here you go, son. Drink up."

Just as Sidney put the glass to his lips, the pair was distracted by the jangle and clattering of an approaching wagon. They looked on as a rickety old cart pulled up close to where they stood at the end of the platform.

Sidney immediately noticed that the man holding the reins was enormous, even bigger than the superintendant back in England. He was a fat, dirty-looking character wearing well-worn coveralls and a torn straw hat under which tufts of wiry, curly black hair stuck out. His scraggly black and grey beard covered most of his round face and hung down to his protruding belly. The large, intimidating man glared down at Sidney through beady, cold blue eyes.

The woman sitting beside him on the wooden bench seemed not to have any expression at all. She didn't even look at Sidney or the station master. She just stared down at her boots.

"Hey boy, you Sid?" the man hollered down as he glared at the pair. His voice was gruff, exactly like what Sidney had expected would emerge from such a grizzly-looking creature.

"My name is Sidney, sir," he responded, wondering why such a motley couple was stopping to talk to him.

"Sidney!" the man laughed. "Who the hell gave you a name like that?" he scoffed.

Not realizing that the big man was mocking him, Sidney politely responded, "Well, sir, my parents named me."

"Oh, you knew your parents, did you?" the man said, turning his stare on the station master. "I thought them kind was all bastards." The man grunted out a loud, smug laugh, obviously pleased with his own witty remark.

Sidney suddenly comprehended that, for the second time that day, a stranger was mocking him.

"How old are you, boy?" the big man asked as he eyed Sidney more closely. "You don't look big enough to be of use around a farm."

"I am eight, sir," Sidney answered. "I'll be nine in November," he quickly added.

The man frowned as he looked over at the woman. "Did they tell ya he'd be so puny?"

Despite the plain and soiled black dress that covered the woman from her neck down to the top of her black boots, her matted hair and shy manner, there was something warm and open about her, Sidney thought. She reminded him of his mother in a peculiar, forlorn kind of way.

The woman kept her head low, only looking up briefly to acknowledge that the big man had spoken to her. The look in her sad brown eyes told Sidney that she was terrified of him. "No, Clarence, I didn't know," she said in a faint, barely audible voice. She briefly glanced down at Sidney, and he sensed that she was afraid for him as well.

Suddenly, it dawned on Sidney who these people were. *The Olson's.* His body instinctively recoiled back toward the station master.

Clarence paused for a moment, scratching at his face through the coarse locks of his whiskers, likely considering whether or not he was going to take Sidney at all. Finally, he looked over at him. "Load your things and get in boy. We're yet three hours to home," he grunted. Clarence gestured with a nod of his head, directing Sidney to climb into the back of the wagon.

The station master cleared his throat. "Uh, pardon me, sir, but do you have some paperwork to show that you are the legal guardian of this boy?" he asked.

The bearded man grunted. "They didn't give us no paperwork! All's they told us was that they wanted him out of the orphanage. Said they was getting another shipment of these poor bastards next week and needed the space."

Sidney bristled at the words. *Surely Mr. Dobbs had not tried to give him away so carelessly, had he?*

"We didn't even need to have anyone sign for us. That's how bad they wanted him gone," Mr. Olson continued. "All we did was answer a newspaper advert, and--" he snapped his fingers "--he was ours, easy as that."

Sidney looked up at the station master, his eyes pleading. The kindly man cleared his throat again. "Well, perhaps you were right. A boy of this size probably won't be any good to you. If you like, he can stay with me until we can make arrangements to send him back from whence he came. I can keep him busy here at the station until then."

Sidney's heart pounded hard against his chest as he anxiously anticipated Mr. Olson's acceptance of the station master's offer.

"Hold on a minute mister," Clarence yelled. "You want a boy to do your chores, you can send for one just like I did. We'll teach him right quick, won't we?" he called over his shoulder to where the woman was quietly sitting. He looked back at the frightened boy. "Sidney, eh?" he scoffed. "From now on, you'll answer to Sid. That's more like a man's name. Now get in."

The station master hesitated, first looking at Clarence and then back at Sidney. *Please, please let me stay with you, Sidney silently begged.*

The station master cleared his throat. "Well, if it doesn't work out for you over at the farm, bring him back here and we'll sort things out," he said.

Sidney's heart sank. Clarence grunted, dismissing the man's words.

The station master gave Sidney's shoulder a firm squeeze, then picked up the metal trunk. He carried it over to the wagon, carefully setting it on the broken floor boards in back and gently helped Sidney climb in. Sidney grabbed onto the side of the wagon to keep his balance as Clarence jolted the horses forward. "God bless you, son," he called after him.

Without notice, Clarence whipped the reins down on the horse's back. "Get up!" he yelled. Sidney was nearly thrown off the trunk, but he managed to pull himself back into place. He knew in that instance that it wasn't going to be a pleasant trip. The wagon bounced and shook roughly as it rolled down the road leading away from the station.

Sidney looked up at Clarence's broad back. The stink drifting off of the fat, sweaty man attacked his nostrils as the wind blew around him and straight into his face. Suddenly, Clarence twisted around and looked straight into Sidney's eyes, a sinister look that pierced clean through him.

"Boy, reach under the seat and grab that jug," he shouted.

Sidney struggled to maintain his balance as the wagon bounced and shook. After searching for a moment, he saw the earthenware jug wedged between two wooden boxes. He reached under, stuck his finger through the small handle, and dragged the container out. It was full of liquid and quite heavy, but Sidney managed to get it close enough for Clarence to grab. *I hope he offers me a drink of water*, Sidney thought, too nervous to ask but so thirsty that his tongue was sticking to the inside of his mouth. He wished he'd had enough time to drink the water that the station master had brought him.

Clarence grunted and jerked the jug from Sidney's grasp before turning back to the road. He pulled the cork out and took a big swallow. No offering of a drink was made to Sidney or the woman before he jammed the cork back in.

The woman slightly lifted her head and glanced back at Sidney, then up to Clarence. Her fear seemed to have intensified. She lowered her head again, looking back to her feet, not uttering a word.

Sidney made himself as comfortable as he could. There was no shelter from the hot sun in the wagon and the dust from the dirt road swirled around him, covering him like a sooty, grimy blanket. The grit wafted into his mouth and grinded between his teeth, forcing his thirst to an even more intolerable intensity. He squinted his eyes to keep the dust out and braced himself for a long, torturous ride.

The blistering heat of the late-afternoon sun continued to beat down on them. Clarence, after quite a few more swigs from the jug, turned the reins over to the woman. By the time they reached the farm, Sidney had deduced that the jug wasn't carrying water. Clarence had drunk most of it and was by then quite unsteady in his seat. The woman steered the wagon onto a dirt lane that cut through a thick stand of trees and eventually led up to the farmhouse.

This place is so far away from everything, Sidney thought as they bounced along the rutty road and through the stand of mature trees, the shade of which finally offered a break from the searing heat. Sidney had been paying close attention to the surrounding countryside for the duration of the journey and had noticed that there were fewer and fewer farmhouses the farther along they travelled. A feeling of uneasiness slowly overwhelmed him as they seemed to plunge deeper and deeper into an isolated wilderness that took him further and further away from safety.

When they finally reached the lane, Sidney calculated that the closest neighbour was about two miles back down the road, *a long way off if I ever need help*, he concluded.

As they exited the shade of the grove and travelled further up the drive, Sidney saw a huge, well-tended garden plot alongside the lane that seemed to be abundant with foods that he, like most other eight-year-olds, generally disliked. At that moment, however, he would have given anything for a raw carrot. His stomach churned as he recalled eating the last of his bagged lunch hours earlier.

Sidney saw another sight on the other side of the lane that made his stomach rumble: fruit trees with apples and pears pulling down on the branches, begging him to run over and get his fill. Assuming that Clarence would not tolerate such behaviour, Sidney restrained his urges, thinking that he would have plenty of the juicy treats soon enough.

A little farther down the drive and facing the garden was an old rundown farmhouse sided with the same weathered brown board Sidney had seen on plenty of barns during the three-hour trip. The house was badly in need of repair and a coat of paint. And the stone chimney that stuck out through the roof looked as if it could topple over at any moment.

The front porch slanted severely to one side, the same side that accommodated a large stack of split firewood. An axe was buried in a chopping block near another huge mountain of logs that were piled up in front of the house. One old chair and a wooden barrel sat tilted on the other end of the cockeyed porch. There were two windows in the front of the house, one on either side of the door and two more on the side that faced the lane. Sidney looked uncertainly at the dwelling, trying to imagine where his room would be.

"Whoa," the woman softly mumbled as she pulled back on the reins, bringing the wagon to a stop near the house. She sat for a moment, glancing over at Clarence as if waiting for instructions. He finally looked over to her and then back at Sidney and snarled, as if they were troubling him in some way.

"Take the boy out to the barn," he slurred as he struggled to figure out the best way to get off the wagon. "Cow needs milk'n. Show him his place," he grunted. Finally, after getting one of his big boots onto the footstep, he pulled himself off his seat, violently tilting the wagon to one side as he clumsily stumbled down. After taking a moment to steady himself, Clarence staggered on towards the house. "Eggs need gathrin' too," he shouted without turning back to look at the pair. They watched as Clarence fumbled with an armful of logs, shouldered his way through the front door and disappeared into the shack.

Once Clarence was inside, the woman quickly slapped the horse with the reins and started the wagon towards the barn, which stood with a prominent lean a short distance down the lane. Sidney noted with some surprise that it was in considerably worse shape than the house. The woman drove straight into the big opening where, Sidney deduced, a barn door likely hung in better days. She pulled back on the reins and brought the rig to a sudden halt. The two sat on the wagon in the cool shade and for an extended moment, neither spoke or moved.

The smell of horse shit and cow dung hung heavy in the air as Sidney glanced around the dank, foreboding structure, taking particular note of the thick layer of wet, manure-filled straw that covered the wooden floor. He recalled helping clean the barn at the home in Toronto, but he had never seen a mess quite like this.

Suddenly, the woman turned to him. "You ever milked a cow before?" she asked.

Sidney was surprised by the gentleness in her voice. "No, ma'am," he casually replied. "I've never seen a cow before ma'am, except for the one my father made," he added.

The woman looked down at him with a puzzled look and then shook her head. "Well, we're gonna have to remedy that right away," she said. "I hope you learn fast. Clarence won't take kindly to it if you don't have milk to the house first thing in the morning. We'll unhitch the horse first."

The woman hesitated as she looked at him as if silently telling him that she was afraid on his behalf. Sidney looked back into her sad brown eyes and, for a fleeting moment, imagined that she was his mother.

She quickly turned away. "Let's get started then," she said as she jumped off the wagon.

Sidney followed, watching closely as she removed the harness and hung the jumbled mess of leather straps on a rusty nail hammered into a post.

"I don't suppose you've seen a horse either, then?" she asked with a feeble smile.

"Oh, yes ma'am, I have," Sidney piped up. "I helped Mr. Dobbs with the horse almost every day in Toronto," he bragged. He didn't mention that his only equestrian duties there were to brush and feed the animal, and occasionally lead it to and from its stall. Sidney had never actually harnessed the horse to the wagon before, although he did watch closely when Mr. Dobbs did it.

"Well, good. Hitchin' the wagon won't take much teach'n then." She started to lead the horse to its stall, then paused and looked back at Sidney. "Come on, you might as well do it," she instructed, handing him the rope. "I'll show you what to feed her. Feedin' the animals will be one of your chores," she added. "Let's get Nel put away, then I'll show you how to milk Bess."

After the long, silent wagon ride, Sidney was enjoying the chatter. "Do all of the animals have names?" he asked.

The woman smiled. "Just the horse and the cow," she chuckled. "I named them. Clarence just calls them 'the horse' and 'the cow'," she half-heartedly joked. "Not many folks come by to visit, least wise none that I want to see," she said. "I don't get to talk to folks much. I'm Elizabeth," she spurted, extending her hand to the boy.

Sidney quickly gathered himself to respond in kind. "I'm Sidney," he said, smiling as he reached out to accept her hand.

"Pleased to meet you, Sidney. But I think we'd better call you Sid, like Clarence wants," she firmly suggested.

Sidney sensed the insistence in Elizabeth's tone. "Yes, ma'am. Sid."

Despite the air of fear and sadness that shrouded her, Sid felt unusually comfortable and safe in her presence. In a down-to-earth way, Elizabeth had a gentle side to her. *She seems to like me*, he thought.

Nel was put into her stall and Elizabeth pitched a forkful of hay onto the floor. "You'll need to haul water from the well near the house and dump it in the trough," she advised. "She'll drink six or seven pails a day."

After the horse was tended to, Elizabeth picked up a small stool and a pail from the corner and, with Sid close behind, carried them over to the animal that Sid presumed was Bess. "Okay, watch closely. Set the stool here," she instructed, "and put the pail under here."

Sid squatted down beside her for a better view of the procedure, close enough to see what she was doing but far enough away, in his mind, to avoid injury if the black and white beast decided to attack.

Elizabeth looked over and grabbed his arm. "She don't bite. Now get in here so you can see what I'm doin'," she said as she pulled him directly under the cow. Elizabeth reached up and grabbed two of the four teat's that were hanging below the heavy, milk-laden sack. "Grab here with your thumb and finger, like this," she instructed, "and squeeze gently." Elizabeth started milking Bess with both hands, carefully directing each stream into the pail. After a few squirts from each teat, she stopped, stood up, and gestured for Sid to sit on the stool. "You try now."

Sid crawled back out from under Bess and cautiously took his place on the seat. He looked back under the cow and then up to Elizabeth.

"Just reach under and start milking," she said on the verge of impatience. "And make sure it all goes in the pail."

Sid squeamishly reached up, grabbed one teat, and gave it a sharp tug. Suddenly, a stream of milk shot out at him, splashing directly into his face. The sudden and aggressive action startled Bess, causing her to take a half-step sideways in Sid's direction. At the same time she swished her tail around the back of his head, and the end of it slapped him squarely in the face. These sudden and unexpected movements startled Sid, causing him to jump back with all his might and land flat on his back and directly at Elizabeth's feet. Shocked, he stared up her with a look of terror in his eyes and milk dripping from his face, expecting to be punished for causing such calamity.

A big smile spread across Elizabeth's face and she started to laugh. "Well, that's not exactly how you do it, but you did get some milk out." Her gentle response made Sid feel better and he picked himself up off the floor. Elizabeth used the bottom of her ragged dress to wipe the milk from his face. "Let's give it another try," she said with a smile.

Sid got back on the stool and slowly reached under Bess again, grabbing her with a little more tenderness this time. Elizabeth kneeled in beside him, close enough that she could reach up and take his hands in hers, and together they started milking. Sid focused intently on the task and, after a few minutes, Elizabeth stood back and watched as he almost hit the pail with nearly every pull.

"You've got it, Sid."

Pride surged in him. He could barely believe that he was milking the first cow he had ever seen.

"She'll fill that pail twice a day," Elizabeth said. "Once in the mornin', and once at night. When you're done milk'n, you bring the pail up to the house. And don't spill any of it," she warned, her eyes flashing towards the farmhouse.

"Yes, ma'am," Sid acknowledged.

Suddenly his stomach rumbled so loudly that even Bess turned her head in his direction.

"Oh my, you must be hungry, Sid," Elizabeth said as she grabbed his arm and pushed him towards the door. "But first we need to collect the eggs. I'll get you started and then go to the house and start supper. Clarence'll be getting hungry, too." She suddenly seemed to be in a rush.

"Should I leave my trunk here, ma'am?" he asked. Sid looked towards the back of the wagon to where his metal trunk waited, still covered in dust.

"Oh, right," Elizabeth said quietly, as if talking to herself. "Set the pail down." She took Sid's hand and escorted him to the ladder that led up to the hayloft. "You will sleep up there," she said, pointing towards the empty space above.

Sid blinked twice, hard. *I am supposed to sleep up there*? he thought, not quite believing.

"And I stitched some sacks together and stuffed them with straw for a mattress," Elizabeth rushed on in an embarrassed voice. "I left a wool blanket there for you as well."

"Thank you," he managed. For all of his life, Sid had slept in a room with other boys. For as long as he could remember, and even before that, he had shared a bed with his older brother, George. Panic began to set into his chest and he tried to hold back the tears.

Elizabeth's eyes wandered across his face. They were full of compassion and concern. Sid could tell that his sleeping arrangements were not her decision. "You'll be fine out here," she assured in a quiet, firm voice. She took a deep breath, grabbed him by his shoulders and looked him straight in the eye. "If I could live up there rather than in that old shack with him, I would," she sobbed, tears welling in her eyes.

Sid felt lonely and abandoned, and thoughts of mother hurried through his head. *If she would only send for me*, he thought. But salvation seemed to be drifting further and further away. His hopes of ever being with his mother again were swiftly fading.

"Ma'am, does he hate me?" Sid asked the question that was burning inside him.

Elizabeth took a deep breath. "No, Sid, Clarence doesn't hate you. He's that way with everyone. You just mind yourself and tend to your chores and hopefully he won't treat you too badly. Come along now. We have chores to finish," she said with forced cheer. "We'll put your trunk up after."

Elizabeth led the way to the chicken coop, which was back up the lane towards the house. The small square shed was elevated off the ground, balanced on six rotten posts sticking out of the ground. Three crumbling wooden steps led up to the only entrance. Elizabeth climbed the steps and unlatched the door, allowing a foul smell to escape. Sid was immediately reminded of the two weeks he had spent at sea.

"Always, always, always make sure this door is latched tight when you leave," Elizabeth warned. "If a chicken gets out or a fox gets in, Clarence is likely to beat you good."

"Yes, ma'am," Sid politely responded as they stepped into the foul-smelling pen. He had never actually seen a live chicken before either. When his eyes adjusted to the dim light, he looked around the small space and saw thirteen, maybe fourteen birds, all bobbing their heads frantically and eyeing him with distrust.

"You'll get about a dozen eggs this time every day," Elizabeth said as she picked up a basket from near the door. She made her way to one end of the coop and pushed a chicken off its nest. It squawked loudly before clumsily flapping its way towards the far corner. "See, there's two here," she announced, gently placing them into the basket. "Come on over here, Sid. You help," she shouted over the squawking of the birds. "And don't break any," she warned.

"Yes, ma'am." Collecting eggs seemed to him to be an easier and much safer chore than milking cows. Without hesitation, Sid went to the other end of the coop and started pushing chickens from their nests and gathering up the eggs. Each time his hands were full, he carefully placed them in the basket Elizabeth was holding.

"Here," she said. "You take the basket and finish. I'll take the milk and go up to the house. And remember, don't break any." Elizabeth carefully closed the door behind herself, leaving Sid alone with the chickens.

It only took a few more minutes before he had finished checking every nest and had gathered all the eggs--thirteen in total. Sid felt a sense of relief that he had retrieved more than the twelve he presumed he would be accountable for when he delivered the basket to the house. *This should make Clarence happy*, he thought.

Sid opened the door of the coop just wide enough to let himself out. He set the basket down and secured the latch, just like Elizabeth had shown him, checking it twice for good measure. He picked up the basket and walked towards the house. He could see that the chimney was emitting a full plume of thick white smoke high into the air, carrying with it the smell of something delicious. Sid imagined that he would soon be sitting down to a hearty meal of meat, mashed potatoes and gravy, followed by a generous helping of some type of scrumptious dessert. *Maybe apple pie*, he envisioned.

As he drew closer to the house, Sid stopped in his tracks, startled by the sound of a thunderous crash coming from inside. He could hear Clarence yelling, and then a loud thud. *Maybe they're being robbed? Maybe the station master has come to take me back?* A million thoughts ran through Sid's head as he drew closer to the house. He snuck up beside one of the windows and peered in. He cringed at what he saw. Sid watched as Clarence grabbed Elizabeth's arm and violently threw her to the floor, her head nearly hitting the corner of the wood stove. Clarence stood over her, shouting like a madman, and continued his rant for a minute or so before walking away.

Sid's eyes were glued to Elizabeth as she slowly wiped her face and picked herself up off the floor. The sight invoked visions of his mother lying on their kitchen floor, blood dripping from her face, and the same hate he felt for his brother that morning burned in his gut. But this time, he was more afraid than he had ever been in his young life.

"Boy, get those eggs up here!" a raging voice growled. Sid looked up and saw Clarence's huge figure standing by the corner of the porch staring down at him. He looked angry.

Sid slowly picked up the basket. "Yes, sir," he said. He warily stepped towards the big man, holding the basket out in front of him, offering it to Clarence, who made no move to meet Sid halfway. When Sid got within arm's reach, Clarence grabbed the basket and looked inside.

"This all you got, boy?" he barked.

"Yes, sir. That's all there was, sir," Sid mumbled as he looked down at his feet.

Clarence glared at Sid for a moment and then turned away. "Fetch some wood for the stove," he yelled as he stomped off. "Bring it to the door."

Sid stepped around to the front of the house and walked over to the pile of split logs on the other end of the porch. He grabbed three pieces and lay them across his arms, then started towards the door.

"Is that all you can carry?" Clarence hollered, stepping outside and blocking Sid's path. His mean eyes were glinting and he raised one hand.

Sid trembled as he looked up at the big man. He suddenly felt sure that he was going to suffer a beating, just like Elizabeth had. Slowly, he felt his pants become soaked, and warm liquid was running down his leg. He stood frozen in the doorway.

Clarence looked at the puddle that was collecting at Sid's feet and his face turned red. "You a coward, boy? Or did they send me a girl?" He abruptly raised his right arm and back-handed Sid alongside the head so hard that his feet left the ground, sending him through the air and off the step, face first into the dirt. Everything went black.

When Sid came to, his ears were ringing and he was completely disoriented. He could feel a rock jabbing into his shoulder and his mouth was full of dirt. Clarence's voice shouted down at him from somewhere close by, "You ain't gonna be much good for anything around here, are ya, ya lazy bastard?" Sid struggled to roll over onto his back. As he did, he saw Clarence looming over him from the porch. "Now pick up those logs and bring them to the house," he ordered as he turned back towards the door.

Sid saw Elizabeth standing in the doorway watching the ordeal. Looking down to her feet, she stepped aside to let Clarence back into the house. Once he was inside, she hurried down to help Sid up from the ground.

"I'm sorry, I'm so sorry," she whimpered as huge tears streamed from her eyes. "You're going to have a dandy of a black eye," she tried to joke as she wiped the dirt and blood from his face. "Here, take these and a couple more," she said as she picked the three logs up off the ground and added two more from the pile. "I'll show you where to put them," she offered.

Sid guardedly followed Elizabeth into the house, where she directed him to put the logs into a wooden box just inside the front door. Sid could feel the intense heat from the fire that was raging in the wood stove. *Why would they keep the house so hot, especially on a day like this*? he thought. He cautiously glanced over at Clarence, who was sitting at a heavy wooden table and stuffing himself with meat and potatoes, oblivious to Sid and Elizabeth.

"I'll get you your supper, Sid," Elizabeth said quietly as she turned him back towards the door and onto the porch. "You better wait here," she instructed. After a minute or so, Elizabeth came out and handed Sid a plate and a spoon. "Here you go," she mumbled.

Before she could say another word, Clarence pushed past her onto the porch. The sight of him made Sid cringe.

"Whatcha doin', hanging around here like some stray dog? You'll eat your meals in the barn, boy," Clarence barked. Sid was so afraid that he nearly dropped his plate. Then, just as abruptly as he'd come, Clarence walked back inside, pulling Elizabeth with him and slamming the door.

Sid stood motionless for a moment, bewildered and in considerable pain. His right eye was swollen shut. All he could think about at that moment was to run. *But there's nowhere to go*, he recalled disdainfully. *And what kind of punishment would Clarence dole out if I get caught*? And he would be caught, he was sure of it. With only a few other farmhouses within ten miles of them, Sid knew he didn't have a chance of escape.

He looked down at the plate Elizabeth had given him: two slices of bread drenched in some thick syrup that looked like molasses. Not the meal he had anticipated, but he was hungry. He made his way back to the barn and climbed up onto the back of the wagon to eat his meal, using his dusty metal trunk as a table. One small spoonful at a time, he forced down the syrupy slop, trying not to pay mind to the almost unbearable animal stench that he inhaled with every breath.

After he finished his meal, Sid made his way to the ladder and climbed up to the loft that was his place. The area was big enough alright, but the only sign that any hay had ever been stored up there was a dusty floor littered with bits of straw. Sid looked up at the roof and could see plenty of sky through large gaps between the boards. He walked over to the wall facing the lane and could clearly see the back of the farmhouse through the cracks. In the most sheltered corner of the loft, he found his bed of straw-filled sacks that Elizabeth had made for him. One neatly folded wool blanket lay at the end of the mattress.

In another corner, Sid found a pile of old rope that would be suitable for pulling his trunk up from below. He scurried down the ladder, getting a bad splinter on the way. Sucking on his finger to ease the pain, he studied the trunk to determine the best way forward. He decided to empty it first and carry all of his belongings up separately.

After all of his things were up top, Sid removed his wet pants and wool coat and changed into the overalls that Mr. Dobbs had given him. He silently thanked Mr. Dobbs for his kindness and tried to push out of his mind the mean things that Clarence had said earlier about how the organization had been more than happy to get rid of him.

Sid crawled onto his straw bed and pulled the wool blanket over himself. The late-July sun was still shining brightly, but he was weary and sore and homesick and afraid. He also knew that he'd better be up early in the morning to start his chores, or surely he'd face another beating.

Once again, thoughts of his mother rushed into Sid's head. He recalled the orphanage in England, a place that suddenly didn't seem so terrible. Even Thelma's brutality paled in comparison to Clarence's wickedness. The horrors of that place seemed trivial now that he was an ocean away from it. There, at least, he'd had his mother to comfort him on the first Sunday of each month. He prayed that she would send him word soon. He was stuck waiting for her letter to come to him--waiting and praying.

Sid lay shivering on the coarse straw mat, surrounded by strangeness and peril as the darkness of night slowly closed in on him. He cried himself into a restless slumber, with the knowledge that morning would bring with it another day of torment and fear.

Chapter Nine

Flames of Freedom

In the following weeks, and with as much help from Elizabeth as she could offer, Sid learned what Clarence expected of him around the farm. His days were long, starting before sunrise and ending after sunset. He tended to the animals, delivered a pail of milk to the house morning and night, gathered eggs and drew countless buckets of water from the well. He spent many hours in the orchard, filling baskets with apples and pears, and his hands were blistered from pitching mounds of smelling, heavy, shit-laden straw from the barn.

There was no idle time. When he might have had a break, Clarence would send him to the garden to help Elizabeth cut down weeds and fill baskets with vegetables destined for market.

Out of hungry desperation, Sid had learned effective ways to sneak a pear or an apple back to the barn now and again and, with Elizabeth's help, sometimes a few carrots or a tomato for his supper. On those days when the hens were generous, Sid even snuck an egg or two to his hiding place in the barn, eating them raw with his daily serving of bread and molasses and carefully burying the shells afterwards so as not to leave a trace of evidence for Clarence to find.

Besides disappearing into the back woods for a few hours every day and drinking with the other vulgar men who frequently stopped by to visit him and to share in some of his legendary homemade hooch, the only thing that Clarence did was split logs to stoke the inferno that he kept blazing in the stove, even on the hottest days of summer. And when

Clarence was close by, he was always watching, ready to pounce whenever he thought that Sid or Elizabeth weren't working hard enough or doing things his way. The beatings became customary for Sid, usually a backhand to the side of his head, sometimes followed by a kick with heavy work boots.

With two victims to maltreat, Clarence's brutality seemed relentless. But with time, Sid, like Elizabeth, learned to anticipate and come to terms with the beatings. There was simply no way to avoid them.

August 28, 1914

Early Friday morning, Sid helped Elizabeth load up the wagon with baskets of fruit and cartons of eggs, jars of maple syrup and garden produce, all to be sold at the public market in Aylmer. Sid looked forward to the weekly trip. He knew that he and Elizabeth would have a chance to talk without Clarence watching over them, as Clarence was usually nowhere to be found during the monotony of vegetable selling. Sid didn't know where Clarence went during those few hours, but he always staggered back smelling of alcohol and barking orders at the end of the day.

Sid had another reason to be excited about these weekly trips, anticipation that he might receive a letter from his mother. Their first stop in town was always at the post office, where Clarence collected a stack of mail, which up until now hadn't included Sid's eagerly anticipated correspondence, at least not according to Clarence.

As they heaved the last heavy crate into place, Sid felt a tinge of sadness come over him. This would be their last trip of the season. Any other produce from the garden would be canned and kept in the root cellar at the farmhouse. Sidney would miss their unwatched hours together. Elizabeth had a way of comforting him and making his situation seem more bearable, even though she herself was subject to more frequent and severe beatings than he. But her sad eyes always looked at him with kindness, maybe even love. Sidney wished he knew the right words to say to console her, but just being together seemed to be comfort enough.

Sid hitched the horse to the wagon, and just as he finished, Clarence showed himself from inside the house. He climbed aboard, roughly grabbed the reins and headed off towards the main road. *The one hour trip will seem like an eternity,* Sid thought as he envisioned opening his letter, and more-so, hearing Elizabeth read to him that his mother had finally made arrangements for him to return to England. This would be his last chance before winter set in.

Elizabeth hesitated for a moment before climbing down from the wagon. She glanced back at Sid with a sad look in her eyes, as if she was certain that he would be disappointed yet again.

"Go on woman, what are you waiting for?" Clarence barked.

Elizabeth glared at Clarence, a contemptuous scowl that Sid had never witnessed from her before. It seemed to him to be a bold display of defiance given the likelihood that Clarence would normally respond with a heavy back-handed blow to the side of her head, even in this public place. But he didn't seem to notice.

Elizabeth slowly climbed down and went into the post office, returning a few minutes later with a stack of mail.

"Give it to me," Clarence growled before she had a chance to climb back up. Elizabeth reluctantly handed the pile over to him.

Sid took a few minutes to work up the courage to ask the same question he asked every week. "Um, is there a letter for me?"

"No," snapped Clarence, without even looking at the pile. "There won't never be no mail for you boy, so you might as well stop asking."

Sid's heart sank as the reality of having to spend the winter under Clarence's cruel control set in.

As usual, after they'd arrived at the market, Sid and Elizabeth stayed in their seats, waiting for Clarence to climb off and start walking towards the gathering place by the river where he and his cronies congregated to consume.

Sid breathed a sigh of relief when Clarence was finally out of view. He looked around, noticing all of the faces that he had become familiar with over the summer. Apart from Clarence and Elizabeth, these were the only people he knew in his new life.

"Let's get to work Sid," Elizabeth said, a subdued but obvious cheeriness in her voice. "Customers are already coming."

Market day, when Clarence was finally gone, was the only time that Sid ever witnessed any real joy in Elizabeth, which in turn made him forget his worries, at least temporarily.

Sid energetically jumped off the cart and he and Elizabeth commenced displaying their goods. As always, before they could get completely set up, customers started gathering around their stall. Molly and Roberta, two frugal but kind widows, were the first ones to arrive.

"Hello, Elizabeth dear," Roberta said as she carefully inspected the small melons, squeezing and tapping them. "And Sid, darling, how are you, son? It's so nice to see a young face."

Sid never understood why the women always spent so much time touching and smelling the produce before making their selections, but the old woman's kind words did make him smile from ear to ear. And they always bought at least two bags full.

"Mmm, mmm, Elizabeth, you've always got the best-smelling herbs. I don't know how you do it," praised Molly as she held a sprig of basil to her long, hooked nose. "You are blessed with a gift, dear."

The ladies continued with their selections, praising Elizabeth the whole time. Sid was happy for her, knowing that she heard far too few kind words at home. He had a feeling that Roberta and Molly knew that as well. The two elderly women paid for their produce, but hesitated before moving on.

"I suppose we won't see you dears again until next spring," Molly said as she delicately picked through the basket of juicy red tomatoes. "We sure do miss you during the winter months," she added, looking up at Elizabeth. *Molly's friendly smile and gentle approach always seemed to bring Elizabeth out of her shell,* Sid noted. *Maybe Molly reminded her of someone from her past, from a happier time when she was treated gently and felt safe,* he thought.

Elizabeth lifted her head, offering a delicate but genuine smile. "That's right," she said, slowly dropping her head as she spoke. "This will be our last trip of the year."

"And are you folks ready for winter?" Molly asked, diverting her attention to Sid. "This will be your first Canadian winter, won't it, young man?"

"Yes, ma'am," Sid responded matter-of-factly.

"Do you have suitable clothing? You know, mittens, a hat, a warm coat?" she inquired, pressing him.

"Mr. Dobbs gave me a pair of overalls and some rubber boots before I left the home," he proudly informed.

Roberta clucked her tongue in what Sid surmised was disapproval.

Elizabeth cleared her throat. "He also has a medium-weight wool coat and wool socks," she informed. Her eyes again sought the ground. "I wish I could afford to outfit him properly, but-" Her voice trailed off.

Sid sensed Elizabeth's embarrassment as she struggled to explain their dire circumstances.

"Well, I might have the perfect solution," Roberta informed in a tone that was meant to lighten the sombre mood that had descended on their small group. "I just so happen to have some extra winter clothes and blankets that I absolutely must get rid of before the moths chew them to pieces. And," she looked back to appraise Sid's size, "I think they might be a perfect fit." Roberta smiled and winked at Sid.

Elizabeth looked taken aback by the offer. "Thank you, ma'am," she said, stumbling over her words, "but I, I mean, Clarence and I, I don't think we can accept." Her cheeks were flushed red and her eyes flashed regretfully at Sid.

"Well, it would be a shame to see such useful things go to waste," Molly said quietly. She stepped over to the wagon and took a look inside. "I think the winter coat and the mittens might fit just nicely inside that box," she said, pointing to an empty vegetable box lying in the back. "And it could slide right up there under the seat so it didn't get in your way," she proposed.

Elizabeth hesitated. Sid knew that she was terrified of Clarence finding out that she had accepted charity, so it surprised him immensely when she finally conceded. "Alright," she said, looking back to the women with a small but genuine smile. "I think we could take the coat and mittens, if they didn't get in the way."

"Wonderful!" Molly exclaimed "We don't live far. Would you be so kind as to lend us that vegetable box to carry our goods in?" she asked, her eyes twinkling. "We'll take our things home and return your box to you within the hour. And don't worry, young lady. We'll use the utmost discretion," she assured.

"Thank you," Elizabeth said softly to the ladies as they bustled away. She turned to Sid and said, "Don't you go saying anything to Clarence about this, you hear!"

Sid nodded, his eyes wide. "No, ma'am, not a word," he promised. The two nervously smiled at each other and then returned to their work.

Not a half hour later, the two elderly ladies came gingerly walking back towards them with the vegetable box. Sid instinctively looked back in the direction that Clarence had gone, hoping not to see him unexpectedly staggering back towards the wagon. The coast was clear.

"Here, I'll just put it in here," Roberta said, lifting the box over the side rail of the wagon and setting it on the floor behind the bench. Sid hopped up into the back and slid it underneath the seat with his foot. He quickly stacked some other empty boxes around and behind it, making sure that the illicit cargo was well hidden.

Elizabeth looked in and gave a quick nod. "That's good," she said as she walked around the cart to get a better look from all possible angles. "Yes, that should be fine." She thanked the ladies for their kindness and offered to give them the last four tomatoes.

"No, dear, but thank you just the same. We already have more than enough," Molly said.

"We surely do look forward to seeing you next spring," Roberta said before she and her companion turned and started back towards home.

"I'll give you three cents for the last of these tomatoes," came a voice, interrupting the silence that had settled around the stall. Sid turned and was greeted by a kindly, well-dressed gentleman who was bargaining for the last of their stock.

"Yes, sir," Elizabeth said, putting on a genuine smile. "Three cents is fine, sir," she agreed, gesturing at Sid to put the ripe fruits into the shopper's bag. The man handed Elizabeth the pennies and wished them a good day.

Elizabeth cautiously scanned the area, then promptly walked over to the wagon and felt amongst the boxes for the coat. Sid watched as she dropped the three copper pennies into the jacket pocket. "You hide them good when we get home," she instructed, trying to suppress a mischievous grin.

As Sid gave her an affirmative nod, he felt a surge of hope. With kind people like Elizabeth and the old ladies around, maybe he had a chance at surviving in Canada after all.

In the following weeks, Sid toiled endlessly, stacking firewood, hauling water and tending to the animals. He helped Elizabeth with the canning, pickling and preserving as best he could, bringing her water for boiling and stacking jars on pantry shelves. Clarence's backhand was finding him less and less often, and Sid was just beginning to feel like he was making an alright farm hand.

And then came killing day.

October 24, 1914

Clarence chopped the first ones while Sid and Elizabeth stretched them out with the twine tied around their necks and legs. The sight of blood spurting everywhere and the unnatural spectacle of headless chickens flapping about, trying to escape the already inflicted blow unsettled Sid immensely. He struggled not to vomit, knowing that Clarence wouldn't tolerate such squeamish behaviour. Until then, he had never witnessed a living creature die, let alone kill one himself. It all seemed so easy for Clarence. It didn't even seem to bother Elizabeth.

"Come on over here, boy," Clarence growled as he leaned the axe towards Sid. "You finish em'."

Sid reluctantly accepted the axe handle, letting the heavy axe head rest on the ground at his feet. There were ten left. Clarence went to the coop to bring out the next victim and stretched its neck out over the chopping block. Sid anxiously contemplated the gruesome task at hand.

"Come on, boy, just pick it up and swing it," Clarence shouted impatiently, rolling his eyes and spitting on the ground.

Sid glanced up and could tell that Elizabeth was nervous. He looked at Clarence, and then down at the chicken, its neck stretched long enough so that even he couldn't miss. *Just do it*, he scolded himself. *Do it now or else he'll make you pay, or worse, he'll take it out on Elizabeth.*

Sid licked his lips and struggled to lift the axe to his shoulder. He recognized the hen that he was about to kill. She was one of the more docile birds in the flock. As he lifted the heavy axe from his shoulder and let it fall down towards his target, he closed his eyes and hoped that it would find its own way.

There was a weak cracking sound as the blade nicked the side of the chopping block and ricocheted downward towards the ground, stopping suddenly with a loud thud in the dirt. Sid opened his eyes to see the chicken still stretched out over the block and still very much alive. He looked up at Clarence, who was already stepping towards the boy.

"You stupid bastard!" he hollered as he drew his right hand back to deliver the customary punishment for failure. Clarence struck him on the side of the head, knocking him violently to the already bloodied ground. Clarence grabbed the axe and flung it down at the boy, its handle striking Sid squarely on the back of the head.

Sid lay cowering in the filthy, sticky dirt, dazed from the attack and flinching in preparation for another blow.

"Pick up the god damn axe and chop the god damn chicken's head off!" Clarence thundered.

Sid slowly got to his feet and reached down for the axe. He looked up at Elizabeth, who by now was wringing her hands and shuffling her feet anxiously. Again, Sid struggled to bring the axe to his shoulder, and again, he took a moment to carefully study his target. This time, when he threw the axe head towards the chicken, his eyes stayed open. The sharp edge struck the chicken's neck directly, cleanly separating its head from its body. The blade buried itself into the chopping block far enough so that it stayed in place when he let go of the handle. With a dazed look, Sid glanced back at Elizabeth, who returned a soft smile and a discreet nod of approval.

Clarence had been holding the twine tied to the chicken's legs and as the chicken continued to flop and flap, he laughed cruelly as he chased Sid with the flailing bird. Sid was quick to run away from the macabre sight, his own arms flailing to deflect any contact with the bloody, headless bird. After the chicken had finished thrashing about, Clarence threw it on the pile and chuckled to himself as he walked back into the chicken house to fetch another one. Within the hour, the remainder of the flock was be-headed and ready for butchering.

It was still early in the afternoon by the time the last head was removed, the pile of them, beaks, eyes and all, mounded around the base of the chopping block. Elizabeth started to take the bodies into the shed behind the house and Sid took his place at the pile, helping her pick up the dead birds. He expected that his day's work was just beginning and was readying himself to help Elizabeth with the de-feathering and butchering that he knew lay ahead.

But when Clarence returned from the house with his rifle slung over his shoulder, he beckoned to Sid to follow him in the other direction. "Come with me, boy," he barked as he wrapped his huge, dirty hand around Sidney's arm and roughly dragged him towards the barn. Sid stood quietly out of the way while Clarence harnessed the horse to the wagon and threw his rifle into the back. "Get on," he growled.

Sid huddled in the back as Clarence led the outfit out through the big barn door. He steered the wagon down the lane behind the barn and towards the thick stand of maple trees about half a mile from the house.

Sid recalled having once overheard Clarence joking with his buddies about a place he called the sugar shack, hidden well out of the sight of the law. Sid had never been back to the shack before, but as the wagon bumped through the red and gold autumn leaves, he knew it wasn't the right time of year for making maple syrup. He shuddered at the thought of being alone with Clarence in such a secluded, out of the way place.

Sid gripped the rails as the wagon squeezed between the tress and bounced roughly down a steep hill, at the bottom of which stood a small wooden structure. *This must be the sugar shack,* he figured. An occasional wisp of smoke rose out of the chimney revealing that a fire was still burning inside. Clarence pulled the rig up in front and brought it to a halt. "Get off," he yelled as he jumped from the wagon and headed for the shed.

Sid reluctantly climbed down and stood back while the big man opened the door, gesturing for Sidney to follow him in. Sid stepped inside and a caustic smell instantly flooded into his nostrils. It was a sour, putrid smell, but a smell that somehow seemed to be agreeable to him. It didn't make him feel ill or make him want to run back outside.

"That's the smell of the best bush whiskey in the county, boy," Clarence loudly bragged, sucking in several deep breaths, savouring each one as if he were sampling the aroma of a fine wine.

Sid studied the odd-looking apparatus that took up most of the inside of the shack, the vats and coiled tubing. He scanned the small room and noticed four large wooden crates stacked against one wall in the corner, and wondered why Clarence had brought him there.

"Stand back, boy, while I get these on the wagon," Clarence grunted as he lifted the first crate from the stack. Sid was confused. *Why did Clarence bring me along if he didn't want me to at least help with the work?* he wondered. Clarence easily handled each crate in turn and quickly loaded them into the wagon. Then he motioned for Sidney to follow him outside.

Sid stood idly by as Clarence closed the door to the shack and latched it behind him. He walked over to the wagon and slid a metal bar under the wooden lid on the closest box and lifted sharply, flipping the cover off and exposing ten jars of his famous homemade brew. Clarence reached in and pulled out one of the jars, holding it up to the sky to check its clarity.

"Ya, just right," he grunted with pride.

"Come here, boy," Clarence barked as he twisted off the lid and took a hearty swig. Sid nervously walked over to him. "Here, boy," Clarence said as he handed the jar to Sid. "This'll make a man outta ya. Go on, take a drink." Clarence seemed to be in an uncharacteristically good mood, which made Sid all the more suspicious. He hesitantly reached up and took the jar. "Go on, take a drink," Clarence insisted, still unusually patient despite Sid's hesitation.

Sid lifted the jar and at the same time lowered his head, trying to smell the liquid before sampling the drink. Quite unexpectedly and much to his displeasure, he took in a mighty whiff and inhaled the powerful vapours, which instantly caused his head to reel back and a stream of tears to pour from his eyes. Despite his sudden reaction, Sid concentrated on not spilling any of the brew, a mishap that surely would have changed Clarence's mood.

As usual, the bootlegger found considerable humour in Sid's discomfort and laughed at the boy, who was still reeling from the acrid fumes.

"Now drink!" he demanded, quickly becoming impatient with Sid's dawdling. Suddenly, Clarence grabbed the jar with one hand and Sid's hair with the other. "Here, I'll help ya," he grunted as he forcefully tilted Sid's head back and poured a generous amount of the concoction into his mouth.

Sid gagged and sputtered. The liquor burned all the way down his throat and into his stomach. He immediately started to heave, causing Clarence to shove him away. Clarence leaned against the wagon, laughing loudly as he watched Sid hunch over and grab his belly, trying desperately not to vomit. Suddenly Sid felt unsteady on his feet and everything around him started to spin.

"How's that, boy?" Clarence laughed as he lifted the jar to his mouth and took another big swallow. "Come back here and have some more," he yelled.

Sid slowly unfolded himself. Each precious breath he sucked in helped to ease his discomfort. He looked over at Clarence and watched him swallow yet another gulp, then hold out the nearly empty jar to Sid. Sid hesitated.

"Don't make me hold you down again, boy," Clarence warned.

Sid slowly wobbled back to the wagon and obediently accepted the container from Clarence. This time, he held his breath as he lifted the jar to his mouth, closed his eyes and gulped down the rest of the brew. For a moment, he couldn't breathe. He shook his head vigorously, hoping that would somehow make things better. Sid tried to stand straight, but instead stumbled backwards, tripping over his own feet and falling heavily onto his back.

When he opened his eyes and looked up, everything was spinning: the sky, the trees, even Clarence. Sid felt as if he was going to be sick, and then everything went black.

Sid wasn't sure how he got into the wagon or where they were, but he did notice that the sun was starting to set. His limp body was bouncing violently in the back while Clarence sat up front, slurping down another jar. Sid's eyes barely opened as the severe pounding beneath him shook him into a state of semi-consciousness. He braced himself as best he could, trying to cushion his head from smashing on the hard wooden boards as the wagon seemed to find every rut and bump on the trail.

Finally, the light disappeared, and a moment later Nel stopped in her usual place in the barn and stood patiently, waiting for someone to remove the harness and lead her back to her stall. Ignoring the horse, Clarence ungracefully climbed off the wagon and staggered off towards the house.

Sid lay paralyzed in the back, unable to make his way to the hay loft. Not even a cold October night could rouse him from that intoxication.

~~~

George fidgeted in his chair, obviously upset at what he was hearing. "Such brutality," he said. "It's unimaginable that no-one intervened. Didn't anyone from the organization come to check on him?" he asked.

"No-one came," Mary said. "Apparently Clarence was right--they were just glad to get him out. And as time went on, things got worse for your father. Shall I continue?" she asked.

"Of course," George said. I want to know all of it."

~~~

It was a bitterly cold winter that year. November came and went. Sid didn't even tell Elizabeth that he had turned nine that month. December passed, and not one word about Christmas was spoken. It seemed that all activity around the farm came to an abrupt halt as the cold winter weather enveloped them.

There were fewer chores in winter, but Sid struggled desperately with the ones that were left to him, spending hours at a time outside in the bitter cold. He was thankful that Elizabeth had accepted the winter coat and mittens from the two old ladies at the market. On most days, the coat, with the proper layering underneath kept him warm enough. Elizabeth was able to knit him a thick wool hat and scarf, all done while Clarence was passed out drunk and none the wiser.

In the early days of winter, when the floor of the hayloft and Sid's bed had become covered with a delicate sprinkling of snow, he was forced to move into the lower section of the barn. A pile of fresh straw in Nel's stall made for as warm a bed as he could hope for. Each night, he buried himself in the pile, fully clothed in his winter attire, and covered himself with the wool blanket and as much burlap as he could find.

Despite the constant risk to herself, Elizabeth helped Sid when she could, sneaking him a decent hot meal and taking his wet clothes inside to dry by the stove. These deceptions were less risky on days when Clarence left for a few hours to shoot rabbits and squirrels.

As winter turned to spring, Sid noticed that something about Elizabeth had changed. She seemed even more detached and the sadness in her eyes deepened with every day that passed. Instead of shying away when Clarence lifted his hand against her, she stood her ground, as if to tell him that he couldn't hurt her anymore. Her change of behaviour enraged Clarence, causing him to be still more violent in his attacks, yet Elizabeth continued to deny him the pleasure of humiliating her.

The only time Elizabeth had any respite was when Sid became the butt of cruelty and humiliation. It was great fun for Clarence and his cronies to witness the youngster stagger and fall down after they'd poured the leftover slag from the bottom of their glasses into him.

Elizabeth helplessly looked on whenever Sid was summoned to the house, the sight of this brutal degradation of her young friend instilling an anger in her that in due time would change all of their lives forever.

March 29, 1915

It was a day like any other. Sid went about his chores, struggling as he trudged through the muck while trying to manage the full buckets of water he needed to deliver to the barn and to the farmhouse. Clarence spent a good part of the day splitting firewood and taking frequent breaks to swill homemade whiskey. Elizabeth worked in the shed out back for most of the morning, cleaning the rabbits that Clarence had snared the previous afternoon. By the end of the day, Clarence was in his usual state of drunkenness, slamming his fist on the table and shouting at Elizabeth to put supper in front of him.

Sid finished his daily routine by filling the firebox inside the shack, avoiding eye contact with Clarence and pretending not to notice the verbal tirade that was taking place in front of him. Elizabeth worked diligently at the stove. She looked over at him and smiled a peculiar, faraway smile. She had a curious look of contentment on her face. Her eyes spoke to him as if to say that she had reached some kind of resolution. Elizabeth looked peaceful. Sid smiled back at her and started for the door.

"I'll bring your supper to the barn," she said, offering Sid another smile as he stepped out of the door. It was an unusually bold offer for her to make right in front of Clarence, for he was normally expected to receive his meal on the porch. Sid quickly glanced back towards Clarence, expecting to see him getting up from the table and angrily stomping towards her. But he didn't seem to have noticed the comment.

"Yes, ma'am," Sid mumbled, looking back in her direction with a baffled smile. "Thank you, ma'am." He quietly closed the kitchen door behind him and made his way back to the barn.

A short time later, as he was huddled in the haystack, he heard Elizabeth enter the barn. "Here's your supper," she said with a smile as she appeared in the stall doorway.

Sid was immediately confused when he saw that she was carrying not one plate of bread and molasses, but two plates, one stacked high with a steaming pile of rabbit meat and the other mounded with mashed potatoes drenched in gravy and two thick slices of bread, both slathered with creamy butter.

As she set the plates down on the floor beside him, her smile broadened. She kneeled down in the straw next to him and took his hand in hers. "You're a fine boy," she said as she gave his hand a firm squeeze. "You'll do just fine."

He could barely hear her as her quiet voice quivered in the cool night air. Sid didn't know what to say. Elizabeth's manner was unsettling. As comforting as her words and touch were for him, Sid sensed that something was terribly wrong. *It's almost as if she's saying goodbye*, he thought.

He and Elizabeth sat in a peaceful silence for a long moment before she gave his hand a final squeeze and said, "Eat up while it's still hot." Without another word, she turned and stepped out of the stall and headed back towards the house.

Sid looked down at the two plates of food that she had left him, but he wasn't hungry anymore. A strange feeling was gnawing at his gut, but he did his best to push it aside. As he slowly ate his dinner, he thought about how kind Elizabeth had been to him over the last months. In many ways, she had been like a mother to him. He was suddenly terrified that he would be taken away from her as well.

He set the empty plates aside and crawled back into the hay stack. As he covered himself, he began to shiver, not from the cold, but from fear. After a long while, he drifted off into a sad, uneasy sleep.

~~~

Thud. Sid was shaken from his restless slumber by what sounded like a heavy log being dropped from a great height onto the hard, frozen ground. It was an eerie sound. He sat up for a moment, listening, hoping that he might have dreamt it. His gut instantly told him that something frightful was happening outside. Then he could hear it, a distinct crackling sound, as if someone had lit a huge fire.

Sid pulled himself out of the hay pile and felt his way out of the dark stall and into the main area of the barn. As he approached the barn door, he was met by a wall of heat. A ghostly bright red and orange glow was coming from the direction of the farmhouse and illuminating the darkness outside. Flames were shooting high into the sky, and crackling sounds and popping noises echoed loudly through the cold night air.

Sidney felt himself frozen to the ground, horrified, as he watched the house being engulfed in flames. He quickly gathered his wits and started to run towards the blazing inferno.

"Elizabeth! Elizabeth!" he cried. As he hurried closer, he frantically scanned the area around the house looking for her. There was no sign of her, or of Clarence.

"Elizzzzzzabethhhhhh!" he screamed, desperately hoping that she had wandered off into the darkness to safety. No response came back to him. As he drew closer, the searing heat kept him at bay, robbing him of any chance to get close enough to help her escape. Coughing and sputtering, he strained to look through the flames and smoke, but all he could see was a silhouette of the old farmhouse, and then it too quickly
~~~

disappeared as the wooden structure began to collapse. Sid stood helpless as he watched the house burn, and most likely Elizabeth along with it.

Sid could hear the jangling sound of the wagon coming up the lane before he could see it. As it emerged through the smoke, he saw that it carried three people, two men and a woman, who Sid took to be the neighbours from up the road. One of the men spotted Sid right away and pointed him out to the driver. "There," he hollered. "There's someone there."

The wagon pulled up close to where Sid was standing and the woman rushed over to him. The men jumped off and ran in the opposite direction, towards the burning pile of rubble. As the woman put a blanket around Sid's shoulders and held him close, he prayed that the men would be able to save Elizabeth.

But their efforts were futile as the blistering heat relentlessly forced them back. "It's no use," one of them shouted as he grabbed his partner and directed him back towards Sid and the woman. "If there was anyone inside, they're surely gone now," he said. "Are you the only one that made it out?" one of them shouted, looking over to Sid.

Feeling numb to everything around him as he watched the flames lick and lap the dark sky above, Sid was paralysed. The man gently grabbed his shoulders and softly spoke again. "Are you the only one that made it out?" he repeated, looking the terrified boy straight in the eyes.

Sid blankly looked back at the man. "Yes, sir. I mean, no, sir. I mean, I sleep in the barn."

The three adults looked at each other in disbelief and the woman pulled Sid closer and held him tightly. No one in the small group said another word. The four of them stood back and watched the last of the flaming timbers give way and crash into the smouldering pile.

"Nothing we can do tonight," one of the men said as he started back towards the wagon. "Son, you'll come home with us. We'll come back in the morning when it's light."

Chapter Ten

Standing Ground

Sid was taken back to the home in Toronto under the watchful eye of Simon, the escort dispatched to retrieve the wayward boy immediately after Mr. Donnelly received the telegram advising of the fire. The neighbours who had taken Sid in that night had wasted no time in getting into Aylmer to report the incident to the authorities and to make arrangements for Sid to stay at the church with the local pastor.

Rumours about the fire had spread quickly around town, and some people pointed the finger of blame squarely at Sid. He was, after all, one from a group of British miscreants widely thought to be trouble. If not for Clarence's reputation as a despicable and disgusting man who certainly would not be missed, the situation for Sid could have been much worse. When questioned, Sid talked about the roaring inferno that Clarence always kept blazing in the stove. He never mentioned Elizabeth's strange behaviour that night. As it was, the authorities were satisfied with his version of events, and as far as the law was concerned, the matter was dismissed as a tragic accident.

It was, however, still an issue for the organization. Innocent of any wrong doing or not, widespread news of the incident would surely solicit much unwanted negative publicity. The sooner Sidney was removed from Aylmer, the better.

So, one week after the fire, a scrawny, pointy-nosed, weasely-eyed little man named Simon surreptitiously arrived in Aylmer to quietly retrieve the boy and escort him back to Toronto. The pastor was thanked for his time with a small donation to the church and Sid was hurriedly shuffled off to a waiting coach. Sid was sad to learn that this gaunt little man had replaced the tender-hearted Mr. Dobbs, who had some months prior resigned his position with the organization. It didn't take Sid long to determine that Simon shared the same scheming and cruel qualities as Thelma.

Before, Sid would have been intimidated by Simon, but after his time with Clarence, he realized that there was nothing that anyone at the organization could do to him that would equal the torment he had already suffered. By the time the pair arrived back in Toronto, even Simon seemed to sense that this newcomer was not like the other boys who were so easily terrorized into compliance. He would need to find new and innovative ways to keep this one in line.

April 13, 1915

Sid lay awake for a full hour, alone with his chilling thoughts before Simon turned on the lights and started his usual trek through the dorm, sharply tapping his cane on the foot-boards and screaming, "Wake up ya lazy bastards! There's work to be done!" It was Sid's second morning back at the home.

The room quickly filled with the sounds of a hundred sleepy-eyed boys moaning and groaning as they were brusquely roused from their sleep for another mundane day of chores, church and school. Sid was the first of the lot to be up and dressed. After having toiled for nearly a year on the farm with Clarence, getting out of bed at five in the morning to scrub toilets was a simple task by comparison. As he looked around the dorm at the group of grumpy, complaining boys, he wanted to shout at them to stop their whining and get on with their daily chores. *What did they have to complain about*? he wondered furiously. The orphanage feeds them well, doesn't beat them and lets them sleep in warm, safe beds.

On his return walk through the dorm, Simon stopped in front of Sid as he was making up his cot. "Mr. Donnelly wants to see you in his office right after breakfast," the small man advised.

Sid glanced up and affirmed with a nod that he had heard him. Ten minutes later, Sid was staring at the heavy oak door that led to the home's main office. As he knocked, he had a sense that this meeting was not going to turn out in his favour. Within a few seconds, he could hear Mr. Donnelly's heavy foot-steps pounding the hard wooden floor. The door slowly opened, and Mr. Donnelly sternly glared at Sid.

"Come in, boy," he commanded. Mr. Donnelly directed Sid to sit in a hard-backed chair in front of the big oak desk. Sid took his place while Mr. Donnelly sat on the edge of the desk and stared down at the boy for one long minute. "You caused quite a disturbance the other week," he finally spoke, furling his eyebrows. "Sidney, we spend a great deal of time and money helping young urchins such as yourself to become decent and productive citizens. We provide you with nourishing meals, clothing and a warm bed to sleep in. We educate you, send you to church and provide you with basic skills and hopefully a good work ethic, all so that you might go out into this world to be a better person than you no-doubt would have been if we had left you to your own devices on the streets of England--"

Sid's attention faded in and out while he watched Mr. Donnelly's large, red nose bounce up and down as he spoke.

"--And how do you repay us for this opportunity?" Mr. Donnelly went on. "With your insolence, defiance and in all likelihood, with murderous deeds. In all my years with the organization, I have never seen such aberrant behaviour and total disregard as repayment for our generosity. You are an embarrassment, and only by the grace of God has word of your behaviour not been too far reaching. We can only hope that it goes no further--"

Mr. Donnelly's face grew redder as the lecture progressed. A generous amount of spittle began to form in the corners of his mouth. Sid sat dispassionately in the chair, his own anger boiling deep inside of himself as he was relentlessly derided.

Mr. Donnelly finally stopped his rant and took a deep breath. Sid glared back at him, his eyes thin slits, feeling nothing but hatred for the man standing before him.

"Do you have anything to say for yourself?" Mr. Donnelly asked.

"No," Sid said simply.

"Nothing at all?"

Mr. Donnelly waited a moment for a response, but none came. He harrumphed and grabbed Sid under one arm, forcefully lifting him from his seat and shoving him out the door. "I'll see to it that Simon assigns you double chore duty."

As the door closed behind him, Sid felt like running as the anger inside of him continued to boil. As he hurriedly hiked through the halls, he could feel the other boys' stares and hear their whispers as he passed. Sid stared blankly ahead, trying to ignore the muted remarks of 'arsonist' and 'murderer'. He felt like lashing out and striking everyone. He wished they all ended up with people like Clarence.

Sid pushed through the door of the dining hall just as the other boys were leaving, having already finished their breakfasts. After turning all the benches up on the tables, he pulled the mop from the bucket and began scrubbing the floor, letting his mind drift away from the moment. Once again he thought back to the night of the fire--the terror of that moment still haunted him. He envisioned Elizabeth screaming, scrambling to get to the door before she was consumed by the roaring blaze. His mind brought him back to the morning after the fire, when he had witnessed the neighbouring men pull two charred bodies from the scorched rubble. The only comfort in all of it for Sid was the knowledge that Elizabeth would go on to live in heaven while Clarence would continue to burn in hell. Tears stung his eyes as he rhythmically dragged the mop over the floor.

As Sid sloshed his wet mop towards the front of the room, his eye caught the wooden carving of Jesus on the cross that, according to Mr. Donnelly, hung on the front wall to remind all the boys at the home of God's unending love. But when Sidney looked at it, all he could see was suffering.

As he went about putting the benches back down beside the tables, Sid's mind turned to his mother. *Where are her letters*? he questioned bitterly. *What about her promises to bring me home*? he asked himself, then dismissed the thought as his own naiveté. *Mother was nothing more than a liar, not to be trusted any more than the superintendant, or Mr. Donnelly, or Simon, or any of them*, he concluded. At that moment, Sid had absolutely no hope, just certainty that his lot in life was to live a wretched and worthless existence forever.

Sid managed to make it through supper without any confrontation. It seemed that as much as the others had things to say about him behind his back, none were prepared to approach him face to face with their skewed judgments and rude remarks. That is, until after the evening chores were completed and the boys had an hour of free time before bed.

Soon after the recreational hour started, the dorm was abuzz with juvenile anticipation. Sid felt his whole body tense as the boys began to congregate closer and closer to his bunk.

"So you think you're bad, do you?" came a voice from somewhere amid the crowd.

Sid quickly scanned the group. All eyes were keenly focused on him. He lowered his eyes and tried to ignore the encroaching gang.

"I said, so you think you're bad, do you?" This time the voice was louder and more threatening.

Again Sid scanned the group, looking for the face that had delivered the words. A much older boy who Sid had heard called Evan emerged from the mob. There was a devious smirk splashed across the bully's face as he menacingly looked down on Sid.

"They say that you burned two people because they made you work too hard. Is that so?" he demanded to know.

The situation suddenly became horrifying for Sid. A hundred boys had surrounded him, all anxious to watch Evan bloody his nose and knock him to the floor. Sid warily looked over at the group and then back at Evan. He cleared his throat. "No, I didn't," he softly defended before he turned back to his bed, futilely hoping that Evan would go away and that the mob would disperse.

"I asked you a question!" Evan shouted as he reached over and grabbed Sid's shoulder. Sid spun around just in time to catch the full force of Evan's fist on the side of his face. The blow temporarily stunned Sid, but it didn't knock him down. Evan's face registered a look of surprise when Sid held his ground. The older boy then quickly unloaded another shot, which struck Sid cleanly on the nose. This time, Sid was knocked to the floor beside his bed. Blood immediately began to gush from his nose, spilling onto his bed sheets as he clambered to get back to his feet.

The only times Sid had ever felt a need to fight were when he had to defend his brother from the neighbourhood tyrant's. Now he was faced with defending himself. Evan had pushed him beyond his restraint and the anger inside of Sid was ready to explode all over his older and much bigger opponent. As he was getting up from the floor, Sid realized that the punches he'd just received had caused him no real pain at all. Even Clarence's most feeble backhand had more sting to it than either of Evan's punches.

Bloodied and full of rage, Sid pulled himself to his feet and stood facing Evan, who in the meantime had turned away to accept congratulations from the others. When he turned back, Evan appeared more than a little shocked to see Sid standing and ready to continue the battle.

Sid suddenly unleashed a flurry of punches, all landing squarely on Evan's face and head. As Evan staggered back into the shocked group and clumsily tried to defend himself from the onslaught, Sid stuck close to him and continued to land solid blows until Evan slumped to the floor, crying and pleading for him to stop. Everything around Sid went silent as he mercilessly pounced on his retreating victim, who by then was feverishly trying to crawl away from his attacker.

Sid continued the assault until Simon and two other staff members hurried into the dorm and pulled the still-swinging youngster off of Evan. Just like that, it was over. There was a deadening hush as two of the men restrained Sid, while Simon helped Evan up from the floor. Evan stood sobbing, his nose bleeding profusely, both eyes turning black as they stood there. With his head hung low, Evan was escorted through the crowd, out of the dorm and down to the infirmary. The other two men ordered the shocked crowd to their bunks for lights out. Sid was taken upstairs to a separate room in the attic where the door was locked from the outside.

~~~

Sid was awake and sitting on the edge of the cot when he heard the jingling of keys on the other side of the door. After a moment, the door swung open and two male staff members entered the room, each one
~~~

taking an arm. Sid was surrounded by hushed chatter as he was led past groups of boys busy with chores--every one of them turned to watch as he proceeded past. He noted with surprise the look of admiration that many boys were directing his way, like he was some kind of juvenile folk hero.

Sid was told to sit in the chair outside the office door and wait until Mr. Donnelly was ready for him. The two staff members silently took their places on either side of him. About ten minutes passed before the door opened and Mr. Donnelly stepped out.

"Bring him in now," came the order. The two men lifted Sid from the chair and escorted him into the office. Inside, Simon and the two other staff members who had broken up the fight were quietly waiting for him to take his chair.

"Well, lad, this is the second time in as many days that you have been in front of me," Mr. Donnelly angrily remarked as he took his own chair behind the desk. "It seems you didn't heed a word I said yesterday," he shouted while laying out some papers on the desk. "What are we to do with you?" His cold, calculating eyes stared straight into Sid's.

A surge of fear overwhelmed Sid as he sat, powerless, surrounded by the four of them. Nobody asked him what had taken place in the dorm, but he quickly came to the realization that his efforts to absolve himself of even some of the blame would be futile. *They just assume it was all my fault*, he realized, not surprised at all. *They'll just use this as evidence to prove what they already believe--that I am no good*. He prepared himself to accept whatever Mr. Donnelly had in mind for him.

"Sidney," Mr. Donnelly continued, "we cannot allow you to stay here to corrupt and lead astray the other young boys who sincerely want to learn," he notified. "Tomorrow morning, you will be taken to a home near Hamilton. I can assure you that Mrs. Connors will not tolerate your insolence," he said with certainty. He stood and leaned menacingly over Sid, pounding his fist hard on the desk. "Is that understood boy?" he shouted.

Sid sombrely looked up at him. He knew that he'd already been beaten. "Yes, sir," he mumbled.

"Good," Mr. Donnelly replied. "You'll spend the rest of the day and tonight locked in the attic to think about how you're going to improve your attitude." At that, Mr. Donnelly gestured to the others to escort him back upstairs.

As Sid was brusquely pushed into his room, the last thing he heard before the door slammed was Simon's smug laugh as he quipped to the others, "We'll see how tough this one is when he faces Mrs. Connors."

Sid sat on the edge of his cot and slowly allowed the emotions flood into him, filling every space inside until at last they pushed a torrent of tears from his eyes. He sat and wept uncontrollably for an hour or more, angry at everyone who had left him behind: his mother, Mr. Dobbs, even Elizabeth. He was lost in an uncaring world and wondering what manner of suffering lay ahead of him. He had absolutely no one to count on and nothing more to hope for. Sid was on his own.

Chapter Eleven

The Outsider

Ruth Connors, one of Hamilton's leading humanitarian and religious personalities, was a force to be reckoned with. Her husband's family owned the most profitable hardware store in Hamilton, but Ruth insisted on keeping a working farm to live in the footsteps of the Lord. She made it her hobby to take in wayward boys and reform them through the tried and true methods of hard farm labour, a healthy dose of religious indoctrination, and the occasional good switching.

Mrs. Connors was a staunch supporter of the prohibition movement and an active member of the Woman's Christian Temperance Union. People either loved her or they hated her, depending on which side of the bar door they stood, but everyone within a hundred miles knew of Ruth Connors. And Sid was about to get to know her a whole lot better than most.

April 15, 1915

Sid sat on his metal trunk waiting for Simon to come out. Once again, it was Simon's task to escort Sid to his new home near Hamilton to meet Mr. and Mrs. Connors. As he waited, Sid tried to imagine what kind of home he was being sent to. The only accounts he had were based on brief remarks made by Mr. Donnelly and Simon espousing Mrs. Connors' expertise in dealing with dissidents such as himself.

Sid couldn't comprehend being sent to a place worse than where he had come from. Of course, Mr. Donnelly had no idea of the hell he had sent Sid to eight months prior, when he'd blindly shipped him off to live with Clarence. It was obvious that Mrs. Connors was known to Mr. Donnelly, and that her skills in dealing with hooligans like himself were highly regarded by him. This made Sid nervous.

Simon exited the back door with his overnight bag in hand and directed Sid to load his trunk onto the wagon. Sid noticed that Simon never looked him in the eye or said any more than necessary to him. His guardedness seemed strange to Sid. He was, after all, only nine years old, and Simon was an adult. *Simon must think I murdered the Olsons*, Sid deduced. The thought angered him.

Sid dragged his trunk across the loading ramp and heaved it into the back of the wagon. After everything was in place, Simon and the driver sat on the seat up front, while Sid took his usual place in the back.

"I'll ride with you on the train to Hamilton," Simon advised as the wagon pulled out into the street. "Mr. and Mrs. Connors will meet us at the station there."

Sid looked back at Simon and offered him a weak nod, affirming that he had heard him.

The pair boarded the train well before the departure time. The run from Toronto to Hamilton was always a busy one and Simon obviously wanted to make sure that they were settled into their seats before the other passengers boarded. The half-hour wait inside was silent and tense. Sid sat anxiously, staring out the window, watching the late arrivals scurry to get their bags checked and other passengers hug friends and family before they boarded.

He didn't notice that the train was full and ready to depart until he was startled by the jerking motion of it pulling away. He looked around and watched as families and couples settled into their seats. Simon briefly glanced over at Sid before turning back to his paper and ignoring him for the rest of the one-hour ride.

Simon insisted that they wait until everyone else was off the train before they disembarked. Sid spent those few minutes scanning the crowd outside, trying to figure out which of the waiting couples was there for him. *At least I won't have to wait for hours this time*, he hoped, recalling how he'd had to wait for the Olsons. The thought made him think of the London station master's offer to take him in to clean the station, and he couldn't help but think about what might have been.

Finally, when the last of the passengers had gotten off, Simon stood up and gestured for Sid to follow him. Simon carried his bag in one hand and grabbed one of the handles on Sid's heavy trunk with the other and the two stepped onto the platform. Sid saw Simon scanning the crowd, no doubt anxious to hand over his charge as soon as possible.

"There they are over there." Simon pointed as he hollered at Sid to grab his end of the trunk. "Mr. and Mrs. Connors!" he shouted while clumsily trying to wave at them with the hand that held his overnight bag. Sid was dragged across the platform as Simon marched ahead with his end of the trunk. He hung on and kept up the best he could, stumbling as they wove in and out of the crowd. Finally, Simon stopped abruptly and set his end of the trunk down in front of a solidly built, stern-looking woman who was standing with her arms crossed over her chest.

"Well, we've arrived," Simon anxiously announced as he wiped a bead of sweat from his brow. He seemed very nervous as he stood face to face with Mrs. Connors. "Hmm, well, I see you're looking lovely as usual, Mrs. Connors," he clumsily complimented. There was a brief moment of awkward silence as the two just stood and looked at each other.

"Um, well, yes then. This is Sidney," he went on as he turned to Sid, who was still standing behind him. Simon grabbed Sid's arm and dragged him in front, placing him directly between himself and Mrs. Connors.

Sid looked up at the woman and immediately thought of Thelma. She stood at least six inches taller than Simon, and, in Sid's estimation, she weighed as least as much as Mr. Donnelly. Her hair was tightly wrapped into a bun on the top of her head and was covered with a fine black hairnet. The intense, stern look on her face led to her ominous aura.

"This is Sidney," Simon continued, "the boy Mr. Donnelly spoke to you about." There was a noticeable quiver in his voice as he forcefully nudged Sid a few inches closer.

Sid, who was by now almost directly underneath Mrs. Connors' nose, felt her roughly grab the top of his head and push him back so that she could get a better overall look at him. "So, you're the young rascal that's causing you so much trouble," she said as she scanned Sid from head to toe. "He doesn't look so bad to me," she scoffed to Simon. "Nothing here that a hard day's work and the good Lord can't cure," she assured. "You've done your Sunday schoolin', haven't you, boy? You are familiar with the teachings of our Lord?"

"Yes, ma'am," Sid politely delivered the half truth. He hadn't been to Sunday school for the past eight months.

Mrs. Connors seemed appeased. She abruptly grabbed Sid by the arm and started to lead him away. "Albert, you help the man with Sidney's trunk," she barked as she started off towards the end of the platform with Sid firmly in tow.

"Yes, Ruth," came an obedient reply.

Sid craned his neck to see where the reply had come from. He hadn't noticed the man standing just behind Mrs. Connors--her presence had been too overwhelming. As he was dragged by, he noticed that Albert wasn't much bigger than Simon and, by first observation, appeared to be even less self-assured.

Mrs. Connors and Sid were already sitting up on the front seat of the carriage when Simon and Albert arrived with his trunk. Sid naturally assumed that he would travel in the back, and started to climb that way when Mrs. Connors grabbed him. "You'll ride up here with me boy," she said. Albert and Simon climbed aboard the buggy, taking their places in back atop of Sid's metal trunk.

"I'll drop you at the boarding house, sir," she hollered to Simon as she commanded the horse to start moving. "You can advise Mr. Donnelly that the terms will be as usual," she informed.

The buggy jerked hard as they set off towards town. Sid quickly glanced behind him and quietly snickered as he watched the two frail men, each with one hand on the edge of the trunk and the other holding down their hats, bounce around in the back of the buggy like two skinny trees being tossed about in a strong wind. After a few minutes of deafening silence, Mrs. Connors pulled the carriage up in front of a large house on quiet street. "There you are, sir. Good day," she said, still looking straight ahead.

Simon grabbed his bag and climbed down from the carriage. "Thank you, Mrs. Connors," he said as he tipped his hat to the matronly woman. "And good day to you, Mr. Connors." Without further adieus, Mrs. Connors slapped the reins down, leaving Simon standing on the curb. Sid looked back and stared at Simon until the three of them disappeared around a corner. He then looked up at Mrs. Connors, and felt a chill run down his spine.

About a mile or so out of town, Mrs. Connors pulled the carriage into a long drive that led up to an impressive, two-storey red brick house that seemed to get even larger as they drew nearer. There were verandas and a balcony, all sturdy-looking and freshly painted. *With all of those windows, it must have held a hundred rooms*, he thought.

The lawns were surrounded by neat and tidy farm buildings, all of which looked suitable for living in. The red barn across the way stood tall and straight. Horses and dairy cattle milled about, and they passed an apple orchard and a good-sized vegetable garden.

As the buggy came to a stop in front of the house, Sid noticed three children standing on the porch, all watching intently. He quickly calculated that the girl was younger than he was, maybe seven years old. One of the boys was about his age, and the other he presumed to be about twelve. All of them looked as if they were dressed for church--their hair was neatly combed and the boys wore suits while the girl was dressed in a pretty blue frock. A young woman of about twenty-five stood beside them. Her attire suggested that she was the housekeeper.

The buggy jerked to a stop in front of the main entrance. Mrs. Connors climbed down and immediately began issuing orders. "Albert, take Sidney's trunk to his room. Sidney, come on down from there. Martha, bring the children over here to meet Sidney. Children, come over here and meet the new boy."

Sid couldn't help but pause for a moment, watching as everyone responded immediately to Mrs. Connors' demands.

"Come, Sidney! Come down from there," she repeated, her sharp voice reaching him like a whip.

Sid climbed off the wagon and nervously stood by as Martha ushered the other children down the steps. He wasn't used to normal children. The only kids he'd interacted with for almost five years had been the other grey-clad orphanage boys. He felt extremely nervous as the Connors children all lined up in front of him, each one measuring him with squinted eyes.

"Children, this is Sidney," Mrs. Connors announced. She took a place behind her children and introduced them one at a time. "Sidney, this is Paulette. This is Francis, and this is my oldest, Paul. Children, say hello to Sidney."

In unison, all three greeted the newcomer with a chorus of, "Hello, Sidney." With their mother standing behind them, their cool expressions didn't match the cordial tone of their voices.

Sid sensed that the young girl, Paulette, was innocent enough, but he immediately had a bad feeling about the two boys. There was an air of mischievousness about them, especially with the oldest, Paul. Paul had a devious smile and a gleam in his eye that instantly warned Sid that he would need to be cautious around him.

"Alright, children, let's allow our guest to get ready for prayers and supper," came a renewed stream of orders. "Martha, show Sidney to his room. Make sure that he knows where to wash up. And Sidney, put on a clean change of clothes. We'll have evening prayers in half an hour."

Martha briskly took Sid's hand and led him into the house and upstairs to his room. She filled the wash basin with water and gave him a clean towel and wash cloth.

"You'd best not be late for prayers," she advised in an unkindly tone. "And make sure that you put on a clean change of clothes," she warned as she walked out the door and let it slam behind her.

He looked around the room. It was a small space, but very tidy. There was no window. He sat down on the edge of the small bed and was surprised at how soft and comfortable it felt. There was even a small night table and a chest of drawers. It was much more comfortable than his place in Clarence's barn.

Realizing that he was wasting time inspecting his new surroundings, Sid hurriedly stepped over to the wash basin and began to scrub his face, neck, and hands. After he dried off, he opened his trunk to look for something clean to wear. He didn't have much to choose from. His eyes passed over the well-worn coveralls that Mr. Dobbs had given him and the winter coat that he and Elizabeth had smuggled back to Clarence's farmhouse. His hand reached for his last grey wool suit. *These short pants wouldn't be warm enough for this time of year,* he thought, but they were the only clean clothes he had. Sid changed, folded his dirty clothes neatly and set them in a corner, and then made his way back downstairs. He paused at the bottom step, searching for a clue as to where he should go.

Suddenly, Mrs. Connors swung open a parlour door and stepped into the hall.

"Oh my Lord," she gasped as she grabbed him by the shoulders and held him out for a closer inspection. "Is that all you have to wear?"

Sidney reddened. "Yes, ma'am. This is my good suit of clothes," he said.

"Well, this is inexcusable! I will certainly be talking to Mr. Donnelly about this," she shouted. Mrs. Connors grabbed Sid under the arm and hauled him through the parlour door and into the sitting room. Mr. Connors and the other children were already there, all neatly groomed and dressed and quietly seated, waiting for her to commence with the evening prayers. All three kids watched Sid as he was being dragged across the room, snickering to themselves. Mr. Connors sat utterly still, his eyes never leaving the carpet.

Mrs. Connors flopped Sid onto a chair, stomped over to the book shelf and grabbed her bible. Then she took her seat at the table.

"All right," she said. "Let's begin." Mrs. Connors led the prayer meeting, zealously reading verses from the bible, praising God for his wisdom and for giving her the strength to carry out his work. The theme of that night's prayer was focused around saving a certain young gutter snipe from his unholy ways. Sid tried not to squirm in his hard chair. According to Mrs. Connors, he had been raised in a cauldron of corruption, violence, and debauchery, no doubt by lewd, sinful, and drunken parents and it was her mission as God's representative to reform the disobedient child and convert him into a God-fearing young man.

Sid felt self-conscious and embarrassed by all of the attention. At first he tried to follow along with the verses as best he could. He frequently glanced up at the other children for cues, for they all seemed to know exactly when to say 'Amen' and 'Praise the Lord'. Occasionally he would catch a glimpse of one of the other boys glaring at him with a malicious smirk.

As the forty-five minutes dragged on, however, the anger began to brew inside of Sid. Just like Mr. Donnelly and Simon, it seemed apparent Mrs. Connors had decided that he was a bad apple even before getting to know him. *Despite her fancy house and tidy clothes, she was no different than them*, he thought. *Nothing she says is going to change anything for me*, he kept reminding himself. Sid realized that his torment no longer came at the hands of a vicious drunken bootlegger, but from the mouth of a scheming religious zealot. He wasn't sure which one he feared more. He resolved then and there not to let anyone keep him under their thumb ever again.

Finally, when it was all over, Mrs. Connors slammed her bible shut, pushed her chair back and quickly rose to her feet. "Let us move on to the dining room and we'll have supper," she said. "And Sidney, we have prayer sessions every morning and every evening. You'll be expected to attend all of them. Is that understood?"

All eyes again focused on Sid, waiting for him to answer. "Yes, ma'am," he half-heartedly replied.

"Okay, let's go in for super then," she said.

The three Connors children raced into the dining room, while Sid hesitantly followed behind them. As he entered the ornate room, his eyes widened and his stomach grumbled. The table was festooned with bowls heaped with mashed potatoes, vegetables, salads and gravy. There was a large plate piled high with slabs of steaming hot roast beef and loafs of warm bread with sticks of creamy butter sitting alongside. In amongst the spread were two jugs filled with fresh, cold milk. There were even two vases of fresh-cut flowers set out on the table to complete the display. Sid had never seen such a feast before, and had never smelled such wonderful smells.

The Connors children took their seats at the large wood table, but Sid hung back in the doorway, unsure of where his place was. Mr. Connors finally stepped up behind and put his hand on Sid's back, gently pushing him towards an empty chair across from Francis and Paul and beside Paulette.

Sid looked down at the table. The place setting in front of him was confusing. There was a large porcelain plate decorated with painted flowers, a smaller plate on top of which sat a bowl, two forks, two spoons, and two knives. In front of his plate was a large glass of water in a fancy crystal glass. As delicious as it all looked, the nervous tension that was churning inside of his gut completely robbed him of his appetite.

"Bow your heads for grace," Mrs. Connors ordered. She went on to again thank the Lord for giving them all another day to worship him and for the food that they were about to eat. She again reassured him that he was doing the right thing by sending her this young hooligan, whom she would surely transform into a decent and God-fearing human being. As soon as she was done, everyone immediately began filling their plates. Sid was glad when the focus shifted from him to the meal.

"Here, Sidney, take some roast beef," Mr. Connors offered as he passed the plate over to him.

Sid carefully took the plate, mindful not to bump anything or spill its contents, and gently slid one slab of meat onto his plate. He hesitated, not sure what to do with the heavy platter.

"Pass it around, boy!" Mrs. Connors shouted.

Sid turned to Paulette and carefully handed her the plate, hopeful that it wouldn't be too heavy for the young girl. She readily accepted it without difficulty and stabbed two pieces for her own plate.

"I understand you've worked on a farm before, Sidney," Mr. Connors cheerily inquired as he handed him a bowl of potatoes.

Sid once again felt uncomfortable as the focus shifted back to him. "Ah, yes sir," he mumbled as he stared down at his plate. He could hear the two boys snicker from across the table, obviously finding humour in his anxiety. Everyone was silent for a moment. For the first time, Sid was glad to hear Mrs. Connors' voice break the hush.

"Tomorrow, after school, you'll meet Mr. Emery. He's the hired hand. He'll show you to your chores," she informed.

Sid looked up at her. *I'll be going to school*? he thought. An anxious and excited feeling rose in his chest at the notion. "Yes, ma'am," he said.

Suddenly he began to feel nervous. The only schooling he'd had up until then had been at the home. Sid wasn't sure how he would fit into a real school. He began to feel overwhelmed as thoughts came crushing in on him. Things were happening so quickly. Not two weeks before, he had been struggling in the cold, the mud and the slop, hoping that Clarence wouldn't beat him too severely. Now all of a sudden he was being inundated with the word of God, filled with roast beef and gravy, and enrolled into school.

It was six o'clock by the time supper was done. After she cleared the table, Martha served up bowls of ice cream, a treat that Sid had only heard about. It was as sweet and creamy as he had been told, but the cold made his head hurt. Once again, the boys across the table snickered as they watched Sid squirm, trying to hide his pain and the tears that streamed out of his eyes.

"You children have an hour to yourselves before bed," Mrs. Connors shouted. "Why don't you take Sidney outside and show him around." The words were not spoken as a question.

"Yes, mother. We'll go out to the stable and show him the horses," Paul decided. The three kids quickly pushed away from the table. Paulette innocently grabbed Sid's arm and pulled him along as she ran towards the front door.

"I'll show you my pony!" she yelled.

There was a biting chill in the night air as the four hiked off towards the stables. Nothing was said during the short walk, except for Paulette's chatter about her new pony. Sid stepped lively behind the two boys. They seemed to be in a hurry to get there. Paulette ran behind them all, out of breath and barely keeping up as she rambled on.

Once inside the stable, Paul and Francis turned and waited for Sid and Paulette to join them, then quickly closed the door behind.

Paulette grabbed Sid's arm again and started to drag him over to a stall in the corner. "Come on! Come and see my new pony," she insisted. Not knowing what else to do, Sid dutifully complied and started to follow the excited young girl.

"Let go of him, Paulette. Who wants to see your stupid pony anyways?" Paul scolded.

Paulette turned and scowled at her older brother, then started to sob. She let go of Sid's arm and went off sulking by herself.

Meanwhile, Francis had stepped away and was rummaging through a pile of hay. "Do you smoke, Sidney?" he asked as he pulled his arm out from between the bales.

Sid paused for a moment, taken aback. "No," he finally answered.

Francis opened the pouch he had retrieved from the bales and pulled out a fat, hand-rolled cigarette, the kind Clarence's drinking buddies would bring over to the rundown farmhouse.

"Hurry," Paul snapped, "before the little brat comes back."

Francis pulled a wooden match from the pouch and struck it. He put the cigarette in his mouth and lit it, feverishly sucking to get it burning. Once lit, he deeply inhaled a waft of smoke and passed it on to his brother. Paul did the same, and then passed the cigarette to Sid.

"Come on, take a puff," he coaxed.

Sid wasn't sure what to do. He didn't want to look foolish in front of the boys, so after a pause he reached out and took hold of the cigarette and held it for a moment.

"Hurry up, before it burns away!" Paul hollered. "Just put it in your mouth and suck on it," he instructed.

"Take a big puff and inhale it all the way in," Francis said, looking at Paul with a devious grin.

Sid slowly put the cigarette to his mouth and copied what he had seen the other two do. He sucked in a generous amount of smoke and inhaled it deep into his lungs. Immediately, he began to choke and started coughing violently. He became lightheaded and felt as if he was going to be sick.

Paul and Francis stood back and laughed hysterically. Francis grabbed the cigarette from Sid's hand and took another puff before handing it back to Paul.

"There, now you smoke," Paul said with a laugh. "And now you can't tell mother about this or you'll be in trouble too," he warned. "Plus, mother would never believe you." He shoved the nearly finished cigarette back into Sid's face, challenging him to take another drag. Sid politely refused and the brothers laughed.

Sid stood by as Francis and Paul finished the cigarette down to a stub. Then Francis extinguished the butt and shoved it into a crack between the wooden floor planks.

"You're the fourth one from the home to live here," Paul said, as he turned to Sid. "But you don't seem so bad. Hell, you don't even smoke. I'll bet you've never had a drink either, have you?" he presumed.

Sid instinctively knew better than to tell the boys that not only had he drank booze before, but he had been drunk, many times. It wasn't something that he liked to think about. He was anxious to change the subject to something other than himself. "What happened to the other boys who stayed? Where are they now?" he asked.

Paul looked at his younger brother, a devious smile once again sprawling across his face. "We're not too sure," he said, looking back at Sid. "None of them stayed any longer than six months. They all just disappeared," he wisecracked, looking back at Francis, who seemed to be finding humour in Paul's banter.

"Ya, they just disappeared," Francis smugly confirmed.

Sid was beginning to feel quite unsettled by the two boys. Paulette's sudden return to the group put him slightly at ease.

"I wanna go back to the house," she whimpered.

"Stop your whining, ya little brat," Paul yelled, raising his hand as if he were going to slap her. Sid immediately tensed. Francis laughed when she cringed and then Paul dropped his hand.

"Come on, then. Let's go back to the house," Paul decided. Just before Francis opened the door, he looked back at Sid. "Remember, don't tell anyone. They won't believe you anyways," he said as he heaved open the door.

The two boys walked on ahead, leaving Sid behind and Paulette running to keep up.

~~~

Sid was awake and dressed in his grey suit before there was any stirring in the house. Without a window, he couldn't tell what time it was. He sat in the dark on the edge of his bed, keenly listening for sounds to indicate that someone else was up and about. Finally, he heard the faint sound of a door closing and footsteps going down the stairs. He took a deep breath, opened his door and stepped out. The rest of the upstairs was still shrouded in darkness, but he was able to make his way to the
~~~

top of the stairs and start down. He could hear the clanging of dishes and silverware.

"You're up awful early, aren't you?" Martha's voice startled him as he stepped into the kitchen. Her tone gave him the impression that she didn't like the intrusion.

"No ma'am," Sid mumbled. "I'm up at this time every morning."

"Well, it's just five o'clock. The rest won't be up for another hour. Not even Mr. Emery will be up this early," she said. "You'll meet him later this morning when you do your chores."

Chores, later this morning, Sid thought. He was puzzled. "No ma'am" he said. "Mrs. Connors said that I start school today."

Martha laughed and looked over at him. "Oh yes, you'll be in school all right," she assured. "But not with the other kids. You'll have two hours of home schoolin' with Mrs. Connors after breakfast, and you won't have breakfast until after you've milked the cows. And before you milk the cows, there'll be morning prayers. And then after your schoolin', you'll have more chores. You're going to be a busy lad," she notified as she turned back to the stove to stir the porridge. "Prayers start at six thirty. I recommend that you stay in your room until everyone else gets up so as not to be in the way."

Sid felt both relieved and disappointed. The thought of not having to meet a new group of children abated his anxiety. At the same time, however, he was disappointed that he wouldn't have the opportunity to go to school like the other children. Once again, he felt like an outsider.

~~~

Every weekday morning at seven forty-five, Sid stood at the barn door and watched with a heavy heart as the three other kids, with books under their arms, climbed into the buggy with their father and headed off to school. Early morning chores were finished by eight-thirty, after which he sat by himself in the kitchen and ate his porridge and bread. Mrs. Connors came in promptly at nine and escorted him to the den where he was tutored for two hours in math, reading, writing, and, of course, religious studies. Mrs. Connors' teaching methods were harsh, and she was unforgiving of even the slightest mistake. Not a day went
~~~

by that she didn't make certain that he knew how stupid, ignorant, careless and outright insolent he was.

And Gus Emery was by no means an easy man to work with. The farmhand tended to be lazy, and like Clarence, he was a drinker. On a normal day, Sid wound up doing most of the work while Gus snuck off behind the barn for a nip of whiskey and a cigarette.

Every day, Sid endured subtle taunts from Francis and Paul. The two always seemed to be scheming some way to get him into trouble. The boys were always polite and courteous with Sid when they were around their mother and father, but as soon as they were left alone together, the goading started. Sid was always wary of them and tried to keep his distance as best he could. For the first month or so, he was able to avoid any serious trouble. But then, just as Sid had somehow sensed they would, the brothers finally had their way.

May 1, 1915

It was a beautiful Saturday morning. Sid was dumping a wheelbarrow load of cow shit and soggy straw out behind the barn. Like usual, Gus was nowhere to be seen. On the veranda, Sid could make out Francis and Paul relaxing lazily, drinking lemonade and watching as he did his barn chores.

Sid watched as Paulette walked up to her brothers and sat at their feet for a while. It wasn't long before she was running away from them, however, tears streaming down her face. She was headed towards the stable. *What sort of mean lies are they telling their little sister now?* Sid wondered, feeling a surge of pity for the defenceless girl.

Paulette reached the stable just as Sid entered to gather up another load. Paul and Francis strolled in a moment later with mischievous looks on their faces. Paulette walked right up to Sid.

"Is my pony alright?" she cried.

Sid looked over at the brothers, annoyed. "Yes, Paulette, your pony is fine," Sid calmly told her.

Paulette grabbed his arm and tried to drag him towards the stall with her. Just then, Francis pushed Sid hard, directly into Paulette. She fell heavily into a heaping pile of cold, wet cow shit and straw, with Sid landing solidly on top of her.

Paulette let out a scream that could be heard clear up to the house. Paul stepped out of the stable and yelled for his mother, who by then was standing on the porch with Martha to see what all the commotion was about.

"Over here, mother!" Paul yelled, waving his arms. Mrs. Connors and Martha hurried across the lawns and into the barn just in time to see Sid standing by the wheel barrow, covered in shit, while Francis helped his sister up from the pile. The girl was covered from head to toe with the sloppy goo, and pieces of dirty brown straw were sticking every which way out of her hair.

"What on earth is going on here?" Mrs. Connors bellowed as she ran over to Paulette. She stopped short of touching her daughter, fearful of getting any of the mess on herself. "Are you alright, girl?" she asked.

Paulette stood there, crying, unable to speak.

"Martha, come and take her to the house and clean her up," she ordered. "There doesn't seem to be any injuries, but have her lie down just in case. And make sure that none of this mess gets inside!"

Martha reluctantly grabbed the young girl's filthy hand and led her towards the house.

"What happened here?" Mrs. Connors screamed.

Sid opened his mouth to give his side when Paul's voice cut through the stable. "Well, me and Francis saw Paulette running to the stable, so we ran out to make sure everything was okay," Paul said, his face earnest. Sid stifled a grunt. "When we got here, we saw Sidney push her into that pile," he said, pointing to the wet mound of shit and straw.

Sid opened his mouth in disbelief at the blatant lie. Paul glanced at Sid with a sly smirk and then looked to his brother. "Isn't that right, Francis?"

"Yes, Mother, that's what happened," Francis confirmed. "He pushed her for no reason at all," he added, his eyes twinkling.

Sid was bewildered. He couldn't move or speak as he looked over at Mrs. Connors, who by then was glaring at him with a look of cold condescension in her eyes.

"Paul, go get a handsaw from the tool shed and bring it to me," Mrs. Connors shouted, her eyes never leaving Sid. She took two steps towards the frightened boy and grabbed him by the ear, nearly yanking him off his feet. "You come with me, boy!" she bellowed as she dragged him out of the stable and over to the stand of willows behind the barn. Paul quickly caught up to them and handed his mother the saw.

"Take this and cut off that branch," she yelled, pointing to a long, thick, tapering switch about five feet off the ground.

"But ma'am, I was just-"

"Mind your mouth, you evil brat!" she cut in. "Now cut off that branch as you were told."

Sid took the saw from her hand slowly sawed through the branch. When it fell to the ground, he handed the saw back to Mrs. Connors.

"Now pick up that branch and give it to me."

Sid's throat tightened. He contemplated trying again to tell her what had happened, but decided against it. *She made her mind up about me a long time ago*, he realized. He braced himself for what was to come.

When Mrs. Connors had the branch in her hand, she once again grabbed Sid by the ear and dragged him all the way across the lawns to the front porch, with Paul and Francis merrily skipping along behind them. "Now bend over," she demanded.

Tears started to well in Sid's eyes. His whole body trembled as he prepared to take his whipping.

He heard Paul and Francis laughing as they watched the spectacle. After the first ten whacks, Sid lost all sensation in his body and slipped into unconsciousness.

When he came to, he found himself in the barn, still covered in shit and straw, his backside bloodied from the beating. The sun was down and everyone else was asleep. He made himself a bed in the straw beside Paulette's pony and remained there for the night.

Chapter Twelve

The Runner

Life at the Connors residence changed for Sid following the incident in the barn. Mrs. Connors became even more determined to whip the boy into shape, but only after a few changes where made to his living arrangements. Sid was no longer allowed to stay in the main house or to be anywhere near Paulette. He took his meals by himself in the kitchen after everyone else had eaten, and he and his belongings were moved into the bunk house with Gus Emery.

Believing that education was a privilege that must be earned, Mrs. Connors decided that Sid's two hours of daily schooling would be replaced with extra time spent working around the farm. She was, however, not willing to let him get away without his religious studies, and decided that what he needed was an even more rigorous dose of God's word. As part of her new lesson plan, the rod wasn't to be spared. Sid dreaded those sessions, and with every passing day he became more and more rebellious towards her.

By the end of May, the fury that raged inside of Sid had become almost unbearable for him. He spent many nights fantasizing about running away, but he always stopped himself, not sure of where he would go or what he would do. And, though he wouldn't admit it, there was a small part of himself that was not yet willing to disappear beyond the orphanage's reach just in case his mother sent him a letter.

He was trapped in that place just as firmly as he had been held hostage on the farm with Clarence.

May 29, 1915

As Sid returned to the bunkhouse after his nightly prayer meeting he was, as usual, full of rage. He touched his shoulder and winced as he rubbed the sore spot where he had received a lashing an hour before for not knowing of Cain's sins. When Sid stepped in, Gus was at his regular place, sipping a glass on whiskey at the table near the window. He seemed unusually jovial that night.

"You have a good meetin' with the ol' battleaxe tonight, boy? She get frisky with ya again?" Gus teased.

Sid was having difficulty finding humour in the situation and disdainfully glanced at Gus before sullenly walking over to his bunk to turn in for the night.

"Come on, boy, lighten up," Gus slurred. "You know, here we are livin' in the same house and we barely say two words to each other," he said as pushed himself up from the table and staggered over to where Sid stood.

That's because I'm always too busy doing all of your work while you're out doing whatever it is you do out behind the stable, Sidney thought.

Gus grabbed Sid's arm and roughly coaxed him back to the table. "Come on, boy, come and have a seat," he insisted as he shoved Sid into a chair. "Tell ya what, boy. Have a drink with me and we'll talk, maybe get to know each other a bit better. Whaddaya say?" he mumbled as he proceeded to fill two large cups with straight whiskey.

The situation reminded Sid of those awful times when Clarence had forced him to drink and he wanted nothing to do with it. But then he thought about how it would be the ultimate disrespect to Mrs. Connors and he warmed up a bit to the idea.

Sid accepted the glass, raised it to his mouth and took a small sip. To his surprise, Gus's whiskey didn't taste nearly as bad as Clarence's moonshine. In fact, it barely burned his throat at all. He took another sip.

"That's the way, boy," Gus laughed as he raised his glass to make a toast. "Here's to Old Lady Connors--may the good Lord have mercy on us all and come for her soon."

They both laughed. Sid held his glass up in reply and they drank. It didn't take long for Sid to down the whole cup, leaving him queasy and unsteady in his chair. When he was able to focus his eyes, he saw that Gus had poured another round.

"Come on, let's celebrate!" the old farmhand hollered.

As Sid was slowly sipping the second glass, the room started to spin. Gus kept on talking and seemed to be getting louder with every word that came out of his mouth. While the drunkard rambled on, Sid was overcome with the urge to lie down and go to sleep in his bed.

He clumsily set the glass down and tried to stand, and for a moment he thought he was going to make it. Suddenly, his legs gave way, causing him to crumble onto the floor. Gus kept talking as Sid struggled to get back to his feet.

"Come on boy, let me help you," Gus laughed as he got up from his chair. He was suddenly looming over Sid, grabbing him by the arm. Sid tried to push him away, sure he could get up by himself, but he wasn't strong enough to overcome Gus's power. Gus kept laughing as he dragged Sid over to the bunks and lay him down. "It's okay, boy," he assured as he started to undo the buckles on Sid's coveralls.

After a moment Sid realized that he was lying on Gus's bed, not his own. He tried to push Gus's hands away from his body, but the whiskey had left him with little strength.

"It's okay, boy. I'm just going to help you get undressed for bed."

Sid tried to yell out, but Gus quickly covered his mouth with his hand. "Now don't start hollering, boy," he warned. "There's no one around to hear." Gus continued to disrobe the boy until he was completely naked. Sid willed his body to move, but his limbs were just too heavy. He began drifting in and out of consciousness as he lay there, exposed and powerless, while Gus removed his own clothing and stood naked over him. Sid lay helpless as Gus moved closer, climbed onto the bed and straddled him. Sid could smell the other man's stinking breath as he squatted over him.

Sid sensed his small hand being forced between Gus's legs before he finally drifted out of consciousness to the low guttural sounds of Gus's moans.

The following morning, Sid awoke naked on his own bed. His head was pounding and he felt dirty. The sun was already beaming through the bunkhouse window. He lifted himself up as best he could and looked around the room. There was no sign of Gus.

Suddenly, Sid had a hazy flashback of the events of the previous night and an awful gut-wrenching feeling crept inside of him. A loud knock at the door brought his mind back to the bunkhouse.

"Are you in there, Sidney?" Mrs. Connors yelled. "It's half past nine!" she hollered. "Come on out here this instant!"

Sid didn't respond. He just wanted to disappear.

After a moment, Mrs. Connors barged into the bunkhouse. Sid used all of his strength and wits to cover himself up. "Why are you still sleeping?" she scolded. "You've missed all your chores this morning, and you were supposed to be at prayers half an hour ago. Now, get up!" she hollered.

Sid's head pounded harder with every piercing sound that came out of her mouth. He lay on his bed, hurting and struggling for something to say. "I'm not feeling well," he mumbled as he pulled the covers up to his chin.

Mrs. Connors stomped over to his bed, causing him to cower further under the sheet, sure that he was about to be assaulted.

"Let me feel your head," was all she said as she lay her hand on Sid's forehead and held it there for a moment. "You do seem to have a bit of a fever," she conceded. "Well, Gus has already gone into town. I suppose you might as well stay in for the rest of the day. I'll send Martha over later to check in on you." At that, Mrs. Connors turned and marched out the door.

Sid lay still for a few minutes, trying to gather his thoughts. Suddenly, he began to heave violently. He somehow managed to roll over, getting his head partly over the side of the bed before the entire contents of his stomach spewed out of him. Vomit splattered all over the pillow and the bed sheets and onto the floor. When he was finally finished, he slowly pulled himself up and sat on the edge of the bed. For a brief moment, a feeling of panic overcame him. He was fearful that Gus would walk in at any minute.

I can't stay here any longer, he realized, and just as the thought came to him, a sense of freedom overwhelmed him. He got up off the bed and found his shirt and coveralls hanging on the back of the same chair that he had fallen out of the night before. He managed to get himself dressed and stumbled to the door, opening it just enough to see out into the yard. When he was certain that there was no one around, Sid slid out and made his way to the barn. He climbed up into the hayloft and buried himself in the straw, *a good place to hide until nightfall*, he reckoned.

Sid heard the wagon pull into the barn later on that afternoon. It was Gus, back from town with a load of supplies. Sid lay in the haystack, stock still, his heart pounding. He listened as Gus unhitched the horse from the wagon and hung the harness on the wall.

"Gus!" Mrs. Connors called from outside the barn. "Have you seen Sidney?" she yelled.

He heard Gus's heavy footsteps pound across the wooden floor towards the barn door.

"Martha went to check on him this afternoon and he's gone!" she hollered. "The brat left an awful mess in his bed and now he's nowhere to be found." Sid could tell from her voice that she was furious.

"Last I saw him, the lad was still in his bed," came Gus's voice. "Said somethin' 'bout not feeling well. I just left him be." Sid's eyes narrowed in hatred as he listened to the words.

"Get that horse hitched back to the wagon!" she ordered. "You're taking me into town. If we can't find him there, we'll see how well the little brat does when the police get hold of him."

Sid heard Gus re-hitch the horses to the wagon and within minutes the two started off for town. Sid stayed in the haystack for the rest of the day and into the dark of night. When he was sure that everyone was asleep, he climbed down from the loft, put Gus's hidden cigarettes in his pocket, and headed off towards the lights of Hamilton.

~~~

The sun still hadn't risen and Sid was a little tender from having slept on the hard ground in the alley behind a blacksmith shop. He furtively looked in every direction before climbing to his feet. *Even at this early hour, there'll surely be someone out and about to turn me over to the police*, he thought. He decided it would be best to get away from the blacksmith shop before it opened, so he brushed himself off and started to make his
~~~

way towards the centre of town. A few scraps of food from a garbage bin behind the café would have to suffice for breakfast.

As he was walking, he was flooded with memories of his days in England when he, his brother George and their mother had fended for themselves on the streets. In a strange way, the thought made him feel at ease, reminding him that he could survive on his own. But it was different this time. He didn't have mother or his brother to turn to for help or comfort. And those thoughts quickly turned to anger as he recalled his mother's promise to write every month, and to bring him back to England. *She meant none of it*, he thought.

As the first light of day began to break, the city of Hamilton started to come alive. Shop doors opened and people hurried to work. After scavenging a few scraps of food, Sid was just wandering the streets, trying not to draw any notice from passers-by.

As he wandered aimlessly, his thoughts turned to the events of the previous night. He recalled vague images of Gus, naked and drunk, sitting on top of him, touching him in ways that he did not like--ways that weren't right. He began to feel sick again and he ducked into an alley to relieve himself of the pain. When he finished, he pressed his back against a brick wall and slid down it until he was in a squatting position. For the first time since the fire, Sid cried.

At that moment, every negative emotion that he held inside poured out of him. He struggled. *Should I just go back.* No matter how he looked at it, he knew that life wasn't going to be good to him. *Maybe a hell with three meals a day is better than the uncertainty of trying to make it on my own*, he thought.

He had just about decided to turn himself in when a sudden realization stopped him dead in his tracks. *I will never return to live with Gus*, he pledged. Sid pulled himself up and pushed all of his negative feelings deep down inside. No matter what, he resolved that he would not stay anywhere that he did not want to be, or do anything that he did not want to do. *I'm through with letting people treat me badly.* Sid decided that the only person he needed in this world was himself.

Brushing himself off, he stood for a moment, trying to determine what he should do next. *The train*, he thought. He had heard of people riding the trains before. *Maybe I could jump on one of the freight cars.* As he headed towards the tracks, careful not to come too close to the main station, Sid felt an overwhelming sense of relief knowing that he was going to get away from everyone who had treated him so cruelly: Mrs. Connors, Mr. Donnelly, Simon. Sid had no idea where he would end up. He just knew that it would be a better place than anywhere he might be sent to.

Sid had never felt that free before. He found a hiding place close to the tracks about a mile out of town. It was thick with brush, just the right amount of cover for him to hide in until the next train left the station. As he lay in the long, blowing grass, he slowly drifted off.

~~~

"Get up, kid!"

The voice jolted Sid out of his sleep. Before he was fully awake, he was up on the tips of his toes, his left shoulder cranked up high over his head by a strong figure standing behind him. He could hear men laughing.

"Gonna ride the rails, were you, lad?" one of them scoffed.

At the men's mercy, Sid was spun around. Bleary eyed, he found himself looking up at two of the biggest men he had ever seen. Both were wearing uniforms. A sense of panic overwhelmed him as the two constables led him away, instantly dashing all his hopes of freedom.
~~~

Chapter Thirteen

The Last Straw

Mary picked up her cup and sipped the last of the cold tea from it. All that was left on the plate were a few cookie crumbs.

"Oh dear!" she gasped. "We need more tea and cookies. How long have I been babbling on?" she asked, looking over at George as if she were embarrassed for going on too long with her story.

George looked at his watch. "Oh, we've been here for about three hours now, I guess," he said with a smile. "But I could sit here all day listening to you if you'd let me," he assured. "I want to know everything there is to know about my father."

George's words made Mary feel more at ease. "Okay, then," she smiled. "I'll just fetch us some more tea before I go on." With that, she headed back to the kitchen.

"Where did they take him?" George asked as Mary set another plate of cookies on the table.

"Where did they take him?" she replied with a puzzled look.

"The constables who found him, where did they take him?" he persisted.

"Oh, yes," she smiled. Mary contemplated for a moment as she seated herself and recalled where she had left off in her story. "Well, let's see now. Oh yes, they took him back to the Connors' farm and turned him over to Mrs. Connors. I suppose they didn't consider that a nine-year-old runaway was worth putting in jail," she said.

"So he stayed with the Connors family again?" George asked. "Did they put him back in the bunkhouse with Gus?"

"I suppose that was the plan," Mary said. "But Sid would have nothing to do with it. That very night, he ran away again, only to be caught early the next morning. And, he was once again returned to Mrs. Connors. But not for long." She smiled.

May 31, 1915

As the two constables pulled their buggy up in front of the Connors residence, the entire Connors clan, along with Martha and Gus, came out to the porch to meet them. Paulette stood back with her father and both wore anxious looks on their faces. Paul and Francis stood together, sporting their usual smirks. Martha and Gus were at the back, quietly watching and, Sid was sure, looking forward to seeing him punished. Mrs. Connors was front and center. Sid slumped down on the bench, anticipating the wrath she was about to unleash on him.

"Good day, Mrs. Connors. Mr. Connors," one of the constables greeted with a tip of his cap. "Seems the lad still wants to ride the trains," he laughed. "What'll you have us do with him today?"

Mrs. Connors did not smile. She looked over to Sid. "Bring him down," she barked. "I'm not done with this one yet."

"Yes, ma'am," the constable replied, then paused for a moment. "You know, Mrs. Connors," he started. "Well, it's just that we can't waste any more time chasing this boy all over the countryside. Something has to be done, ma'am." The man paused, and a grin spread across his face. "Maybe you should chain him to a post in the barn," he joked.

Tight-lipped, Mrs. Connors stared at the constable. "Don't worry, officer. I'll make certain the boy doesn't cause you any more trouble," she assured, coldly glancing over at Sid. "Bring him to me," she demanded.

The two officers climbed down from the buggy, pulled Sid from his seat and dragged him to Mrs. Connors. "There you go, boy," one of them said. "I don't expect we'll be seeing you again."

Sid stood in front of the furious woman, her anger not moving him an ounce. He looked over her shoulder to where Paul was standing with his brother, a smug look plastered on his face. The sight of that smirk fuelled a rage inside of Sid that he couldn't contain any longer. Suddenly, he bolted from the constables' grip, ran up the stairs and grabbed at Paul's throat. Sid pounced on top of the unsuspecting boy and began pummelling him with all his might.

The first to step in was Mr. Connors, who feebly tried to pull Sid off of his son. In his fury, Sid swung wildly at the frail man, knocking him down. Paulette screamed and ran over to Martha. Gus and Francis stepped back and idly watched the altercation unfold. Mrs. Connors, usually not one to be at a loss for words or action, looked on in shock.

The two constables hurried up the porch and pulled Sid off his target. When it was over, Paul raised himself up on one elbow and crawled towards the wall, blood gushing from his mouth and nose.

With Sid firmly in control, one of the constables impatiently looked up at Mrs. Connors. "You still not done with him, ma'am?" he asked.

Mrs. Connors stared at the boy for a moment, her eyes icy. "Take him away," she finally said. "He can't stay here any longer."

"Yes ma'am," the officer replied as he led Sid back towards the wagon. "We'll need to place him in the cells until someone comes for him," he advised over his shoulder.

Mrs. Connors snapped her head up. "Yes, right," she muttered. The usually demanding and forceful woman was speechless. "I'll contact Mr. Donnelly. He'll need to send someone for the boy, I suppose."

The constables took Sid back to the wagon and helped him up to his seat. One of the officers sat beside the boy to keep him restrained, while the other climbed up and took hold of the reins. "Well, good day, Mrs. Connors. Mr. Connors," he said, once again tipping his cap as he turned the buggy around.

Sid didn't look back at the big house as the buggy pulled away. He didn't try to hide the look of triumph that was surely creeping across his face. He felt an enormous sense of relief. He had won.

Chapter Fourteen

Pickled Eggs n' Chicken Legs

"I don't suppose Mr. Donnelly was too happy about that, was he?" George surmised.

"No, I don't suppose he was," Mary chuckled. "But he got used to it. That wasn't the last time that Sid was sent back under, shall we say, difficult circumstances. You see, Mr. Donnelly kept sending Sid out, and Sid just kept on going back. If he wasn't fighting with other children, he was caught smoking or drinking behind a barn. Usually, he just kept running away. There just didn't seem to be anyone who could handle him."

"Was everyone as cruel to him as Clarence and Mrs. Connors were?" George asked.

Mary gave the question some thought. "No, not all were cruel," she finally said. "In fact, he was able to look back on some of his placements and laugh later on. For instance, there was one lady he was sent to named Bertha, a widow. Sid said that she was an odd woman. You see, Bertha raised chickens, and the only thing she fed him was pickled eggs and chicken legs. Sid said that he got so sick of pickled eggs and chicken legs that he would have rather eaten pig's feet." Mary laughed, a faraway look in her eye. "Pickled eggs n' chicken legs, that's all there was to eat. Pickled eggs n' chicken legs, I'd rather eat pigs feet," she sang. "Sid always used to sing that little ditty."

Mary lowered her head and hesitated for a moment. "He also said that when they were at home in the evenings, Bertha would lift her dress and, you know, show him things. Well, that made Sid really uncomfortable. Can you imagine?" she posed. "There he was, barely a teenager, and this forty-year-old woman would stand in front of him with her dress hiked up to her chin showing off her private parts to him. Poor lad."

Mary paused to think for another moment.

"And then there was the brother and sister who lived down near the lake. You know, one of those big lakes there in Ontario. Their parents died in a horrible wagon wreck. Left the two of them alone on the farm to fend for themselves. So, like many others, they turned to the organization for help," she said.

"What were they like?" George asked. "Were they good to him?"

"Well, they weren't mean to him," she said. "But he never felt right living there either. He said there was some strange things going on in that house. They made him sleep up in the attic, and every night he could hear them going at it in the bedroom down below. Even Sid knew that a brother didn't do those sorts of things with his own sister," she said. "He didn't last long there, either."

"And, then there was the time he went to live with that family, the Turnbulls. That couple had seven boys and a daughter. Sid said he knew their horse had a mean streak the moment he set eyes on it. The old man always made Sid hitch it to the plough--never himself or the other boys, always Sid. Well, Sid did as he was told and one day the horse up and kicked him right in the gut. Said it knocked him flyin' clean across the yard. He figured the old nag broke at least three of his ribs. Said he had never felt such pain before."

"Well, the couple refused to take him to see a doctor--told him to be a man. And besides, they said, doctors cost money and he didn't work hard enough to earn his keep, let alone pay for medical bills. Sid was given the rest of the day off and told to go lie on his bed."

"That night the man came in and told Sid to make sure he was up early the next morning and to have the horse hitched to the plough before breakfast. Well, the poor boy could hardly stand. So he snuck out that night and somehow made his way back to Toronto. Said it was eight weeks that time before the police caught up with him and sent him back to the organization."

George smiled. "I can just see Mr. Donnelly's face every time he got a message," he laughed. "And that went on until he was eighteen?"

"Well, no," Mary said. "They struggled with him until he was sixteen. That's how old he was when he met the old man, McTavish. He lived somewhere down near Sarnia," she recalled. "They met quite by chance, but I dare say, it was just the sort of boon Sid needed at that time."

May 1, 1921

Sid was shaken from his uncomfortable sleep by the annoying hack. *What's that smell?* he wondered, irritated as he rolled over onto his back. The cot was hard and he had hardly slept at all for five nights. He rolled over, bleary eyed and tired, and looked at the old man sitting on the edge of the cot across from him. *A new arrival*, Sid presumed.

Sid quickly recognized the strong smell to be pig. He focused his eyes on the man's face to distract himself from the odour. He seemed to be in his sixties and his round weathered mug was covered with scruffy reddish-grey whiskers. The man had a big head, and he was mostly bald with tufts of short, curly grey hair running around the sides. It looked to Sid as if someone had put a horseshoe on the man's head and shaved out the middle.

The old man kept hacking and coughing loudly, casually discharging a chunk of spit onto the floor. When he was finished, the man glared over to Sid. "What you lookin' at, boy?" he bellowed.

"Nothin'," he groggily answered.

The old man straightened himself up, shifting his focus away from Sid for a moment. "Why they got you in here, boy?" he barked. "You seem too young to be in the lockup." His voice was gruff. He coughed up another large gob of green and black spit, which he again spewed out onto the floor.

"What?" Sid mumbled as he slowly sat up and wiped the grime from his eyes.

"Why you in here?"

Sid pondered for a moment how best to tell a stranger that an organization from across the sea had swindled him from his family, shipped him to a new country and doled him out to a series of abusive and hard-hearted individuals who used him like a farm animal. "I'm waiting for someone to come and get me," he replied. "Suppose they'll take me back to Toronto," he muttered.

"You some kind of runaway?" the old man asked as he spewed out another wet mass. "Do ya smoke, boy?"

Sid looked at the old man who was full of questions, wondering why he was taking such an interest in him. "Ya, sometimes," he said.

The old man tossed a pouch of tobacco at him. "Make me one, too," he said. "And don't be stingy."

Sid picked the pouch up from the floor and started to roll the smokes.

"What's your handle, boy?" the old man growled.

Sid looked up from his rolling. "Handle? What do you mean, handle?" he snapped. He was beginning to wish that old horseshoe head would just leave him alone.

"Your name, boy, what's your name?" the old man grunted.

"Sid. My name is Sid."

"Why you in here, boy?" the old man asked again. "First time I ever heard of keeping a boy in jail just to wait for someone to pick him up." Another coughing fit erupted from his lungs.

Sid looked up and tossed him a smoke. The old man pulled a match from his pocket and struck it against a cinder block. "Get over here 'afore I burn my fingers," he yelled.

Sid took the two steps over to the man, put the flame to his own cigarette and then went back to sit on his cot. "I took some whiskey and got drunk," he explained, recalling the events of a few nights ago. "And I guess I hit Mr. Stanley when he found me wandering out behind the barn."

"Mr. Stanley, you mean, Bert Stanley?" the old man said.

"Ya, Bert Stanley," Sid confirmed.

"Now why would you go and do a fool thing like that? I know Bert Stanley. He's a good man. Leastwise, he never done no harm to nobody that I know of."

Sid lowered his eyes to the floor. It was a good question, and one he'd been asking himself quite a bit lately. He just couldn't seem to stop himself from wanting to punish anyone and anything that kept him bounded to a life he didn't want. "I don't know," he finally said. "I was drunk."

"How'd ya come to get drunk and hit a good man like Bert Stanley?" the old man pressed.

Sid sat up on his cot, leaned against the wall and puffed thoughtfully on his smoke. The old man's questions were starting to eat away at him, because he just didn't know the answers. But something about the bald fellow across the cell compelled Sid to open up about himself.

He intended to give only a brief summary, but after ten minutes Sid found that he had told the old man his entire life story, how he'd been separated from George after he'd failed to protect him, how he had been sent to Canada from England by the organization, and how he had been working on farms ever since. His last placement had been with Bert Stanley and his family. "And now they're gonna send me back to Toronto, I guess," Sid concluded with a heavy sigh.

The old man listened patiently, seemingly intrigued by Sid's story. "You know anything about pigs 'n chickens?" he asked.

Sid was surprised by the question but glad to change the subject. "Ya, I've worked with pigs and chickens," the boy replied. "Cows, horses, sheep, and mules too," he boasted. "And I can plough a field and prune an apple tree as good as anyone," he added.

The old man raised his eyebrows and smiled. Just as he opened his mouth to ask another question, their conversation was abruptly interrupted when someone slammed the heavy door of the jail house, sending a loud clanging noise reverberating around the cell. They could hear two men talking, and Sid immediately recognized one of the voices. It was Mr. Donnelly himself who had come to retrieve him this time. Sid's heart plummeted as he anticipated yet another confrontation with the man whose determination to break his spirit was just as strong Sid's resolve to break away from the organizations hold on him.

After a few minutes, the two men stepped into Sid's view. Mr. Donnelly looked tired and furious.

"Is that your boy?" the constable inquired.

Mr. Donnelly stared hard at Sid. "That's him," he grumpily answered. "What did he do this time?"

Sid's cell-mate sat quietly on his cot, keenly listening to the conversation.

"Well," the constable started. "He stole some whiskey from somewhere, got slobbering drunk and was staggering around out behind Bert Stanley's barn. When Bert went back to get him back inside, the boy landed a couple of punches to his face. By the time we got there, the lad was passed out in the hay loft," the constable noted with considerable displeasure. "When we tried to wake him, he started to fight with us. Took two of us to get the irons on him."

The old man chuckled.

The constable snapped his head around. "What's that about, McTavish?" he barked.

"Oh, nothing," the old man chimed with a grin. "Hey Bill, when ya lettin' me outta here? You know I got pigs to feed."

"The pigs'll wait 'til I get this other matter sorted out," the constable barked. "If you'd stay away from Mack's and not get yourself mixed up in drunken brawls, you'd be home right now slopin' your hogs and doin' whatever else it is you do out there, you old fool," he yelled.

McTavish's smile broadened and he sat back on his cot, watching the scene before him like it was appearing on a movie screen.

"Now, Mr. Donnelly, what about the boy?" the constable asked.

"Well, I suppose I'll take him back to Toronto. This one's been nothing but trouble from the day he set foot in Canada," he said. "We'll have to find him another home. He'll be eighteen in two years. After that, I'm done with him."

To Sidney's ears, two years sounded like an eternity.

Suddenly McTavish stood up and walked over to the cell bars.

"What is it now, McTavish?" the constable yelled.

The old man cleared his throat and suppressed a cough. "Maybe it's none of my affair, but if this fine gentleman wants to find a home for the boy, well, I'd be obliged to take him on," he offered. "There's plenty of work for the both of us at my farm, and I have plenty of room for him. I'd make sure he'd earn his keep and then some," he assured.

The constable's face was turning red. "You're right, McTavish," he spat, "this here is none of your business--"

The young constable was interrupted when Mr. Donnelly held up his hand. He looked at McTavish, then at Sid, and then to the constable. Sid could plainly see the wheels turning in his head. "You do understand that there would be some conditions that you'd be required to agree to?" Mr. Donnelly asked McTavish.

McTavish nodded.

"You'll need to see to it that the boy is fed and that you pay him a small wage for his labour," Mr. Donnelly went on. "In this case, the boy will be expected to look after his own needs in terms of clothing and the like."

Sidney could tell that he was sweetening the pot so that McTavish would agree.

"Fine," agreed the old man.

"Fine," echoed Mr. Donnelly.

The constable looked on with a bewildered expression. Sid sat on his cot and watched while his next placement was being negotiated. Something in his gut was hoping that McTavish would be successful in his bid.

Mr. Donnelly contemplated the offer for a brief second. "Alright, then. You've got yourself a boy."

The constable shook his head and reached into his pocket for the keys. "Okay, McTavish, you and the boy can go, I guess. But I'm holding you personally responsible for his behaviour from now on, and as for you," he narrowed his eyes at McTavish, "you stay away from Mack's, you hear?"

"Yes, of course Bill," McTavish said with a chuckle, then turned to Sid. There was a newfound spring in his old body's movement. "Come on, boy, get your things. We got work to do."

Outside the jail house, the old man shook Mr. Donnelly's hand, then motioned for Sid to climb aboard an old rickety wagon that was sitting nearby. It was hitched to a bored-looking horse that resembled a donkey. As the horse slowly pulled the wagon forward, Sid looked back at Mr. Donnelly, who was standing on the steps of the jail house. The look on the orphanage master's face told Sid that he was happy to be rid of him. Sid couldn't have seconded the feeling more.

~~~
~~~

Sid caught the strong stench of swine long before McTavish pulled the wagon up in front of the cabin he called home. Sid looked around the property, noting an old log shelter where the hogs were kept and three outdoor pens. Next to the pig shelter stood the chicken coop. An old rickety barn and a horse corral stood further behind the cabin. The rest of the property looked as if it had been ploughed up with some kind of crop planted.

"We got ten acres here, lad," McTavish boasted. "I been workin' this piece of dirt for over thirty-five years," he said. "Raise hogs and chickens and grow potatoes and beets. Not much, but enough to keep me in tobacco and booze."

The old man passed the reins over to Sid and jumped down from the wagon. "Take the rig out to the barn. Unhitch the horse, put it in the stall and give it some hay and a cup of oats. I'll go start us some supper. Like eggs, don't ya, boy?"

Sid nodded.

"Good. I'll get eight of 'em, then," he shouted as he headed for the chicken coop.

Sid whipped the reins down on the horse and started for the barn. He tried to hold back the feeling of hope that had been building inside of him ever since he'd left the jail house with McTavish. The whole arrangement seemed too good to be true. *Something's gotta give, and soon,* he figured.

"What's wrong with old horseshoe head, eh, girl?" Sid murmured as he nuzzled the horse's nose. "I bet he's a real mean drunk or something, eh?" He finished tending to the horse and made a mental note of the best corner of the barn to sleep in, then headed back to the house.

"Good, you're here," McTavish called over his shoulder. "You can wash up over there." He pointed to a basin of water sitting on a bench in the corner.

The smell of bacon sizzling and cornbread baking made Sid's stomach growl. He hadn't had a decent meal in almost a week. As he was drying his hands, Sid noticed a dusty old photograph sitting in a wood frame on the shelf above the bench. It was a picture of a young man, a young woman and two small children--a boy and a girl. He studied it for a moment, noticing that the man and the children were all smiling, all seemingly happy and content. The woman didn't appear to be nearly as happy as the rest. She had a long, drawn-out look on her face, as if disappointed that life hadn't turned out the way she had hoped it would.

Sid took the photograph down and blew the dust off. "Who are these people?" he asked as he carried the fragile print over to the old man.

McTavish glared at him, his eyes suddenly darkening. "Put it back," he barked. "That's none of your business. Put it back." The old man quickly turned away. Sid cursed himself for his misstep and hoped that the punishment wouldn't be too severe. He put the photograph back on the shelf right where he had found it.

"Come and eat your supper, boy," the old man said, his voice still gruff. "We still have a day's worth of chores ahead and the day's almost gone."

Sid took a place at the table where McTavish had set down a plate, and the two ate their meals in silence. After they finished, the pair went outside to tend to the animals.

As the afternoon became evening, Sid keenly observed that McTavish was a hard worker. And, for an old man, he was strong. His fingers were as thick as tree branches, and he swung a hundred-pound bag of feed over his shoulder like it was a pound of flour. Sid kept up with the old man as best he could, but it was all he could do not to let his fatigue show. Just as darkness began to fall, McTavish patted him on the shoulder. "You're a hard worker, boy," he said. "I can tell by the way you handled yourself tonight, you're gonna do good here."

Sid hid his smile, but the praise felt good.

"Come on, let's turn in for the night. I'm beat."

Sidney followed McTavish towards the house, glad that he wouldn't be expected to sleep with the animals. Once inside, the old man went to a cupboard and pulled out a bottle. "We'll have a nip or two before bed," he said as he looked over at Sid with a grin. "Make ya sleep better."

Uneasiness flowed through Sid as he watched the old man carry the bottle to the table. He thought back to what had happened with Gus in the Connors' bunkhouse and began to consider his best plan for escape.

McTavish poured two shots and then pushed one towards Sid.

"Go ahead. Drink up boy. You'll be glad to have it when yer head hits the pillow," he said. "We've got a full day tomorrow. Up before sunrise," he added. "Go ahead, drink."

Never taking his eyes off McTavish, Sid put the glass to his mouth and took a sip. He watched as the old man sat quietly, sipping on his own drink, his thoughts seemingly drifting to another place. When he suddenly stood up, Sid felt a surge of fear rush through him. He squirmed in his chair as McTavish started in his direction. He let out his breath as the old man kept going past him and walked over to the shelf with the photograph. He gently brushed it with his sleeve and carried it back to the table.

"I s'pose you were good enough to tell me your story this morning, lad," he said. "Guess it wouldn't hurt none if I told you mine." McTavish turned the photograph towards Sid and pointed to the man. "That's me," he smiled, "thirty years ago now. Handsome devil, eh?" he joked with a laugh.

Sid looked closely at the picture, then glanced up to McTavish. It was hard for him to see any resemblance at all, except for the eyes. Years of hard work and hard living had obviously taken their toll on the old man.

McTavish pointed to the woman. "And that," he said in a humourless voice, "that was my wife Gloria. Ran off with a travellin' salesman just after that picture was took, the whore." The old man looked off out the window. "Guess pig farmin' weren't good enough for her. Took the kids, too, the bitch."

Sid watched the old man closely. It was clear that he had been deeply hurt. He didn't know what to say.

McTavish gently set the photograph down on the table and raised his glass. "Here's to bitches!" he shouted. The old man looked Sid directly in the eyes. "Don't ever trust a woman, Sid," he advised. "They're only good for three things I reckon: cookin', cleanin' and screwin'." A broad, wily grin stretched across the old man's face. "And here's ta screwin'!" he shouted.

Sid felt relieved that the old man's stormy mood seemed to have passed. He raised his glass and the pair gulped down their drinks.

McTavish grabbed the bottle and put it back on the shelf. "C'mon, boy, time for the sack. We've a long day ahead."

McTavish directed Sid to a small room off the main area of the cabin. "I don't go in here much," he said. "It was the kid's room. I s'pose it'll be comfortable enough for ya. Might be a little dusty," he added.

Sid pushed the door open and his attention was immediately drawn to the bed, which looked to him to be big enough for four. As far as he could tell, there were two, maybe three heavy quilts on top, and a feeling of elation overwhelmed him as he contemplated curling up under the inviting layers. Up against the far wall was a chest of drawers, with a mirror. *My own room,* he thought. It was the first time he had truly felt at home since arriving in Canada. The grin that stretched across his face was obvious that Sid was happy with his new accommodation.

"Well, good night then," McTavish said with a satisfied smile, indicating that he sensed Sid's satisfaction. "Go on now, get to bed. We got us a full day tomorrow."

Sid was tired and McTavish was right, the whiskey had sedated him well. He pulled back the bedcovers, laid his head on the pillow and quickly passed into a deep, peaceful sleep. Sid felt safe.

Chapter Fifteen

Life According to McTavish

Over the next few months, Sid and McTavish worked tirelessly together. The labour was hard and the days were long, but Sid was used to that. The old man pushed him to work harder than he'd ever worked before, but Sid didn't mind. If there was one thing that he admired about McTavish more than anything, it was that the old man never expected Sid to do anything that he wasn't willing to do himself.

Almost daily, folks stopped by to purchase a hog for slaughter, some eggs, or some butchering hens. McTavish also sold off some of his root crops, keeping only what he and Sid could use. Every Friday, the pair hitched up the wagon for the weekly supply run into Sarnia and at the end of each month, McTavish gave Sid ten dollars, more money than he had ever earned in his life. The old man always told Sid that he was worth at least fifteen, but that he needed to dock him five for all the whiskey he drank and the tobacco he smoked. That seemed fair enough to Sid.

McTavish always took Sundays off and insisted that Sid do the same. "The pigs 'n chickens can fend for themselves on the Lord's day," he would say. It wasn't that McTavish was a religious man by any means, but that was his excuse to sleep until the afternoon on Sundays. And that was because Saturday nights were set aside for drinking whiskey, smoking cigarettes, and arguing about important matters such as the best time of year to plant beans or the best way to dig a post hole. Both were equally as stubborn when it came to being right--McTavish because he was older and more experienced, and Sid because he was young and knew everything.

But as Sid would soon find out, he still had a lot to learn.

August 27, 1921

The sun was setting in the Saturday evening sky as Sid and McTavish finished up their supper.

"I'll just get these dishes cleared away," Sid offered, having just shovelled away his final mouthful.

"Don't bother, lad," McTavish mumbled, his mouth still full of mashed potatoes and pork chops. "Just pile 'em on the shelf there. We'll clean up this mess tomorrow. Come on, sit. I'll pour you another shot. And grab the crib board on your way over."

Sid was happy to comply. He was tired from harvesting beets all day and didn't feel like scrubbing pots while the old man sat there drinking whiskey. Sid retrieved the crib board, took his place at the table and lit a smoke. After taking a long drag, he sipped on his whiskey and looked forward to the night ahead.

The two sat in silence as McTavish shuffled the cards and dealt them each a hand.

"Don't think I'll let you run away with this one as easy as you did last week's game, boy," McTavish warned. "I weren't feeling well was all."

"Whatever you say, old man," Sid said as he lay his cards on the table with a flourish. He counted out his score, "fifteen two, four, six, a pair, ah, twelve."

The old man looked over at the cards. "Twelve my ass!" he yelled. "Where the hell do you get twelve from that?"

Sid looked back at the cards and recounted. "Fifteen two, four, six, ah, oh, eight," he muttered.

"Is that the only way you can beat me at this game, boy--by cheating?" the old man yelled. "Do that in a poker game and yer liable to get yerself shot."

Sid shrugged the old man's rant off and pegged his points on the board. "Okay, that's eight for me, old man," he declared. "I'm still ahead."

McTavish continued to fill the glasses as the banter went from the subject of the weather to the difference between a donkey and a mule. Then came the subject of what a man needed to know in order to look after himself. It was a topic that Sid felt quite qualified at discussing considering all that he had gone through during his yet young life.

Sid was adamant that he had what it took to go out into the world and fend for himself. "After all, I've sailed across an ocean and lived in hen houses and barns," he argued. "I've survived some of the meanest people you're ever likely to meet, and I've beat my share of them, too," he proudly declared.

McTavish bristled. "Ha! You've still got a lot to learn about life," he counselled. "There's them out there that would soon stab ya in the back as look at ya. Yer not man enough to deal with that yet, my boy," he hollered.

Sid rolled his eyes. "You don't know shit, old man," he countered in an exaggerated tone. "I've fought with the best of them." Sid glared at McTavish, goading him to challenge that particular point.

"Hell, I've seen a bag of pig feed get the best of you, you snot nosed brat!" McTavish joked, and then laughed so hard he nearly fell out of his chair. "Don't be tellin' me how tough ya'ar," the old man went on as he slammed his fist hard on the table. "You'd be better off if you had your mama around to wipe your arse!" McTavish hollered in laughter.

Suddenly the smile fell off Sid's face and his blood began to boil. *Who the hell is he to mention my mother?* Sid raged. *Who the hell does he think he is?* Sid couldn't contain his anger any longer. "Is that right, old man?" he thundered, pushed beyond his restraint.

McTavish's face immediately registered the change in Sid's mood, but it was too late. The damage had been done. Sid grabbed the edge of the table and lifted it up, flipping the whole thing over towards McTavish. Everything flew off, covering McTavish in cigarette butts and soaking him in whiskey. The old man stared at Sid for a moment before getting up from his chair.

"Why you little shit!" he yelled as he leapt from his chair. Sid was surprised by the old man's show of agility as he scrambled over the upturned table and pounced. "You wanna go with me, boy?" he roared as he flew towards Sid with all his strength. "Then we'll go!"

McTavish landed on Sid and the two slammed heavily to the floor, rolling in the whiskey and the ash, both wildly swinging and grabbing. They smashed into the wood stove, sending the coffee pot crashing down on them and covering them with spent grounds. They rolled over broken glass and leftover chunks of ham. Spit and blood gushed out of both of them, but Sid was not willing to concede. He was determined to teach the old man a lesson, although it wasn't going quite as easily as he'd anticipated.

After about three minutes of violent thrashing, Sid felt his hand slip on the wet floor and the old man immediately got on top of him, pinning him down. Knowing he was beat, Sid stopped fighting and desperately tried to catch his breath.

McTavish coughed and sputtered as Sid looked up at him. "Well boy, you do have some fight in ya after all," McTavish conceded, then laughed. "That's good."

McTavish rolled off him and crawled away, releasing an enormous weight off Sid's chest. He leaned his back against the wall and gave Sid a wink. Sid crawled over and sat beside the old man, still trying to catch his breath.

"You're not so bad yourself. For an old man, I mean," Sid acknowledged, a broad smile stretching across his face. Sid reached up and pulled the hand towel off the counter, then handed it to McTavish. "Here, ya got some blood on your face. Not sure if it's yours or mine," he chuckled.

McTavish took the towel and laughed. "Not likely mine," he said. "Your nose is bleeding like a tap. But I gotta say, ya do have some scrap in ya. I thought ya had me there for a while," he admitted. His look suddenly turned serious. "You'll do just fine lad," he said, his words full of feeling. "You'll do just fine."

Sid smiled, suddenly feeling very lucky that he'd met McTavish all those months ago.

Suddenly, the old man backhanded Sid across the side of the head. "But remember, keep your guard up," he reminded, then laughed.

Sid looked at McTavish with a haughty grin and quickly delivered a backhand of his own. "You keep your guard up old man," he quipped.

McTavish returned the smile. "C'mon boy, help me up," he moaned, struggling to get to his feet. "And get that table sorted. We've got a crib game to finish."

~~~

The autumn brought with it an early and bitterly cold winter. Sid and McTavish worked endlessly, making sure that the hog shelter was warm enough so that the hogs they kept over winter wouldn't freeze. The old man boarded up the windows in the cabin and Sid split and stacked nearly double the usual amount of firewood.

During the cold winter months, chores still needed to be done and the occasional trip to town was necessary, but there was also plenty of time to just sit in the warmth of the cabin, drinking whiskey, playing poker for cigarettes and talking about everything under the sun.

McTavish had become like a father to Sid, and Sid sensed that the old man liked having him around as well. *Maybe I remind the old man of his own son,* he thought.

April 2, 1922

"Here, boy, take your wage for March," the old man said, handing Sid ten dollars as they were about to enter Tonner's Dry Goods Store. "And here's an extra two dollars. Take it and buy yerself a shirt. A good one," he offered.

Sid took the cash with a smile. "What's come over you, old man?" he asked. "I usually have to fight you for my regular earnings," he joked.

"Just take the money and stop yer complainin' before I change my mind," McTavish growled. "Lucky ya get anything at all, lazy as ya'ar."

Sid smiled and passed through the screened door of the store, immediately sauntering over to the clothing section.

"Make sure you pick out a dressin' shirt, not one for workin' in," the old man hollered after him.

Sid stared back at McTavish through the screen with a puzzled look, but he'd learned long ago not to question him. "Whatever you say, old man," he muttered. He quickly found a black and red shirt that caught
~~~

his eye and pulled it from the rack. "Never had a shirt like this before," he mumbled to himself. He draped the shirt over his arm and, satisfied that it would fit, took it to the counter. "This one," he said, handing the shirt to the clerk. "And I'll take that there pocket knife for the old man."

After Sid's purchases were wrapped and paid for, McTavish sauntered over with a crateful of supplies. He paid for the goods while Sid loaded them into the wagon. When everything was secured, the two climbed aboard and set off for the cabin. The pair enjoyed a comfortable silence for the first fifteen minutes of the trip. McTavish seemed lost in his thoughts, and Sid was more than content to enjoy the spring warmth and the clean air.

Suddenly, McTavish's voice broke the quiet. "You ever been with a woman before, boy?" he blurted.

Sid stared at the old man, puzzled by the sudden and strange question. He instantly felt uncomfortable and embarrassed. He hung his head to hide his blush.

"C'mon, boy," McTavish persisted. "You ever been with a woman before? Ain't such a hard question, is it?"

Sid paused for a long moment, considering his options. He had very little to tell, considering that he had spent half of his youth locked up in a boys' orphanage and the other half in the back of animal stables. Finally he decided that a white lie would appease the old man. "Well, I kissed a girl before."

McTavish glared at Sid and angled himself in his seat to get a better look at him. "No, ya daft idiot," he yelled. "I asked if ya've ever been with a woman. Kissin' some farmers daughter out behind the wood shed ain't the same as bein' with a woman." McTavish squirmed in his seat, obviously frustrated that he hadn't gotten his point across. "Boy, did ya ever stick yer dick in one?" he hollered.

Sid felt his face grow hot. He wished for the wagon ride to end. No one had ever talked to him like that before and he wasn't sure what to say. He hesitated for an agonizing moment. "No, I never done that before," he finally replied.

The old man smiled. "Didn't think so," he smugly proclaimed. He reached back and groped around in one of the crates. "Here," he said as he handed a can to Sid.

Sid took it and turned it around in his hand, feeling the weight. "What's this?" he asked.

"You can read, can't ya? What's it say?" the old man barked.

Sid studied the label for a moment and started to sound out the loopy letters. "Ha-hay-hayr-ah-hair-cra-cre-crea... Hair cream!" he shouted. "Hair cream." After a brief moment of triumph, Sid was overcome with confusion. "What's it for?"

"Whaddaya think it's for? It's for yer hair!" McTavish shouted. "After chores is done on Saturday, wash the stink off with lots of soap," he said. "Put on that new shirt I bought ya, and put some of that grease on your head. We're goin' to Mack's. Gonna get you laid, boy. You ain't a man 'til ya screwed a woman."

Sid blushed and tried to conceal his excitement. *The old man's gonna take me out for my first night on the town, and I'm gonna get laid!* Sid looked up at McTavish and shyly smiled.

"Ya, you're gonna get laid," McTavish sang, "Gonna get you laid on Saturday night." He started to whistle a tune that stuck in Sid's head for the rest of the night.

~~~

On Saturday morning, Sid was up an hour before McTavish. He had the coffee on and was ready to work before the old man had even climbed out of bed. *The sooner the chores are done, the sooner we can head off to town,* he reckoned. He started banging pots around to wake McTavish from his sleep, growing more and more impatient as each minute passed.

Finally, after what seemed like an hour to Sid, McTavish sauntered out of his room, still half asleep. "Boy, what's all the noise for?" he growled. "Sun's barely up. You ain't gonna have enough energy left by the end of the day to pound your own dick if ya don't slow down."

Sid looked away, embarrassed that he was so easy to read.

The old man smiled at the boy. "But okay, as long as we're both up, we might as well get started. Just let me have a cup of coffee before ya put me ta work, won't ya?"

Sid poured the old man a cup, mixing in the canned milk and sugar just as he liked it. "Oh, and here," Sid mumbled, suddenly embarrassed all over again. "This is for you." He slid the pocket knife over the table
~~~

towards McTavish, then quickly slipped out the door, letting it slam behind him.

Just before seven that night, Sid wiped the dirt off of his boots with plenty of soapy water and put on the cleanest pair of denim pants he had. He smoothed down the front of his new red and black shirt before he climbed into the wagon.

"You coming or what, old man?" Sid called towards the house. His body was tingling all over, whether from the better part of an hour he'd spent scrubbing in the wash tub or from the nerves, he did not know. He tentatively raised his hand to his head, checking that the generous amount of hair cream he'd slathered into his hair was still there. It was.

"Well, look at you boy," McTavish beamed as he sauntered up to the wagon and took his seat. "I wouldn't have recognized ya if I didn't know for sure who it was," he said. "You're gonna turn the ladies' heads tonight, lad." Sid began to blush and was glad when McTavish set his eyes on the road. "Get up!" he shouted, slapping the reins down hard on the horse's back. "We got us some dancin' to do!"

Half an hour later, McTavish banged hard on the heavy wooden door. After a few seconds, a small peephole opened and a large eye peered out.

"Who is it?" came a muffled shout.

"It's me, McTavish," the old man said. "C'mon, open up. It's cold out here."

"Who's that with ya?" the man queried, turning his eye towards Sid.

"Why, this is my boy, Sid."

"How old?" the voice asked.

McTavish looked at Sid and smiled. "Why, he turned twenty a week ago," he lied. "Boy's been stuck on the farm with me all winter. Can't expect him to stay shut in all his life, can ya?" he argued. "'Sides, the boy can handle his drink. Now open the door, will ya?"

The small peep hole slammed shut and Sid could hear the loud clang of a bolt being slid open on the other side. They were in. The door swung open, and a big man stood fast before them, closely studying the pair. "Evenin' McTavish," he greeted. "No trouble from you tonight, you hear?" he warned.

McTavish smiled earnestly at the man. "Not tonight," he assured. "Got my boy with me."

Sid liked the way that McTavish kept referring to him as 'his boy'. He followed the old man into the large smoke-filled room, sticking close to his side. As they moved through the crowd, McTavish cordially greeted old friends.

"Hey McTavish, haven't seen you in a while," one large, red-nosed fellow said, belly laughing and smiling wide.

Just then, another man came up and slapped McTavish hard on the back. "Ya old bugger, where ya been hidin'?" he asked. The old man only grinned.

Sid noticed that a few men were glaring at the old man as they casually sauntered through the room, but their looks didn't seem to bother McTavish. He looked at home there, which was the stark opposite of how Sid was feeling. He'd never been in a place like this before--a place for men, not boys.

"C'mon boy, I'll buy the first drink," McTavish offered as Sid followed him to the bar. "You got the ten dollars I gave ya today?" he asked.

"Ya, it's right here," Sid said, nervously pulling the cash out of his pocket.

"Whoa, boy, don't be flashin' it around like you was some kinda big shot!" McTavish cautioned. Sid slowly eased his hand with the cash back into his pants pocket. McTavish nestled in close and lowered his voice to a conspiratorial tone. "Now boy, when you see a woman you like, make sure you buy her some drinks. A woman'll take quick interest in a man who buys her drinks," he advised. "C'mon, I'll introduce you around." McTavish stepped up to the bar.

"Good evenin' McTavish," the barkeep greeted. "What's your poison?"

McTavish ordered two whiskeys. "One for me, and one for my boy Sid," he shouted over the noise.

Sid grinned. He was about to make a joke about McTavish being more like his grandfather when he looked over at a heavy-set woman in her forties staggering up behind the old man. His eyes widened to take her all in. Her lips were painted bright red, and she walked with a swagger that was a borderline waddle.

"My-oh-my, it's my favourite gal Margaret," McTavish greeted her as he reached around and slapped the woman on the ass. Sid's mouth dropped open in surprise. McTavish looked over at him and winked.

Margaret laughed. "Oh, you dirty old bugger," she slurred. It was obvious that Margaret had been there for a while, and that she'd already had her fill of drink. The woman turned to Sid and flashed him a crooked smile. "And who's your young friend?" she asked.

McTavish looked back at Sid and winked again. "Why, this is Sid. Lad's been stayin' with me at the farm, helpin' with chores 'n such. A good strong lad he is," he boastfully added. "Healthy too, if ya know what I mean," he snickered.

Sid squirmed uneasily and started to blush as the woman slyly looked him over like he was an item for sale. "Evenin', ma'am," he finally said.

The woman laughed. "And polite, too," she hollered. "Why don't you fellas come and sit with us? Me and Luanne got a table over there by the dance floor. You remember Luanne, don't you, McTavish?" she asked, pointing over to a table where an even older and heavier woman sat alone, all painted up like Margaret. Sid didn't like the looks of her, but he felt sure that tonight was not the time to be choosy. "C'mon! The band'll be startin' soon. Maybe this young man knows how to turn a step," she said, then began to stagger through the crowd.

Sid's feet were stuck to the ground. With all the anticipation leading up to the evening, he'd forgotten about the dancing. *Maybe I'll be able to get a woman without dancing,* he hoped. All of a sudden, the whole night started to feel very overwhelming.

McTavish suddenly reached over and grabbed Sid by the shoulder. "Now there ya go, boy," he whispered into his ear, nodding towards Margaret's retreating back. "That one's already got you picked for the night."

Sid nervously smiled at the old man. He couldn't think of anything to say. He was relieved when the band started to play. McTavish laughed again and shoved the boy towards the table. They both took a seat, McTavish next to Luanne and Sid next to Margaret.

Sid squirmed anxiously in his seat as he looked around the room, trying to avoid eye contact with Margaret, who was staring at him with a glazed look in her eyes. Sid looked over to McTavish, who by then had struck up a conversation with Luanne. The two laughed loudly. Sid felt abandoned by the old man in this strange new world.

Suddenly Margaret slid her chair closer to Sid and put her hand on his knee. His heart exploded in his chest. "Well, you bein' a workin' man and all, don't suppose you'd mind buyin' a lady a drink, would ya?" she slurred, batting her eyes at him.

Sid sat up straight in his chair. "Ah, no ma'am," he blurted as he reached into his pocket and pulled out some cash. Sid held out the money, not quite sure on how to go about buying a drink.

Margaret laughed like it was the funniest thing she'd ever seen. "You're too cute!" she squealed. She looked around and waved to the woman carrying a tray of beer. "Over here!" she yelled until she got the waitress's attention.

The waitress walked to the table. "How many ya want?" she asked with a gravelly accent.

Before Sid had a chance to speak, Margaret shouted out, "Four beers, Gerda." After Gerda walked away, Margaret turned to Sid to explain. "It saves her a trip if we order more than one each."

After another few minutes of awkward silence, the waitress returned and set four glasses of beer on the table. "That'll be sixty cents," she said.

Sid gulped. *That's a day's pay!* he thought as he reached into his pocket and pulled out some coins. He handed sixty cents to Gerda, suddenly feeling glad that McTavish had given him an extra ten dollars to spend that evening. She put the money in her pouch, but didn't make a move to leave.

"Ya need to give her a little somethin' extra, honey," Margaret informed in a loud voice. "You know, so she'll come back when these are done."

Sid reached into his pocket and pulled out another nickel and he nervously handed it to the woman.

"My, ain't this one a big spender," Gerda grumbled as she flipped the coin onto her tray before walking away.

Sid felt flushed, sensing his misstep. He looked down at the table to the four beers and the half glass of whiskey that sat between him and Margaret. He quickly threw back the rest of the liquor and grabbed a glass of beer. He glanced over to where McTavish and Luanne had been sitting. They were gone.

Sid looked around the room and finally spotted the two of them on the dance floor. McTavish was stomping his feet and swinging his arms wildly, occasionally grabbing Luanne and tossing her about like a rag doll. *So that's dancing*, he thought. McTavish seemed to have all the steps. He looked over to Margaret, who by then had finished one glass of beer and was halfway through another. He briefly thought about asking her to dance, but she seemed more interested in drinking beer. He decided to wait.

A half hour or so passed, but it seemed more like three. He and Margaret continued to sit there, not saying a word. Margaret made sure that there was always beer on the table at Sid's expense, and he was getting bored. He looked over to the dance floor and watched McTavish and Luanne dancing and laughing. *Maybe I should ask her to dance*, he thought. It looked like McTavish and Luanne were having a much better time than he was.

He turned back towards Margaret and found her passed out. Her head was on the table and she was snoring like a man, but still she had a firm grip on the full glass of beer in front of her. Sid looked around the room, embarrassed and hoping that people weren't staring. He was glad to see that no one seemed to be paying attention.

He reached over and pulled the beer from her hand. "No sense in letting it go to waste," he mumbled to himself. He looked back to the dance floor just as the band stopped playing. Luanne walked off towards the lavatory and McTavish was heading towards the table. Sid got up to meet him halfway. It was the first time he had been out of his chair since they'd sat down.

"Why ain't you up dancin', boy?" McTavish shouted.

Sid looked pointedly at the old man and then back to the table. "She drank almost two dollars of beer herself," he moaned, pointing to Margaret. Her head was still on the table and by then there was a generous amount of slobber oozing out of her mouth.

"You idiot!" McTavish yelled, laughing so hard he brought on a coughing fit. "You're s'posed to buy 'em enough booze to loosen 'em up, not poison 'em half to death!" he joked. "Well, ya ain't gettin' nothin' from that one tonight, are ya?" he said.

Sid looked over at the old man, pleading for help with his eyes. He felt utterly lost.

McTavish laughed gently and put his arm around Sid's shoulders. "Listen, son. This is what ya gotta do," he explained. "Ya buy 'em a few drinks and get 'em up dancin'. That way they get loose, you know, they have some fun but they ain't so drunk afterwards that they can't screw, and you still have a few bucks left in your pocket at the end of the night for a room."

Sid nodded. It all seemed so simple when the old man explained it.

McTavish looked around the bar. "See that one over there? The one sittin' by herself." He casually pointed to the younger, dark haired woman sitting alone. "I been watchin' her and she's been watchin' you, boy. Now, go on over and buy her a drink. And get up her up dancin'," he scolded.

Just then, Luanne returned and put her arm around the old man. "You just gonna stand there talkin' all night or are ya gonna buy me another drink?"

McTavish put his arm around the woman's waist and pulled her close. "C'mon woman," he bellowed into her ear, "let's dance some more. I like the way you move." McTavish winked at the boy as he staggered back to the dance floor with Luanne on his arm.

Sid looked over at the young woman McTavish had pointed out, and was surprised when he caught her staring his way. She blushed and immediately looked away. *Maybe the old boy's right*, Sid thought. *It's at least worth a try.* He straightened himself up, took a deep breath and walked over to her table. "Ahem, ah, hi, name's Sid," he blurted. "Can I buy ya a drink, miss?"

The woman bashfully looked up at him with big brown doe eyes and smiled. "Sure. Yeah, that would be real nice. My name's Connie. Go on, sit if you like," she offered.

Sid accepted her offer. As he sat down beside her, he was abundantly pleased that she was much better looking than Margaret. Connie was a slender girl, and her pretty face wasn't painted like the others' in the joint. He calculated her to be about twenty-seven, maybe thirty years old.

He paid for two beers, gave the lady ten cents extra, and set one in front of Connie. Before long the two were telling each other about themselves and laughing. Sticking with McTavish's earlier lie, Sid presented himself as a twenty-year-old hired hand. He mentioned nothing about the organization, and felt glad to be free of his past for the night. Remembering the old man's advise, he finally summoned the courage and turned to her. "Ah, do ya dance?" he timidly asked.

"Ya, sometimes," she answered, her pretty pink lips stretching into a smile.

There was a long pause. Sid shifted. "Oh, ya? Well, would you like to dance then?" he finally blurted.

"Ya, sure," she quickly accepted.

Sid stood and politely waited for Connie to get out of her chair. He escorted her towards the band and felt nervous as they stepped onto the dance floor. The music sounded foreign to his ears. Sid recalled watching McTavish earlier and decided he would just do the same.

Connie turned towards him, his queue to start, he presumed. Sid began to stomp his feet and swing his arms, trying desperately to keep in time with the music, but it seemed to him that he was moving much too fast for what the band was playing. He was also confused as to why she hadn't yet started moving.

Connie leaned towards him and whispered, "This is a slow dance. We're supposed to hold on."

Sid looked around at the other dancers and saw that the men were holding the women close and slowly shuffling their feet. He looked back at Connie, his face flush. She was patiently waiting for him to grab hold of her. *I can do this!* he coached himself. *Just get through one dance, and the rest of the night will be easy.*

Sid carefully stepped towards Connie and clumsily put his arms around her, glancing back at the other dancers to make sure he had it right. It seemed he did, because Connie returned his embrace, buried her face in his shoulder and began to move to the slow beat of the music. As they started to move around the dance floor, she held him tighter, pulling him closer to her.

Sid whiffed the scent of perfume on her hair, and he had a feeling in his gut, an excited sense of anticipation like he had never felt before. As they moved, their thighs rubbed together. She seemed to want to pull him even closer as the bulge in his pants grew. *She likes dancing*, he thought. He did, too.

It was after midnight and they'd all had their share of drink. Sid looked across the table and saw McTavish and Luanne huddled close together, whispering to each other. He wondered what the old man was saying to make her giggle. Suddenly, McTavish turned his chair to Sid and pulled himself close. "Listen up, boy," he said. "Luanne has a place not far. We're headin' on over there now." The old man reached into his pocket and pulled out ten dollars. "Take this and get yourself a room over at the hotel."

Sid accepted the money gratefully, though he thought it was an extravagance to pay for such an expensive room for one boy alone.

As if he was reading his mind, McTavish elbowed Sid in the ribs and looked over towards Connie. "She likes ya, boy," he whispered. "Take her along." McTavish pulled himself out of the chair and grabbed Luanne by the arm. "C'mon woman," he hollered. Luanne clumsily pushed herself away from the table and dutifully followed McTavish to the door. Sid and Connie were left alone, and the moment became awkward.

After a minute or so, Sid finally leaned towards Connie and mumbled. "You wanna go, too?"

She smiled shyly. "Ya, sure," she replied.

Following McTavish's lead, he stood up, grabbed Connie by the arm, and led her to the door. As the pair stepped out into the alley, the cool, quiet night enveloped them. It seemed to magnify the silence.

"I, um, I s'pose I'm heading for the hotel," Sid stuttered. She took his hand and pulled him in the right direction, seemingly having already agreed to a question he hadn't yet asked. Sid's heart was pounding. He couldn't believe that he was walking to a hotel with a lady, much less a lady as beautiful and sweet as Connie. He reached one hand up and smoothed down the red and black dress shirt that McTavish had bought him, silently thanking the old man.

Early that morning, Sid got laid for the first time. He was a man.

Chapter Sixteen

Gud Man Gud Fater

Over the next two years, Sid and McTavish worked hard and played hard. The hogs, chickens, beets, and potatoes earned them a decent profit, at least by their standards. They drank and womanized, and often fought, sometimes with each other, but mostly side by side. The pair even spent the occasional night together in the Sarnia jailhouse. On those mornings, Bill would give them his standard lecture before letting them out--"And stay away from Mack's."

"Ya, sure Bill," they would say.

He'd be turning nineteen that year. He was officially released from the organization's thumb, but he hadn't even thought about leaving McTavish's. It was his home now. For the first time since he was five years old, Sid felt a true sense of peace inside himself. He actually had hope for his future. He could see himself working alongside McTavish until he had saved enough to buy an adjoining lot, and together he and the old man would grow their farm to an even larger operation, maybe even hire on some hands to ease the old man's workload. Sid could finally see a future for himself in this new land.

August 3, 1924

Even before the sun was up, the hot, sticky summer heat found Sid. This was the third day of a heat wave that was enveloping the region and Sid was praying for rain to bring them some relief soon.

Still half asleep, Sid bellowed out a big yawn before sitting up on the edge of his bed. He stretched, wiped the sleep from his eyes and twisted his neck from side to side, trying to get rid of the stiffness that gripped him. Yawning again, he stood up and grabbed his work shirt from the chair and pulled in on. He stepped into his overalls, letting the straps fall loose for the time being and then sat back on the bed to pull up his socks. He stretched out his right leg and wiggled his big toe, which stuck all the way through the hole. *Hmmm, I'd better get a new pair next trip into town,* he thought.

He reached up to his chin with his left hand and rubbed the coarse whiskers. *And better shave one day soon, too.* Though he'd never admit it when McTavish teased him about it, Sid was proud of the thick beard he was able to grow.

Suddenly Sid looked up, noticing that he couldn't smell the aroma of fresh-brewed coffee that normally wafted into his room by that hour. He cocked his head again, listening for the annoying hack that usually woke him up. There was silence. He stood up, walked over to his door and opened it. The dim morning light inside the cabin's kitchen revealed no movement.

"Lazy old bastard," he mumbled to himself as he walked over to the wood stove. "C'mon, old man, time to get up," he hollered as he opened the door to the stove. Sid bent down and saw that there were still some red-hot embers burning from the night before.

Hating to add to the heat but knowing that McTavish would complain all day if they didn't have their usual bacon and eggs breakfast before work, Sid tossed in another log and poked at it with the iron. Even in the humid air, it didn't take long before it caught.

He grabbed the coffee pot and filled it with water from the hand pump, added a scoop of grounds and set it on the stove. He walked over to the ice box, opened the door and pulled out a platter of bacon and six of the eggs he'd collected the day before. He carried the plate to the counter and set it down beside half a loaf of dried-out bread. *Better pick up some bakery goods in town as well,* he thought.

He grabbed the handle of the big cast iron frying pan, which was still full of mushy white and black bacon grease from the day before, and carried it to the stove. Immediately after he set it on the stove top, the grease started to melt.

Maybe he started the chores early before it got too hot out there, Sid thought, before coming to the conclusion that the old man would never start the day without at least one cup of coffee.

"Wake up, old man," he yelled again.

By then, a small puff of white steam was beginning to rise from the pot and the inviting smell of fresh-brewed coffee reached his nose. "That'll get the old man up," he mumbled. The bacon grease in the cast iron frying pan started to crackle, notifying Sid that it was ready for more bacon.

Sid looked over towards the old man's bedroom door. He still hadn't heard as much as a cough. Suddenly, something didn't feel right. He slowly walked over and pushed the door open a crack. "McTavish, time to get up!" he yelled into the room. Still nothing. A lump of anxiety formed in Sid's throat. He pushed the door all the way open and looked over towards the bed. He could see the McTavish-sized lump under the covers. The lump didn't stir. He slowly walked towards the bed, and then hesitated. "Hey, McTavish, you awake?" he called. The old man had the blanket pulled up over his head and he still didn't answer. Sid slowly reached down and put his hand on McTavish's shoulder to give it a gentle shake. Even through the blanket, Sid could tell that something wasn't right. McTavish's body was cold and rigid.

Sid slowly peeled down the blanket to reveal McTavish's still face, his eyes and mouth wide open. His right arm was splayed across his chest, his right hand clutching his nightshirt. Hardly able to breathe, Sid stared down at the old man for a long minute, then walked back into the kitchen, sat down, and cried.

~~~

The undertaker had given Sid a good deal on a small plot in the back corner of the cemetery. He stood there, shuffling his feet in the newly
~~~

dug dirt, feeling totally lost. He looked around at the small gathering at the grave site: the preacher, Constable Bill, the grave digger and the two drifters that had accepted the job of lowering the simple pine box that Sid had made into the ground. All Sid could think was that McTavish deserved much, much more.

After the preacher said a short prayer for the old man and Sid had thrown a handful of dirt on the lowered coffin, the small crowd began to disperse.

"I'm real sorry, son," Bill said, clapping Sid on the back. "He was good to you, I know that. You got a plan?"

Sid shook his head. "All's I know is I got chickens and hogs to feed tonight, and the beets and spuds to bring in soon," Sid said. Something about keeping to the old routine helped to ease the heavy sadness that was crushing down on Sid's chest.

Sid watched numbly as the small party dispersed and the grave digger filled in the hole. When he was finally alone with the old man, Sid walked over to the wagon and pulled out the marker that he had made the day before: a cross fashioned from some black cherry wood that Sid had sanded until it shone in the sunlight, just like he'd seen his father do when he was a young boy. He knew that McTavish wasn't a religious man, but Sid thought he might appreciate some kind of Christian remembrance.

Sid stood the cross at the head of the grave and pounded it into the loosely packed dirt with a hammer. Carved into the cross were the simple words:

norman mctavish

1855 – 1924

gud man gud fater

rest n peese

Sid stood back and looked at the marker for a moment. He wished he could have done better by McTavish, but he also knew that the old man would understand.

Sid walked back to the wagon. He laid the hammer in the back, reached inside his tool box, and pulled out the old photograph. He wiped it gently with his sleeve as he carried back to the grave. Sid took a moment to look at the picture one last time, then carefully placed it at the base of the cross, gently mounding a small pile of dirt around it to hold it in place.

He stood up and paused for another moment, staring down at McTavish's final resting place. He could almost hear McTacish's voice in his head, cracking some crude joke about getting laid, finally. The young man smiled. "Goodbye old man," he whispered before walking away.

~~~

As autumn settled in, Sid stayed on the farm, tending to the animals and working the fields. People still came by for their purchases, most offering their condolences for his loss. He still felt very much at home in the cabin, and he knew that McTavish would have wanted it that way. In Sid's mind, he felt certain that he too would surely die there someday, and the thought brought him a strange sense of comfort.

September 30, 1924

Nearly two months had gone by since McTavish passed. Sid had just finished doing his usual morning chores of slopping hogs and gathering eggs, and was busying himself snooshing stove wood before lunch.

The sound of the axe splitting wood brought him comfort and kept his mind free of more difficult subjects. As he looked up to wipe his brow of sweat, a trail of dust rising off the dirt road caught his eye. There was a motor car coming his way.

Sid leaned the axe against the wood shed, lit a smoke and waited for it to pull into the lane. When it came to a stop, Sid could see that there were two men in the car. He recognized the passenger. It was Constable Bill.

"G'day, Sid," Bill greeted as he stepped from the vehicle. He had a solemn look about him that made Sid uncomfortable. A tall, well-dressed man stepped out from the driver's seat. *A man of means*, Sid
~~~

thought. He carried with him a leather satchel, shuffling through it as he walked towards Sid.

"Is this Sid?" he asked, addressing Bill.

"Yes," Bill acknowledged. He looked over at Sid with a look that seemed almost apologetic.

"Sid, my name is Terrance Crawford," he said, forcing a smile. The man didn't offer his hand. "I am the solicitor for the children of Norman McTavish, the rightful owner of this property, correct?"

Sid gave a slight nod, but the man's eyes had already returned to his paperwork. Sid looked over to Bill, wishing he could ask him what was going on.

"I understand that Mr. McTavish passed away some-" He trailed off as he searched his papers. "Some seven weeks ago."

Sid grunted. He desperately wanted Bill to take this fellow back to wherever he came from.

"The constable tells me that you were quite close to Norman. My condolences for your loss," he said hollowly.

Spit it out and then get the hell off my farm, Sid fumed silently. He shot Bill an exasperated look, but the jail keeper wouldn't meet his eyes.

The stranger kept talking. "I'm here to advise you that his children, being Mr. McTavish's only next of kin, are now the rightful owners of this property. And as such, the property has been legally sold."

"What are you talking about?" Sid couldn't contain his confusion. *No kids of McTavish's have set foot on this farm for over forty years,* he mused. *There must be some mistake.*

"The property has been sold to some migrants from Holland, sight unseen," the solicitor clarified. "They also purchased the adjoining lot just up the road. Going to make it all a dairy farm, I suppose," he joked. Neither Sid nor Bill was laughing. "I have the legal documents here," he said, his voice suddenly sober. He pulled a pile of papers from the bag.

Sid looked over to Bill, hoping that he might have something to say in his defence. But Bill avoided his gaze and lowered his head. "You'll need to be off the property by Friday," he mumbled. "There'll be some trucks here the day after tomorrow to pick up what's left of the stock. It's all been sold to the meat packers in town."

Bill's matter of fact words felt like a slap in Sid's face. He felt his eyes begin to sting.

Bill raised his face and finally met Sid's gaze. "Sorry, Sid," he said quietly. "There's no other way. It's all legal."

The solicitor clapped his hands together, clearly ready to wrap the meeting up. "The next of kin have very generously agreed to let you keep what money you've made off the property these past few weeks," he offered. "Anything from today on will go to the estate. Do you have any questions?"

Sid dropped his cigarette butt and crushed it into the dirt with his foot. Without a word, he turned and walked into the cabin. A few minutes later, he heard the motorcar drive away.

That night, Sid packed a few belonging into a duffel bag, took one last look around, and walked out the door. He didn't look back as he walked down the road towards Sarnia.

Chapter Seventeen

The Reunion

Sid stayed around Sarnia for the next three years. Finding work was never a problem for him, for most of the local farmers knew him and respected his work ethic. McTavish had taught him well in that regard. In fact, Sid took after the old man in many regards. It didn't surprise anyone when he disappeared for a day or two after payday, but he always came back, ready to work and to do it all over again.

But all the while, Sid was mourning the loss of McTavish. It felt like he'd been orphaned all over again. With time, however, Sid's sadness began to ease. He filled in his lonely times at Mack's, where there was always someone around who was eager to lift a glass with him, and a woman eager to share a bed with him at the end of the night. In fact, he had earned himself a reputation as a womanizer before he even reached his twenties.

Sid was also well known to be a fighter, a characteristic that regularly landed him an overnight stay in the Sarnia jailhouse, where every morning as he opened the door, Bill would announce, "And stay away from Mack's."

"Ya, sure Bill," Sid would dutifully reply, and he would swear he could hear McTavish laughing from wherever he was.

Despite his wild ways, Sid always managed to squirrel away five or six dollars a month, saving for the day when he could afford to buy a Model T Ford, the one luxury that would satisfy his notion of success.

By all accounts, Sid was happy to stay in Sarnia. It was home, or at least it had been, before he got the biggest surprise of his young life.

July 7, 1927

"Over here Buck," Mack yelled, as he rose half way out of his chair to get the big man's attention.

Sid looked up and watched as Buck pushed his way through the crowded room. By this time of the evening, most of the people there had already had their fill of beer and whiskey, and it was Buck's job to see that none of them got out of hand. *Any man in the place would have to be drunk or mad to challenge that giant,* Sid thought. And Sid knew first hand that Buck was good at his job, having tangled with him on many occasions himself. But still, Sid was always welcomed back into the joint, as long as he had cash to spend. And this night, like many other nights, Sid was sharing a table with the owner himself, and two familiar ladies, one of whom he was certain to take home at the end of the night.

As Buck manoeuvred his sizable frame from his post at the door, people stepped aside and politely paid their respects, a tip of the hat or a nod and a friendly smile.

"Hey Mack, how's things?" Buck cheerfully enquired as he stepped up to the table. "Place is busy tonight," he said as he took long, serious look around the room.

"Yep, we're gonna do good tonight, Buck. I hope they never legalize booze in this province again," Mack quipped. "Got the cops on our payroll, the mayor's a regular, hell half the town council is here tonight," he laughed. "I love this country. How's thing's up front, Buck? Any trouble?"

"Quiet," Buck calmly replied. "Haven't had to bust any heads yet tonight," he laughed. "But I just had a strange thing happen at the door," he said, averting his attention to Sid. "Some guy outside wants to see you Sid. Says he's your brother."

All eyes at the table turned to Sid. "Didn't know you had a brother," Mack said. "Thought McTavish was the closest you had to kin."

Sid was dumbfounded and momentarily at a loss for words. He immediately thought of George. *No, it can't be him,* he thought. The idea of George travelling to Canada and actually finding him was too implausible to even consider. "Probably someone's husband come looking for me," he half-heartedly joked.

"Well Sid, you can go outside and talk to this guy if you want, but I don't want him in here until I know he's okay," Mack insisted.

Sid sat motionless for a long moment, looking up at Buck through his bloodshot eyes. "And he says he's my brother?" he confirmed.

"Ya, that's all he said," Buck replied with a shrug of his big shoulders. "You gonna go see him, or do you want me to get rid of him?"

Sid sat still for another long moment before looking up again. "No, I'll come out to see who the guy is," he decided. Sid looked back at the table and grabbed a shot glass full of whiskey and quickly downed it. He was glad when Buck grabbed him under one arm to help him from his chair.

Once on his feet, Sid took a moment to balance himself. "Okay, you ladies wait right here," he mumbled as he twisted back towards his two companions, stumbling and nearly knocking over a glass half full of beer in the process. "I won't be long," he assured. "My brother, eh!" he laughed as he followed Buck to the door.

Outwardly, Sid made light of the situation, but the mere thought that it might be possible terrified him. *What if George is out there?* he thought. *What would I have to say to him after all these years, after I abandoned him back in England?* Suddenly Sid felt queasy. For a moment, he thought about going back to his table and ignoring the whole episode, but something stopped him. He was curious.

Buck opened the small trap door and they both peered through the tiny hole out into the dark alley. "That's him over there, standing under the street lamp," Buck said, pointing towards the tall silhouette of a man.

"Ya, I see him," Sid replied. Buck unlocked the door and slowly pulled it open. Sid staggered out and stood staring at the tall shadowy figure standing on the other side of the alley. The sudden clang as Buck slid the bolt back into place startled him.

The man across the way stood straight and tall. *A stature not likely suited to George,* he thought. *At least not the George I left. But why would a stranger suddenly show up and claim to be family?* he wondered. Sid slowly started towards the man, straining to get a better look at his face before he got too close.

"Sidney, is that you?" the man called out through the dim light.

"Who the hell are you?" Sid yelled. By then, he was able to see the man more clearly under the light. He vaguely recognized the face. *I should know this man,* he thought.

He stopped six feet short of reaching the stranger and took a closer look. The man was well-groomed and stylishly attired. He wore a simple but finely tailored suit. Sid whiffed a familiar aroma, one that he recognized whenever he was near a man of means, the scent of cologne. *This is no one from my family,* he thought as he took one step closer.

"Sidney, it's me. Reginald."

Sid took another step forward and looked closely at the man's face. His gut started to churn.

"Sidney, it's Reginald," the man repeated, smiling as he reached his hand out to shake Sid's. Sid did not return the gesture.

Suddenly, Sid realized that the man standing in front of him was, in fact, his oldest brother. He could only stare as his mind went completely blank. He felt like a child, terrified of the man standing in front of him. Memories of cruelty and pain rushed into Sid's head, memories so vivid that he wanted to cringe in fear. He felt sick with anxiety as an image flashed before his eyes, the picture of his mother cowering in the kitchen, her face bruised and bloodied by the hand of the man who stood before him now.

All of the muscles in Sid's body began to tense and his fists clenched tight as a rage unlike any he had ever felt before boiled inside of him. His face glowed red as he hollered out, "You bastard!" He instinctively drew back his arm and swung, unloading a punch that connected squarely on his brother's jaw.

The blow knocked Reginald heavily back against the brick wall, but it didn't knock him down. The jolt stunned him for a moment, but he quickly regained his footing. But instead of trying to return the punch, as Sid expected, he hung his head and wiped his bloodied mouth with his hand. The wallop had split his lip wide open, causing blood to gush over his chin and down the front of his suit. Reginald calmly raised his fingers to his face and checked them for blood.

"I suppose I deserved that," Reginald mumbled as he pulled a handkerchief from his pocket and pressed it tightly against his lip. "You throw quite a punch," he lamely joked.

Sid just stood there, stunned and confused as to what had just occurred. He was unsure of what to do next. He'd imagined being reunited with his mother and George a thousand times over the years, but never in his wildest dreams had he thought that Reginald would come into his life again.

"What the hell are you doing here?" he finally shouted. "How did you find me? Why did you want to find me?" His head was swimming with unanswered questions.

The stress of the unanticipated meeting suddenly overwhelmed him. Sid walked over to a bench near the lamp post and sat down heavily. He put his elbows firmly on his knees and buried his face into his hands.

A few seconds passed before Sidney heard the echo of his brother's footsteps coming towards him. The wooden bench gently lurched beneath him as Reginald's weight descended onto it.

"Well Sidney, it sure has been a long time," his brother's quiet voice reached him.

"How did you find me?" Sid repeated, still unbelieving that the scene before him was actually happening.

"A Mr. Donnelly at the home in Toronto let me look through your files," Reginald informed. "But even so, it wasn't easy finding you," he chuckled. "You move around a lot."

There was a long moment of silence. Sid did not return the laugh.

"Well Sidney. I guess all of this must be quite a shock for you, me showing up like this and all," Reginald said. He paused for another moment, but Sidney was determined not to make it any easier on him. He just sat there. "Look. I know that things haven't been easy for you," Reginald ventured.

Sid quickly sat up and glared at his brother. "How the hell would you know how things have been for me? How would you know anything about me?" he hollered. After the short outburst, he quickly reburied his face in his hands, hoping that Reginald would just get up and leave.

"I saw your file," Reginald quietly repeated. He paused for a moment, then sighed. "You're right, Sidney. I really don't know how things have been for you. How could I?" he conceded. Reginald took a deep breath. "I suppose I was one of the luckier ones," he muttered.

Sid sat motionless. He tried to seem uninterested in Reginald's words, but he was in fact listening intently to everything that his brother was saying now. He was curious as to why his brother had bothered to track him down.

"I stayed at the home myself," Reginald went on. "I wasn't there long, before they found a place for me. I wish I'd been there when you arrived," he whispered almost inaudibly. Reginald leaned back on the bench. "I know I was a bit of tyrant in those days, but I have to tell you, I sure was afraid when they sent me out," he admitted.

Sid twisted his head and quickly glanced up at Reginald. "So what the hell did you come here for, all dressed up in your fancy clothes, makin' like you're some kinda big shot?" he shouted. His anger building, Sid turned fully towards his brother now and looked him over. He felt the muscles in his body tighten, ready to strike again. "What do you do now?" he yelled. "Rob banks? Mug old people?"

Reginald looked at Sidney and forced a dull smile. "Ya, I suppose you might think that of me after knowing the way I was when I was a younger," he said. Reginald hung his head and looked at the ground. "Looking back on those days, Sidney, well, I'm not proud of the person I was. I was a mean and cruel boy. I know that I hurt you and George." He hesitated for a moment. "And mother," he whispered. "Especially mother. I'm ashamed for all of it," he admitted. Reginald raised his head and looked back at his brother. "Coming to Canada changed me, Sidney. Not at first," he noted. "But, like I said, I was one of the luckier ones. Mr. and Mrs. Jenkins--the couple I was placed with in Winnipeg--they treated me as one of their own." He paused for another moment. "I wasn't the best behaved kid at first. I caused them plenty of problems in the beginning, you can be sure," he chuckled. "But those folks, well, there was something special about them," he reminisced, a gentle smile stretching across his face.

Sid sat up straighter and looked at Reginald, curious to know how the vicious boy that he knew twelve years before had changed into the man sitting beside him on the bench. "What makes these Jenkins people so special?" he asked, trying his best to sound disinterested.

Reginald looked into the distance thoughtfully, and a minute passed before he answered. "They were different, I suppose. They disciplined me, but they weren't cruel. I had to work hard, but no harder than anyone else in the family," he said. "They showed me a way of life that I didn't know before." Again Reginald paused for a moment to reflect. "I don't exactly know how to explain it, except to say that they treated me as one of their own. I felt like I belonged."

Sid was bewildered as he struggled to comprehend what was happening. Not just that his brother was sitting next to him on the bench, but taken aback at complete transformation that seemed to have come over him. Once more, rage started to fill Sid. His fists clenched, ready to strike out once again. "Why are you here?" he hollered. "You come to tell me how good your life has been?"

Reginald looked at his brother, making no motions to protect himself from another blow. "No, Sidney," he flatly replied. "That's not why I'm here." Reginald took a deep breath and paused for a moment. "I came to take you home, Sidney. Home to England. Home to mother. I've got your fare right here," Reginald finished with a note of triumph in his voice, patting his right breast pocket.

Sid froze. The words rang through his head like a hundred church bells all clanging at once. He couldn't lift his head or open his eyes. A thousand chaotic thoughts raced through his mind at the same time. He wanted to run, but he couldn't move. A long minute passed before he regained some composure, at least enough to challenge Reginald. "How would you know where home is for me?" he shouted, lifting his head and looking Reginald directly in the eyes. "There's nothing in England for me," he mumbled as he lowered his face back into his hands. "Mother made sure of that eleven years ago when she sent me away."

Sid felt Reginald get up off the bench and heard his footsteps pacing the pavement. "No Sidney, you're wrong," he scolded. "Mother wants you home. She always has. You should know that as much as anyone," he yelled. "Up until your eighteenth birthday, she wrote to you every month."

"She did not!" Sid shouted, his voice cracking. "I waited for her letters for almost ten years, and she didn't write me a single time!"

"She did too, Sidney. She wrote you every month, care of a Mr. Dobbs at the home."

Reginald's voice reached Sidney as though from a great distance away. He wanted to believe his brother's words, but he'd learned enough since arriving in Canada to know that he simply couldn't.

"Why didn't you at least write back to let her know that you were alright?" Reginald's voice reached him again, lapping against his ear-drums like they were both underwater. "Mother worried sick over you all those years. She always wanted you home."

Sid lifted his head and glared at Reginald. "I never received one letter from her," he yelled. "Not one. If she told you different, she's a liar." A sudden surge of guilt rushed through him as the disrespectful words gushed out of his mouth. Sid quickly stopped and put his head back into his hands. He thought for a moment, wondering how Reginald even knew anything about their mother. He slowly straightened up and looked back to Reginald. "How the hell would you know what she did or didn't do?" he snapped. "How would you know anything about our mother after what you did to her? What you did to all of us?" he yelled.

Reginald hung his head. "You have every right to be angry at me, Sidney," he conceded. "And for that matter, so do mother and George. I was a rotten boy in those days. There's not much from my youth that I am proud of today," he said. Reginald's voice hushed, but he kept on. "How I treated mother. How I treated you and George." He stared down at the ground for a long moment.

"So how dare you tell me about her like you've been a dutiful son all along?" Sid spat.

"Because I've done my best to make amends," Reginald defended. "Six years ago, I joined the Canadian Navy," he informed. "And as luck would have it, my first posting was in England." Reginald looked at Sid pointedly, but was met with silence. "Well, to make short a long story," he said, "you might say that I went back to England a different person than I was when I left." He smiled a genuinely happy smile that made Sid feel sick. "Sidney, I have always carried guilt for what I did in the kitchen that night," he confessed in a voice that sounded on the verge of tears. "For everything I've done. And I have always wanted to make things right for that. So while I was in England, I found mother. And George. They are both very much alive and well," he informed.

Sid sat there, stunned.

Reginald chattered on, oblivious to the torrent that was ripping through Sid's gut. "We all got to know each other again, and we've managed to put the past behind us. We keep in touch regularly and I see them every time I go back to visit."

Sid sat motionless, a rigid young man with his face buried in his hands. He wished his brother would stop talking.

"Mother is doing very well, Sidney," Reginald continued. "Did you know she remarried?" he asked, then immediately flushed at his mistake. "I'm sorry," he said. "Of course you didn't."

Sid clenched his jaw and said nothing.

"Well she did, almost ten years now. To a fine man named Derrick Woolmar, a baker. Owns his own shop. They're doing very well, very happy and prosperous," he cheerfully declared. "And George, George is doing well, too. He's married and has a son of his own. He's one of the most sought after gardeners in London."

"Why are you here, Reginald?" Sid muttered.

"Well, Sid, the very first day that I saw mother, she asked me about you, asked if I'd seen you. She had a thousand questions about where you might be and what you might be doing," he said. "Of course I couldn't tell her what she wanted to hear. So she asked me to find you and bring you home. I promised her that I would and I've never stopped looking for you since."

Sid sat there trembling, his face still buried in his hands. He felt as if he were in a fog, his thoughts all mangled together, all muddled up. Nothing made sense to him. He was numb. It was like he was dreaming but he couldn't wake up. Sid's mind suddenly took him back to the days at the home in England and his monthly visits with his mother. He began to recall all of the thoughts he'd pushed out of his mind over the years, thoughts that were too painful for him to hang onto any longer. He remembered her holding him tightly in her arms and telling him that everything would be alright. He remembered hoping with every visit that she would take him away. And then he remembered the men pulling him away from her on the dock, both reaching out to each other, both trying desperately not to let go. He saw her standing on the dock as the ship pulled away. He remembered the loneliness he felt on the ship and how he had longed to be back in England, to be with her.

Sid looked up at Reginald, uncaring that tears were streaming from his eyes. His gut was tied in knots as he tried to think of what to do. After all those years, he had finally heard from her. He finally had his chance to go back to England. *But things are different now*, he thought. He could barely remember what his mother looked like. *Would he even recognize the sound of her voice*? Sid had long ago pushed any notion of ever returning to England, and of ever seeing her again out of his thoughts.

Reginald reached out to touch Sidney, but Sid jerked his shoulder away.

"I am a cabinet maker now, like father, and I have my own place down near Toronto," Reginald informed. "I'll take you there tomorrow. We can leave for England in a week. I'll look after it all," he assured, beaming with restrained delight.

Suddenly, Sidney felt a sense of relief. A glint of happiness rushed into him as he slowly began to comprehend what was being offered to him. *Home*, he thought. *Home to mother. It would be good to see George again.* Sid quickly contemplated what he would say to them when he saw them. *What would they say to me?* he wondered. *Would they recognize me? Would they accept me?*

Anxiety and fear suddenly fuelled his thoughts. He began to reflect on his life, on the misery and the loneliness and the cruelty. Suddenly he felt angry again, angry at the people who took him away from her, angry at Reginald for his contented life, angry at George for not having been sent away, angry at mother for letting them take him. His feelings of happiness were quickly devoured by the rage and hate he had learned to live with all those years ago. It was all too much.

Sid scornfully glanced up at Reginald and without warning, jumped up and bolted as fast as he could down the alley towards the dimly lit street at the end. Before long, he could hear Reginald's footsteps pursuing him, but they quickly faded into the distance. His brother's calls of, "Sidney, wait! Please come back," reverberated off the alley's cold stone walls, but fell on deaf ears.

Sid never considered turning back as he rounded the corner onto the main street, running as fast as he could to nowhere in particular. His brother's calls faded into the foggy night as he turned blindly towards the rail yard.

Chapter Eighteen

Westward Bound

July 8, 1927

"What the hell?" he shouted as he rolled over onto his back. The smell of hay and horse shit filled Sid's nostrils as he painfully opened one eye. He wasn't sure where he was, but the man standing over top of Sid, and poking him with the pointy end of a pitch fork was about to get poked himself if he didn't stop, that is if Sid could muster the strength to get up. He was a big man and his girth easily blocked out the sun that was just rising behind him.

Sid tried his best to scramble to his feet and immediately tripped over himself, stumbling back into the haystack. Laying flat on his back, he squinted up at the figure. "Who are you? And why the hell are you poking me with that fork?" he hollered.

"Sid, is that you?" came the silhouetted figure's voice.

Sid wiped his eyes. "Pat? Pat O'Brien?"

"Well, who the hell else would be here at six-thirty in the morning? Besides you, I guess," Pat scolded, his voice determinedly rough. "Now what the hell are you doing sleeping in my haystack? C'mon, let me help you outta there." Pat reached down and took Sid's hand and pulled him up to his feet. "My God, boy," he groaned. "You look like you seen a ghost. Musta been some night, eh!" he laughed.

As faint recollections of the previous night's events returned to him, Sid scowled. Not even an all-night session of drinking near the rail yards could help him forget his brother's visit. "Ya, it was a night," he mumbled. He steadied himself, brushed the hay dust off his front, and thanked Pat for helping him up.

"C'mon boy, I got some coffee over at the office," Pat offered. "Could use a cup myself." Pat stuck the fork into the haystack and started towards the stable. Sid followed behind him, his whole body aching.

The two sat quietly at the shaky wooden table, sipping black coffee out of tin cups. Pat rolled a couple of smokes while Sid stared blankly at a poster on the wall that displayed alluring pictures of rolling wheat fields and cloudless blue skies.

"Here ya go, kid. Take this," Pat said as he handed Sid a smoke. "Looks like ya got things on your mind," he said. "Somethin' wrong?"

Sid didn't respond for a long moment. "You ever been out west before?" he finally asked, looking at the poster behind Pat's head as he spoke.

"Ya, I was there once. Saskatchewan, bout ten years ago now I guess. Had a brother out there. He's gone now. Why ya askin'?"

"What's it like?" Sid asked. "I hear there's lotsa work out that way come harvest time."

Pat followed Sid's gaze and looked over his shoulder at the poster. "Pretty sight for a farmer, eh? They put them posters up all over the place. Advertising for workers to help with the grain harvest in Saskatchewan," he explained. "There, a man can look out over his crop and never see the other side of it," he said. "And when the wheat gets high and blows in the wind, it looks like a golden sea gently rolling across the prairie." Pat looked at Sid, leaned towards him, and said with stark frankness, "And in winter, it gets so cold your spit freezes before it hits the ground, and the snow gets so deep you gotta dig your way outta your own house. And when the wind blows-" Pat started to laugh and looked at the boy. "But ya, Sid," he said softly. "A young fella like yourself can make some real money out there, if he's willin' to work and he ain't a complainer. Thinkin' a goin' there?"

Sid looked over at Pat and shrugged his shoulders. "Maybe. Maybe someday." He stood up, thanked Pat for the coffee and smoke, and walked to the stable door. "See ya 'round, Pat," he said, smiling back at the man.

"Ya Sid, see ya 'round."

Sid knew he'd never see Pat O'Brien again.

~~~

Sid put on his best suit, threw his duffle bag over his shoulder and walked out of the bunk house without once looking back. He noticed the old Ford farm truck rolling down the laneway and hitched a ride into town with the bosses' son. "Just drop me off there," he said, pointing to the confectionary on the corner.

"Want me to wait for ya?" the kid shouted as Sid climbed out of the truck.

"No, that's okay," Sid hollered. "I'll walk from here." Sid stood and watched as the truck drove away. He casually scanned the area as he walked towards the little shop and then quickly stepped around the corner and headed towards the Sarnia Rail yards. Making sure that nobody was watching him, he hurriedly strolled up the street and slipped into the station. Sid stepped up to the ticket agent and reached into his pocket. Pulling out a wad of cash, he laid it on the counter in front of the man. "That enough to get me to Saskatchewan?" he asked.

The man nonchalantly looked at Sid and then down at the money. He licked his fingers and picked up the bills, counting out loud as he flipped through them, "ten, twenty, thirty, forty, fifty..."

Sid furtively looked right, then left.

"One hundred... one hundred and thirty, one hundred and forty... ah, one hundred and forty-three dollars," the agent announced. The man looked down at a chart and then back up at Sid. "Yep, that'll get you all the way to Regina and then some."

"But I want to go to Saskatchewan," said Sid.

"Regina is Saskatchewan, kid," the ticket agent said, his expression never wavering. "Saskatchewan's the whole province, and Regina is its capital city."

Sid felt the colour flooding into his face.

"Well, do ya want the ticket or not?" the man snapped.

Sid stood motionless for a moment, staring at all the money he'd saved over the past three years. Looking back up to the agent, he said, "Ya, one ticket to Regina."
~~~

The man looked back to the schedule and cheerfully proclaimed, "Well son, this is your lucky day. The two-o-seven leaves in twenty minutes," he advised. "That'll get you to Toronto just in time to catch the Trans-Canada twenty-two-twenty-seven. Nice train it is, the twenty-two-twenty-seven. Fine food, sleeping berth, observation car--you'll be in Regina in three days. Yep son, this must be your lucky day."

The agent handed Sid his ticket, gave him forty-five dollars back, and told him that the conductor would be around in a bit to announce boarding.

Sid folded the ticket, stuffed it into his pocket and then walked over to a bench and made himself comfortable. As he looked around the terminal at all the other travelers, a feeling of apprehension overwhelmed him. *Am I doing the right thing?* he wondered. He had, after all, been quite content living in Sarnia. At least he had been until two days ago, when his brother had found him.

Sid was still confused in that regard. *Maybe it isn't too late to find Reginald again,* he thought. *Maybe I should have accepted his offer.* He looked back to the agent, mulling over the idea that he might return the ticket. Then he saw him, from the back, the well-dressed man standing at the counter purchasing his own ticket. Sid immediately knew that it was Reginald. He slumped down in his seat and pulled his duffle bag up on his lap, holding it to his chest in an attempt to conceal his face. He watched as Reginald picked up a newspaper and walked over to a bench on the other side of the terminal. Reginald unfolded the paper and held it up, covering his own face. Sid felt nervous, and suddenly had an urge to go over to him. He squirmed in his seat, and sweat rolled from his brow as he struggled with indecision. A few minutes passed before he slowly lowered the duffle bag and convinced himself that the best thing to do would be to stand up and walk over to where Reginald was sitting. His gut churned as he started to lift himself from the bench.

Suddenly, a man's booming voice crackled from all corners of the building. "Attention all passengers for the two-o-seven bound for Toronto. The two-o-seven is now boarding." The faceless voice continued to bellow out instructions, most of which Sid didn't clearly understand. His head spun as people around him stood up and started to gather their belongings. He'd seen Reginald briefly look up from his paper when the announcement had sounded, but he didn't notice Sid.

Sid stood, looking over at Reginald. He could feel his knees trembling. He reached into his pocket and pulled out the ticket. Looking down, he read the bold letters: REGINA via TORONTO. People bumped into him, knocking him about as they scrambled for the train. Sid looked back at the ticket, slipped it into his pocket, threw the duffle bag over his shoulder and discreetly blended into the crowd. Without looking back, he turned and started for the train. It was as if an unseen force was pulling him away from his brother, and most likely his last chance to ever see his mother again.

~~~

On a bright and sunny Monday morning, Sid stepped off the train. As his foot touched Saskatchewan soil for the first time, he felt a surge of hope run through him. He was a man of his own making now. By then, he'd had a good taste of what the west was like, having spent much of the journey in the observation car, looking out over the seemingly endless prairie, astounded by the vastness of the wheat fields that seemed to reach beyond the horizon in every direction. *It's just like Pat said,* he thought, reflecting on the old farmer's words about the golden sea. Sid shuddered to think that if Pat had been right about the wheat fields, maybe he was being truthful about Saskatchewan winters as well. The thought chilled him to the bone, even on that hot July morning.

Sid stepped onto the platform, fresh from sleep and a full belly. As he looked around him, he reached into his pocket and pulled out the last of his money: twenty-eight dollars. *Enough to get by for a few days*, he thought. He looked off towards the city, *a small town by Ontario standards, but still quite busy*, he thought. A few motor cars vied for their place on the streets amongst the horse-drawn carriages. Sid had a pleasant feeling as he watched the people go about their business. He was certain that life would be good for him there. He grinned, picked up his bag, slung it over his shoulder, and started for town.

Sid walked around the cluster of main streets for nearly an hour, taking in the sights and looking out for posters advertising for farm labourers. He looked up at the huge grain elevators and walked by the
~~~

livery stable and the blacksmith's shop, aiming to acquaint himself with the surroundings of his new life. He watched as farmers loaded their trucks with supplies at the hardware store. Time passed quickly.

It was early afternoon when he stumbled upon a sight that made his gut rumble and his mouth water, the Pioneer Hotel and Tavern, which beckoned him closer. He peered through the large street-facing window, hardly believing that people were having a drink in the broad daylight. Sid knew that the west had abandoned prohibition, but it was an odd sight for him just the same.

Sid's cheeks warmed as he pushed open the heavy oak door and walked into the saloon, pausing for a moment to look around the huge, dimly lit room. The place was quiet apart from the chatter of twenty or so men, all scattered throughout. Some were farmers wearing straw hats and dusty coveralls, and others obviously worked for the railroad, their faces all black and grimy with soot.

Sid felt comfortable enough there. He sauntered over to the bar and set his bag on the floor. "Glass of beer," he ordered as he sat up on one of the tall stools. The bartender filled a glass from the tap and slid it over to him.

"That'll be fifteen cents," he said.

Sid threw two dimes on the bar and told him to keep the change. He lifted the cold frothy brew to his lips and gulped down half of it in one swallow. "Ahhhh," he sighed, holding the glass up and toasting no one in particular. He put the glass back to his mouth, gulped down the rest, and slammed it on the bar. "That tasted like another one," he shouted to the bartender.

The bartender stared at Sid for a moment and then smiled. "You new in town?" he asked as he pulled another beer.

"Ya, just come in on the twenty-two-twenty-seven this morning," Sid replied. "Thought maybe I'd find work in the harvest. You know of anyone hirin'?" he asked.

"Nope, not right off," the bartender said.

Sid's heart sunk. *Maybe my expectations were too high,"* he thought.

"But Slim down there," the bartender continued, pointing down to the other end of the bar, "he might be able to help ya."

Sid looked down the bar and saw a tall, skinny man sitting there, a clean-shaven man, maybe a couple of years older than himself. The man seemed to be taking an interest in the bartender's conversation. Sid gave him a friendly nod and raised his glass in greeting.

The man similarly greeted Sid, then stood up and walked over. "Hi, name's Slim," he said as he extended his bony hand.

Sid reached out to shake Slim's hand. "Name's Sid."

"Couldn't help but overhear your conversation with Sam," Slim said. "You just got in today, eh?"

"Ya, on the train this morning," Sid replied. "Bartender says you might know of some work around."

Slim smiled and turned to Sam. "Two more beers," he hollered with a wink. "Ya, I might know about a job or two. Got any farmin' know-how?" he asked.

Sid smiled back. "Yep, farmin's all I done since I was eight years old," he replied. "Pigs, cows, chickens, crops. Done all of it, I reckon," he bragged.

Slim smiled back at the boy. "Ever worked on a steam thresher?" he asked.

"A steam thresher?" Sid repeated, his voice cracking slightly. He cleared his throat. "Can't say as I ever worked on a steam thresher before," Sid admitted.

"Too bad," Slim said. "Just so happens I run a threshin' crew. I'm engineer on a twenty-two Goodison 'bout fifty miles north of here, near Liberty," he went on. "Just getting' ready for harvest and lookin' for a few good men." Slim looked at Sid and smiled. "Too bad you never worked on a steam thresher before. Mighta bin able to use ya," he said as he took a swig of his beer.

Sid felt downtrodden as he sipped his beer. *What the hell is a Goodison?* he wondered. "Well, thanks anyways," he said. "Maybe you know of someone who'll need field workers, or drivers?" he asked, not yet ready to give up. "I can drive trucks: Internationals, Fords, Averys, you name it. I don't mind workin' hard. I--"

Slim cut him off in the middle of his pitch. "I was just kiddin' ya, mate," he said. "I could tell you're a good worker soon as you walked in here. I'll hire ya on as a waterman," he offered. "We work fifteen, sometimes sixteen hours a day, seven days a week, 'til the crops are all off. Pays three dollars a day. We'll even bunk ya up and feed ya," he laughed. "Whatdaya say, mate? Ya want the job?"

Sid took another sip of his beer and smiled. "When do I start?"

Slim raised his glass in a toast to seal the deal. "Tomorrow morning," he advised. "Harvest won't start for another month yet, but I'm in town all this week picking up spare parts and camp supplies. You can help with that. We'll head north on Sunday." Slim flashed Sid a devious grin and lifted his glass again. "Meanwhile, mate, we'll drink as much beer as we can fit in and dance with all the women that'll dance with us," he howled. "Once harvest starts, there won't be any drinkin' or womaniz'n 'til it's done." Slim moved in closer. "Come Saturday night, this place will be packed with guys like yourself that come lookin' for work, and it'll be crawlin' with women wantin' to hook up with 'em," he laughed.

Sid grinned and raised his glass, and the two chugged down what was left of the beers. "Two more," Sid yelled, then turned to Slim. "These ones are on me." Sid leaned back in his chair and smiled. *Booze, women, and work. Just like home*, he thought. He was getting off to a good start in the west.

~~~

Grace? Gloria? Wilma? It was ten o'clock on his first Sunday morning in Saskatchewan. Sid had just rolled over and was staring at the naked body lying next to him. He vaguely remembered bringing her back to his room. *What's her name*, he silently struggled. *Wendy? Jill*? Nothing rang a bell. *Maybe it doesn't matter anyways*, he thought. She was passed out and snoring like a logger, her matted black hair wrapped around her face like a tattered scarf. Sid gently pulled himself out of bed and snuck into the lavatory for a quick wash before putting on his clothes.

"Well, thanks for the night, whoever you are," he whispered as he grabbed his duffle bag and quietly pulled open the door. Sid slipped out of the room and made his way downstairs to the restaurant, where he was supposed to have met up with Slim a half hour earlier.

Sid looked around the room, which was by then bustling with regular Sunday morning patrons. Slim wasn't anywhere to be seen. A nauseating
~~~

feeling overcame Sid as he imagined his new employer already halfway to Liberty, fuming that his green employee hadn't made it on time.

"Damn it all to hell," he muttered as he felt his shoulders fall towards the floor.

Suddenly a hand grabbed his arm. "Jesus!" Sid shouted, spinning around to face whoever had interrupted his melancholy. It was Slim. He couldn't remember feeling more relieved in his whole life.

"Take it easy," Slim laughed. "Sorry I'm late. Had some broad in my bed this morning. Couldn't for the life of me remember her name."

Sid grinned.

"C'mon, let's get some breakfast and get outta here before she comes down lookin' for me," Slim said.

The two found a table tucked away in the corner and ordered breakfast. Forty-five minutes later, the pair was headed northward. The stake bed truck was laden down with oil and grease, spare machinery parts and food stuffs.

"Thanks for breakfast," Sid said just as they hit one particularly fierce bump on the gravel road. Sid had worked three days the previous week, helping to load the supplies as they came in. Slim had paid for his room at the hotel, but they had spent every night at the saloon, swilling beer and shamelessly flirting with women. By Sunday, Sid's pockets were empty. He was glad to be on the road and on his way towards a steady paycheque.

The two were silent as they trundled on. Sid was quite hung over, his headache amplified as the beat-up Ford truck clanged and rattled, bouncing roughly down the dirt road. Sid looked out at the expanse that surrounded him, anticipating many prosperous days ahead. As he stared off into the distance, his thoughts drifted back to his unexpected meeting with Reginald back in Sarnia. He thought about what his brother had told him, of how his mother had remarried and was happy. *She's certainly not in the same circumstances as she was when I left England*, he thought. He tried to picture her in his head, suddenly needing to remember what she'd looked like the last time he had seen her. But all he could see was the faceless silhouette of a woman with long, thick black hair. *What did her face look like?* he probed himself, but no image came. It was almost as if she'd never existed at all. Sid shook his head as he came back to the moment and looked over at Slim.

"How long before we're at camp?" he asked.

Slim kept his eyes fixed firmly on the road. "About an hour now," he replied. "You never did tell me where you came from. What brings you out here?" he asked.

Sid pondered for a moment. *Where should he begin this story*? "Well, I came from Ontario. Been livin' 'round Sarnia for the past three years," he said. "Before that, well, I moved around a lot."

"Why'd ya come west now?" Slim asked, his eyes still fixed in front of him. "You must have folks, people back east," he presumed.

Sid looked down at the mud-caked floor, unsure of how to respond to Slim's assumptions. "Well, no," he started. "S'pose anyone I'd call family is still in England. Haven't seen any of them in over ten years," he lied. Sid didn't want to talk about Reginald.

Slim took his eyes off the road to look at Sid. "Did the organization bring you here?" he asked.

Sid was taken aback by Slim's question. It was the first time anyone on the outside had ever mentioned the organization to him. "Ya," he said. "In nineteen-fourteen. I was eight. How do you know about the organization?" he asked.

"Nineteen-ten," Slim said. "I was nine."

Sid stared at Slim, unbelieving.

"You stay in Toronto?" Slim asked.

Sid grinned. "Yep, I was there lots," he boasted. Sid thought for a moment. "Nineteen-ten, huh? Was that bastard Donnelly there then?" he inquired.

Slim cocked his head as if straining to recall that far back. "It's been a long time now. I don't recollect a Donnelly," he said. "Of course, I was only there for a week or two before they put me out. Sent me down to a farm near Niagara Falls, with a family named the Burkes." His voice carried no harshness as he spoke.

Sid looked at Slim, wondering whether his friend had been through the same sort of hell that he'd been through. As the truck jolted on, he began to vividly recall his own dreadful encounters with the likes of Clarence, Ruth Connors, and the others, like the lady who'd lifted her dress.

"Pickled eggs n' chicken legs, that's all there was to eat. Pickled eggs n' chicken legs, I'd rather eat pigs feet," he muttered to himself. Sid furled his brow. *How strange that I can so clearly remember the people who treated me poorly, but I can't remember what my own mother looks like*, he thought.

Slim was looking at him sideways. "What the hell you talkin' 'bout? Pickled eggs, chicken legs, pigs feet."

"Oh, nothin'," Sid said. "Just rememberin'. So the Burkes, were they good to you?" he asked quietly.

Slim glanced over to him. "Ya, I s'pose they were okay," he responded, not sounding totally convinced. "They didn't beat me, if that's what you mean. A willow-switch now and again when they thought I deserved it," he went on, "but they didn't beat me. What about you, Sid? Were you treated well?" he asked.

Sid turned away to look out the passenger window as a rush of emotion welled up inside of him. "No," he mumbled. "At least, not at first." He took a deep breath and straightened up in his seat. "McTavish was a good man," he said, a smile spreading across his face. "McTavish was a good man."

"Well mate," Slim said. "Next year this time, I plan to have my own operation. Just about got the down payment. Should have it all after this season," he cheerfully declared.

Sid forced a smile. He was still thinking about that horrible morning when McTavish had never woken up. "That sounds great, Slim," he replied. He thought for a moment before venturing, "What about the thresher you have now? Isn't it yours?" he asked.

"Nope," Slim piped. "This'll be my fourth harvest working for Mike Chalmers," he said. "Chalmers is one of the biggest grain farmers in the province. We'll thresh his wheat, and then other farmers will pay him for us to thresh theirs. It's all big business out here, mate," he claimed with an air of importance. "Besides, I don't plan on buyin' a thresher." His grin widened. "Combines, Sid, combines. That's where it's all going now," he boasted. "Combines'll cut a field and thresh the wheat, all at the same time." Slim was becoming more energetic with every word. "You know, mate, farmers out here are ploughing up every inch of prairie that they can get at. You think these crops are big now, just wait five years," he assured. "There'll be more work here for guys like us than you can shake a stick at. Yessiree, contract combinins' the way of the future," he declared. "Ain't nothin' but money to be made here if a fella has any ambition at all. In three or four years, mate, I'll be cuttin' all the grain from Manitoba clear to Alberta." Slim leaned back in his seat. A sprawling smile lit up his face and he started to whistle a lively tune.

At that moment, Slim's good mood wrenched Sid out of the gloom that he'd just fallen into. His new employer's confidence and enthusiasm made Sid feel even better about his own decision to move west. It all sounded so easy for Slim, being part of the prairie boom. *Could there be something in it for me, too?* he thought. *There must be, if I put my mind to it.* Sid straightened in his seat and looked out the window, not paying any mind to the rattles and bumps of the truck. Suddenly, he was able to picture himself behind the wheel of a brand new Model T. He liked the image.

"Whatcha whistlin'?" he shouted over the noise as they traversed a section of particularly loose gravel.

"Four Cent Cotton, a Skillet Licker's tune," Slim called back, hardly missing a note and barely watching the road.

Sid listened for a moment until he got the tune in his head, and then he started to hum along. Slim whistled and Sid hummed hillbilly tunes for the next hour as they drove northward to Liberty.

Chapter Nineteen

Prosperity Abounds

Nineteen twenty-seven was a good year for prairie grain farmers and for those who worked for them. Crop yields were high, people talked about how well the weather had cooperated, and Sid and Slim became best friends. The two worked long days, side by side. Slim took extra time to show Sid the more detailed particulars of the steam thresher, and Sid was an eager student. There were five men on the crew in all, but no bonds were struck like the one between those two. They were a pair destined to conquer the west.

During those two months, Sid and Slim constantly talked about their plans. With help from the bank, Slim would purchase his first combine in time for next season's harvest. Then the two would take turns operating the machine for eighteen or, more likely, twenty hours a day. In two years, maybe three, they would buy another machine, and then another and another until they had the prairies covered from Winnipeg to Calgary. It was a plan that couldn't fail. It was Sid's chance to make something of his life.

Harvest was over by mid-October that year. Sid had managed to set aside one hundred and fifty dollars, more money than he had saved in three years back in Sarnia. Of course, he hadn't seen the inside of a tavern for almost three months, either. He would rectify that when he and Slim took the rest of the crew back to Regina. With pockets full of cash, the others were heading back to Ontario to be with their families. With no wives or kids waiting on them and no homes to return to, Sid and Slim decided to spend a few nights on the town, sowing some oats of their own. The pair dropped the others off at the train station, bid them farewell, and headed directly to the Pioneer Hotel.

October 21, 1927

Sid looked around the crowded room, full of well-to-do grain farmers boasting over yet another profitable year. He smugly chuckled. *It's like these men think they have control over the weather and other circumstances that contributed to a successful crop*, he thought. And the weary, but flush harvest hands yakked loudly amongst themselves, generously buying rounds of drinks for each other and for the young ladies that came to town to share in their fortunes and maybe snare a good husband in the bargain. Sid and Slim easily mingled among them all, enthusiastically swilling beer and whiskey as if someone had declared that there would be no more of their favourite beverages made ever again. Sid was happier than he had ever been. He felt at home.

In the group of well-to-do's was Mike Chalmers, himself already well into the celebrations. "C'mon over here, boys," he shouted in his gruff, commanding voice.

Sid and Slim casually walked over to Chalmers' table, not expecting anything more than a thank you for a job well done. But it seemed that Chalmers had other motives for beckoning them.

"Hey, boys, come meet some of my friends," he shouted as they approached. Introductions were quick and the pair was offered chairs. Chalmers reached around and grabbed Slim by the back of his wiry neck and pulled him close. "You know, son, you've done a hell of a job on that thresher these past few years," he slurred. "Made me a lot of money." Chalmers pulled Slim even closer and looked over at Sid with a big, wily grin splashed across his face. "How'd you fellas like to work for me all year 'round?" he offered. "Got plenty to do around the ranch when we ain't growin' wheat. Pays twenty-five dollars a month, room and board included. You won't get a better offer from any of these two-bit crooks," he laughed a sort of glib, high-pitched laugh as he looked around the table at the other farmers. The rest of the men laughed along with him, all seemingly wrapped up in some sort of conspiracy with him.

Slim pulled himself away from Chalmers, looked at Sid and shrugged his shoulders. "Sounds like a good deal," he supposed. "Gotta do somethin' until next harvest."

Sid didn't have to think twice about the offer. He immediately raised his glass and proposed a toast. "Here's to working for Mike Chalmers!" he roared.

Glasses around the table clanged and everyone laughed heartily. For Sid, it seemed that life was good for one and all on that day.

When the revelling was winding down, Chalmers pulled his chair closer to the boys. "You know, son," he said, staring directly at Slim through tiny bloodshot eyes. "I hear you're looking to buy a combine. Thinking about doing some contracting with it, I understand."

Slim looked nervously over at Sid. Neither had anticipated that Chalmers knew of their plans, and neither had considered how their boss might take the news if he found out. Sid took a deep breath and swallowed hard, silently praying that Slim would know how to handle Chalmers.

"Well, yes, sir," Slim began, his voice an octave higher. Sid's ears shut out all other noise as he strained to hear Slim's words. "I, ah, I mean, me and Sid here, we were thinkin' of buyin' a combine," he conceded. "You know, maybe workin' for ourselves someday," he timidly finished.

Chalmers glared first at Slim, and then at Sid. Suddenly he sat straight up in his chair and laughed out loud. "That's what I like!" he yelled as he looked around the table. "Men with vision, ambition. Entrepreneurs, just like all the great men who built the west. You boys get your combine. I'll even help you along the way, under one condition, your first contract is with me!" he declared as he raised his glass to celebrate their newly formed business venture.

Sid breathed a sigh of relief and looked over at Slim, whose face was beaming with delight. Sid knew they were thinking the same thing. *With that year's harvest barely hours behind them, their business venture for the following season was already starting to show promise.* They had secured a contract with one of the biggest grain farmers in the province. The two young men simultaneously reached over to shake Chalmers' hand.

"Yes, sir," they accepted in unison.

"You won't be sorry, sir," Slim added.

Chalmers flashed the boys a cunning smile. "I'm sure I won't be," he laughed. "I'm sure I won't be at all." He winked at his fellow farmers and raised his glass once more. "Now you boys get on back to your celebrations. I'll expect you to be sober and on the ranch day after tomorrow," Chalmers light-heartedly ordered.

Sid and his best friend graciously said goodbye and triumphantly strutted back to their companions across the tavern.

"Now let's find us some women," Slim whispered slyly to Sid.

Sid returned a wide grin. "No better way to cap off this day," he said. It had been a fine day indeed.

Thirty-six hours later, Sid and Slim arrived at the Chalmers ranch near Liberty, sober and on time. The following months brought even more prosperity: good food, comfortable bunks, and of course a steady paycheque. The work was quite undemanding, almost effortless given that they had access to the most modern equipment that money could buy. When it came to farming and ranching, Chalmers spared no expense. And every Saturday night, the two budding tycoons could be found at the Liberty Hotel, proudly bragging about their business enterprise, flaunting their fortunes and buying drinks for the ladies. Life couldn't get better.

January 24, 1928

It must have been about three-thirty in the afternoon. Sid could tell because the mid-winter sun was just beginning to fade for the evening. He sat patiently in the lobby of the Regina branch of the Weyburn Security Bank, anxiously waiting for Slim to come out of the manager's office. *He's been in there for over three hours*, Sid thought. *They wouldn't be talking to him about combines for that long if they weren't planning on financing him. Right?* His stomach flipped as doubt crept into his gut with each passing minute.

Finally, at a quarter to four, Slim emerged from the back offices, slow paced and long faced. He casually ambled up to Sid and stood silent for a moment. Disappointment flooded into Sid's mind.

Suddenly, Slim swung his arms into the air and let out a loud bellow. "I got it!" he shouted. "I mean, *we* got it!" he rectified. Slim pulled a stack of papers out from under his coat. "We got us a combine," he joyously proclaimed. He looked up at Sid and smiled. "I don't think I coulda' done it alone," he admitted. "You've been a good friend, Sid. We're in this together, mate. Partners. Next harvest, we'll be makin' the big dough!" he yelled.

Sid reached out and grabbed Slim's hand, slapping him hard on the back. "Partners," he proudly proclaimed.

"Partners," Slim echoed.

"Well, this calls for a celebration," Sid declared. "Drinks are on me today."

Slim wholeheartedly agreed. The two walked out of the bank, a lively spring in their step as they made their way to the Pioneer. A prairie partnership had been born.

~~~

Six months later, a large flatbed truck hauling a brand new combine pulled into the Chalmers ranch. Considering that his would be the first crop it harvested, Mike Chalmers agreed to keep the machine on his property free of charge. It was an unusually generous offer coming from an astute businessman like Chalmers, but his kindness was greatly appreciated by the up-and-comers.

During the next couple of months, Sid and Slim got to know their new piece of machinery inside and out, top to bottom. Chalmers had already given them a sizeable down payment on their contract with him, so they stocked up on oil, grease, and fuel. They also secured contracts with other farmers in the area, and the pair were ready for an abundant and prosperous harvest.

And prosperous it was. Nineteen twenty-eight brought with it one of the best grain harvests in Saskatchewan in recent memory. Sid and Slim worked tirelessly and fulfilled all of their contracts, and word of their work spread quickly. Even Chalmers was astounded by how efficiently
~~~

and timely their new combine got his grain out of the fields and on its way to market.

That first year was a financial success for the determined pair. By mid-October, the machine was shut down for the season and it was time to tally up the year's take. Considering that Slim had made the initial outlay for the down payment, he was also entitled to the lion's share of the profits. But neither Slim nor Sid would get anything until all of their expenses were accounted for.

October 29, 1928

Sid waited impatiently in a dark corner of the Pioneer for Slim to return from the accountant's office with his cut. He sipped on his beer, blissfully imagining himself behind the wheel of his very own car, and of the women it would bring his way.

Two hours passed before Slim walked through the door, all serious and stoic. "Hey Sam, couple of beers," he hollered to the bartender as he made his way to the table where Sid sat alone. He took the chair next to Sid and looked over to him, his face giving away nothing. "Well, anything exciting happen while I was gone?" he nonchalantly asked.

Sid glared at Slim. "Whaddaya mean, did anything exciting happen? I've been sitting here waiting for you!" he shouted. "How'd it go? How'd we do?"

Slim couldn't maintain his charade any longer. A big smile spread across his face as he reached into his pocket and slapped a thick brown envelope down onto the sticky table top. "This is your cut," he announced.

Sid stared at the envelope for a moment. He slowly reached over and grabbed the packet, feeling its thickness and trying to estimate how many five dollar bills were inside. *Three, maybe even four hundred dollars,* he silently hoped. He slowly peeled back the seal and reached inside. When he pulled out the contents, he felt his mouth fall open. It was the thickest wad of cash he had ever held in his hands at one time. He began to fan out the bills with his fingers. *All tens and twenties*! He flipped through the bundle and slowly started to count it.

"For Christ sake, mate," Slim hissed. "If ya want someone to take it off ya, just give it to charity!"

Having momentarily forgotten where he was, Sid cautiously pulled the envelope close to prevent prying eyes from viewing his bounty. Both men warily scanned the room to make sure no one was watching. When they were satisfied that their fortunes had not been made public, they let go with a victorious laugh and a hearty punch to each other's arm.

"There must be almost five hundred dollars there!" Sid exclaimed in a hushed voice.

"Six hundred," Slim corrected with a spreading smile.

Six hundred dollars? If Reginald could see me now!, he thought.

Sam approached and set the two beers on the table. "You boys wanna run a tab?"

"Yeah, we'll be here awhile," Sid piped, sharing a grin with his buddy. "Start us a tab."

When Sam was out of ear-shot, Slim pulled his chair close to Sid and leaned into him. "What ya gonna do with your cut?" he asked.

Sid didn't have to think about the question for long. "Well, first thing I'm gonna do is buy me an automobile," he beamed. "S'pose I'll open a bank account, too. Gotta start savin' for another machine."

Slim raised his glass and smiled. "Here's to partners," he toasted.

"Here's to partners," Sid echoed as their glasses clanged together. It seemed that their business plans were right on track.

Chapter Twenty

Shattered Dreams

The two friends were kept busy enough working for Mike Chalmers again that winter. With steady employment, along with a hefty down payment of two hundred and seventy-five dollars, Sid persuaded the bank to loan him the balance for his car, a 1927 Ford Sports Coupe complete with rumble seat. He was on top of the world. On Saturday nights, the pair proudly drove into Liberty flaunting their prosperity. They quickly became the objects of desire for many of the eager and naïve farmer's daughters who frequented the Liberty Hotel, most of whom went there to escape the boredom of a prairie winter as much as to look for an eligible bachelor. When two handsome young businessmen like Sid and Slim came along, their choices for female companionship were limitless. And so it went during the winter of nineteen twenty-eight and into the spring of nineteen twenty-nine. There wasn't anything that could hold these two back from achieving their dreams. It was the spring of twenty-nine that Sid met Eva, the most striking young woman he had ever seen.

It was at the spring dance, held early in April every year at the Liberty Community Hall. Folks from as far north as Imperial and as far south as Penzance showed up for the annual shindig. The spring dance was the traditional farewell-to-winter party and the formal welcome of the spring planting season, which according to who you listened to wasn't looking very promising that year.

But Sid and Slim were so much blinded by their own accomplishments that no worrywart, no matter how astute, was going to sway them in a direction that didn't fit with their plans. So they strode forward, confident that another successful harvest was only a few months away. In the meantime, there was beer to drink and women to court.

April 13, 1929

Sid noticed Eva as soon as she walked into the hall. She looked to be only sixteen or seventeen years old, but she was a remarkably pretty girl. She was a petite woman, but carried herself with a fitness that one might expect from a prairie farmer's daughter. Her long black hair flowed down over her shoulders, and for the first time in his life Sid understood how a smile could quite literally light up a room. She reminded him of someone he should have known from his past, but couldn't place.

She was with two other men. One man looked much older, *her father*, he presumed. The other man was only slightly older, a *brother or a cousin*, he hoped. Suddenly, he was keenly aware that she had spotted him as well. He caught her sneakily glancing his way when the others weren't watching, her inviting smile deviously encouraging him to make his move.

As he contemplated how to approach the young beauty, Sid noticed that another young man in the room was also taking a keen interest in her. He was about eighteen or nineteen years of age and as big as an ox. Sid inwardly groaned as he watched the young man hurry over to greet her. From the way he looked at her, his gentlemanly mannerisms, and his politeness towards the other two men, it was obvious to Sid that he was interested in being more than friends with her. The boy's apparent interest in the young beauty made her even more desirable to Sid, and he became determined to woo her away from the big buffoon.

Sid kept his eyes on the girl as he elbowed Slim in the side. "Hey, you know that one there?" he asked as he discreetly nodded in her direction.

Slim looked across the room. "Oh ya, that must be William Evans' daughter. What was her name again? Eliza? No, Eva. Wow, I heard she was a looker," he said and whistled low under his breath. "A bit young, but a looker." Slim threw Sid a cautious glance. "You ain't plannin' on goin' after her, are ya?" he asked. "I hear old man Evans watches her like a hawk," he warned. "And the other guy, that's her brother, Wilf. Good guy. Likes his beer, but that is his little sister you're gawking at," he laughed.

Sid looked up at his friend and smiled. "Ya, just might go after that one tonight," he declared. "Who's the other guy? The big one?" he asked, pointing as casually as he could to the hefty boy who had run to greet Eva at the door.

"Oh, that's Oly Swanson's boy. I don't know his name. People just call him Tank, you know, because he's as big as a tank." Slim stared at the group for a few seconds and then looked back at Sid. "Looks like Tank's already got her staked," he laughed. "Don't think ya otta be messin' with that," he advised with a wink.

Sid smiled, taking his friend's warning as a dare. "We'll see, we'll see," he said as he started to walk away.

Slim leaned against the wall and watched as his friend sauntered over to the group. He couldn't hear what was being said but he could imagine what Sid might have been saying, having listened to him turn on the charm many times before. It wasn't two minutes before Sid was shaking her father's hand and sharing a laugh with her brother. A few seconds later, he was holding Eva's hands and politely introducing himself to her.

The smitten look on Eva's glowing face was obvious as she looked up into the young man's eyes. The darting stare from Tank was also obvious as he was being ignored and hastily pressed further into the background. And just at the right moment, the band started to play.

"Mr. Evans, sir. May I have the first dance of the night with your daughter?" Sid politely asked.

Mr. Evans warily studied Sid from top to bottom, and then looked into his daughter's pleading eyes. "Well, I suppose," he guardedly consented.

Eva wasted no time in grabbing Sid's arm and leading him to the dance floor. Tank helplessly looked on as Sid wrapped his arms around the eager young woman and gracefully moved her about, Eva submissively allowing him to take charge, her face aglow, her broad smile unashamedly exposing her infatuation. She was love-struck. Sid was in.

And on went the night. Everyone danced and laughed, well, everyone except for Tank, Sid noticed with a note of triumph.

As Sid spun Eva off the dance floor following a lively polka, they broke into peals of laughter. He put his arm around her shoulders as he led her towards her father and brother.

As they approached, Eva's father eyed Sid with a look of cautious approval. "Well, that seems like a good note to end the night on," he said, looking at Eva. "We'd best get going."

"Oh, father," Eva groaned with a tone of disappointment. "It's still so early yet!"

"It'd be such a shame if she had to leave now," Sid piped up. "I can assure you, sir, I'll bring her home safe and sound as soon as the band stops playing."

"That'll be a bit late for a seventeen-year-old, don't you think?" her brother Wilf put in his two cents.

Eva slapped his arm playfully. "No way, Wilfred! If I'm old enough to cook and clean all day for you and father, then I am certainly old enough to be out without you two looking over my shoulder every second! And besides, if mother was still alive, she'd want me to be enjoying myself."

William Evans looked unsure of what to do, but mention that his late wife would approve seemed to tip the scales. "Well, Sidney, you seem like a stalwart young man," Eva's father said. "A gentleman who by all accounts is ambitious and prosperous. I suppose I could trust you to take good care of my daughter for another hour or two."

"Oh, yes!" both Sid and Eva proclaimed at once.

And so it was settled. Eva reached up to give her father a kiss on the cheek before Sid led her back onto the dance floor, where they danced for three hours more.

~~~

Sid turned off his headlights as he pulled up to the farmhouse in his 1927 Sports Coupe complete with rumble seat. He let out a sigh of
~~~

relief to see that no lights were on in the house and no smoke was coming from the chimney.

Eva giggled. "They must both be asleep," she whispered conspiratorially. They tried to muffle their laughs as they stumbled towards the door, Sid clumsily tucking his shirt back into his pants, Eva hastily combing her hair with her fingers and carefully checking to make sure that all of her clothes were in the proper place.

Sid had not yet considered how to end the evening. Unlike the other times that he had seduced a woman, he felt different that night. He wanted to see her again.

Finally at the door, she bashfully glanced up at him. "I had fun tonight," she said with a laugh as she gently rubbed his hands. She lowered her head and raised her eyes towards him. "Maybe you'd like to come for super one night next week? Maybe Tuesday?" she asked.

At the thought of seeing her again, Sid suddenly felt a sensation that he had never felt before. It was a pleasant feeling, a rush that permeated throughout his whole body as if someone had lifted a heavy weight off of him. He looked back at her and smiled. "Yes, that would be good," he said. "Ya, Tuesday night would be good."

Eva smiled, turned, and quickly stepped into the house. After the door was closed behind her, Sid stood on the porch for a moment, feeling satisfied with the way the evening had gone. *Tuesday,* he thought to himself with rising anticipation. *We can do it all again on Tuesday.*

Suddenly, he realized that he had not only accepted an invitation to have dinner with Eva, but undoubtedly with her father and brother as well. He abruptly found himself facing the unsettling idea that he would have to live up to the standards that he had placed upon himself earlier that night. He was a smooth operator, but he wasn't sure for how long he could fool them all.

~~~

The two squinty pink slits on Sid's face desperately tried to block out the dim light streaming into the bunk house. He slowly looked around to see who else was still in their beds. As far as he could tell, he was alone. He lay his head back on the pillow and struggled to remember the night before. Much of the evening was a blur. He recalled being
~~~

with Eva and standing on her porch. He also recalled her inviting him to supper on Monday night. *No, Tuesday night. One of those nights,* he thought.

Suddenly, the muffled voices of two men shouting caught his attention. Sid jumped out of bed and stumbled to the door, opening it just enough so that he could see what was happening. He looked out and across the yard to see Slim and Mike Chalmers involved in a heated discussion, both men wildly gesturing with their arms and pointing at the combine. Sid strained to hear what was being said. Suddenly, Slim stopped shouting, lowered his head and angrily walked towards his truck. He jumped inside, slammed the door and sped off down the lane towards the dirt road, spewing a heavy trail of dust in his wake.

Sid hastened to get into his clothes and ran out of the bunk house, calling after his friend to come back. But Slim kept going.

Chalmers looked over at the bunk house, striding with determination towards Sid. Chalmers' face was red with anger.

"Good morning, Mr. Chalmers," Sid cautiously greeted. "What was that all about, sir?" he asked.

Chalmers looked directly into Sid's face. "Won't be needin' you any longer, either," he barked. "Get your gear together and be off my property by this afternoon," he ordered.

Sid looked up at Chalmers, his eyes glazed over and not entirely sure that he had heard the man right. "I'm sorry, sir," he said, his voice crackling. "You want me to leave?"

"You heard me, boy," Chalmers growled. "Don't need ya anymore."

"Well, okay, sir," Sid mumbled. He looked up at the unyielding figure glaring down at him. "Can I ask why?"

Chalmers glared at him. "Got no work for ya this year," he shouted.

Sid stood dumbfounded for a moment and then looked over to the machine. "What about the combine?" he asked. "When's Slim comin' to--?"

"He's not," Chalmers interrupted. "Combines' mine now. The bank would have taken it back anyways if I hadn't paid off the loan," he growled with a frown. "You two have been too busy philandering about to pay much attention to what's been happening around here," he sneered. "There ain't gonna be much of a crop this year. Grain bins and elevators are still bustin' at the seams with last year's crop. No one's buyin' our wheat anymore. They're all growin' their own now." Chalmers looked at Sid like it was all the younger man's fault. "Anyways, boy, I got no work for you this year, and you got no combine," he snapped. "You're gonna have to go somewhere else." Chalmers glared at Sid for another moment and then stomped away.

Chapter Twenty One

A Sure Thing

Chalmers was a shrewd businessman and knew how to go about acquiring things such as cheap labour from naïve young men and top-of-the-line farm machinery in legal, if not slightly underhanded ways. In his mind, business was business, and every man needed to look out for himself. But even Mike Chalmers couldn't have anticipated that not only would nineteen twenty-nine be a bad year for grain farmers such as himself, but the following nine years would see operations like his all across the west crumble like parched, useless dirt.

If it had only been the Great Depression that they faced, people like him might have survived those years. But like many other prairie folk during the thirties, he too helplessly stood by and watched as his once fertile land turned into a desert, its precious topsoil picked up by the slightest breeze and carried off in huge black clouds, some of it drifting on the high winds to as far away as the eastern cities, darkening the skies over Toronto and Montreal before being dumped into the Atlantic Ocean to be lost to grain farmers forever.

Yep, nineteen twenty-nine brought with it an abrupt end to Sid's short-lived prosperity and the beginning of a whole new era for up-and-comers on the plains and across the country. Men like Sid, it seemed, were to become forever destined to a life of relentless hardship.

November 12, 1929

He could smell it. It was the same smell that greeted him almost every night since he and Eva had married almost four months earlier: stewed rabbit and turnip. He kicked at one of the rotted posts that barely held up the crumbling roof over the front porch, knocking frozen clumps of wet, dirty snow off his boots. He couldn't see into the old shack of a house, the windows having been boarded up for the winter, but the sweet smell told him that Eva was at her usual spot in front of the stove.

His feet were cold and he was hungry. "What's for supper?" he hollered as he pushed the door open and slammed it shut behind him. He started to take off his winter clothes: first the two pairs of worn wool mittens, then the heavy wool coat and cap, next the moth-eaten sweater, and finally the torn coveralls. He threw the heap of wet, dirty clothes on top of the old piano bench that one of their kindly neighbours had given to them. The piano bench was one of the many odds and ends donated to the young couple after they'd moved into the old farmhouse on her father's property, just a mile up the road from him.

Sid stood just inside the door for a moment, clad only in his stained long johns and wool socks pulled nearly up to his knees. *At least the house is warm enough,* he noted with satisfaction. That was Eva's job--to keep the fire burning, as well as have supper ready when he got home. An impulsive rage overwhelmed him as he looked around the room. The table hadn't even been set.

"What's for supper?" he yelled again, even though he could tell from the smell that it was the same dish they'd been eating all month. He just wanted her to hear the harsh reprimand in his voice.

"Sorry, Sid," Eva apologized as she hurried out of the bedroom. "I just lay down for a moment. I'll have your supper on the table in just a minute." She waddled over to the wood stove, careful not to rub her big belly against the hot metal, and gave the stew one more stir before scooping two big ladles of the steaming hot potage into a bowl.

Sid poured himself a glass of beer before taking his place at the table.

"Here ya go," she said as she dutifully hurried to the table with his supper. "And there's fresh bread in the oven," she announced as she ran back to the stove to fetch it.

Sid quietly watched as Eva wrapped a towel around her hand and cautiously opened the oven door. As Sid silently watched his wife wait on him, he wondered why she still doted on him after the way he had been treating her those previous few months. He knew that he had been distant, and when he did speak to her, it was usually to shout out an angry command or to make a degrading comment. He hadn't touched her for months, not even to feel the child, his child that was growing inside of her.

He watched as she slowly bent down and reached into the oven to pull out the piping hot pan, being careful not to drop it even though it was obvious that she had already burned her hand. From somewhere deep inside himself he knew that he should offer to help her, to bring in a bucket of snow for her blistering hand, but his mouth and body would just not respond. The restlessness inside of him seemed to hold him back. He had cut back on his drinking, mainly because he didn't have the money to sit at the Liberty Hotel every night. He resented her for that. He did, however, make sure that there was always beer in the house. His line of reasoning was that if he had to spend his hard-earned money on things such as flour, sugar, coffee, and the occasional slab of pork for his wife, he at least deserved something for himself.

Eva cut a thick slice of steaming bread and hurried it over to him. After he was taken care of, she went back to the stove and fixed a bowl for herself, brought it to the table, and took her place across from him. They sat in silence for a few minutes, the clanging of their spoons against their bowls the only sound in the room.

Sid looked up from his stew to find Eva staring at him through big, timid eyes. "We need more wood for the stove," she nervously whispered before lowering her eyes back down to her meal. "Dad stopped by today. He said we could pick some up from his place."

Sid stared at her hard. He felt an indescribable feeling rising up his throat. "I'll go by tomorrow and get a load. Got no work, anyway," he grumbled. He paused for a moment, set his spoon down, and looked over at Eva. "I'm takin' a job up north," he blurted. "There's a lumber camp near Carrot River that's hirin'. Pays twenty-five dollars a month," he snarled, talking to her as if he already needed to defend his decision.

He could see that his sudden announcement stunned her. She looked at him with a confused twist on her normally pretty face. "Carrot River! How far is that?" she asked, her voice strained.

"Far enough that I can't come home at night," he snapped, upset at her useless questions. He forced his voice to soften. "Forty, maybe fifty miles, I'd guess. I'll be ridin' with Jack Wilson and Frank Morley. We'll be staying in the camp there. Most likely be gone for a month or so," he figured.

"A month?" she gasped. "When will you be leaving? You will be home for Christmas, won't you?" She looked down at her belly and Sid could see the spots forming on her apron where tears were falling. "The baby," she bawled. "The baby is due in January. You'll be home for that, won't you?" came her muffled voice.

Sid's face flushed red with anger as he felt Eva's interrogation run through him. He jumped up from his chair, his fist clenched tight as he pounded it heavily on the table. "Shut up, woman!" he yelled. "Just shut up!" He leaned over the table and glared at her for a full minute before speaking. "What the hell else do you think I should do?" he hollered. "There's no work here. Jesus Christ, half the dam farmers in the county'll be headin' off to the bush this winter just to put food on the table," he shouted.

Sid continued to glare at her and then slowly settled back into his chair. "We'll be leaving the day after tomorrow. I'll send word as soon as I find out when we'll be coming back," he assured. He paused for another moment. "It might be best if you stayed with your father while I'm gone," he suggested. Just the thought of her being dependent on somebody other than him lifted a huge weight off his shoulders. The comfort didn't last for long.

Eva met his eye with a hint of defiance that was unusual for her. "This is our home and I'm not going to leave it," she stubbornly declared.

Sid groaned. "Be sensible woman," he shouted. "I can't run home every time you can't figure out some stupid little thing." The cruel words popped out of Sid's mouth before he could stop himself.

His words didn't halt Eva's persistence. "No. Father and Wilf are close by, and the neighbour women will lend a hand if need be," she reasoned.

"Besides, I want to have our home ready and waiting for you when you get back, and for the baby when it comes."

Her words closed in on him like a straight jacket.

"And maybe your boss will let you come home on the weekends, you know, if you tell him that your wife is expecting."

Sid stifled his annoyance as he watched Eva wipe her tears with her sleeve, her hopeful eyes boring into him. *Why can't she see that I'm only doing what I have to do?* he thought. *Why is she making everything so damn difficult for me again?* He got up from his chair and started for the bedroom, stopping just before he opened the door. "Don't expect it. I won't be home for at least a month, and that's that," he said, without turning to face her. He pushed open the door and disappeared into the bedroom. Sid never knew when, or if, Eva came to bed that night.

November 14, 1929

Sid's duffle bag sat next to the door, all packed and ready to go. They had both been up since six. Eva had baked bread and made porridge while Sid spent the morning outside, stacking the load of firewood that he had split the day before. Not much was said while Sid ate his porridge and Eva prepared food for the long trip. She filled the canvas bag with pork sandwiches, a loaf of freshly baked bread, a thermos of coffee and five of the ten Hershey bars they'd bought the day before.

Sid pushed his porridge bowl away and slammed three of the five dollars he had left on the table. He'd save the other two for a nip when he got into the camp that evening. "You'll have to make do with that until I return," he spoke harshly to Eva's turned back. "Your father and the neighbours will need to contribute whatever else you need, I guess."

Eva carefully folded the top of the bag over and set it on the table beside the small pile of coins. She stood by his chair and looked down at him, tears welling in her eyes.

"You make sure Frank and Jack don't get their hands on this bag," she teased. The quiver in her voice sent chills down Sid's back.

"I'm sure they'll have their own," he muttered. He sat for a moment, looking up at her, and then he slowly got out of his chair. "Will your father be by today?" he asked.

Eva nodded and smiled at his diminutive display of concern. "Yes," she replied. "He'll be by later this morning."

He reached out and put his arms around her, and as he felt her body pressed against his, he realized that it was the first time he had held her in months. The two held each other for a brief moment, and then they heard the crunching sound of hard-packed snow under the wheels of a truck pulling up outside. Sid was the first to pull away.

"That'll be Jack and Frank," he said as he picked up the bag of food. He walked to the door, pulled on his coat and picked up his duffle bag. He paused for a moment and looked down at the floor. "I'll let you know when I'll be home," he muttered softly as he opened the door. He quickly glanced back at her one more time before walking out.

After the door closed, Eva ran over and opened it again and watched Sid greet his two friends as he climbed into the truck. As they pulled away, he briefly glanced back towards the house and then turned away. Eva stood and watched until they disappeared down the road.

January 1, 1930

Sid picked up his cards and slowly bent up the corners just enough so that he could see what he held. Not even Luanne, who was standing right behind him, one hand on his shoulder and the other holding the beer that he'd bought for her, could see his cards. It was six o'clock in the morning at the Carrot River Hotel, New Years Day. He'd barely heard the jovial countdown to nineteen thirty and best wishes for a "Happy New Year!" a few hours before. His mind was fully focused on winning back the money he had lost over the last eight days of nineteen twenty-nine.

Finally, things seemed to going his way. It was the best hand he'd been dealt since he hit the poker tables the night after the logging camp had shut down for the holidays, two days before Christmas. Most of the others had left camp that afternoon to be with their families, all of them with twenty-five dollars cash in their pockets. Sid had already drunk away most of his earnings and was determined to win some of it back before returning home to Eva, and her father.

"C'mon on guys, just a few more hands," he'd begged as Frank and Jack pressed him to get up from the table. They had waited a full day before finally giving up on him and driving Frank's truck back to their prairie homesteads for Christmas Eve without him.

Since then, Sid had been up and down and was struggling to make the most of his last ten dollars. But by New Years Day morning, the other gamblers were getting tired of playing.

He slowly peeked at his cards again and a rush of excitement came over him: an ace, a queen, a ten, a five, and a seven, all hearts. He had been dealt an ace-high flush. He looked at the pot--two dollars and fifty cents sat in the middle of the table, the fifty-cent antes that each of the five players had already contributed.

Sid put on his best poker face and nonchalantly looked at the others. He tapped his fingers on the table, doing his best to look confused, and then he took a swig of beer. "What the hell," he shouted. "Five dollars." Sid threw his five in the middle, challenging any of them to match his bet. In a game where the bets had typically been no more than two dollars and the largest pot of the week had been fifteen dollars, it certainly was an intimidating wager.

One by one, the others folded their hands in order. Then it came to the last man to make his decision, the big bull-headed man to Sid's right, Harry Adams. Instead of throwing his cards in the middle, Harry slowly bent them over, took another look, and then stared long at Sid. Sid tried hard not to show any emotion, although inside he was desperate that Harry would match the bet. Sid knew that he had the best hand, and he would gladly take another five dollars if Harry was willing to throw it in. Harry looked at Sid's last five dollars and made his move.

"I'll see your five and raise it five," he announced loudly, throwing a ten-dollar bill into the middle of the table. In no time, the gamblers were surrounded with onlookers, curious to see who was going to win the massive pot.

Sid could barely contain a smile. He grabbed his last five dollars and tossed it in. "I call," he smugly announced, silently counting the pile of money in the middle of the table. Twenty-five dollars, a full month's pay back to him in just one hand. *I won't go home with empty pockets now*, he thought. He paused for a moment, still feigning indecision. "I guess I'm good with these," he said as he kept both hands over his cards, fearing that someone might see through them and reveal his unbeatable hearts to the chump sitting beside him.

"I'll take two," Harry declared, his deep voice steely. He threw two cards away and was dealt two back. He bent his new cards over, looked at them, and deftly inserted them into his hand. He looked over at Sid with a self-assured expression, waiting for him to make his final bet.

This guy won't even know what hit him, Sid thought as he rummaged through his pockets, hoping to find another dollar or even fifty cents. He anticipated that Harry would certainly call and he wanted to build the pot up as much as he could. He pulled out a handful of lint. "I have no more to bet," he groaned. "I'll have to pass."

Harry tapped his cards on the table, then threw in some more bills. "Twenty more," he announced. He looked up at Sid and grinned. "I'll take your IOU," he offered.

Sid's heart skipped a beat as he once again calculated the winnings in his mind. He quickly motioned for Luanne to fetch him a pencil and paper. The crowd was silent as they waited for her to return. As she set a pencil and a piece of newspaper in front of him, Sid made a mental note to leave her a dollar on the bedside table later on that morning.

'Twenty dollars', he wrote in his childish hand. He quickly scribbled his mark on the note and threw it into the pot. "I call," he yelled, then threw his ace-high flush face up on the table. Sid looked around the room with a haughty smile as he started to reach for the money.

"Hold on there, Sid," Harry calmly interrupted. One at a time, Harry placed his cards face-up onto the table: six, six, six, king, king.

Sid felt the burning bile rising in his throat.

"That's a full house," Harry informed, as if Sid might not know. "Full house beats a flush every time," he chuckled as he reached in and started to gather up the cash. "You owe me twenty dollars," he reminded Sid as he waived the IOU in front of him. "You can pay me next month," he said with a wily smirk.

Sid sat dumbfounded and stared into the middle of the table, watching Harry scoop away all his money. A sickness filled his gut as he felt Luanne's hand leave his shoulder. He silently watched as she walked around the table and nuzzled up to Harry, congratulating him on his win and unashamedly soliciting her next drink from him. The crowd quickly scattered and the mumbles and mocking laughter faded. No one stood by Sid.

Chapter Twenty Two

The Family Man

February 3, 1930

It was a dark winter night, about seven o'clock, Sid supposed, when they finally arrived. He reached into the box of the truck and grabbed his duffle bag. "Thanks for the lift," he said before slamming the passenger door shut. The old timer just smiled, and then drove away, leaving Sid standing alone in front of the farmhouse. It looked peaceful. A full plume of thick white smoke rose out of the chimney and he could smell the rabbit stew. His stomach growled in anticipation. He hadn't eaten in two days. Sid slowly started up the path that had been cleared through the deep snow right up to the front porch. He hoped that she was alone.

The place looks smaller than it did before I left, Sid thought. It was the first time he had been home since leaving the previous November. He knew that Eva would certainly have learned the truth, why he stayed away so long, that he wasn't asked to stay on because the logging company needed him. He knew it was time to face the lies he had told her in his letter. But he had money, forty dollars in his pants' pocket, and he smiled at the recollection of how good the card tables had been to him over the last month. *Surely that will gain me some favour with Eva,* he reasoned. *And, more importantly, with her father.*

Sid stepped lightly as he climbed the steps onto the front porch. He slowly pushed open the door and looked inside. "Eva! I'm home!" he yelled. "Eva!"

Suddenly Eva rushed out of the bedroom. "Shhhh! You'll wake the baby!" she scolded in a whisper. "I just got him down." She stood there and looked at him, her hard face revealing nothing of the hopeful girl he had left three months earlier. *Her big belly is gone, but she's still fat*, he thought. She was still pretty enough, he decided, but something about her was different. She looked older.

Sid felt awkward, a stranger in his own home. He set his bag on the piano bench and took off his boots. "Smells good," he said softly, looking over to the stove. He hoped that Eva would tell him to sit down and eat.

"You want to see him?" she asked instead.

He was surprised by her question. "Ya, sure," he replied. He felt like he was walking in another man's body as he slowly made his way towards the bedroom door. He stopped and waited for her to lead the way in.

Eva gently pushed open the door and started into the bedroom. Sid followed her to the bassinette that sat next to their bed. He got as close as he dared and craned his neck to look into the tiny basket. There wasn't much to see as far as he could tell, just a small pile of blankets.

Eva reached in and carefully pulled back a flap, revealing a tiny face. She looked back at Sid. "His name is William," she whispered, "after my father. People are already starting to call him Bill." Her quiet voice rang with pride.

Sid stared intently at the little face for a minute, and an unexpected surge of emotion rushed through him. As the first hint of wetness began to prick at his eyes, he abruptly turned and walked out of the room. *I have a son*, he thought. *I have a son and his name is William.*

Of the complex tangle of emotions washing over him, he latched onto feelings of anger and shame. He had missed the birth of his first son and, worse yet, he didn't even have a say in naming the boy. He quickly wiped the tears away before Eva could see them, hurried to the front door and started to put on his boots.

"Where are you going?" Eva called, running out of the bedroom after him.

Sid didn't face her as he pulled on his jacket. "I'm going into town," he growled, trying to muffle the quiver in his voice. "Man has a right to celebrate the birth of his own son, don't he?" He pulled open the door and started out. Suddenly he stopped, and without looking back he shouted, "the next one we name George, after my brother."

Sid slammed the door and walked the two miles into Liberty to temporarily abandon the confines of marriage and fatherhood. He returned home the following day, impassively ashamed and thirty dollars poorer.

July 11, 1930

Once again, a sickening terror filled Sid's gut and he needed to step around back for a few minutes. And of course, once again, his first thought was to keep on going into the hot July night and never turn back. Those two words kept bouncing violently inside of his head, as if someone was relentlessly beating him with a club.

"I'm pregnant," was all she said.

Since February, everything had been good for Sid. He and Eva had come to some sort of truce, and she was for the most part good about keeping the baby out of his way when he was at home. When he was away, the only things that concerned him were making it out of the bush alive every day and hoping that the stories of his clandestine evening escapades never made it back to Liberty. Focusing his affections towards Eva for a couple of days at a time at the end of each month was a small price to pay for that, or so he thought. But the confines of marriage and fatherhood quickly closed in around him once again. The freedom he had always enjoyed was destined to come to an end and he could feel the uneasy truce with Eva crumbling within himself.

The warm days of summer turned to chilly autumn nights, and then back to the bitter cold winds of winter. Eva struggled to maintain their home, her belly growing larger every day while Sid stayed away for increasingly longer periods at a time. The usual four weeks turned into six weeks, and then to eight. The stories of her husband's indiscretions soon made their way back to Liberty. And when he did return home, usually with his tail tucked between his legs after having lost his paycheque in an all-night poker game or having been jilted by a casual lover, Sid would cozy up to Eva until the monotony of sobriety and home life caught up with him again. That's when he would turn on her, blame her for all his woes, pack his bags and leave. So it was no surprise to anyone that Sid wasn't there on February fifth, nineteen thirty-one, for the birth of their second child, George.

February 21, 1931

The hour was late and there was no light coming from the cabin. Sid opened the door and stumbled out of the truck, hoping that his arrival hadn't stirred Eva from her sleep. The woman who stumbled out after him clumsily tried to grab him to keep from falling over herself. Sid struggled to keep her on her feet and then fought to push her back into the truck. She struggled to get her arms around him and kiss him.

"Shudup ya drunk bitch!" he yelled. "My wife's right inside." Sid pushed her back into the truck, slammed the door on her skirt and stepped back so that she couldn't reach him from the open window.

"You bastard!" she yelled as she leaned out through the window, wildly flailing her arms trying to grab, hit, scratch and poke him all at once. "You lying bastard," she yelled again. The woman looked over at the house and cupped her hands around her mouth. "He's a lying bastard!" she screamed.

Sid reached over and grabbed the woman's face and pushed it hard back into the truck. He looked in through the window and hollered to the driver, "get her the hell outta here!" The driver laughed loudly, obviously finding great humour in the situation.

"Right, Sid. See ya next week. C'mon, get in here Luanne," he shouted as he pulled the still-flailing woman back into the truck. The pair drove off, leaving Sid standing alone in the lane.

Sid took a moment to gather his wits and then staggered towards the porch, carefully negotiating his way to the door. Just as he pushed it open, he stumbled and fell heavily onto the piano bench, causing a loud, heavy thump when his head hit the floor. He slowly picked himself up and starred at the closed bedroom door, hoping that Eva hadn't heard the commotion. Satisfied that she was still asleep, Sid clumsily made his way to a shelf near the stove and reached for a loaf of bread. Now he was certain she would wake as the loud crash of the pots and pans falling from the shelf shattered the silence. Suddenly, one of the babies began to cry. The child's annoying screams immediately infuriated Sid.

"Shut him up!" he yelled as he stormed into the bedroom. Sid glared at Eva with an angry stare through his red, bloodshot eyes. He propped himself against the door frame and held the partially eaten loaf of bread in one hand. "Get up and look after the kid," he shouted.

Without a word, Eva quickly rushed over to the crib and grabbed William and held him close, rocking him vigorously. It was the first time since they'd been together that Sid sensed that she was truly fearful of him. In his drunken state, he cruelly took pleasure in the control his rage seemed to have over her.

Eva looked into the bassinette, worrying that George would start as well. "Shhh," she whispered. "Everything's okay," she quietly assured. William seemed to understand and he fell silent in her arms.

Sid just stood and stared at her for a moment before staggering back into the kitchen. He stumbled to the table, sat down and started ripping pieces from the loaf, stuffing them into his mouth. Eva stepped into the room, holding William close. He wondered if she was going to say something about what had just happened outside, but she just stood there, watching him as he awkwardly tried to steady himself into his chair.

Sid looked up at her. "What are you staring at?" he yelled. "Go on back to bed and keep those ones quiet."

Eva didn't move. Her eyes bore into him icily. *Here it comes,* Sid thought to himself with a groan.

"Who was that you were with?" she finally blurted. "Outside in that truck, who is she?"

Sid glared up at her. In his hazy mind he decided that the best course of action would be to deny everything. "What the hell you talkin' about, ya stupid bitch?" he yelled. He could feel his face turning red as anger rose inside of him. He grabbed a tin coffee cup from the table and brought it back behind his head. "I said, get on back to bed!" he yelled again as he threw the cup in her direction. It crashed hard against the wall just above her head.

Eva froze. She held William even tighter and pressed her back firmly against the kitchen wall. She started to cry, but stood her ground and hollered back at him, "I want to know who she is."

Sid glared at her and violently slammed both of his hands on the table as he pushed himself up from the chair. His body tensed and he kicked the chair across the room. "Get the hell out of here!" he yelled, just as high-pitched wails started coming from the other room. *I thought I told her to shut those damned kids up!* his mind flashed with anger.

Suddenly, he spun around and grabbed the shotgun from the rack behind him and turned towards her. "Ain't none a yer business who my friends are, you stupid bitch!" he hollered. "I ought to finish you right now," he shouted as he pointed the barrel directly at her.

Eva froze and she instinctively covered William's head with her hand to protect him. Her body trembled and she wept as she slid down the wall and squatted onto the floor.

Sid held his position for a few seconds and then started to laugh. "Ya stupid bitch," he grunted. "Damn thing ain't even loaded." Sid cracked the barrel to reveal an empty chamber. He glared at Eva again, shook his head, and tossed the gun onto the table. "Stupid bitch," he mumbled again as he started for the bedroom. "Now shut that damn kid up before I do." The last thing Sid recalled was sitting on the edge of the bed, trying to remove his boots.

~~~

Sid's body shook violently as he slowly lifted his head. He could see the vapour from his hot breath drifting out of his mouth every time he exhaled. He slowly rolled over and looked at the window. It was covered in frost.

"What the hell?" he mumbled as he struggled to pull the blanket out from under himself. "Throw some wood in the stove," he yelled. He lay there for another few minutes before finally sitting up on the edge of the bed. "I said throw some more wood in the fire!" he hollered again. There was no response. Sid stood up and slowly staggered out of the bedroom. Eva wasn't in the kitchen. He scrapped some frost off the window and looked outside. *Still early*, he thought. He opened the stove door to find a heaping pile of cold, white ash. "Where the hell is she?"
~~~

he mumbled to himself. And then he looked over at the table to where the shotgun still lay, and it all started to come back to him. Suddenly, he knew where she must be.

Still dressed from the night before, Sid quickly put on his outerwear and headed out the door. After what he had done, he knew better than to be there when William Evans showed up. Sid had stepped over a line that not even he was likely going to be able to talk himself out of.

~~~

Two days had passed since the incident at the farmhouse. On the morning that he'd left, Sid went straight to the Liberty Hotel and woke one of his drinking friends. "I need a ride to Regina," he pleaded. Three hours later, he had a room at the Pioneer. And there he sat, at the bar with his second beer of the day in hand, looking around the familiar room. It had been almost three years since he had been there last. He remembered the first time he set foot in the Pioneer Hotel, the day that he'd met Slim. *And now I'm sitting at the same place at the bar, probably on the same stool,* he presumed. *Life seemed to hold so much promise back then,* he recalled with a smirk.

Sid took a sip of beer and wondered how he was going to make things right with Eva. She had always taken him back before. *This will pass too,* he thought. *After all, I'd never really intended on shooting her. I just wanted her to stop nagging me. Surely everyone would understand that,* he reasoned. He took another sip of his beer. *But convincing her father and her brother, that would be another matter,* he thought. He needed more time to think.

"Another beer!" he yelled. As Sid looked around for the bartender, he glanced out the window that faced the main street. He immediately recognized the truck that had pulled up on the other side. It was Eva's father, and he hadn't come alone. William and Wilf Evans, Tank and another man all climbed out of the truck and started for the hotel. Sid momentarily froze in his chair, unsure of whether to stay and try to explain his way out of the mess, or get up and run out the back door. He looked back out the window and saw the look on William's face as he drew closer. *Not a man who is coming to talk,* he decided. Sid was out the back door before they reached the front entrance.
~~~

Sid wasn't really sure where he would go, but as he raced past the rail yard, the box car seemed like a good place to ride out the next hour or so. But as soon as he climbed in through the open door, the train jerked forward and started to pull away from the station. Shocked, Sid just sat there as the engine chugged louder and louder, slowly picking up speed. The next thing he knew, it was moving too fast for him to get off.

His destiny, it seemed, had suddenly fallen into the hands of the Canadian Pacific Railway.

Chapter Twenty Three

Riding the Rails

George hung his head and stared at the floor. Mary could sense that he was distressed at what she was telling him. She gave him a minute to gather himself, and then asked, "are you okay?"

George sat quietly for another moment, and then looked up at her. Tears welled in both eyes. "Yes, thank you," he replied. "I'll be fine." He took a deep breath. "I suspected that things didn't end well between them, but I had no idea. No wonder mom never wanted to talk about him."

"I understand George," Mary said, "but if it's any comfort, Sid felt terrible for what he had done, and for what he had lost. Your dad cried when he told me that story."

George nodded and smiled. "I suppose that is some consolation. So, I guess that's when Sid moved here to Princeton," he presumed.

"Well, yes," Mary started. "That was the beginning of the journey that brought him this way. But your father had other adventures before ever arriving here in Princeton. If you want, I'll continue."

George didn't speak, just offering an affirmative nod.

March 15, 1931

Sid hung his head halfway out the partially open door of the box car and watched as the familiar scenes of Regina slipped out of sight. The car roughly swayed back and forth and he held on tight as he looked down and watched the ground swiftly pass underneath, far too fast for him to safely jump off. The wide open space of the snow-covered prairie opened up in front of him and all he knew was that he was heading west.

He pulled his head back in and looked around the dimly lit rail car. *It must be twenty-five below in here*, he thought. He tried to pull the door shut, but it was frozen in place. He pulled the collar of his coat up around his chin and ears. He didn't have a hat or gloves, which was not a good state of affairs for him, considering that it was the middle of a prairie winter.

At either end of the car were some large wooden crates. Sid decided he could huddle in behind those to at least shield himself from the strong, cold wind that whipped in through the open door. He squeezed in between the crates and the wall of the box car and squatted, his knees pulled up tight to his chest and his arms wrapped tightly around them. At that moment, Sid truly believed that he would die that day.

"You'd better get out of there," a husky voice called out over the loud screech of steel on steel. "If those crates shift, they'll crush you like a bug," the voice laughed. "C'mon over here, boy. These ones are tied down."

The voice sounded friendly enough, and Sid needed all the help he could get right then. He stood up and slipped out from behind the crates, straining to see where the voice had come from. The piercing wind made it hard for him to keep his eyes open.

"Over here, boy," the raspy voice called again. "The other end of the car," he yelled, now seemingly annoyed at Sid's confusion.

Sid carefully made his way to the other end of the rail car, struggling to maintain his balance with every step. He grabbed onto one of the crates and made his way around, and found himself looking directly into the red, squinty eyes of an old man. The man's weathered face was covered with bristly grey whiskers and long tufts of matted grey hair stuck out from under his thick wool hat. His bulbous nose was big and red, as big a nose as Sid had ever seen on a man. The man sat comfortably on a large soft sack of grain.

"C'mon, boy," he said, waving Sid over with a gesture of his hand. "These sacks are mighty comfortable once you get settled into them. And they'll help keep your ass warm," he added.

Sid hesitated for a moment before quickly taking up the offer and plunking himself into the middle of the pile. He immediately felt the warmth as he nestled in. The two sat quietly for a few minutes.

"What's your name, boy?"

"Sid," he replied.

The old man reached into his coat pocket. "Here, put this on," he offered, handing Sid a wool toque.

Sid hesitated for a moment, shocked that a wayward stranger would offer him something so valuable.

"Don't worry, boy," the old man said. "It's an extra. I can get another one. Take it," he offered again.

Sid reached over and took the hat. "Thanks," he said as he pulled it over his ears. The heavy, thick wool hat warmed his head instantly.

"You haven't ridden the trains much, have you Sid?"

Sid looked over to the man. "No, not too much," he admitted.

"I could tell the moment you jumped in here," the old man chuckled. "Jumping into a boxcar right in the middle of the rail yard, and in broad daylight too. We're both lucky the bulls didn't catch you and me in the process," he scolded. "Do you know what they do to the likes of us when they catch us?" His tone was a shade less friendly.

Sid stared at the old man. "No," he timidly answered.

"You keep doing foolish things like that and you'll find out soon enough," the old man warned. He reached into the small sack sitting next to him and pulled out a loaf of bread, then tore it in two. "Here," he offered, passing one half over to Sid. "You probably haven't eaten in awhile either," he assumed.

Sid eagerly accepted the bread. He didn't admit it, but he hadn't eaten since the previous day, and he was famished. He ravenously tore into it. "Thanks again," he mumbled.

The two sat quietly for another few minutes, the old man studying his new travelling partner. "What are you running from?" he finally asked.

Sid stared at him, feeling a resurgence of the panic he'd felt when William Evans and his crew had climbed out of the truck a few hours before. "What makes you think I'm runnin' from anything, old man?"

The old man smiled. "Boy," he started, "I've been riding these trains for over fifteen years. I've travelled from the east coast to the west coast and back again more times than I can count. Along the way, I've met all sorts. Some are in it for the adventure, some to get from one job to the next. But most are running away from something," he said. "I can tell that about a man," he assured, "and boy, you're a runner."

Sid looked down at his lap. As much as he didn't want to admit it, the old man did seem to have him pegged. His words struck a chord in Sid, conjuring up memories of his youth and, more recently, of running out the back door of the Pioneer Hotel. It suddenly occurred to Sid that for as far back as he could remember, he had in fact always been running from something. "You seem sure of yourself, old timer," he replied, struggling to insert confidence into his voice.

The old man looked at Sid and smiled. "I'm not asking you to tell me your story, boy," he said. "That is, unless you want to," he added. "That's your business."

"Not much to tell," Sid quipped. "Just lookin' for work is all, like everyone else." He hoped the man wouldn't be able to detect his lie.

Sid shivered and curled himself up into a ball, settling himself as comfortably as he could onto the sack. He thought about Eva and the old farmhouse near Liberty. He suddenly missed the crackling sounds and the aroma of the fire burning in the wood stove with its heat radiating out into the small room. He even missed the smell of rabbit stew simmering away. *How could I have let all that slip away from me so quickly?* he wondered. One day he was married and the father to two boys, and the next day he was cold and hungry, huddled up in a boxcar with a strange old man, his destination a mystery to him. Even with his sordid past, Sid had to shake his head at that.

He looked over to the old man. "What about you?" he asked. "What are you running from?"

The old man looked up and away for a moment, as if to reflect on days gone by, and then smiled at Sid. "Boy," he said as he straightened himself, "I had a rather conventional life at one time. An education, a family, a home." The old man's face lit up as memories of happier days seemed to come back to him.

Sid sat quietly and listened as the stranger started to tell his story.

"I had a beautiful wife. Her name was Maria. We met at a picnic, on a sunny day in Halifax. June of o-three," he said. "Got married in o-five, in Montreal." The old man's smile grew even larger. "Maria was my life. We had two sons, twins," he noted. "Albert and Timothy. And we had a beautiful daughter whom we named Gwen, after Maria's mother." The old man beamed as he spoke of them, as if they were sitting right beside him on the sacks of grain.

Sid sensed that this story didn't have a happy ending, considering that the old man was telling it to a stranger inside a cold and dark boxcar in the middle of winter. But talking about his past seemed to make him happy, and Sid was desperate to keep his own thoughts off of Eva.

"So, what did you do?" he asked, to keep the conversation going. "You know, for work."

The man looked straight at Sid and furled his brow. "I was a minister," he calmly replied, "in a small Baptist church in a village back east. A place called Fort William, on the big lake," he clarified. "It was a small congregation, but a fine bunch." A smile crossed his face. "I was a believer then. I had it all." The old man fell silent, staring off into the dark as if he were suddenly somewhere else.

Sid studied the scruffy, weathered face, the big red nose, and the red squinty eyes. He cleared his throat. "And your family? Where are they now?" he cautiously asked.

The old man looked directly at Sid. "Well, boy, the good Lord in all of His infinite wisdom decided to take my family in a fire. June twenty-second, nineteen-fifteen," he recalled. "That's the day I stopped believing, and that's the day I started running." The old man quickly sat up and seemed to come back to the moment. "Haven't looked back since," he quickly added.

Sid didn't know what to say. He had never had anyone tell him their story like that before. He sat silently for a moment, trying to recall what he had been doing in nineteen-fifteen. All of a sudden it dawned on him that nineteen-fifteen was the same year that Elizabeth had died in the fire. The memory suddenly brought back the hurt and pain of those days, days that he would just as soon have forgotten and could surely never talk about.

The old man looked over at him and smiled again. "So, where you headed, Sid?" he asked. "Calgary, Vancouver maybe?"

Sid thought for a moment. "Not sure," he replied. He looked at the old man, feeling somewhat embarrassed. "I'm not even sure where this train is going," he admitted.

The old man laughed. "Well, boy, this one'll go straight into Calgary," he advised with all the confidence of a conductor. "You might have a good chance at picking up some work there, if that's what you're looking for." The old man stared at Sid for a moment, as if trying to determine if he was worthy of the wisdom he was about to impart. "Four things you need to remember when riding the trains, boy." He began to count items off on his gloved fingers. "Stay warm, fill your belly whenever you can, always help your fellow travelers and don't get caught. You remember those things and you'll do just fine," he assured as he curled up on the sack and started to close his eyes. "Oh ya, and get lots of sleep when you've got a comfortable bed to sleep on, like these sacks."

Sid nodded and closed his eyes. The swaying motion and rhythmic sounds had made him tired, too. He pulled his coat up around his head as far as it would go and he drifted off into a deep sleep. The next two hours were lost to him.

~~~

His eyes slowly opened and, for a moment, he forgot where he was. He stretched his arms and craned his neck, trying to get the stiffness out. He was cold. The coat had slipped down from around his head and some of the buttons had come undone.

Oh ya, the train, he abruptly recalled as the metrical clatter of the steel wheels reached his ears. He sat up on the sack and looked over to where the old man had fallen asleep, but he wasn't there. Sid looked around, but couldn't see him. He stood up and made his way out from behind the crates. "Hello?" he yelled. There was no response. Sid made his way to the other end of the boxcar and looked in behind the crates. "Hello?" he yelled again. No response. *He couldn't have just disappeared*, he thought.
~~~

Sid stepped over to the partially open door and looked out. It was pitch black outside. There were no lights in the distance to signify that even a small town was close by, there was only blackness. Sid felt his way back to the grain sacks and sat. After his eyes had adjusted to the dark, he noticed something sitting on the sack next to where he had fallen asleep. He reached over and picked it up. It was a full loaf of bread. Sid ripped off a piece and stuffed it into his mouth. He settled back onto the grain sack and thought about the old man, wondering why he'd gotten off the train, and where. Sid didn't even know his name. He thought about the old man's story, about his wife and family and how talking about them seemed to make him happy. Sid wished he had told the old man more about himself.

~~~

Burn barrels and makeshift tents lined the banks of the Bow River, Calgary's place for the hundreds of transients that passed through that city every day. It was a true hobo jungle, and that's where Sid found himself after arriving on the train that had taken him out of Regina and away from Eva and his sons, and his father-in-law.

Sid quickly learned that work was scarce and charity was almost non-existent during those Depression years. During the days, he sometimes picked up an odd job sweeping floors at a bakery for a loaf of bread and a cup of coffee, or cleaning up scraps of meat from the killing floor at the slaughterhouse in exchange for whatever scraps were salvageable. The men on the banks of the Bow, at least most of them, shared what they had with their friends. Sid had something to eat almost every-day. His nights were spent huddled around fires drinking coffee made from used grounds found in restaurant garbage pails and sharing stories and laughs.

Sid listened, mostly. He didn't have the experiences of rail riding that most of the others had. He just knew that it wasn't the life for him. But he needed all the hints he could get about finding steady work, so he listened closely to the others. Any jobs that did become available were usually kept as closely guarded secrets to those who found out about them first.
~~~

March 25, 1931

It was another bitterly cold March night. Sid hustled to the barrel and briskly rubbed his hands over the flames.

"Any luck today, Sid?" a man who was drying his toque over the flames asked.

Sid stepped closer to the barrel. He needed some more time to warm himself before he could stop his teeth from chattering long enough to answer. "No work today," he finally replied. He reached into the deep pockets of his coat and pulled out a bag. "The woman at the bakery gave me these, though," he said with a triumphant smile. Sid held up the coffee grounds and a loaf of bread. "What about you Tom? Anything?"

Tom couldn't hide his smile any longer. "We're eatin' like kings tonight!" he declared as he reached down and picked up a slab of bacon from the snow. "There's enough here for all three of us," he added with pride, referring to himself, Sid, and their friend Sam.

Sid had met a lot of men in the short time he had been in Calgary. Most were friendly enough, but he had bonded most closely with two, Tom and Sam. Tom was a small man but always seemed to be full of energy and ideas, most of which were a little far-fetched as far as Sid and Sam were concerned. But he did have a good sense of humour that lifted their spirits during some of their more desperate moments.

Sam was a big man, at least six foot six. And he was as solid as a locomotive. Sid thought of Sam as a gentle giant, but not one that he'd want to rile, as they had all witnessed the night when someone had tried to steal their coffee pot.

Like Sid, Tom and Sam went out everyday and brought back what they could to share with the others. They talked incessantly about finding work and vowed to stick together. They helped each other survive.

Sid's stomach growled as soon as he saw the big hunk of meat that Tom was holding up. "There must be five pounds of bacon there," he gasped. "Where did you get that?"

"It's more like ten pounds, and don't ask where I got it," Tom chuckled. "Let's get this feast started," he said as he set the meat on a stump and began cutting it up with the rusty old pocket knife that he carried with him. "You get that old fryin' pan heated up. We'll have coffee and bacon ready by the time Sam gets back. God knows he'll likely eat half all by himself," he prattled on. Suddenly Tom stopped for a moment and looked over at Sid. "I got some other good news, too," he beamed, "but I ain't sayin' nothin' 'til Sam gets here."

Sid saw the glow on Tom's face and stifled a groan. *Another crazy scheme*, he thought, not paying much mind. He was more anxious to dig into the pile of bacon. "I'll get the coffee on," he said.

Just then, Sid heard a familiar voice in the darkness and the loud crunching of snow underfoot as Sam and another man approached the fire. Sid and Tom looked at each other, wondering who else they might be sharing their bounty with. As the pair approached, something about the other voice caught Sid's attention. It was one that he recognized.

As Sam came into the light of the fire, calling out greetings, Sid squinted to see the face of his companion, who was hanging back slightly. As soon as the stranger's features came into focus, Sid instinctively rushed over to greet the man.

"Slim!"

Sam looked surprised. "You know this guy?" he asked, staring at Sid.

Sid reached out and put his hands on Slims shoulders. "What the hell!" he shouted. "What the hell are you doin' here?"

"What the hell are you doin' here?" Slim echoed. Slim had a look of shock on his face as he reached up and grabbed Sid's shoulders. A broad smile stretched across his face as he greeted his old friend. "Well I'll be dammed," he shouted. "Never thought I'd ever see you again," he said laughing.

After the greetings were finished with and introductions had been made, Slim stepped closer to Sid. He looked at the fire and then over to the makeshift shelter near the tree line. "I thought you would have married that Eva girl and been settled down in Saskatchewan with a houseful of kids by now."

The comment made Sid's heart sink. He briefly turned away to hide his pain and then looked back at Slim with a crooked smile. "Ya, well, that didn't work out." Sid forced a smile. "I'll tell you all about it sometime," he said. "Meanwhile, get yourself over by the fire and warm up. We've got lots to eat tonight," he offered, pointing over at Tom, who was putting the first slices of bacon in the pan.

Sid caught the unmistakable glean of hunger flash over his old friend's eyes.

"You sure you fellas wouldn't mind if an old bugger like me joins ya?" Slim asked.

"Not at all,"Tom shouted.

"Well, better add these, then," Slim called as he pulled his own bounty out of his pocket. "I got a block of cheese, and Sam there got a dozen or so eggs," he bragged.

"We spent the day unloading trucks at the grocers," Sam informed. "There must've been forty guys showed up there this morning, and lucky for us, me and Slim here got picked."

Tom looked up from the frying pan for a moment and looked from Sid to Slim. "So, how do you guys know each other?" he asked.

Sid smiled broadly and looked over at Slim. "Old Slim here and me go back a few years. Had a good thing goin' once," he boasted.

"Yep, sure did," agreed Slim, his voice becoming a bit distant.

Sid looked at his old friend with a frown pulling at the corners of his mouth. "Where the hell did you get to that day?" he asked. "You know I went all the way to Regina lookin' for you. You just up and disappeared."

Slim looked away. "Ya, well I'm sorry bout' that," he said with a hint of embarrassment in his voice. "When Chalmers told me that he'd paid off the loan for the combine and that I was no longer needed, well, if I had a gun I would have killed him right there on the spot," he said. "Thought it best that I get out of there before I did something stupid. Guess I should have come back for you," he apologized. "Next thing I knew I was working on a ranch down near Lethbridge." Slim's voice brightened again. "Turns out I ain't much of a cowboy," he laughed. "So I've been travelin' 'round ever since, picking up work here and there. But like you fellas know, ain't much out there for guys like us." Slim paused again and stared at his old friend. "But it sure is good to see you today, old friend," he said with a smile.

Sid smiled back. "Ya, you too, old friend. Partners again?"

"Ya, partners again," Slim grinned, reaching out to slap Sid on the back.

"Bacon's almost cooked,"Tom cut in. "Let's get those eggs in the pan. My, oh my, it is a fine night tonight, and things'll only get better."Tom began to hum an upbeat tune as he pulled the first pieces of cooked bacon from the pan and put them on a tin plate. Sid heard Slim's stomach rumble loudly.

"What the hell are you so happy about, Tom?" Sam barked. Sid had been wondering the same thing.

Tom stepped in close to the others, his excitement clear on his face. He looked over his shoulder as if to make sure that nobody else was listening. Sure that they were alone, he took a deep breath. "Got some good news today," he proclaimed as he looked over at Sid. "You've worked in lumber camps before, right?" he asked. Before Sid could answer, Tom stepped in even closer. "I overheard a couple of guys talkin' today," he whispered. "Seems there's a big timber operation out in Revelstoke that's hirin'. And they need men now!" he emphasized. "Word is the wages are good and they provide food and lodging. Hell, they'll even give you clothes and a new pair of boots. I figure we head out that way and get us some real work," he proposed, clapping his hands together like it was already a done deal.

The others looked at each other and stood silent for a moment. Sam was the first to speak up.

"Well, Tom," he began in a patient voice, almost as though he were talking to a child. "It sounds good, but how do you suppose we're going to get there? If there are any jobs, they won't last long."

Tom flashed a cocky smile. "I got that figured, too," he assured. "There's a coal train heading out to Revelstoke first thing in the mornin'," he informed. "It leaves before sunrise. I say we bury ourselves in the coal, have ourselves a little nap, and before you know it we'll be stompin' around Revelstoke in a new pair of warm boots!"

Sid looked between Sam and Slim, seriously considering the idea.

"When did you work in lumber?" Slim asked him.

"After you left, when there was no farm work," he said. "I worked in the bush cuttin' and draggin' for a couple of years." Sid looked pointedly at each of the others, revelling in the chance to be an expert. "It's hard work," he informed, "but it does pay well and they treat you well if you get on with a good outfit. And I've heard that the camps in B.C. are the best. If Revelstoke's hirin', it might be a good set-up."

Tom whooped, pleased that Sid seemed to endorse the idea. "It'd be better than working for scraps and trying to stay warm around this old barrel," he pitched in as though an extra ounce of enthusiasm might tip the scales in his favour.

Sam looked between faces. "Any of you guys ever rode in a coal car before?" he asked.

Sid shook his head and Slim followed suit. Not wanting to sully his newfound expert status, Sid didn't mention that he had only ridden the rails once.

Sam looked at Tom, who seemed to have all of the answers. "What about you?" he asked.

Tom busied himself with the coffee for a moment. "Well, no," he finally admitted, "but I heard that if you bury yourself deep in the coal, it'll keep you warm. And besides, the bulls never check the coal cars. Too dirty for them." He scanned the group with a sober gaze. "Train leaves at five. If we're gonna do this, we need to decide now."

"Anything beats this," Sid shouted. "I'm in." He looked over at Slim and Sam.

"Guess if we're gonna be partners, I'm in too," Slim declared.

"What the hell," Sam yelled. "Count me in."

Tom had a grin from ear to ear as he began cracking eggs into the frying pan. "Okay then," he shouted. "Let's get our bellies full and nab a couple hours of sleep. We've got a five o'clock train to catch."

It was like old times for Sid, his old friend and partner by his side, and the real possibility of success just down the line.

~~~

Sid squatted behind a stack of railroad ties that were piled along the tracks, with Slim and Sam huddling close behind. Tom had gone around to the other side to make sure the coast was clear.

"Be quiet," Tom whispered as he appeared around the corner on his hands and knees. "There's a couple of cops headed this way."

The group crouched low so as not to be detected. They could hear the two railroad policemen talking as they stopped to have a smoke on the other side of the pile. Sid's heart was beating ferociously. *We're gonna get caught for sure,* he thought as he struggled to calm his breathing.
~~~

"Damn! It's cold out here. Must be forty below," came an officer's gruff voice. "I don't know why we need to be out here at this time of morning, freezin' our asses off," he grumbled. "No one rides these coal cars anyways, least wise no one in his right mind." Both men laughed.

"Ya, you're right," the other man agreed, "'cept most of those damn vagabonds is two bits short of a dollar. Come on. Let's get back inside before we freeze to death."

One of the men flicked a cigarette butt over the pile of ties, landing it right in front of Sid. He slipped off his mitt and took a quick drag, then passed it to Slim to finish off. Sid listened as the crunching sound of the police officers' boots slowly faded as they rounded the end of the train.

"Okay," Tom began, his voice still hushed. "The last car before the caboose is right on the other side of this here pile. We'll go one at a time," he instructed. "Slim, you go first. Get as far to the front of the car as you can. As soon as you get in, dig yourself in all the way," he advised. "Sam, you'll go next, then me, then Sid."

Sid looked around at the anxious group. *Are we really out of our minds to try riding the coal car?* he wondered, then forced the thought out of his mind. He spat on the ground and the frothy gob froze instantly.

"Are you guys ready?" Tom asked, a false enthusiasm permeating his voice.

Sid and the others nodded reluctantly.

"Okay then, let's go!"

Sid followed close on Tom's heels as the group slowly crawled around the end of the wood pile. He could see Slim peeking around the corner, looking up and down the track. When he determined that is was clear, he scrambled towards the awaiting train. Sid inched forward and watched as his friend scurried over to the ladder affixed to the open rail car and climbed up it. With a brief look back, Slim jumped from the top of the ladder and let himself drop down into the awaiting bed of coal. As soon as he was out of sight, Sam began to make his way to the ladder. He, too, quickly disappeared over the top, with Tom close behind.

When it was Sid's turn, he froze. Suddenly he wasn't sure if they were doing the right thing. He squatted down beside the wood pile, carefully scanning the tracks in both directions. He realized that he was afraid, afraid of being caught by the bulls. A memory from his childhood flashed into his mind, taking him back to the time when he had hidden in the long grass near the tracks, waiting for the train to come and take him away. A chill went through his body as he recalled the two policemen pulling him up from the ground and laughing at him before turning him over to Ruth Connors. Suddenly, Sid wasn't sure if he could make it to the top of the ladder.

Sid looked up and saw Tom peering over the side of the car. "Come on, Sid!" Tom loudly whispered. "Get up here! Quick, or else this train is leaving without you!"

Sid gathered himself, took a deep breath and looked hard at the ladder. "Well, here goes," he muttered to himself. He pushed off and started for the train, grabbing hold of the first rung with his gloved hand just as the whistle sounded, signalling that the train was set to pull away. Clinging to the ladder, he could hear the loud clang of the iron couplings smashing against each other as the cars ahead started to roll. Just as he reached the top of the ladder, the open-air coal car jerked hard as it was pulled to life by the procession.

Sid fell heavily onto the pile of coal beneath him, stirring up a cloud of dirty black dust. The soot quickly filled his lungs making him cough. *No wonder people avoid the coal cars,* he quickly decided. By then, the screeching sounds coming from the tracks below muffled any noise that he made. Comfortable that he was not in danger of being caught, Sid settled back for a moment, oblivious to the cold and relieved that he had made it. As the train picked up speed, he slowly pulled himself up and squinted towards the front of the car. Through the blowing coal dust he could barely see Sam and Tom, both of whom were not far from where he was at the back of the car. They were already buried up to their necks in coal, and their faces were black with soot, making them nearly invisible. The sight would have made Sid chuckle if he hadn't been preoccupied by thoughts of Slim.

Sid strained his eyes, trying to see where Slim had wound up. But with all the coal dust their troupe had stirred up, he couldn't see his friend at all. As the cold began to chill him, Sid started to dig himself in. It was a more difficult task than Tom had made it out to be, for chunks of coal fell back into the hole he was digging nearly as quickly as he could remove them. It may have only taken a few minutes to complete the entire task, but to Sid it seemed like an eternity. When he was finally buried up to his chin, he reached up and pulled his thick wool hat down over his ears and his bulky winter coat up as far as he could around his face. While the surrounding coal made for a pleasant weight around his body, being buried in it wasn't nearly as warm as Tom had said it would be. He shivered uncontrollably.

Sid looked ahead to where Sam and Tom's faces were visible. "Where's Slim?" he whispered loudly.

Tom strained his neck for a better view. "He's way up front. He's okay," he assured after a moment.

Sid could feel the cold biting at his hands and feet. He tried to take shallow breaths so that the piercing cold wouldn't hurt his lungs. "Tom, you said it was going to be warm in here," he hissed. "My feet are freezing!"

"Just give it a few minutes," Tom whispered back, sounding self-assured.

Sid groaned. *This is the last time I'll ever listen to him,* he vowed. He looked up into the clear night sky, noticing the big dipper over his head. He might have been cold, but at least he had a great view.

Sid could see the whites of Sam's eyes darting towards Tom. "Why are we moving so slowly?" Sam asked. "I've never seen a train leave a station this slowly before."

Tom stretched his neck to look forward towards the engine. "I don't know. Looks like something's goin' on up ahead," he said. "It's too dark to see up there."

Sid strained to see if he could make out what was happening. As the train slowly trudged forward, he could hear what sounded like the gush of heavy-flowing water. *What the hell is going on?* he wondered, wishing that he knew more about coal trains. The sound grew louder and louder as they moved ahead.

Suddenly he saw it. The boom from the water tower was directly ahead, fully open and spewing a torrent of water into each car as it passed underneath. Sid looked over at Tom. "They're watering down the coal," he yelled ahead of him. "You never said anything about water!"

Sid frantically struggled with all his strength to free himself from the heavy grip of the coal.

The car in front of them had already passed under the boom and their car was about to get its soaking. The water came crashing into the front part of the car, thundering down ahead of him as though the big dipper had upturned an ocean of water right in front of his eyes. The relentless stream of water was inching towards the back of the car and Sid was powerless to do anything to save himself.

All of a sudden, the pounding water stopped. Only a slight trickle was left by the time the boom was over the back of the car, and not even a dribble emerged by the time the caboose rolled underneath. Sid, Sam and Tom had been spared the soaking. The engine chugged loudly into the night as it prepared to push full speed ahead on its journey to the mountains.

Sid's joy that he remained dry was quickly replaced by the realization that Slim might have taken the full brunt of the water flow. He called out to his friend, panic gripping his throat. "Slim, are you alright up there?" he shouted as he redoubled his efforts to dig himself out of the coal. There was no response. "Slim!"

"Shhh!" Tom hissed. "Stay down, and be quiet! The bulls are still around!"

Sid scowled at Tom and then looked over at Sam. "Come on!" he hollered. "We've got to crawl across. Slim won't last two minutes if he got wet!"

Sid and Sam dug themselves out and started to crawl towards the front of the car. By the time they were half way there, the top layer of coal became a solid frozen mass. Fear engulfed Sid.

"Slim! Slim!" he yelled at the top of his lungs, dragging his knees along the unforgiving surface of the frozen coal. He felt a burst of relief when Slim's face came into view, his head and shoulders visible above the mound, his face wearing an expression that seemed to be mock amusement. "Thank god, Slim! I thought you might be--"

Suddenly Sid's voice turned into a dry, heaving sob as he fully processed the scene before his eyes. Slim was encrusted in a thick layer of coal and ice. The whites of his eyes glowed amidst the black of his face like two tiny lights shining in the dark. His mouth had been solidified in a surprised and pained 'O' shape that marked a frigid realization that came too late.

Sid pushed forward, frantically trying to dig his friend out from underneath the frozen mass. "Come on!" he yelled over his shoulder. "Help me get him out!" Sid pounded on the frozen mound of coal, desperately trying to loosen its hold on Slim. It wouldn't budge.

Sam joined in, and the pair pounded and chipped away at the ice-covered heap with their bare hands, trying to free their friend from his icy prison. "This isn't working!" Sid wailed after a minute, and decided to switch tactics. He cupped his hands around his mouth and breathed the warm air from his lungs onto Slim's face, hoping against hope that he might be able to thaw some of the icy layer that was suffocating his friend. But the night was so cold that the fine film of water that he did manage to generate froze again within seconds. "Damn it!" Sid cried, openly bawling now but refusing to give up.

Sid and Sam worked in vain for five, maybe six minutes, long enough for both of them to work up a profuse sweat.

Finally, Sam sat back, exhausted. He tried to pull Sid away. "He's gone," Sam whispered over the wind that roared in their ears. "There's nothing we can do now." Sam took hold of Sid's arm and tried to pull him towards the back of the car.

Sid ripped himself away, unable to take his gaze from his friend's eyes. "He might be still alive in there!" he cried. "We can't just leave him like this!"

"Sid, we can't get him out." Sam was hollering to be heard now as the train reached full speed, causing a bitter wind to whip over the car. "We need to get back to where it's dry, or we'll all die up here. Come on, Sid. We can't save him."

Sid's body went limp as he reluctantly gave in to the inevitable. His friend was gone. He took a last look. "I'm sorry, Slim," he whispered. "I'm sorry."

Sid slowly turned towards Sam. The tears froze to his cheeks as fast as they gushed out of his eyes. Sam put his arm around Sid and the pair slowly crawled towards the back of the car. Tom watched them from beneath the mound of coal where he'd buried himself ten minutes before.

Reaching the back of the car, Sid pulled his wool hat down around his ears and his collar up past his chin, covering as much of his face as he could. He dug into the coal and again buried himself until only his face peered out through the blackness. His body shook violently as he closed his eyes to the whipping wind, not caring if they ever opened again.

~~~

Sid awoke, groggy and frostbitten, to the sound of Sam's shouts. "Any of us'll be lucky to get out of this alive!" he yelled. "We should've known better than to listen to you."

What's going on? Sid wondered, before the horror of the night before crashed into his mind. *Slim is gone.*

Sid forced his eyes open, pushing his hand up through the coal mound to shield his eyes from the sun. "Slim!" he shouted. He looked up towards the front of the car and saw no trace of his friend. Sam and Tom were sitting atop the coal, in front of a larger mound.

"Where is he?" Sid hollered. "Where did Slim go?" *Did he manage to escape?* he wondered, his heart rising in his chest.

Tom stared hard at Sid. "We buried him," he said matter-of-factly, jerking his thumb over his shoulder towards the larger mound.

Tom's crassness immediately struck a chord in Sid that made his blood boil. "You son of a bitch!" Sid yelled as he wildly started to dig himself out from the weight of the coal. "I'll kill you for getting Slim into this mess!" he screamed.

Tom scurried to the farthest corner of the coal car, as far away from Sid as he could get. "I didn't know," he yelled back. "I didn't know about the water. I'm sorry about your friend."

"Why the hell'd you tell Slim to go up front? If it was your bright idea, why didn't you go first?" Sid screamed. He could feel the last pieces of coal around his legs about to give way.

"I didn't know!" Tom repeated, real fear in his voice now.

Just as Sid was about to free himself, Sam jumped in. "Hold on," he shouted as he pulled Sid back. "It wasn't anyone's fault. None of us knew about the water. It could have been any one of us up there."
~~~

Sid slumped back onto the pile, all the fight suddenly drained from him. "It just ain't right," he moaned. "Slim goin' like that. He was a good fella. A good partner. He deserved better than to die like he did."

Sam reached out and put his hand on Sid's shoulder and looked him straight in the eye. "Sid, men die every day ridin' these trains. Hundreds of 'em every year," he said quietly. "It's a risky business."

Sid looked towards his feet. He knew what Sam said was true, but none of those other men could be half the friend Slim was to him.

"We can't just leave him in there," Sid said, nodding towards the mound. "The railroad guys'll never do right by him when they find him." His voice was little more than a whisper.

"We ain't got no other choice here, Sid," Sam replied.

Sid knew he was right. He sank back into the shallow hole left from where he had dug himself out. He felt numb as he reflected back on his life. He remembered the few people who had cared about him over the years. He always seemed to push them away, that is, if they didn't die on him first.

As the train chugged towards the mountains, taking him further and further away from England, Sid thought about what a harsh country he'd ended up in.

The sun shone brightly on them and the temperature had risen considerably. Sid made himself as comfortable as he could, half buried in the coal. He looked out at the scenery around him. It was the first time he had ever seen mountains. The air was calm, crisp and clear, and a deep blanket of pure white snow covered everything. A forest of massive pine trees surrounded him for as far as he could see. The only sound was the distant echo of the steam engine bouncing off of the rising slopes. It was peaceful.

"The tunnels'll be comin' up soon," Sam called over to him. "It's always rough goin' through the tunnels, even if you're inside the boxcars."

"Tunnels?" he yelled back.

Sam grinned. "Yeah, the tunnels are cut right through the mountains. They fill with smoke from the train," he said. "Ridin' in the open air like we are is likely to choke you up really bad. Most don't make it through without pukin' out their guts," he warned. "Keep your face buried in your coat. That's about all you can do." Suddenly, the echoing sound of the engine far ahead of them changed to a dull rumble. "Here we go!" Sam yelled.

Sid stretched his neck, trying to see the front of the train, but it had disappeared around a curve. As the back end rounded the bend, he could see the gaping black hole in the mountain side, swallowing the train one car at a time, reminding him of a giant snake slithering back into its hole.

As they drew closer, he could see the black and yellow smoke billowing out of the tunnel. He inched himself deeper into the coal and pulled his coat up over his head, sealing off his mouth and nose as best he could. Just as they were about to enter, he took a deep breath, and then everything went black.

It didn't take long for the acrid smoke to breach the protective barrier of his wool coat and flood into his nostrils and his mouth. As soon as he sucked in his first breath, his lungs filled with the caustic fumes, immediately choking him and causing him to sputter and cough. Instantaneously becoming nauseous, he started to heave. He tried desperately not to vomit, but the corrosive gases relentlessly billowed over him, uncaring of anyone or anything in their path. When Sid couldn't hold it any longer, he spewed all over himself and the inside of his coat.

Finally, after about fifteen suffocating minutes, the sun suddenly reappeared and they were clear of the tunnel. Sid poked his face out of his soiled coat, his face still green, vomit dripping from his mouth and nose. He looked over at Sam to share a look of mutual agony. But both he and Tom seemed fine. Seeing Sid, they broke out laughing.

"Guess you're just not doin' it right," Tom joked tentatively. It was the first time they'd spoken since their altercation earlier on that morning. "Ya gotta hold your coat tight to your face, you know, breath through it."

Sid glared back at him, still not ready to forgive his friend. "Thanks for tellin' me now that we're through," he chided. "Seems there's a lot about this trip that you're not saying."

Sam laughed, lessening the tension. "Don't worry, Sid," he yelled. "Sounds like the other tunnel's comin' up. You can practice in there."

Just as Sam spoke, Sid looked up to see the front end of the train disappear into the second tunnel. Fifteen minutes later, he still hadn't gotten it right.

Chapter Twenty Four

Poverty to Prosperity

Clock. Clock. Clock. Sid was immediately calmed by the rhythmic sound of the cold, dry wood splitting. The reverberation of each strike was carried cleanly to the mountain and back on the heavy, crisp winter air. The warmth of the newly risen sun had just started to filter through the morning haze, its rays reflecting off the ice crystals that danced all around. It was the kind of quiet morning that Sid enjoyed most.

He had been the first one awake. The vacant cabin that the men had stumbled upon the previous evening after they had jumped from the train just outside of Revelstoke provided a more than comfortable spot to rest their tired bodies after the long, gruelling, and devastating ride from Calgary. A can full of coffee beans, plenty of firewood to stoke the stove, and four bunks with plenty of bedding was miraculously awaiting their arrival. By sundown, their clothes were dry, their bellies were full, and each had a soft pillow on which to rest his weary head. It seemed that lady luck had finally found them. Revelstoke and employment were only a short hike away.

As Sid stepped back into the cabin with an armful of firewood, he paused briefly to look at the tidy, un-slept in fourth bunk where his friend Slim should have been sleeping. His anger towards Tom had subsided, but the ache at losing Slim still burned.

"You gonna get up today or not?" Sid hollered at the snoring mound that was Tom. He dropped the wood noisily by the stove, but Tom didn't stir.

Sam walked in from the tiny back kitchen with a coffee pot. "You'd think he ran all the way from Calgary, the way he's been sleeping," Sam joked.

"We're walking into town within the hour," Sid yelled in the direction of the bunks. "With ya or without ya."

Tom slowly lifted his head. "I'm comin'," he grumbled.

Sid sat down at the table with Sam and poured himself a coffee. He looked at his friend and smiled. "Thank you for trying to help with Slim," he said quietly.

Sam met his gaze before taking a sip of his coffee. "We did what we could," he assured. "You know that, right?"

The men were silent for a few minutes, lost in their own thoughts. Finally Sid's mind came back to the purpose of their journey. He glanced over at Tom, who was just then crawling out of his bunk. "You think there are really any jobs in Revelstoke, like Tom said?" Sid asked Sam.

Sam shrugged his shoulders. "S'pose we'll find out soon enough," he replied. "Soon as Tom there gets his ass out of bed, we might as well go in and see what's there."

~~~

The snow was deep along the path that led them down into the valley that was Revelstoke. The three men trudged along, Sid breaking trail and Sam's massive form keeping a steady pace while Tom struggled to keep up. Sid stopped and turned to watch Tom fight his way through yet another snow drift. "You'd best be able to move a little faster than that in deep snow if you think you're going to work in the bush," he yelled.

"I'm comin'," Tom grumbled as he struggled to follow the narrow path that had already been trampled down by the other two men.

After about forty minutes, Sid pointed through the trees. "That must be it," he called out. "That must be Revelstoke."

After another couple of minutes, the three men stepped out of the trees and onto a narrow, abandoned street. After taking in their surroundings, they headed towards what looked to be the centre of town. When they reached the main intersection, it was obvious that they were in the right place. The building at the end of the street displayed a huge sign that read McSorley Lumber Co. Under that sign was another, in
~~~

big bold letters: HIRING – QUALIFIED MEN ONLY. At least fifty men were lined up in front of the building.

Sid looked at his pals, silently cursing Tom for having delayed them. "Well, I guess we're in the right place," he said. "S'pose we'd best be getting in line."

Just as the three of them approached the back of the line, the front door to the building swung open. Two big men stepped out onto the porch and scanned the ragged looking group of men before confidently stepping into the street. "Let me make this clear," one of them yelled. "We're only hiring men with experience." He was a huge intimidating figure. Even the bulk of his heavy fur coat didn't conceal his muscular build. His booming voice carried up and down the line. "Those men that have worked in a logging camp before, step forward."

Without thinking about his friends, Sid advanced to claim his spot amongst the qualified. As he scanned the other twenty or so men who'd stepped forward with him, he realized that Sam and Tom were still behind him. He looked back and waved his hand, furtively gesturing for them to join him. Just as he turned back to face the front, the two company men strode up to him.

"And what kind experience do you have, boy?" the man barked.

Sid was instantly reminded of Clarence's interrogation after he'd stepped off the train in London nearly twenty years before. Like a trembling boy again, he was suddenly stumped for words.

"If you don't have any experience," the man in charge hollered impatiently, "then don't be stepping out here and wasting our time." He started to move down the line with the other man close on his heels.

"Wait!" Sid hollered after them. "I spent three years in the bush near Carrot River in Saskatchewan," he exaggerated.

The two men turned back and looked at him. "Is that so? What can you do?" the big man tested Sid, looking him square in the eyes.

"I can fell, buck, rig, choke, and grease skids," he quickly blurted. "I can operate and fix almost any piece of equipment, and I'm good with horses. And I've driven logging truck and I even did some cruisin'." By the end of his spiel, Sid's half-truths had become full-blown lies.

"That's enough. We'll know soon enough what you can and can't do. Sign up here with Everett and then stand over there," he ordered, pointing his thick finger to a spot near the main office building.

"Yes, sir!" Sid smiled.

As the two men started to walk away, the man in charge turned back and looked Sam up and down. "Big fella like you never worked in a lumber camp before?"

Sam seemed startled to be singled out. Sid wished for Sam's sake that he'd stretch the truth a little, but he knew his friend well enough to know that he couldn't lie to save his life. "Done a lot of things," Sam replied, "but I ain't never worked in a lumber camp."

The man took a moment to look around. "See that stump?" he asked, pointing to a massive log lying on the ground about thirty feet away. "Go on over, pick it up and bring it to me."

It must weigh at least two hundred and fifty pounds! Sid thought, sure that not even Sam could handle such a weight. But Sam dutifully walked over and easily picked up the log, slung it over his shoulder and carried it back. "Where do you want me to put it?" he asked, his voice even. He hadn't even broken a sweat.

"Just drop it there and sign up with Everett. You're hired," he said. The two men turned away and continued down the line.

Sid looked over at Sam and flashed his stunned friend a big smile. They were in. Then they noticed Tom, who stood by silently watching as his friends each got the job that he had been hoping for. Sid followed as Sam walked over to him, not sure of what to say.

"Hey, it's okay," Tom started. "There must be other work around here," he presumed. "Someone has to look after all you lumberjacks, right?" he tried to joke, but his voice was strained. "You guys go on. I'll see ya around. Go!"

Sid and Sam shook Tom's hand, wished him luck, and then turned and headed off towards the lumber company's office building.

In the short time it took for them to get to the spot, the two big men had already weeded out most of the remaining applicants. In all, only eight men stood waiting in front of the building for their instructions. The two men stepped up onto the porch and turned back to the small group, again scanning them closely as if they hadn't yet made their final decision. Fearful that he might still be cut from the group, Sid's stomach churned.

"My name is Eric McSorley," the man in charge finally announced. "I own this company. This man is Everett Oldman. Mr. Oldman is the camp push."

Oldman tipped his hat in acknowledgment.

"It's plain and simple," McSorley barked. "We have contracts with the railroad and the power company. You men work hard to help us fill those contracts and you'll be treated well," he said. His voice suddenly lowered and his eyes flashed fiercely. "Anything less than an honest day's work and I'll personally see to it that you're run out of town with less than what you came in with. Is that understood?"

A collective nod and a few guttural sounds came from the small group.

"We have a few rules around here," he continued. "When I'm not around, Everett here is in charge," he shouted. "We work six days a week, ten hours a day, except Fridays, when we work eight hours. Payday is every Friday night. If you don't fill out a pay sheet every day and pass it back to your foreman, you won't get paid. Understood?" he shouted.

The group again nodded and grunted.

"That's the pay office there," he said, gesturing towards a small building next to the main office. "We start cutting at six o'clock no matter how damn cold it is. Show up on time for work, and show up sober," he emphasized. "We don't tolerate drinking or fighting on the job. Do what you want on your own time."

Sid listened intently and silently vowed to himself that he wouldn't fall into his old Carrot River habits.

"We don't work on Sunday's," McSorley continued, "and there is a house of worship in town for those of you who are so inclined. You can buy whatever clothes you need at the company store, right over there," he motioned listlessly to another building across the way. "You'll be deducted a portion of your pay every week until it's paid off," he advised. McSorley stopped and looked his new crew over. "Any questions?" he asked.

Sid looked around at the others, hoping that someone else would ask the question that was on his mind, but nobody spoke up. The two men looked at each other, and then they started to laugh. Everett Oldman looked out at the group and pointed at one of the men. "Where are you sleeping tonight, boy?" he shouted.

The stunned man just stared back. "Uh, I don't know, sir," he sheepishly mumbled.

"Well, that might be a question then, might'n it?" Oldman retorted.

"I suppose so," the man said.

"And that's part of the reason you're here, ain't it?" Oldman pressed.

"Yessir," the man mumbled.

The two men started laughing again. Oldman pointed to a row of buildings behind the pay office. "Those are the bunk houses," he informed. "And that's the refectory," he added, pointing to another building nearby. "The crummy'll be parked there at a quarter to six, and it leaves at six sharp. If you ain't on it, you might as well start packing. Is that understood?" he shouted.

The chorus of grunts sounded on cue.

"You've got the rest of the day to pick your bunk and get whatever clothes you need from the store," McSorley barked. "The refectory is open now and will stay open until eight o'clock this evening," he said. "Now get goin', and don't make me regret hirin' ya!"

Just as the group was about to disperse, the man who had been singled out before stuttered out the question that had been burning in Sid's own mind. "I was wondering sir, what is a refectory?"

The two big men started to laugh once again. "That's a good question," Oldman replied. "Can anyone help this poor fella out?"

Feeling ignorant, Sid looked down at the ground. He was relieved when it became apparent that no one else in the group knew the answer, either.

"Well, I guess it wasn't such a dumb question after all," Oldman said. He looked around the group and smiled. "It's the mess hall."

"I know some of you men haven't had a decent meal in awhile," McSorley calmly added. "Make sure your bellies are full. You have a hard day ahead." Oldman and McSorley turned and walked into the office.

McSorley's kind words and sudden change of demeanour put Sid at ease. *Maybe it was worth coming all this way after all,* he decided. Then he, along with Sam and the others, headed straight for the refectory.

~~~
~~~

The following months were good to Sid. The work was hard, but the benefits were first rate. He made sure that he ate his share at the expense of the company, and he paid off his debt to the company store quickly. In the beginning, he and Sam maintained a close friendship, but Sam's reserved lifestyle didn't fit well with Sid's boisterous, if not self-destructive personality, a trait that in the past had cost him plenty. But there he was again, in the midst of prosperity and a man like Sid just couldn't help but celebrate his success at every opportunity, which for him was almost nightly. So it happened that Sam and Sid slowly drifted apart, cordial in passing but otherwise detached.

Sid's charm and sociable ways did, however, serve him well in establishing other friendships, friendships with people who shared his comfort in a more raucous lifestyle. And one of those people just happened to be the man who got them there in the first place, Tom. When Tom didn't get a job at McSorley's, he wasted no time in sourcing other possibilities, one of which was a vacancy at the local tavern, the only drinking establishment in town. As it turned out, Tom knew how to work the bar crowd--he could convince a drowning man that he needed another drink. Those poor patrons never knew what hit them. Within two months, he had not only become the bar manager, he was well on his way to becoming part owner of the place. It was no wonder that, when free drinks were in sight, a guy like Sid would gravitate so quickly back to a guy who not so long before had been in his sights for causing the death of his best friend.

Despite the reputation that Sid had quickly acquired around town as a hard-drinking, poker-playing womanizer, he was also developing an equally impressive reputation at the McSorley Lumber Company for his work ethic and his wide range of skills in the business. McSorley quickly pegged Sid as a valuable asset to his company, as long as he could keep his work life separate from his unruly private life, that is.

And Revelstoke, like many other towns in the thirties that boasted prosperous men with free-flowing cash, attracted its fair share of single young women. Some came strictly for the revelry, while others came seeking a suitable husband. It didn't matter to Sid why they were there. As far as he was concerned, if a woman was willing to let him buy her drinks all night, she'd better be prepared to share her bed with him.

There weren't too many women in Revelstoke who had the pleasure of more than one encounter with him, in fact, there was only one.

Wanda was a petite, pretty woman, but plain by the standards of the other ladies who frequented the pub. Wanda found herself alone in Revelstoke after her husband, a railroad man, never returned from a run to Calgary the year before. She had agreed to travel all the way across Canada and move to Revelstoke with her husband of two years in 1930, on a promise of prosperity and eternal adoration. During his frequent trips away from home, however, he had apparently found greener pastures and decided to permanently graze there. So, after she had gotten over the initial shock of being abandoned, Wanda took a job as a seamstress and found social refuge at the inn. She only slept with men that she felt sure would stick around, but even so, she was relentlessly disappointed. That is, until Sid came along.

Although she knew Sid was a player, she could tolerate his faults. He did seem to want to spend more time with her than the others. Moving into a small, two-room cabin on the edge of town with him was the best offer she'd had in over a year.

June 4, 1932

Mosquito-bitten, dirty, and tired, Sid began his long walk home from a full day in the bush. His stomach growled as his thoughts turned to the meal he knew would be waiting for him at home. *I hope she cooked up those moose steaks*, he thought. *And a cold glass of beer would go down good just about now.* Sid's saunter quickly turned into a brisk walk as his stomach churned even more.

After supper, he and Wanda would take their regular Saturday evening stroll down to the Timberline and gather with their friends for an evening of drink, song and dance. Sid felt his heart beat quicken with anticipation. *Maybe she'll leave early tonight*, he thought. *Give me a chance to play some poker with the guys. Hmm, maybe even get a little on the side.* Sid always felt guilty after his one night stands, but that never stopped him from surrendering to an interested woman's advances if her touch was inviting enough. He didn't get far before he heard his name being called.

"Sid! Come on over here. I need to talk to you for a minute." It was Everett Oldman, calling to him from the front porch of the main office.

Sid groaned silently and abruptly changed course. "Mr. Oldman. What can I do for you, sir?" Sid hollered with as much good cheer as he could muster at the end of a long day.

Oldman motioned to a couple of chairs on the porch. "Have a seat," he offered. "I need to talk to you about some company business."

Sid warily took his seat, a little taken aback that Oldman wanted to consult with him on company matters.

"Well, kid," Oldman started as he took the seat next to Sid. "You've proven yourself to be a valuable employee with this company," he commended. "You're a hard worker, always on time, and you have learned the business well." Oldman's eyes bore into him.

Sid was momentarily stumped. "Um, thank you, sir," he finally mumbled.

"As you know, Sid, we have substantial contracts with both the power company and the railroad. Problem is, we need to start looking to other areas from which to harvest our timber. So, we have secured the potential rights to an area up in the high country, about forty miles west of here, near Sicamous," he said. "If it looks good, we'll be setting up a new camp in there sometime next year."

Sid started to relax, confident that this discussion had nothing to do with any indiscretions.

"What we need is for someone to go in there and assess it for us," Oldman went on. "You know, survey the stand and mark trees. Sid, we think you're the man for the job. You're the best cruiser we've got." Oldman wasted no time in sweetening the pot. "If you want the job, we'll double your pay from the outset, and when the new camp is set up, you'll be hired on as a foreman."

Sid's mouth fell open. He was completely stunned by the offer. He was proud that he was being considered for the job, but anxious about taking on such a big responsibility.

"You will have to live out in the bush, mind you, at least until next year," Oldman notified. "There is a cabin on Yard Creek, about five miles from the area you'll be surveying. I've been assured that it would be quite comfortable for you and Wanda, and Sicamous is only another ten miles up the road."

Sid's mind suddenly started to race as the offer ran through his mind while Oldman continued to speak.

"We have accounts with most businesses in Sicamous," Oldman said, "and all your supplies will be covered."

By this time, Sid had already decided that he couldn't pass up the offer, but he put on his best poker face anyways. "Does the job come with a company truck?" he nervously ventured. He'd been aching for his own vehicle since he'd lost his coupe in Saskatchewan.

"'Course," affirmed Oldman. "You'll need it to get into Sicamous for supplies."

Sid scrunched his brow and pretended to ponder the offer. After a few seconds, he looked up at Everett and smiled. "I'll do it."

Everett smiled back. "Don't you want to discuss it with Wanda first?" he asked.

Sid hadn't even considered Wanda. "No, she'll go," he confidently replied.

"Alright then," Oldman said. "First thing Monday morning, we'll have a meeting and get you set up with a map and some supplies. You'll be gone by Wednesday."

The two men stood and shook hands before Sid started back towards home. He hadn't felt so euphoric since the day he and Slim decided to go into the combining business together.

June 8, 1932

Sid walked out the front door of the company store with the last box of supplies and loaded it into the back of his company-issue truck. Wanda stood quietly by with a look of bewilderment on her face as Sid checked his list one more time.

"All set to go?" came McSorley's raspy voice as he and Everett Oldman walked up.

"Yep, looks like that's everything," Sid yelled back.

Just then, the store manager came sauntering out carrying a shotgun and a box of shells. "Hold on there, boy," he shouted. "Might need a twelve gauge." He looked over at Wanda. "To shoot rabbits," he clarified.

Sid glared at him. "No rabbit for me," he snapped. "I ate enough of those back in Saskatchewan."

"Better take it all the same, boy," Oldman advised.

Sid grinned and looked over at Wanda. "S'pose I could use it to scare away the bears," he said with a laugh.

Wanda's mouthed dropped and her face turned white. "There's bears?" Her voice was quavering.

Everett quickly stepped up and put his hand on her shoulder. "Don't listen to him, ma'am," he said. "The bears'll stay up in the high country as long as there's food there. You've got nothing to worry about."

The terror on her face suggested that she didn't believe him. Sid just laughed. *She'd better snap out of it if she's going to survive one night in the woods,* he thought with annoyance that he strained to hide from his bosses.

"Okay, Sid," McSorley said. "The cabin's not hard to find. Turn south off the trail to Sicamous just before you get to Yard Creek. It's all been marked. I'll have the truckers stop by from time to time to check on you. You can send your reports back with them," he instructed. McSorley looked over to Wanda. "You'll be fine, ma'am," he assured. "Sicamous is only ten miles away. You make sure Sid takes you in now and again for a nice supper," he said.

McSorley's words of encouragement put a smile on Wanda's face, and she looked over at Sid. "You hear that, Sid?" she said. "You'll be taking me out to supper."

Everyone said their last goodbyes as Wanda and Sid climbed into the truck. Two hours later, they pulled up to their new home in the woods.

Chapter Twenty Five

The Cabin

It didn't take long for Sid to get started at his new job. If he did have one redeeming quality, it was his work ethic. As usual, he was up before sunrise the very first morning, studying the maps and readying himself to set off up the mountain. Wanda dutifully prepared his breakfast and packed his lunch, and then stood on the porch of the small one-room cabin and watched as he drove off into the dark morning, leaving her to what must have become a lonely, tedious and demanding daily routine of chopping wood, hauling water, washing clothes and preparing meals. As devoted and obedient as she was, Wanda surely envisioned that their time in the wilderness was not going to be easy for her.

The small cabin itself was nestled in a large clearing next to Yard Creek and surrounded by a forest of lodge pole pine and cedar trees. It was comfortable enough for the two of them. The wood burning stove on which Wanda cooked Sid's meals also kept them warm on cool nights. If not for the isolation, it would have been an idyllic place for an adventurous young couple to call home.

But it was the isolation that captivated Sid the most. He enjoyed his days working alone in the bush, and as long as he had a hot meal, a generous supply of beer and liquor, and a warm body to curl up to every night, he was happy. But even in that paradise, Sid still missed the excitement of Saturday nights at the inn and the occasional untried woman. It wasn't long before both he and Wanda yearned for a night away.

June 24, 1932

Sid couldn't help himself from displaying outward signs of excitement as he sat in the company truck, waiting for Wanda to come out.

"Come on, woman!" he yelled, revving the engine to make her move faster.

Sid's eyes moved to the still-bright evening sky above his head. *Must be darn near close to the longest day of the year,* he thought. It was Friday night, and earlier that week he had promised to take Wanda for supper when they went into Sicamous for supplies. Her face lit up when he also told her they could get a room for the night so they could check out the night life.

Sid's eyes shot back to the cabin. "Damn woman's had days to get ready," he muttered to himself. "What the hell is taking her so long?"

Finally, Wanda came running out of the cabin with her overnight bag in hand and jumped into the truck, squeezing in close beside him.

"What the hell took you so long?" he snapped. "You only got two dresses, and I don't think you'll be needin' both of them."

"Never mind," she chided. "A woman needs more than a man when they go on a trip."

Sid shook his head. "A trip," he mumbled. "More like a supply run, and we're only staying over one night." He put the truck in gear and started down the trail towards Sicamous.

The couple had only been to Sicamous once for supplies since settling into the cabin, and much to Sid's dismay, a stop at the local watering hole wasn't in the cards that day. They had hitched a ride with Ted, one of the company drivers who had stopped by to check on them. Sadly for Sid, Ted was neither a patient man nor a drinking man and they only stayed in town long enough to get the supplies they needed.

Tonight, I'm in charge, he contemplated. The only nagging thought he had was that he wouldn't likely have an opportunity to sample any of the women from Sicamous, *an inconvenience that I'll put right when I make the trip alone*, he assured himself.

"My-oh-my!" Wanda gasped, as they pulled in front of the hotel. "Is this where we're staying?"

"Says Sicamous Hotel on the sign," Sid returned, as he stared in awe at the massive structure. They both just sat there for a moment, silent and mesmerized. "Well, I s'pose we'd best see if they have any rooms," Sid finally said.

As they stepped into the lobby, Sid couldn't help but feel out of place in such elegant surroundings. At the same time, he felt a sense of pride in that he could afford to treat his woman to such luxury. It was the first time that he truly felt successful since arriving in British Columbia.

"Pardon me. Are you folks looking for something?"

"Oh, ya!" The man's deep voice startled Sid. He turned to find himself face-to-face with a tall, very well dressed and neatly groomed man who seemed to have somehow snuck up on them. "Ah, yes. Do ya have any rooms for tonight?" Sid asked, trying to make himself sound as polished as he could.

"Of course sir," the man haughtily replied. "This is the Sicamous Hotel. We have many rooms."

The two looked at each other in a moment of uncomfortable silence.

Sid cleared his throat. "Well, alright then. We'll take one for tonight." Sid looked at Wanda, who returned him a starry-eyed gaze. "Make that for tonight and tomorrow night," he jubilantly declared.

Wanda rushed over, wrapped her arms around Sid and squeezed him tightly. "Oh, thank you Sid," she gushed, holding him even tighter and standing on her toes to reach his ear. "I love you," she whispered.

A warm rush shot through Sid's body and his heart started to beat faster. Eva was the only woman to ever utter those three words to him. Suddenly, he found himself in the arms of another woman who proclaimed her love for him, a circumstance that he had never really thought much about, until now. The spontaneity of the moment caught him off guard.

"I love you too," he instinctively replied. As awkward as it was for Sid to say the words, it also felt right. He squeezed Wanda even tighter, smiled, and then turned his attention back to the clerk. "Yes, we'll be staying until Sunday. Now, is there a dance hall in this town?" he confidently enquired.

That night, Sid spared no expense, treating Wanda to the best offerings from the menu in the elegant dining room at the hotel. Afterwards, the couple enjoyed an evening of dancing, drinking and socializing in the ball room. And despite the many temptations that confronted him: flirting glances from other women and the poker room just down the hall, Sid found himself to be truly satisfied enjoying Wanda's company all evening.

That night in Sicamous was the first of many weekend trips the couple would enjoy together that summer and into the fall of nineteen-thirty-two.

~~~

As the evenings became cooler and the frosts set in, Sid and Wanda prepared for the impending isolation of winter. Their leisurely weekend trips to Sicamous became monthly expeditions, exhausting trudges through deep snow on the trail between the cabin and the main road to hitch a ride with one of the scheduled truck runs from Revelstoke.

Anticipating the difficulties of working in extreme winter conditions, Sid made an extra effort to complete much of his work in the bush during the fall. The fewer days he needed to spend tromping through the snow, the more time he had to help Wanda around the cabin. At any other time during his life, being stuck with one woman for an entire winter would have driven Sid to insanity, but the hardship just seemed to bring them closer together. Sid was happy with his life and Wanda was happy with Sid, and they both excitedly looked forward to the abundant opportunities that lay ahead when the new camp was set up. The couple had even started looking for a home in Sicamous.

Sid turned twenty-seven that November, and for the first time since he could remember, he enjoyed a birthday celebration. He spent the day looking ahead to all he might accomplish with Wanda by his side, and didn't once think about all the people who had been taken from him along the way. The future held nothing but promise for him.

April 16, 1933

"Come on out and sit, Wanda," Sid called through the screened door. "I'll help with the dishes later."
~~~

Sid leaned back in his rocking chair and took a sip of his coffee. The night had a pleasant coolness in the air, and the crickets in the clearing in front of the house were in the middle of their particular kind of symphony.

Just as the sun was going down, Wanda gently closed the door behind her and took up her rocker beside Sid. She gave his hand a squeeze. "This is nice," she said in a quiet voice. "Look at those colours bouncing off the mountain." She gestured with her coffee cup towards the snow-capped peak about twenty miles off.

They sat quietly and listened to the soothing sound of water rushing over the rocks in Yard Creek, watching the deer graze in the scrub just thirty yards in front of them. A calmness washed over Sid. *So, this is what it's like to be happy,* he thought. Just then, something caught his eye.

"What the hell?" he muttered, straining his eyes to see. "Something's out there." He pointed to a spot just beyond the trees.

Wanda quickly sat up and looked out. "What is it, Sid?" she said.

"Shh."

Sid watched for another few moments to be sure. His heart was pounding hard against his ribs. "It's a god damn grizzly," he whispered.

Wanda gasped and raised her hand to her mouth.

"Look, there it is," he said, pointing with his outstretched arm. "Standing on its hind legs, right there. Jeeze, it's a scrawny little bastard."

Wanda stepped in close and grabbed onto Sid's arm. He could feel the fear coming off her in waves. "What are you going to do?" she whispered, her words trembling in her throat.

"Quick, run in and get the twelve gauge. I'll chase that damn thing right back into the high country where it belongs." Despite his own fear, Sid tried to muster some bravado behind his words. Just as Wanda was getting out of her chair, he grabbed her arm. "And make sure you bring the box of shells," he hissed.

Sid kept his eye trained on the bear, not wanting to let it out of his sight for a moment.

As Wanda rushed back out to the porch with the shotgun, she dropped the box of shells, spilling them all over the porch. The clamour made Sid start in his chair and set his heart racing. He took the gun, which was clumsily straddled in Wanda's arms, and cracked open the barrel. He kept his eyes on the tree line. "Pass me some shells," he anxiously whispered.

Wanda crouched down and picked up a handful of shells, dropping some from her shaking hands and passing the others to Sid. He shoved one into the barrel and slammed it shut, then slipped the other shells into his trouser pocket.

"Damn bear," he cursed, forcing a nervous laugh. "I'll give it a whole bunch of reasons not to be comin' round here no more."

Sid stepped down off the porch and strode towards the animal, which was still standing at the edge of the trees, sniffing precisely in Sid's direction seemingly trying to figure out what all the commotion was about. Sid's heart pounded hard against his chest as he crept in as close as he dare and took aim.

Kaboom!

The recoil caused a shooting pain to run through Sid's shoulder. "I think I hit it," he shouted as he cracked the barrel and loaded in another shell. "Damn well better kill him now or we'll have an angry bear on our hands," he mumbled under his breath. Sid raised the gun again. His heart was pounding so wildly that he could barely keep the business end of the barrel fixed on his target. *Come on, now. You can do this. One clean shot is all it takes.*

Kaboom!

Damn it! The bear slowly started to amble back into the woods as Sid ran back to the cabin, yelling for Wanda to give him more shells.

"He's gone, Sid," Wanda called, relief in her voice. "He went back into the woods."

Sid turned back to face the tree line. "Ya, well, I think I hit it with both shots. Don't think we'll be seein' that one back here again," he said, trying to sound confident.

Sid cracked the barrel to expel the empty shell casing. Before closing it, he looked up at Wanda. "You ever shot one of these before?" he asked.

Wanda nervously looked back at him. "No," she replied, her voice full of unease.

"Well, you might as well learn now," he said.

She took two steps back. "Nope, nope, I don't think so," she screeched. "I've gotten along just fine until now."

Sid started to laugh. "Come on," he said, "it won't hurt you. And besides, you should learn how to shoot. You never know when you'll need to protect yourself." He picked up a shell from the porch and shoved it into the barrel. "Come on. I'll stand right behind you." Sid slammed the barrel closed.

A tentative smile twitched at Wanda's mouth as she slowly started down the steps. "Well, alright. But I have to warn you, if I have to protect myself, it just might be from you," she joked.

Her teasing words momentarily shocked Sid, and he felt himself redden. Suddenly he was back in the Liberty farmhouse kitchen gazing at the cracked shotgun on the table and wondering where Eva was. He managed an uneasy smile and then reached out to her. "Come on. Everyone out here knows how to shoot," he said. "It's part of the life." He turned Wanda back towards where the bear had been and pointed to a branch on a nearby tree. "See that branch?" he said. "See if you can hit that." Sid braced himself behind her and helped her bring the gun into position. "Okay," he said. "I'll pull back the hammer, and when you're ready, pull the trigger. Just hold it tight to your shoulder, and--"

Kaboom!

The kick sent the gun flying and both of them stumbling backwards. Sid clumsily tried to keep his footing but slipped, causing him to fall, with Wanda landing heavily on top of him. The pair lay dazed on the wet ground. After a few seconds of stunned stillness, Sid gently pushed Wanda off him. "I think we need to practice a little more," he said, and they both started to laugh.

May 3, 1933

It was a welcome surprise for Sid when Frank, one of the company drivers, pulled up on the sunny afternoon. Sid walked out to greet the exhausted man with a glass of whiskey and a freshly rolled smoke.

Wanda waved hello from the porch. "Will you stay for supper," she yelled.

"Yes ma'am, thank you," Frank hollered back. "I'm famished."

Eva stepped back into the cabin to prepare supper for them all.

"Well, how was the winter here, Sid?" Frank asked. "I see you two haven't killed each other yet," he laughed.

Sid smiled. "Nope, it's been a good winter," he replied. "How's things back in Revelstoke?"

"Good," Frank said. "Real good. Sounds like everything's a go with the new camp. Bosses are real happy with the work you've done in getting things set up here," he informed. "In fact, they're gonna give you a brand new truck."

Sid grinned. He was proud of the work he'd done up there, and he was glad that his efforts weren't going unnoticed. "So, they're gonna go through with the new camp eh! Wanda'll be happy to hear that."

"Yep. They're gonna build it right here in this clearing," Frank said, gesturing to the area in front of the cabin. In fact, that's what I've come to tell you. They want you to come back to Revelstoke for a day or two to fill them in on the last details before they start construction. They thought that Wanda might appreciate a little break as well."

Sid smiled. Suddenly the old, familiar ache to get back to his old stomping ground and enjoy the revelling it had to offer was tugging at his bootstraps. "Sure! That would be great," he said, visions of winning big at the card table filling his head. Sid looked back at the cabin, and then stepped in close to Frank. "About Wanda," he said, lowering his voice so as not to be overheard. "Maybe we can tell her it's just business, you know, only a day, in and out." Sid stepped even closer. "To be honest Frank, it'd be nice to get away by myself, you know what I mean?" Sid winked at Frank conspiratorially.

Frank looked back at Sid with a doubtful frown. "You sure it's a good idea to leave her here by herself?" he asked. "Maybe she'd like to spend some time in town."

Sid feigned a self-assured smile. "Aw, she'll be fine. She'll have her fill of town soon enough when we move to Sicamous," he assured. "Besides, she'll enjoy having the cabin to herself. And once she hears that the camp is a go, she'll want to get things organized before we leave." As he spoke, Sid convinced himself that there was at least some truth in his words.

Frank didn't look all that convinced, but nothing more was said on the subject.

Early the following morning, Frank sat in his truck, waiting for Sid to come out. The plan was for Sid to follow him back to Revelstoke in his own truck. He could see the two of them through the open door. Wanda had been crying all morning, and Sid was taking a few extra minutes to comfort her before he left. Sid finally stepped out and waved to Frank, signalling that he would be along momentarily.

"It's just a quick meeting," he assured. "I'll leave Revelstoke as soon as we're done tomorrow afternoon, and I'll be home for supper tomorrow night. You'll be fine. Come on, give me a hug."

"Are you sure I can't come?"

Sid suppressed an annoyed sigh. "I wish you could, but it's company business. Company men only."

Wanda reluctantly stepped closer to Sid and put her arms around him. "Alright. But you'll be home tomorrow night?" she confirmed as she wiped a tear from her cheek.

"Tomorrow night," he promised as he disentangled his arm from her grip and quickly stepped out onto the porch.

Sid walked over to his truck and threw his duffle bag in the back. He started up his engine and stuck his arm out the window to wave goodbye as he drove off down the road. He looked in the rear-view mirror and watched Wanda as she stood on the porch, her blue dress flapping in the breeze, staring at the back of his truck as he drove away. He wished she'd go inside. *A man's gotta get away every once in a while,* he reasoned. *Ain't no fault in that.* He turned out onto the trail and she disappeared. An uneasy feeling rushed over him as he drove away.

Both Eric McSorley and Everett Oldman were there to greet Sid as he and Frank pulled into the company yard. They shook hands and exchanged warm greetings, and Sid was commended for the work he had done at the new site.

"I'm glad you and Wanda survived the winter without killing each other," McSorley joked. "Speaking of Wanda, where is she?"

Sid avoided Frank's gaze. "Oh, she decided to stay on at the cabin," he lied. "Lots to do there before we move out."

Mr. McSorley furled his brow. "Do you think it's wise to leave a woman alone out there?"

"Well, sir," Sid began, clearing his throat. "I asked her to come, but she said she needed some time away from me or else she'd go insane. You know women," he joked, hoping that the subject would be put to rest.

McSorley raised an eyebrow. "Well, you'll go straight back with Frank on his run first thing tomorrow morning," he said. "Your new truck won't be ready for another week. Make sure you bring that young lady back with you when you come to pick it up. She probably deserves a break more than you do," he laughed. "Understood?"

"Yes, sir," Sid replied.

"Come on up to the office now," McSorley said. "We'll have our meeting this afternoon."

~~~

Sid rolled over on the firm bunk mattress and groaned. His head pounded and he could barely open his eyes. He hadn't had a hangover like that in a long time. It took him a moment to figure out where he was. He looked at the clock that hung on the far wall of the bunk house. Ten-thirty.

"Shit!" he yelled, realizing how much he'd overslept. *Frank leaves at six!*

He scanned the bunk house. There was no one else there. Sid climbed down from his bed and staggered over to the mirror. His hair was sticking up every which way, his eyes were bloodshot, and he had bright red lipstick smeared across his face. He recalled being at the Timberline the night before and quickly throwing back the first few beers, but he couldn't remember much after that. But none of that mattered now. What he needed was to clean himself up and find a way back to the cabin without Mr. McSorley seeing him.

Suddenly the door swung open. "Sid, that you?" the voice called.

"Ya," he answered, hoping with all his heart that McSorley hadn't sent someone after him. "It's me." Sid's eyes adjusted to the light to see old Butch Walters standing there. Butch had been with the company almost as long as the company had been around.
~~~

"I heard you were still in here," Butch scolded. "McSorley told you to catch a lift back to your woman with Frank, and Frank left hours ago. What the hell you still doin' here?" he yelled.

Sid squinted up at Butch with a sheepish grin. "Kinda got bush-whacked down at the Timberline last night," he said, self-consciously covering the lipstick smudge with his hand.

Butch chuckled. "Ya, I guess you did. So, what are ya gonna do now?" he asked.

Sid hung his head. "I don't know," he said. "I need to find a way back before McSorley sees me."

"Well, my friend, you're in luck," Butch said with a grin. "I just happen to be haulin' a load of logs up to the mill in Salmon Arm this afternoon. S'pose you could sneak along for the ride," he slyly offered.

"S'pose you could use the company, too," Sid retorted.

Travelling in a loaded log hauler wasn't nearly as fast as Sid was used to. By the time they left the yard, it was nearly mid-afternoon. And at the rate they were moving, Sid figured they'd be at his turn-off by early evening. When they finally reached the trail, Sid grabbed his duffle bag and jumped down from the rig, readying himself for the two-mile hike up the track that led to the cabin.

"Thanks for the lift, Butch," he called as he headed towards the path. "And for keeping this between us."

"No problem, Sid. I've forgotten all about it already. Sorry I can't take you all the way."

"It's alright, Butch. There was no way this heavy load could make it up that soggy road."

As he walked the last two miles, Sid became keenly aware of the sights and sounds around him. It was a beautiful night. The sky was clear, and the late-spring sun was still hanging in the air. *It's eerily quiet*, he thought. Sid had always enjoyed the peace and quiet, but that night, the silence was peculiar. There was no wind and the trees were motionless. Not even the birds were singing. Once again, just like the previous morning when he was driving away, an uneasy feeling rushed over him.

As Sid turned onto the short path that led up to the cabin, a pang of excitement rushed over him. He was looking forward to holding Wanda and he wanted to tell her that he was sorry for not taking her along.

As he drew closer, he shouted out, "Wanda, I'm home!" He expected to see her run out of the cabin at any moment, her arms open to greet him. But there was no movement at the small shack. He looked up at the chimney--there was no smoke. As he got closer, he could see that the front door was wide open, and still she hadn't rushed out to meet him. *Maybe she's waiting inside to surprise me*, he thought, trying to keep himself calm.

"Wanda, I'm home!" he shouted again, this time louder.

Still nothing.

He slowly stepped up onto the front porch and then turned back towards the clearing. "Wanda?" He looked over towards the creek and saw no sign of her there. "Wanda!"

Sid slowly stepped into the cabin and looked around. He stepped over to the table and found a full plate of bacon and eggs sitting there. He reached down and touched them. They were cold. *It isn't like her to leave a plate of food on the table, or the front door wide open*, he thought. He walked over to the wood stove and looked inside. Nothing but a pile of cold, white ash. Panic started to rush over him.

"Wanda!" he hollered again.

Sid quickly ran back out onto the porch. "Wanda! Wanda!" He looked back over to the clearing and scanned the area. He saw the late-evening light reflecting off something lying on the ground near the scrub and he squinted for a better look. *What in the world-?* his mind raced. He jumped off the porch and ran towards the object. As he got closer, he could see it, the twelve gauge, just lying there, the barrel cracked, one spent shell laying on the ground beside it and two more live shells a little farther away.

Sid let out a sound that his ears did not recognize. He picked up the shotgun, rammed a shell into the barrel and quickly slammed it shut. "Wanda!" he hollered again as he looked towards the tree line. Silence.

He took a few tentative steps towards the edge of the clearing. Suddenly he could see something hanging from a branch, moving in the slight, cool breeze that had just started to blow. As he got closer, he strained to see what it was. It looked like a piece of cloth, blue cloth, dangling from the low branches of a pine tree just inside the woods.

A full-blown surge of panic rushed through him as he slowly walked over to the tree. He reached out and grabbed the cloth and pulled at it. Out from the branches came her blue dress, shredded and covered in dried blood. Sid looked down at the soggy ground and could clearly see the bear's paw prints, and the drag marks where she had been pulled into the woods.

Everything started to spin around him. He didn't know which way to turn. Instinct shouted out to him, telling him that he needed to find her. Common sense shouted back, telling him that she was gone, that there was nothing he could do. He took a few steps into the woods, and then a few steps back towards the cabin, and then to the woods and back to the cabin. He hadn't felt helplessness like this since he and Sam struggled to dig Slim out from under his frozen grave in the coal car.

Finally, after feverishly pacing between the bush line and the cabin for what felt like an eternity, Sid pulled himself together as best he could and walked through the darkness back to the cabin. He closed the door and walked directly to the shelf on which they kept the whiskey. He cowered down in a corner and cracked open the bottle. It didn't take long for it all to be gone.

The following morning, when he finally awoke, Sid slowly pulled himself up off of the floor, picked up his duffle bag, calmly walked through the door and started down the trail towards Sicamous. No one from the McSorley Lumber Company ever saw him again.

Chapter Twenty Six

The Box

"I'm sure I'm the only one he ever told that story to," Mary said. "And now you know, George."

The anxious look on George's face was obvious, and his hands trembled as he set down the cup before tea spilled all over the floor. "Still such a young man and yet so much tragedy. I suppose much of it was his own doing," he added. "Where did he go after that?" George asked, his voice quivering.

"I don't know," Mary said. "I suppose he spent a couple more years just wandering around. That's the only time in his life that he never talked about. All's I know is, he showed up here in Princeton in the spring of thirty-six, took a job at the mill down below and bought this old shack. He lived here right up until I drove him to the hospital in Penticton a week ago."

"What about his daughter, Lauren? And his son, Frederick?" George asked. "He must have married again," he presumed.

"The kids came along a few years after he moved to Princeton," Mary explained. "True to form, it didn't take Sid long to find the local watering hole, and the ladies. He wasn't in town a year before he hooked up with a local gal named Bertha. From the stories I heard, she was just as wild as he was," Mary recalled with a laugh. "They fought like badgers, too. But they stuck it out until she died in sixty-one. They never did marry, but Bertha and the kids lived with him up until she passed. After she was gone, well, Fred and Lauren had no more use for Sid and they both ran off to Vancouver."

"He never saw them after that?" George asked.

"Not Fred," she replied. "Fred was as wild as his father. Got himself hung up with a bad crowd in the downtown and started using drugs. That's what took him in the end, the drugs and the booze," she said, shaking her head sadly. "Sid didn't even know Fred had died until a year after he was gone. And as for Lauren, well, you talked to her last night George. I suppose you can guess how she felt about Sid. It's a shame that she doesn't even want to attend his funeral, but he wasn't much of a father to her either," she said. "He had a hard time being there for people, you know? Maybe because he'd lost everyone he'd ever loved in life," she supposed.

George looked at his watch. "Oh my," he said. "I've taken too much of your time."

"Nonsense," Mary replied. "It was my pleasure to meet you George, and to tell you about your father. And, now that you know about his life, well, maybe it'll give you some peace of mind, an understanding of why he was the way he was." Mary looked directly into Georges eyes and smiled. "You know George, Sid wasn't a bad man. He just didn't have a good go of it right from the beginning. You did a good thing, being there for him in the end."

George pushed himself out of his chair and reached out to shake Mary's hand. "Thank you, thank you for everything," he said, as their hands clasped. "Now, we have a long drive ahead," gesturing to his son that he was ready to leave. "Guess we should be on our way."

"Just hold on a minute," Mary excitedly blurted as she lifted herself out of her chair. "I almost forgot. I've got something that I think you should have." Mary rushed to her room and quickly returned holding a small wooden box, its lid firmly secured with two pieces of twine. "I think it's an old cigar box," she said. "Sid gave it to me about a month ago. He told me to burn it after he died. I suppose I would have opened it myself sooner or later," she admitted, "but I think you should have it George. Maybe there's more answer's in there," she said, handing him the box.

George enthusiastically accepted the package, examining it from all sides, estimating its weight, and then gently shaking it, hoping for clues as to its contents. "Letters?" he mumbled.

"That would be my guess," Mary agreed. "Take it with you. You can call and tell me after you've opened it."

"I will," George said, as he tucked the box tightly under his arm. He opened the door, and then turned back to her, tears streaming from his eyes. "I've dreamed my whole life that I would someday know about him. I can't thank you enough for giving me that," he sniffled.

Mary smiled. "Just meeting you George, is thanks enough," she sincerely replied.

George acknowledged Mary's gratitude with a nod, and then left his father's home for the first, and the last time.

Epilogue

He was lying there motionless, eyes closed, desperately sucking in shallow gulps of air over his toothless gums. He was gasping for every breath that he knew might be his last.

His eighty-eight-year-old withered arms lay limp by his side, over top of the single white bed sheet that covered him up to his chin. He was tucked in like a little boy--he was seen, and not heard.

Isn't it funny how we leave this world the same way we entered it? he thought in a fleeting moment of clarity. If that was the case, then perhaps all of his sins would be forgiven. Though he knew that they would never be forgotten.

He gave them no indication that he could hear them, those nurses who were always hovering, suctioning the saliva from his mouth and checking the machines that told them he was still alive. They weren't aware, or maybe they just didn't care that he might be listening as they talked amongst themselves, about their families, about their children. It was cheerful chatter, and they always seemed anxious for their shifts to be over so they could get home. *That's nice*, he thought. *There are children out there with mothers excited to get home to them*. He silently envied them, those children.

Did I have a childhood? he struggled to remember. *I must have. Everyone had a childhood, didn't they*?

He heard the quiet shuffle of feet and the clearing of throats. Then came the soft whispers of strangers. He wondered who they might be. *Maybe a priest coming to give last rites?* he thought. If he could have muttered a word or lifted a finger, he would have sent them away.

Whoever they were, they seemed to gather close to him, closing in on both sides of his bed. He sensed that there were two of them. What did they want? He could feel their stares.

"What should I say to him?" He heard the question being asked, but the voice seemed very, very far away and unfamiliar.

"Just introduce yourself," came another man's voice, a younger man.

Who are these people? he silently wondered. And then it came. The words he didn't know that he'd been waiting over sixty years to hear.

"Hi Sid, I'm George. I'm your son."

Sid sucked in so much air it almost choked him. *George. My son George.* And then from somewhere, a surge of life flowed through him. He somehow mustered the strength to lift his withered arm and hold open his hand, silently pleading that his son would take it. *Forgive me.*

A warmth rushed through his body as he felt his son's hand grasp his own. A quiet peace filled him as he listened to their quiet murmurs. *So this is what family is about*, he imagined.

He didn't know how long they stayed for, the men, his son George. In his mind, he imagined that it was long enough to toss a ball, to learn to skate on a pond, to tussle in the grass, to make a toast at a wedding. It was long enough, but it was much too short.

As the warmth left his hand and the murmurs retreated, Sidney whispered goodbye, but no one heard.

CPSIA information can be obtained at www.ICGtesting.com
Printed in the USA
LVOW051843280213

322139LV00008B/888/P